# Secrets of the Railway Girls

Maisie Thomas was born and brought up in Manchester, which provides the location for her Railway Girls novels. She loves writing stories with strong female characters, set in times when women needed determination and vision to make their mark. The Railway Girls series is inspired by her great-aunt Jessie, who worked as a railway clerk during the First World War.

Maisie now lives on the beautiful North Wales coast with her railway enthusiast husband, Kevin, and their two rescue cats. They often enjoy holidays chugging up and down the UK's heritage steam railways.

## Also by Maisie Thomas

*The Railway Girls*

# Secrets of the Railway Girls

## MAISIE THOMAS

arrow books

5 7 9 10 8 6

Arrow Books
20 Vauxhall Bridge Road
London SW1V 2SA

Arrow Books is part of the Penguin Random House group
of companies whose addresses can be found at
global.penguinrandomhouse.com.

Penguin
Random House
UK

First published in Great Britain by Arrow Books in 2020

www.penguin.co.uk

A CIP catalogue record for this book is available
from the British Library

ISBN 9781787463974

Typeset in 10.75/13.5 pt Palatino by Jouve (UK), Milton Keynes
Printed and bound in Great Britain by Clays Ltd, Elcograf S.p.A.

The authorised representative in the EEA is Penguin Random
House Ireland, Morrison Chambers, 32 Nassau Street,
Dublin D02 YH68

Penguin Random House is committed to a
sustainable future for our business, our readers
and our planet. This book is made from Forest
Stewardship Council® certified paper.

*To the memory of Bernard Bourke (1927–1946), who died in a tragic accident during his training to be a Royal Marine.*

*And to Jacquie and Annette, whose friendship has seen me through so much.*

# Acknowledgements

My agent, Laura Longrigg, and my editor, Jennie Roth-well, both helped to make this a better book. Thank you, Laura, for making an important decision about Joan.

Thank you to Emma Grey Gelder and Silas Manhood, who created this book's wonderful cover. Thank you both for your patience with all those little tweaks. Much grati-tude goes to Caroline Johnson, my copy editor, whose eagle eyes spotted my mistakes; and Rachel Kennedy, whose expertise and commitment got the series off to a flying start.

Thanks to Kevin, my tech elf, who saved the day on the occasion of the Great Apostrophe Disaster and also when something unspeakable happened to the copy-edits docu-ment; and to Julia Franklin, for narrating the audiobooks. I am proud to have such a talented reader as the voice of my stories.

Love and thanks go to Jen Gilroy. Also to Beverley, aka Booklover Bev, my first reviewer.

# Chapter One

Well! Wonders would never cease. Dot stared across the kitchen at Reg. Gawped would be a better word. There stood Reg, her not-so-loving husband, in his Sunday suit, holding his homburg in his hands, his slicked-down hair thinner than it used to be and his once firm neck looking stringy above his collar and tie, just come home from being interviewed to be an ARP warden. Reg – working for Air Raid Precautions.

Reg looked from Dot to Sheila and Pammy, their two daughters-in-law, who were sitting with Dot at her kitchen table, here to enjoy a secret meeting about Christmas while the children played tiddlywinks in the front parlour. Other folks kept their front parlour for best, meaning it was hardly ever used, and Dot, nothing if not house-proud, had been the same for years, but once her family had expanded and a new generation had come along, she had adopted a more flexible approach.

'Really, Mother,' Pammy had once remarked, 'it would be far more appropriate for us to sit in the parlour and the children to play at the kitchen table.'

But that wouldn't have suited Dot. Her kitchen was her natural place. She had grown up in a kitchen, enveloped by the aroma of onion stew, with a bottomless basket of darning in the corner, and more sharp elbows and scabby knees than you could shake a stick at. Meat had been

1

scarce for the likes of her family and what meat they did have went on Dad's plate and then, later, in smaller portions, on the plate of each son as he started work. Working daughters were expected to get by on bread and carrot-and-swede mash, same as always. Folk today didn't know they'd been born.

Anyroad, she loved her kitchen, did Dot, and she loved nowt better than having her family crammed round her table, tucking into a tasty meal into which she had poured all her loving skill. When she dreamed of the end of the war, that was what she imagined. Not bunting and street parties; not deliriously happy crowds whooping and singing as they surged through the middle of town; but her beloved family squeezed around her kitchen table – all of them. Please let her boys come home. Archie and Harry, her sons, both safe and sound, with no nightmares and no missing limbs – that was what she prayed for every night.

'What do you think?' asked Reg. 'Of me being an ARP man – what do you think?'

Dot blinked. Was he really asking her opinion? Ever since the boys were small, he had derived pleasure from doing her down in front of them. Did he even care what she thought? And what *did* she think? She could hardly say, 'You spent the first year of the war at my kitchen table, waiting for me to put your dinner in front of you, and I thought you'd be there for the duration.'

'I think it's grand,' Pammy declared.

'Aye, Reg,' said Dot. 'Good for you. We all have to pull our weight.'

'I reckoned it was time for me to sign up,' said Reg, 'after all the air raids we've had.'

God, yes. They had lived with air raids since late summer. The whole of Manchester had been affected one way or another as bombers had flown over time and again, dropping their deadly cargo of oil bombs and high explosives, the intimidation increasing after the Battle of Britain ended. In recent weeks, the abattoir had been hit, as had the Brooke Bond Tea Warehouse. The damage to Salford Town Hall had resulted in the burial of many records, though not in the burial of any people, thank God; and, mercifully, there had been no casualties when Manchester Royal Infirmary's nurses' home was hit.

After the numbers of dead and injured in the bombings throughout October, it seemed there hadn't been so many casualties in November, and that was a blessing. Mind you, friends and relatives of the Winter family of 74 Button Lane in Wythenshawe probably wouldn't appreciate Dot's verdict. She had heard about the Winters from someone at work. That was how it was when you worked on the railways. You were surrounded by folk from all over and so you heard the details from all over; but as shocking and heart-rending as it all was, you had to be grateful that Manchester hadn't been Coventrated.

Coventrated. A cold shudder passed through Dot in spite of the fire crackling in the grate and the heat from the oven in which she was cooking steak and kidney pie and baked potatoes. Poor Coventry had had seven bells bombed out of it two weeks ago.

Pray to God they would never have cause to coin the word 'Manchestered'.

Dot's heart swelled with love and concern for her young colleagues, Joan, Mabel and Alison, who were members of first-aid parties, heading out each night they were on duty, not knowing whether they would spend a restless night where they were stationed, or whether they might be called upon to brave the streets during an air raid. Alison lived to the north of Manchester and did her first-aiding over that way, but Joan and Mabel's depot was

St Cuthbert's School, which wasn't more than a hop and a skip from Dot's house. It hadn't always been Joan and Mabel. It used to be Joan, Mabel and Lizzie, but all too soon and far too young, Lizzie had lost her life in an air raid. Poor Lizzie – and poor Lizzie's mum.

'I'm proud of you, Reg,' said Dot.

She waited a moment. Would it happen again, that surge of love that had come over her during the Dunkirk evacuation? Along with hundreds of thousands all over the country, Reg had mucked in during that national emergency, helping local soldiers get home. He had even carried his shaving tackle in his pocket, just in case any of the filthy, battered, exhausted lads wanted a shave. Soppy old bugger. But he had done his bit and old remembered love had ballooned inside Dot's chest.

Would it happen again now? Did she want it to?

The door burst open and the kids threw themselves in.

'Mummy!' Jenny launched herself at Pammy. 'Jimmy's cheating.'

'It's only tiddlywinks—' Dot began.

'Jimmy would cheat at solitaire,' said Sheila, unperturbed.

'Never mind that now,' said Dot. 'Grandpa's going to be an ARP warden.'

'Will they give you the money back on your gas mask?' Jimmy demanded, his blue eyes, just like Harry's, sparkling in his freckled face.

'What on earth is he talking about?' Pammy looked at Reg.

Jimmy burst into song. He had a surprisingly good voice. It was a shame that when he'd been invited to sing in the choir, he had taken some indoor fireworks with him. He hadn't been asked back.

> 'Under the spreading chestnut tree,
> Neville Chamberlain said to me,
> "If you want to get your gas mask free,
> join the blinkin' ARP." '

Jenny gasped. 'Jimmy said "blinking".'

'It's the words of the song,' Jimmy protested.

'It's swearing,' Jenny retorted. 'It's a pretend-polite way of saying the B word.'

'That's enough,' said Dot.

'Anyway,' said Jenny, 'it shouldn't be Mr Chamberlain. It should be Mr Churchill. You can't even get your facts right.'

'It's the song,' said Jimmy. 'Anyroad, are you going to get your money back, Grandpa?'

'The song's wrong, son,' said Reg. 'No one has to pay for gas masks.'

'Can we play air raids?' asked Jimmy.

'That's irresponsible,' said Jenny.

Oh, heavens. There were far too many times when Jenny opened her mouth and Pammy's words spilled out. Dot wanted her granddaughter to have fun and enjoy her childhood, as far as it was possible these days, but Pammy seemed more concerned about having a child who was perfect and clean and good. Back when Jenny was a toddler, Dot and Reg had taken a day trip to Southport, where Archie had taken his little family for a week's holiday. Dot and Reg had offered to take Jenny off her parents' hands for the afternoon and had secretly taken her to the beach to make sand pies, and took her paddling in the shallows and generally let her get covered in sand and ice cream before cleaning her up and returning her to her unsuspecting mother. Dot felt the same impulse now.

'Irresponsible?' she exclaimed. 'To play a game? Nonsense! Reg, take the kids in the parlour and you can all practise shouting "Turn that light out!" Me and the girls have business to discuss.'

'That means they want to talk about Christmas,' said Jimmy.

'Christmas? It's far too soon to talk about Christmas.' Dot made shooing motions with her hands. 'Get gone, the lot of you.'

She shut the door on them and returned to her seat at the table.

'It's going to be a good Christmas this year,' she told her daughters-in-law.

'I hope so.' Pammy's voice was more refined than necessary. She had been fetched up by a mother whose status as the wife of a master butcher had given her ideas. 'Last Christmas was too awful for words.'

'Now then,' Dot said briskly, 'we'll have none of that, thank you. We want to make this Christmas . . .' Just in time she stopped herself from saying *perfect*. '. . . As good as it can be, for the children's sakes.'

Aye, for the kiddies, her beloved Jimmy and Jenny. Their similar names might make them sound like brother and sister, but they were cousins. Jenny's real name was Genevieve, but that was Posh Pammy for you.

Posh Pammy and Sheila the Slattern. Dot dropped her gaze to the tablecloth, making a play out of straightening her cup in its saucer. Mrs Donoghue up the road's daughters-in-law were sensible, house-proud girls who knew their place. Why couldn't Archie and Harry have brought home girls like that, girls Dot could have taken to her heart as real daughters? Instead, she had been lumbered with Pammy, of the flawless make-up, perfect vowels and fancy ideas, and Sheila, whose idea of housework was

6

to wait for the spiders to choke on the dust before she ran round with a cloth.

Dot made sure she had a smile on her face before she raised her eyes again. It was a wise woman who loved her sons' choice of wives, something she had reminded herself of more than once over the years. Did other mothers-in-law feel this way? It wasn't summat you could ask.

'You'll do the Christmas dinner, won't you, Ma?' asked Sheila.

'Don't I always?' Dot flapped her hand in front of her face, wafting away the smoke from Sheila's cigarette. Sheila always blew her smoke right into the middle of the conversation. 'I'm all set with my mock-turkey recipe.'

'I take it that means the rabbit is going to meet its maker,' said Sheila. 'There'll be tears from the kids, you mark my words.'

'No, there won't,' Dot countered. 'And keep your voice down. They're in the front parlour, in case you've forgotten.'

'I thought mock turkey meant rabbit.' Pammy frowned, but only for a second. She was strict with herself about not getting lines. She was a pretty girl whose skilful use of make-up turned her into a beauty. She wore her golden hair parted in the centre and drawn back from her face in waves so tight they almost counted as ringlets.

'It does.' Dot dropped her voice. 'But we shan't be eating our rabbit come Christmas. We'll be eating Mrs Donoghue's and her family will be eating ours. So I'll be able to tell the children, hand on heart, that it's not our rabbit on the table.'

'Are you still having Jimmy on Sunday?' Sheila asked.

'Of course – and Jenny. It's Stir-up Sunday. I've got a simple recipe for the Christmas pud. I hope you two will be here to give it a stir an' all.' It was really Sheila she was asking, but it wouldn't do to be so blatant.

'I already said I'd be here.' Pammy enjoyed doing special things with her daughter.

Sheila made a fuss of stubbing out her cigarette and managed to avoid a direct answer. 'I s'pose we should be grateful there's a pudding at all.'

'My lads always enjoyed their Christmas pudding,' said Dot, 'or at least they always enjoyed digging around trying to find the silver thrupenny bits.'

Sheila laughed. 'Young Jimmy made a point of reminding me that new thrupenny bits aren't suitable for putting in the pudding. It has to be sixpences these days.'

Dot managed not to roll her eyes. As if Sheila would go to the bother of making a pudding. If she and Jimmy hadn't been invited round here, she would have bought one of those tinned puds for a shilling.

'When are you two going to put up your trees?' Dot asked. Warm memories filled her of her two as little lads begging for the tree to go up in October.

'I can't find one anywhere this year.' Pammy fetched a sigh.

'Well, if you will insist on having a real one,' said Sheila.

'I can't say I'd feel like decorating a tree anyway, with Archie away.'

'Put like that, none of us feels like it,' said Dot, aiming for a tone that combined sympathy and common sense. 'But that makes it all the more important for us to do it.'

'For the children,' said Pammy. 'I know.'

'And now you've ended up with no tree at all,' said Sheila, 'and all because you've never been happy with an artificial one.'

'Trees are important for us adults an' all,' said Dot. 'We could all do with a pick-me-up in these dark days. I hope you'll still get your string of electric lights out this year, Pammy, and let me put 'em on the tree here. It'll be a tree for all the family, with us spending Christmas Day together.'

Electric lights on Dot Green's Christmas tree – fancy that! Plenty of folk still had candles, but it was only the best for Posh Pammy. Trust her to have spent Archie's hard-earned wages on the smartest, swishest decorations imaginable. Dot couldn't quite come to terms with the notion of electricity being used for summat so frivolous. In the poverty-stricken neck of the woods where she had grown up, they had had oil lamps that gave off sooty smoke when the wick needed trimming. To this day, she remembered her dear mam's mouth dropping open, her jaw practically landing crunch on the floor, the first time she had clapped eyes on a room illuminated by electricity.

Dot pictured Pammy's electric lights on her own old but much-loved tree. Fairy-sized lanterns in red, yellow, green and blue, their soft lights aglow, making the tinsel sparkle and the string of silver bells glimmer. Tiny lights of love and hope in the darkness of wartime.

# Chapter Two

Joan pushed her sack barrow through the teatime crowds on the concourse of Victoria Station, skilfully weaving her way around pinstriped gentlemen with bowler hats and briefcases, ladies carrying smartly wrapped parcels that showed they had done their Christmas shopping in the best establishments, and boys in uniform arm in arm with pale-faced girls doing their best not to cry. A young couple came running past, hand in hand, laughing, he in uniform, she in a pink and fawn flecked tweed suit and pillbox hat, both of them with confetti on their shoulders. Confetti! Where had they got that? Following them came a string of friends, all smiles, a couple of chaps carrying cardboard suitcases with red paper hearts dangling from the handles.

Smiling, Joan stopped to let the happy group pass by. Would that be her and Bob one day? Her skin tingled as self-consciousness washed through her. How lucky she was. Bob was a signalman, but she had met him through being a first-aid volunteer. He was lovely to be with, and no wonder when you thought about the loving family he came from. The Hubbles were good-natured, considerate folk who enjoyed nothing more than being together, and they had welcomed her into their midst. Having the Hubbles made her feel even luckier. She didn't just have a kind, thoughtful boyfriend, she had gained a whole family.

She pushed her sack barrow past the long, elegant sweep of woodwork that fronted the line of ticket-office booths and threaded her way through the milling travellers towards the platform where she was scheduled to meet the train from Leeds. She loved helping people with their luggage, but oh, wouldn't it be wonderful if folk got used to the sight of a girl working as a station porter. There had been lady porters for months now, yet there were still far too many passengers who thought it wasn't proper for girls and women to do the job. Gentlemen passengers often declared it inappropriate that a slip of a thing like Joan should heave their luggage about; sometimes one would even try to do the job for her. It was common for female porters to be referred to as porteresses or porterettes. Why couldn't they be plain old porters, for heaven's sake?

Joan stationed herself halfway along the platform, in front of the empty space where, until last summer, a sign had proudly proclaimed MANCHESTER VICTORIA, before all station platform signs had been painted over or removed – along with road signs – so as to confuse the enemy in the event of invasion. Joan had to suck in her cheeks to quell a grin. Never mind Jerry, the home population was finding it confusing enough.

Eager to do well in her porter's job, she had started learning the place names along as many routes out of Victoria as she could, so she would be able to tell passengers, 'You want the fourth stop, madam,' and she had felt pleased with herself until Bob's mum, who had a job working as a lengthman on the permanent way, which was what Joan and her colleagues had learned to call the railway tracks, had pointed out to her, 'That's all well and good in broad daylight, love, but it's not so helpful on a dark winter's afternoon. What if a train makes an unscheduled stop between stations? In the blackout, the passengers won't know it's not a station and goodness alone knows where the ones doing the counting according to Joan Foster will end up.'

'They'll be lucky not to end up flat on their faces on the embankment,' said Bob.

Joan caught her breath. 'I never thought of that.'

She was instantly consumed by guilt, but, true to form, the Hubble clan had started chuckling and pretty soon everyone, Joan included, was howling with laughter. Oh, how good it felt to be part of a happy family.

Her heart lifted now as she caught the sound of the rhythmic *chuff . . . chuff . . .* of the approaching train. Lifting her chin, Joan sniffed like one of the Bisto kids as aromatic white clouds filled the air. The sound stopped as the engine pulling its line of dark red coaches ran alongside the long platform, heading for the buffers. Even as the brakes shrieked, doors were hurled open and passengers were already jumping down and hurrying on their way while the train came to a standstill with an echoing *clunk*.

'Excuse me, miss. Would you mind?'

Joan wheeled her barrow to where an elderly couple stood next to a pair of suitcases, which a young Tommy had plonked on the platform for them. Once she had seen the elderly couple to a taxi, she checked the time on one of the huge circular clock faces with Roman numerals that hung from the metal gantry beneath the station's gently arched canopy. Good: time to clock off. Better still, this was an evening for meeting up with some of her chums in the buffet, which was always a highlight of her day. When they had all started work together back in March, Miss Emery, the assistant welfare supervisor for women and girls of all grades, had given them what had turned out to be the best possible piece of advice: stick together. Regardless of age or class, stick together. Regardless of being assigned vastly different jobs, stick together. And they had.

It was mainly thanks to the older ladies of the group, who were of an age to be mothers to the younger ones. Joan was always fascinated by mothers. Her own, Estelle, was supposed to be dead. That was what she, Gran and Letitia told anybody who asked. She and Letitia were orphans: that was the official story. The truth, the shocking, shameful truth that they kept to themselves and never shared with anyone, was that years ago, when her daughters were tiny, Joan a baby and Letitia just twelve months older, Estelle had run off with her lover, her fancy man, as Gran called him in a voice that burned with scorn. Even just thinking of it made Joan's blood turn to sludge in her veins. Estelle had abandoned her children, abandoned her husband, and poor Daddy had ended up dying of a broken heart, leaving Gran to step in and be both mother and father to her darling son's two babies.

Anyway, the group of railway girls was led by Dot and Cordelia. Even now Joan felt surprised at how she had taken to using their first names instead of calling them Mrs Green and Mrs Masters. It had been Dot's idea. If they were to be friends, then using everyone's first names, however uncomfortable it felt at first, was one way of ensuring closeness. In front of others, they all 'Miss'd and Mrs'd' one another, but when it was just them, first names was the rule.

The other good idea that held them together had come from Cordelia. She had instigated the meetings in the buffet for around six o'clock in the evening. Not all of them could attend every time – in fact, one of them, Colette, hardly ever came at all because she was always met after work by her attentive husband – but the hit-or-miss element made the meetings feel more special. They kept a notebook under the counter in the buffet and the friendly staff had got used to them asking for the book so they could read the messages and add their own as they made their arrangements to meet up.

Before she entered the buffet, Joan checked that her coat buttons were fastened so that her uniform wasn't on show. She had exchanged her peaked cap for her felt hat with its shallow crown and narrow brim. Had she still been in her uniform, she wouldn't have been allowed to sit at the table with her friends in case it looked to the public as if she was slacking. Lizzie had always had to stand in the corner beside their table, but it had been spring and summer back then, so of course Lizzie wouldn't have worn a coat over her porter's clobber. Sweet little Lizzie, the baby of the group. Her tragic death had hit them all hard. Was it selfish or big-headed of Joan to imagine that it had hit her, if not hardest, then in an extra way, because she had subsequently been given Lizzie's job? For weeks beforehand, she had ached for a 'proper' railway job instead of sitting behind a typewriter in the charging office – and then her wish had been granted in the most horrible circumstances possible. Bob and his family, especially his mum, had been sensitive and supportive – certainly more sensitive and supportive than Gran, who was sharply disappointed by Joan's 'demotion' to being a mere porter – but it had been Mrs Cooper of all people, Lizzie's poor, bereaved mum, who had helped Joan the most by telling her she must do her new job in honour of Lizzie's memory. Whether it was those brave, generous words or the warm hug that had accompanied them that had been the greatest help to Joan, she couldn't have said. That hug had meant the world to her.

As the buffet's quietly busy atmosphere greeted her, she looked around for the others. Yes, there was Cordelia at a table in the corner, with Dot opposite her. The two women couldn't have been more different: Cordelia with her middle-class poise, her ash-blonde hair perfectly coiffed, looking elegant in her wine-coloured wool coat with its top-stitched collar and buttoned wrist straps, her grey felt hat with its upswept brim tilted fashionably forwards; and Dot in her faithful old overcoat and a hat that had lost whatever crispness of shape it had ever possessed. But it would be a foolish person who underestimated Mrs Dot Green based on her appearance. If she looked a bit run-down, it was because every penny she was able to save went on her family, never on herself. And she didn't just care about her own folks. She cared about her fellow railway girls too – as Joan had good cause to know.

At the table with Dot and Cordelia was Alison, and there was no mistaking Mabel, even though she had her back to the room. Her dark brown curls fluffed out prettily below her hat with its jaunty rosette attached to the band.

Joan bought her cup of tea and wove her way between the tables, taking care not to jolt anybody in passing or trip over their bags. She exchanged smiles with her friends. One of the best things about their group was the feeling that you could just sit down and join in.

'Did you see the bridal couple?' she asked and, when the others said they hadn't, went on to describe them.

'How romantic.' Alison sighed, her brown eyes turning misty.

'That'll be you and Paul one day,' said Mabel.

'After waiting to get engaged,' said Cordelia, 'I'm sure Alison has planned a bigger wedding than that.' She smiled. Her smile was cool, as were her grey eyes, but that didn't mean she was unfeeling. 'And I'm positive her mother will have.'

Alison laughed. 'Definitely! My mother can't wait for us to make it official. Neither can Paul's mother.'

'You should get engaged and put them out of their misery,' said Joan.

'Organising a wedding will cheer them up no end,' chimed in Mabel. 'Us too. We can all be your bridesmaids,' she finished with a laugh.

Dot placed her hand over Alison's for a moment. 'Pay them no heed, love. You do everything in your own good time.'

'I'm sure he'll pop the question at Christmas,' said Alison. 'That would be so romantic.' She looked at Joan and Mabel. 'Who knows, I might not be the only one.'

'Hold your horses,' said Mabel. 'Harry and I haven't been seeing each other for more than five minutes.'

'That's long enough for many couples these days,' Cordelia observed drily. She looked at Dot. 'Just like the last war. The world is divided into two types of people: the do-it-now-because-you-never-know brigade and the save-it-up-and-make-it-special people.'

'There are plenty of do-it-now folk around,' said Dot, 'and you can see why. All these young couples falling in love and dashing off to the registry office, waving their special licences.'

'Before they have even found out how many sugars their intended takes,' Cordelia added, 'or whether they want the same number of children. What a spoilsport I sound. But I do feel concerned about these wartime marriages. What's going to become of them in the long term?'

'But if you don't grab your chance while you can . . .' said Mabel.

Joan felt a flutter of apprehension. That was the trouble with being in the save-it-up-and-make-it-special group. You risked the chance that you might not live to see tomorrow.

In spite of living in a world of danger and uncertainty,

she believed in saving up the special things, thereby making them even more special. Her heart beat faster. Even thinking of Bob made her cheeks glow. She hadn't told him how she felt about him. She was saving it up for Christmas. You had to make everything as meaningful and memorable as you could these days.

And she was going to tell Bob Hubble that she loved him.

With their work shifts and their night-time first-aid duties, Joan and Letitia had to plan the evenings out together that they used to take for granted. This evening, they were going dancing as a foursome, Letitia and Steven, Joan and Bob. They got ready together, easing past one another to take turns at the dressing table.

Putting on her white-spotted navy dress, Joan drew up the concealed zip in the side of the bodice that made the garment a perfect fit. Before joining the LMS Railway, she had worked in the sewing rooms at Ingleby's, where she had enjoyed sewing made-to-measure garments. She still made her own clothes and Letitia's. She also made things for Gran occasionally, though it was always disconcerting when Gran's response to the finished item was 'It'll see me out', as if she was doomed to drop dead next week.

This evening, a dress that Joan had made for Letitia was to have its first airing – a rayon-crepe garment in green and cream stripes, with elbow-length sleeves, padded shoulders, fitted bodice and a slender belt of self-fabric above a skirt that was a mass of tiny knife pleats. Not long ago, Bob's mum had speculated about the rules that were bound to be introduced concerning the use of dress fabrics, which had given Joan food for thought and resulted in her determination that her beautiful sister should have a fashionable dress before the new rules came in.

'Some girls wear home-made clothes and you can tell,'

said Letitia. 'Me, I wear home-made and look like I've stepped out of the pages of a fashion magazine.' She kissed Joan's cheek.

'I could happily make us dresses till the cows come home,' said Joan, 'now that Gran lets us wear our hems at the proper length. It was horrid when she made us dress like old biddies.'

'You should make a new dress for yourself next. I could get you the material for Christmas, if you like. We could choose it together.'

Joan glanced down at her white-spotted navy, with its V-neck and panelled skirt. It suited her, but wouldn't it be grand to have a brand-new dress for going out? 'A printed cotton, perhaps, or a silky rayon. That wouldn't be too frivolous, would it?'

'Frivolous?' Leaning towards the dressing-table mirror to apply her lipstick, Letitia paused to raise an eyebrow at Joan via her reflection.

'With this being wartime.'

'Nonsense. You still have to have fun. Some would say fun is even more important these days. You need to look your best too. It makes you feel better and it's your patriotic duty. It shows you're in good spirits and it gives our servicemen something to feast their eyes on.'

'The only chap I want feasting his eyes on me is Bob.'

Letitia groaned, but it was only pretend. 'Likewise for me with Steven.'

Joan bumped into Letitia as she stepped across to the dressing table at the exact moment that Letitia bent down to pick up her shoes.

Joan laughed. 'We could do with a bigger room.'

'I know. Believe me, I've tried. I asked Gran if she'd swap with us.'

Joan stopped in the middle of putting on her necklace,

arms raised, fingers not quite meeting at the back of her neck. 'You didn't.'

'I jolly well did. Gran having the big front bedroom while we're crammed into the smaller room was fine when we were kids, but not now, and that's what I told her.'

Letitia was much braver than Joan when it came to making suggestions to Gran, but then Letitia could afford to be braver. As the favourite, she was permitted more leeway. She was the clever one who had gone to grammar school; the beautiful one, with the same expressive eyes, narrow face and pointed chin as Daddy. Joan hadn't progressed beyond elementary school, while her seamstress job, for all that it had filled their wardrobes with well-made garments and resulted in a new lining for their heavy old curtains and fresh piping on their cushions, instead of being praised to the skies by Gran was more likely to be dismissed as Joan being 'good with her hands' – in other words, too dim to achieve a place at grammar school.

As for her looks – well, just where did she get her brown hair and blue eyes, her softly squared jawline? Not from Daddy, as their stunning studio portrait of him testified. In the black-and-white photograph, his hair appeared black, though, according to Gran, it had been the darkest of browns – nothing like Joan's distinctly ordinary mid-brown hair – and his eyes were dark too. Letitia's fair colouring couldn't have been more different, yet the resemblance between them was strong. Joan resembled him in neither her colouring nor the cast of her features.

Did her looks come from Estelle?

As a child, she had dared to ask the question, only for it to be brushed aside, not merely with a sharp reply but with a swipe of the hand.

'I don't recall what your mother looked like,' had been Gran's brusque response. 'I've cast her from my mind.'

Joan fastened her necklace and positioned the silver filigree heart below the dip in her collarbones. 'What did Gran say?'

'No.' Letitia plonked herself on the bed and leaned forward to slip on her shoe. 'She said the head of the household sleeps in the master bedroom.'

'Did she say anything else? Such as she would think about it?'

Letitia grinned. 'Only that I shouldn't push my luck.' She put on her other shoe and stood up. 'Let me do your hair.'

Joan slid her snood off. Gran insisted they wear snoods over their hair every day and also when they were on first-aid duty at night. The only times they were allowed to leave the house without snoods was to attend church or to go out in the evening. Gran wasn't just strict about behaviour, she was strict about their appearance too. Joan was madly envious of girls who wore their hair free at all times. She had a secret longing to wear her hair in curlers under a turban all day. Never mind made-to-measure clothes in the height of fashion. She couldn't imagine anything more modern or dashing than a working girl in a turban.

She wore her hair swept back from her face, tumbling in waves that finished in curled-up ends that brushed her shoulders.

'I see you're wearing your silver heart,' Letitia remarked as she combed Joan's hair.

'Alison, Mabel and Persephone have all asked me whether it was a present from Bob.'

'And you had to say no, it came from your sister when you were sweet sixteen. Poor you!'

But there might be a piece of jewellery among her Christmas presents . . .

'Of course,' Letitia went on, 'you never know what Bob will get you for Christmas.'

Heat crept across Joan's cheeks. Was Letitia a mind-reader?

Letitia's face appeared beside Joan's in the mirror. 'Why the blush? Don't say you're expecting a ring.'

'I won't say it, because I'm not.'

'Are you sure? Only that's quite a blush.'

'I'm sure. But it would be nice to have a piece of jewellery from him – a brooch or a necklace, perhaps.'

Letitia resumed hairdressing. 'Preparing to cast my necklace asunder, are you?'

'Idiot,' Joan laughed.

After she had returned the compliment by doing Letitia's hair, Letitia got out their precious bottle of lily-of-the-valley scent, which Gran said they had to make do with until the end of the war. It was Letitia's turn to use it. She pressed the tip of her finger to the bottle's opening and upended it, then dabbed her fingertip behind both ears and, bending her head, brushed her finger against the back of her neck, shaking her head gently so that her hair wafted a subtle trace of fragrance around her.

Turning to Joan, she used up the last breath of perfume by touching behind Joan's ears. Joan longed to have scent beneath her hair too, but never dared say so. There was something especially romantic about putting scent at the back of your neck, beneath your hair, as if . . . as if you wanted a fellow to turn his dance hold into more of an embrace and . . . well, *nuzzle* was the only word she could think of.

And she didn't want that.

Yes, she did.

With Bob, she very much wanted it and she shouldn't be ashamed to say so to her sister. The trouble was she dreaded being like her mother. Was she, in her heart of hearts, given to tarty inclinations like Estelle? And that wasn't her only trouble. Before Bob had come along, the man of her dreams, the man for whom she ached to wear scent on the tender flesh at the back of her neck, had been Steven. Oh, the shame and the guilt of loving her sister's boyfriend – but she hadn't been able to help herself. Thoughts of him had consumed her, and knowing that he saw her as his little sister had made the pit of her stomach tense in agony.

Thank goodness for Bob. Not only was he affectionate, considerate and good fun, not only had he provided her with a whole new family to love and appreciate, he had also rescued her from being a complete twerp.

# Chapter Three

Lying on her side, half awake, Mabel snuggled down deeper beneath the bedclothes. Today she had the whole day off work and she could afford the luxury of a lie-in. No, she couldn't. It would be a criminal waste of precious time to spend it in the land of nod. With a groan, she threw herself onto her back, her face immediately feeling the tingle of cold that meant the inside of her bedroom window would be covered in frost again.

She grasped a handful of layers – knitted patchwork bedspread, soft eiderdown, blanket and sheet – and threw the lot aside, rolling out of bed, her bare feet landing on the soft strips of the rag rug that had been made by her landlady. As far as Mabel could see, Mrs Grayson spent every waking hour knitting – bedspreads, cushion covers, coasters, tea cosies, you name it, as well as all the covers on the coat hangers, hot-water bottles, waste-paper baskets and even the doorstops. In a house stuffed to the gunwales with knitted items, the rag rug was an anomaly.

Snatching up her quilted silk dressing gown, Mabel wrapped it around herself, tying the belt. Weren't you meant to spring out of bed and greet the new day with cheer in your heart if you were from the country? But this country girl loathed getting out of bed and always had. Although she lived in Manchester these days, courtesy of her job as a lengthman on the railways, she hailed from Annerby, up in Lancashire, where her father had made a mint from his factory and turned the Bradshaws from an ordinary family who got their hands dirty for a living into that scorned phenomenon known as new money.

After a hurried wash, Mabel dressed in a tailored wool jacket and matching skirt, with a silk blouse. She preferred to wear simple clothes, not wanting to stand out from the other girls, but you couldn't beat silk for warmth. She brushed her hair, sweeping it up from her temples and ears by inserting dainty tortoiseshell combs that toned with her dark brown waves. A dab of powder was followed by the careful application of lipstick, then she went downstairs.

Warmth greeted her as she opened the door to the kitchen, where a chirpy little fire was doing a splendid job. Her landlady was lightly coating herrings with flour.

'Morning, Mrs Grayson.'

'Good morning, Miss Bradshaw. Close the door or you'll let the warmth out.'

Mrs Grayson's skin was pale, not to say pasty, from lack of fresh air, as she never set foot outdoors. One of her conditions for accepting Mabel as her lodger was that Mabel would be responsible for the household shopping. Why Mrs Grayson stayed inside her own four walls was anybody's guess. Mabel had never enquired. When she moved in, she'd had no intention of forming any kind of bond with her weird landlady. Indeed, she had been dead set against becoming close to anybody, up to and including her fellow railway girls, but the determination had faded away now, at least as far as her colleagues were concerned. Prior to that, she had battled her way through a desperate year in which she had let herself be eaten alive by grief and guilt following the tragic death of her oldest, dearest friend. Althea had been more than a friend. They had called themselves sisters and, thanks to the freedom with which they had breezed in and out of one another's homes, both sets of parents used to joke that they had two daughters.

Then Althea had lost her life in a motor accident and Mabel, the driver, had blamed herself. Fleeing her moorland home, she had started work as a railway girl in Manchester, where eventually the companionship of the other railway girls had proved irresistible and she had confided the truth of what she had done to her best friend. The others had been quick to support her, but . . . but how quick would they have been if they had known the real truth, the full truth, of what she had done?

'Take a seat, Miss Bradshaw. The fish won't take long to fry.'

With its black range standing against a blue-and-white tiled wall, its row of copper-bottomed saucepans hanging underneath a shelf of jugs and jars, and its wooden plate rack, Mrs Grayson's kitchen must have looked the same way for donkey's years. It couldn't have been more different from the dining room in which breakfast was served at Kirkland House in Annerby, where, against a background of wood panelling and oil paintings, meals were taken at the mahogany table, complete with a full array of gleaming cutlery and the finest Irish linen. Even when the fire was roaring up the chimney, it didn't stop your toes turning to ice. Mabel glanced about her. Give her Mrs Grayson's kitchen any day. There was a lot to be said for having warm toes. She seemed to have more in common with her dear old grandad than she did with her parents. Darling Grandad, her friend, her storyteller, her comforter, her silly old softy – most of the time, anyhow. He had never let her get away with anything, not when it mattered. She still missed him. She had become a railway girl more or less by accident, but Grandad had been a wheeltapper and she was proud to follow in his footsteps.

Mrs Grayson laid a plate of fish in front of her. Mabel waited until her landlady had served herself and sat down.

'I take it from your clothes that you're not going to work this morning,' said Mrs Grayson.

'I hope to get my Christmas shopping done.' Good manners compelled her to add, 'If there's anything you'd like me to get for you . . .'

'Thank you,' said Mrs Grayson, 'but I don't exchange gifts with anyone.'

God, how sad. Mabel bent her head over her breakfast in case the pity showed on her face.

'I give the milkman and the postman half a crown inside a Christmas card,' said Mrs Grayson, 'though I suppose I ought to say the postlady and the milklady these days. I used to give to the window cleaner as well, but he was called up. I have some Christmas cards left over from previous years, but frankly, I'm worried they'll think I'm unpatriotic if I use them.'

'Why?' Mabel looked at her landlady. The best Christmas present anyone could give Mrs Grayson would be a decent hairstyle instead of that ghastly old-fashioned bun that put years on her, but apparently not even a weekly shampoo and set was worth leaving the house for.

'Mrs Rafferty popped in the other day. She says this year's cards are flimsy and smaller than usual.'

'You won't look unpatriotic,' said Mabel. 'It'll be obvious your cards are pre-war.'

'Maybe I shouldn't send any at all. The Sunday paper said a single bullet made in the munitions is of greater importance to your friends and relatives than receiving twenty Christmas cards.'

'It's up to you, of course,' said Mabel, 'but if I were you,

I'd definitely write cards for the milklady and the post-lady and pop the money inside. How else are you going to give them their Christmas boxes?'

'True. What gifts are you going to buy?'

Mabel felt a tad iffy about saying, now that she knew Mrs Grayson wasn't going to give or receive any presents, poor love. Well, she would receive one present anyway, from her lodger. Mabel mentally added Mrs Grayson to her list.

She had given a lot of thought to her present-buying. She could easily afford decent gifts, even costly ones. Money was no object to a girl who received a generous allowance from her father on top of her weekly wages, but it was important not to seem to show off. With an inner sigh, she compared herself to Persephone – or, to spell it out in full, the Honourable Persephone Trehearn-Hobbs. Persephone could give anybody any gift at all – costly or cheap, practical or purely indulgent – and she would do it with unselfconscious grace and charm. That was the dif-ference between an old family, its name stretching all the way back to an illegitimate child of the Merry Monarch, and new money, who had nothing more than a well-thumbed etiquette book and a permanent feeling of teetering on a social tightrope.

'It doesn't sound awfully imaginative, but I think scented soap would be appreciated in these days of ration-ing. Everyone needs something that's a bit special. And possibly chocolate, although it's devilish hard to come by, even though it isn't rationed – yet.'

After breakfast, Mabel dashed down the garden to the privy. It was a grey morning with tendrils of fog lingering in the air. It didn't seem fair to have fog and frost at the same time. Still, it was a vast improvement on this time last year. The first winter of the war had seen deep snow and severe cold.

Back inside, she headed straight upstairs. She had time to kill before the shops opened, but she didn't intend to spend it with Mrs Grayson. Was that mean? She felt sorry for Mrs Grayson, at the same time as feeling frustrated by her. The poor lady must be lonely. Mabel couldn't help remembering the old folks in Annerby whom she had taken such pleasure in visiting. Not that Mrs Grayson was elderly, but she seemed to be as cut off as some of those old people whose freedom had been stolen by arthritis and failing eyesight. That, in turn, roused Mabel's annoyance: what was wrong with the dratted woman that made it impossible for her to go out?

She made her bed. That was one skill boarding school had taught her. Then, ignoring the chill, she settled down to write a couple of letters, the first to her boyfriend – her boyfriend! That was something she had never expected to happen. After losing Althea, she had believed that she didn't deserve to have anything good happen to her ever again, but Harry Knatchbull, cheeky blighter extraordinaire, had determinedly wormed his way under her defences and, encouraged by her railway friends, she had given in and decided to give the relationship a try – and, oh, wasn't she glad she had! It was as if all the time that she had held out against him, her feelings were hers to command, but the instant she'd decided to go out with him, they simply ran riot. Even picturing Harry's dark eyes and handsome face sent tingles pitter-pattering up and down her arms. An RAF man, he had the regulation short back and sides, while the beginning of a widow's peak served only to highlight the broad forehead above his Roman nose and generous mouth.

Harry was stationed at RAF Burtonwood near Warrington, which wasn't all that far away, but there were times when it might as well have been a thousand miles distant. In the few short weeks since she had started seeing him, Mabel had astonished herself by being so eager for his company. He was the one who had chased after her, for heaven's sake, even finding out her parents' address and driving all the way up there when she was at home recuperating after a spell in hospital. When she had started going out with Harry, she had expected this state of affairs to continue – him being keener and her being more in control – but instead, her emotions, deadened for so long, had sprung back to life, ripping through her with a power that took her breath away.

She dashed off her letter to Harry, her pen nib flying across the page. In these days of shortages, she had trained herself to use smaller handwriting, and she wrote on both sides of the page instead of on one side only, as prescribed by Mumsy's etiquette book.

'You write to one another a couple of times a week?' Persephone had exclaimed just a day or two ago in the buffet. 'It must be serious.'

'Whatever do you find to say?' asked Dot. 'Or shouldn't I ask?'

Mabel had shrugged, self-conscious and pleased at the same time. 'Oh, this and that.'

The others laughed, but Alison leaned forward.

'If Paul and I were separated, we'd be writing all the time.'

Dot had shared a look with Cordelia across the table. 'Young love, eh? My Reg could be away for a year and a day and I swear all I'd get would be a postcard the day before he came home, asking what's for tea.'

A tug at the corner of Mabel's mouth stretched into a smile at the memory of she and Harry together. They were never stuck for something to say. Warmth radiated through her. After the vile year she'd had following Althea's death, she would never have believed life could be this good.

After she had folded her letter to Harry and put it into an envelope, it was time to write home. She took out the latest letter Mumsy had written. She didn't need reminding of what it said because she had read it a dozen times already, but she lapped it up all over again. For all her social pretensions, Mumsy was a sensitive correspondent. She understood how much it meant to Mabel to hear the smallest details about life in her old home and she had taken over Mabel's routine of visiting housebound old folk so she could pass on news from them. Mabel loved her for that. Mabel sometimes wrote to Mrs Kennedy, her special favourite, but Mrs Kennedy's poor hands, painfully twisted with arthritis, meant she could never reply other than via the occasional message passed on by Mumsy.

Mabel read on. Pops had pulled all kinds of strings and cobbled together a mountain of sleeping bags, blankets, Thermos flasks and siren suits, which he had sent to the Quakers in Liverpool to help those people who had lost their homes in the relentless air raids. Mabel's heart swelled with pride. Good for Pops. He was determined that the hated words 'war profiteer' would never be levelled against him. And wasn't it good to feel that she was playing her own small part in keeping the railways running to send much-needed supplies around the country?

Other than that, since the fall of France, French goods had all but vanished from the shops, according to Mumsy, so the family's traditional champagne toast after returning home from church on Christmas morning was in serious jeopardy – *though perhaps a toast wouldn't be quite the thing this year. Or maybe it would? I hardly dare commit these words to paper, but the prevailing attitude seems to be that, with the coming of winter, the imminent threat of that dreaded event beginning with 'i' has been postponed until next spring.*

Even though she had read the letter before and knew exactly what was coming, goosepimples burst up all over Mabel's arms, but beneath the fear was a tiny flutter of hope. Wherever she was these days and whoever she spoke to, she sensed gratitude and relief in the air, not to mention a hint of surprise, that the country had got through this year intact. They had pulled together and withstood the calamity of Dunkirk, turning it into a source of everlasting pride. They had come through the Battle of Britain and there wasn't a heart in the kingdom that hadn't swelled with dignity and honour when Mr Churchill had uttered those unforgettable words, 'Never in the field of human conflict was so much owed by so many to so few.' Good old London had withstood nightly bombing raids for weeks on end at the expense of goodness alone knew how many lives.

But they were still here. Herr Hitler had done his worst, but they were still here. The invasion hadn't happened, and please God, the threat was now considerably less, thanks to the onset of winter.

*Oh, I pray so. God bless you, darling, and keep you safe – keep us all safe.*
*My best love, now and always,*
*Mumsy xxx*

# Chapter Four

'I'm sick of this weather,' Alison declared, plonking her cup and saucer on the buffet table with a rattle of crockery before sinking onto the wooden chair. 'It's either hour upon hour of drizzle or else it's inches thick with fog. I feel as if the world has turned grey.'

'It's an improvement on last year,' Cordelia replied. 'We were up to our necks in snow for weeks on end.'

'I hope it won't stop your Harry getting here to take you out,' Dot said to Mabel.

'Never fear,' said Joan. 'The force of his love will blast a way through the fog.'

'Very funny,' said Mabel, but she didn't mind. Quite honestly, she would have run through the fog to meet him halfway.

'Seriously,' said Joan, 'I imagine it's no joke for you being out on the permanent way in this weather?'

'We all wear our thickest overcoats and woollies,' said Mabel, 'and the work keeps us warm.'

'I was thinking more of the trains coming along while you're working,' said Joan.

'That took some getting used to,' Mabel admitted. 'I'm glad I had the experience of packing the tracks through the light days and better weather earlier in the year. Even in those conditions, it took a while to get used to the trains racing past. If you're not far enough away, they thunder past with a terrific whoosh and you feel as if you're going to be sucked along in the rush of air. Everyone has to be much more careful in the fog. The trains don't travel as fast, but even so.'

It was hard work out on the permanent way, but Mabel had grown to love it. Repacking ballast under the sleepers to shore up the trackbed might not sound like much, but it was an essential part of keeping the trains running safely and the crucial transport system operating. The war couldn't be won without the railways.

Mabel liked the other three in her gang. Louise was the nearest to her in age, her slender figure owing as much to a hard-up background as it did to physical labour. With her fair hair tied up beneath a turban, the sharp lines of a young face that ought to have been more rounded were plain to see. Bette was older, in her thirties, with an hourglass figure that probably used to have men's eyes out on stalks back in the days when she was a barmaid. In charge of the gang was Bernice. She was level-headed and compassionate, but her kind streak didn't make her a pushover. She was mother to Joan's Bob. Lucky Joan. What were Harry's people like? All Mabel knew was that his father was something in the City and they lived in Surrey.

Pushing back her chair, Mabel stood. 'Excuse me, all. I have to dash. I need time at home to get myself ready for my night out.'

She walked out of the station into the blackout, taking care as she went. She had tripped over her fair share of sandbags and walked slap bang into pillar boxes and lamp posts, not to mention other people doing their best to get home in the pitch-black. At least there was no fog this evening, so her journey home wouldn't drag on.

Home . . . Did she regard Mrs Grayson's house as home? Not really. Home was just a useful label for the place where she stored her possessions, hung up her clothes and sat down to eat her meals. The only truly homely part was that Mrs Grayson was an inventive cook, undaunted by the shortages and rationing that, as Mabel understood from conversations in the shopping queues, had some women tearing their hair out. It was sometimes tempting to refer them to Mrs Grayson for a few lessons in how to produce mutton broth, baked stuffed tomatoes, and date and apple pudding.

At last Mabel was in her bedroom, getting ready. For once, she was blind to the awfulness of the ubiquitous knitting – the knitted patchwork bedspread, the dandelion-stitch curtain around the lower half of the washstand and the fern-lace mats on the dressing table and the chest of drawers. Even the lampshades had clover-stitch coverings. All she cared about was what she was going to wear for Harry. Her velvet rayon in two shades of green with buttons down the bodice, or her mauve wool jersey with its collarless neckline and patch pockets? Harry would admire her appearance whatever she wore. He always noticed.

Dressed in the mauve, she put on her brimless fur hat, together with her gloves and her ribbed-wool coat. One of the nice things about going out with Harry was that she was free to dress up and wear some jewellery. She was perfectly happy dressing simply so as to fit in with her railway chums, but there was something special about wearing her smarter, more expensive clobber, which she felt comfortable doing in Harry's company because he came from money too. The chap who could afford to drive his motor all the way up to Annerby wasn't short of a bob or two.

'Not that I could make a habit of it,' he had remarked when she mentioned the Austin Ten in which he had taken her out for a spin along the moorland roads at the end of her convalescence. 'Petrol shortages, you know. I've put the little beastie up on bricks for the duration.'

Checking the contents of her handbag, Mabel descended the stairs, called goodbye to Mrs Grayson, and set off. Harry would gladly have come to pick her up, but she didn't want to introduce him to her landlady. Anything that might encourage closeness between her and Mrs Grayson was to be firmly nipped in the bud.

Instead, she made her own way to the cinema. Harry came hurrying towards her the moment she turned the corner. That was Harry for you, the perfect gentleman, getting there early so she wouldn't be kept waiting. His warm smile set her pulse racing. She might have rushed into his arms, only she couldn't be so bold. Public displays of affection weren't the thing at all, not if you were respectable, but just look at that couple over there, and that couple further along, not just linking arms but practically snuggling up to each other – in public! The war was changing things, there was no doubt about that. The sense of there being no time like the present, and knowing that tomorrow would not happen for some people, was making couples fling old-fashioned decorum to the winds. Fortunately for her and her racing pulse, Harry was a true gentleman and never tried to take advantage, because she wasn't sure she would be able to resist. As it was, their goodnight kisses on the doorstep left her shaken up and hungry for more.

Inside the cinema, they held hands with their gloves off in the smoky darkness while gazing at the screen. Sitting through the sobering scenes depicted in the Pathé newsreel of the morning after blistering air-raid attacks had showered death and damage on 'a port town on the south coast' and 'a town in the heart of England', Mabel had a sick feeling in her stomach. Those places might be a lot further afield than Liverpool, which had taken many a hammering courtesy of the Luftwaffe, but frankly, any-where that wasn't London felt very close to home. Dear old London had withstood the onslaught night after night for weeks on end, but there was something scary about other places being targeted. It made you feel as if your turn couldn't be far off. Manchester had borne the brunt of repeated raids since the summer, though nothing on the scale of what had happened to London and Coventry.

When the lights came on for the interval, the uniformed usherettes made their way to the front of the aisles, their trays hanging by straps that went round their necks. Harry joined the queue and presently returned with two small tubs of vanilla ice cream and two little wooden spoons. When Mabel finished hers, Harry produced a handkerchief for her to wipe her fingers. She loved small attentions like that. She didn't know whether that particu-lar one featured anywhere in Mumsy's etiquette book, but if it didn't, it ought to.

At the end of the evening, they stood for the national anthem, then joined the lines filing out, nodding to the commissionaire when he touched his peaked cap to them as they left the building, swinging their gas-mask boxes over their shoulders and clicking on their torches, the tissue-dimmed beams providing a comforting glimmer to guide them.

'Did you enjoy the film?' asked Harry, taking her free hand and slipping it into the crook of his arm. This was something else that she enjoyed. His taking her hand so confidently made them look like a real couple.

'Very much. I always do, even though after sitting through the newsreel, I always think I won't be able to concentrate on the story.'

'It's important to have that escape.'

'It's part of being at war, isn't it?' she said. 'You see the horrors, but you learn to take them on the chin, and then you throw yourself wholeheartedly into the good things.'

'I take it Clark Gable counts as a good thing?'

Mabel laughed. 'He was perfect as the test pilot.'

Harry laughed. 'Perfect casting, you mean? Don't tell me you care a fig about that, my girl. You like him for the same reason as all the other girls in the audience – because he's so good-looking.'

'Lucky Myrna Loy, being cast as his wife,' Mabel replied with a hint of mischief.

'Fancy him for yourself, do you?' Harry squeezed her arm. 'I don't think it's a good idea for you to marry him.'

'Why not?'

'Firstly, I don't think Carole Lombard would stand for it, and secondly, you'd be Mabel Gable.' Whatever Harry said next was lost beneath her gurgle of laughter. '. . . But that's a good thing, because it leaves hope for me.'

Mabel's senses scattered to the four winds, then just as suddenly were flung back into a sharpened focus that left her breathless. Did Harry mean . . . ? Was he suggesting that he thought marriage might be on the cards?

It was one of those days. Dot's train from Southport to Manchester Victoria was held up for no discernible reason, which presumably meant it was giving way to a train carrying freight essential to the war. Without a word to her, Mr Bonner, the train guard, had implemented Rule 55, which Dot knew about because another guard had explained it to her. Mr Emmet had said it was the most important thing a guard ever had to do, and given that it was to do with making sure a stationary train wasn't hit from behind by the following train, Dot agreed one hundred and ten per cent. When a train had to stop between stations, the guard had to put on the handbrake, then walk back up the permanent way to fasten small detonators to the track. If another train came along, the three small sharp explosions would warn the driver to apply the brakes immediately.

How late was she going to get home after this shift? She pictured Reg sitting at the kitchen table, scanning the *Manchester Evening News* while he waited. They were having their Jimmy tonight. Would Reg stir himself to do summat useful like pop a hot-water bottle in the spare bed or switch on the gas under the pan of carrots? Not likely. That was women's work and he had more self-respect.

Well, grafting on the railways was women's work an' all these days, along with the housework, shopping and cooking . . . Oh aye, and the small matter of getting ready for Christmas. This Christmas was going to be a good one after the strain and sorrow of last year's when the kids had been away, evacuated to the countryside. It had felt like part of herself had been ripped away, so goodness knows how painful it must have been for Sheila and Pammy. When the two youngest Greens had, along with many other children, been brought home again in the new year, Dot had shed secret tears of gratitude, but every time Manchester had suffered an air raid, she had questioned the wisdom of fetching them home. Ought they to be evacuated again? It wasn't her decision to make. They had been kept safe so far. The thought of not watching them grow up was enough to tear her heart open.

The train breathed out its high-pitched whistle and there was the sound of clouds of steam hissing followed by a massive puff followed by the comforting *puh* . . . *puh* . . . that meant the train was getting under way. With a gentle lurch, it pulled forwards and they were on their way again. The train was packed solid this afternoon, every corridor and compartment filled with passengers politely endeavouring not to step on one another's toes or elbow one another in the ribs. In one compartment, some-one had even stuffed three children into the net luggage racks above the seats. It took Dot a heck of a time to make her way down the length of the train to enforce the black-out and no sooner had she done that than it was time to deliver the next set of parcels to the appropriate door, ready for the staff at the next station to remove them from the train and send them on their way to their final destinations.

'Life would be a lot easier if every station platform was arranged so that all parcels could be handed out from the guard's van,' she said to Mr Bonner.

He eyed her balefully. 'Life would be easier if women weren't being foisted onto us to try to do men's jobs.'

Dot let that wash over her. She had known from day one precisely what Mr Bonner's opinion was of women in the workplace – any workplace, but his precious train in particular. Dot didn't claim to be perfect, but she was sure she did her job well. Not that you'd know it from Mr Bon-ner's narrowed eyes and tight jaw.

As if he hadn't spoken, Dot added, 'I suppose it's what comes of having everything designed and built by men. Now, if the job had been given to a handful of women, the result would have been a lot more efficient.'

Grabbing her first armful of parcels, she marched out of the van, leaving Mr Bonner doing a splendid imperson-ation of a goldfish. No doubt he would make her pay for that later. There was no chance of transporting all her par-cels in one go on the sack trolley, not with passengers packed like sardines along the corridors. In fact, as she stepped unevenly through the swaying connector that linked the guard's van to the next coach, she saw that even getting her parcels through by hand was going to be nigh on impossible. Even so, she squeezed and squashed and excuse me'd her way slowly down the length of the coach before doing jiggly steps through the connector into the next coach.

And here it really did become impossible to get through, which was doubly frustrating, as the door she needed to reach was at the far end.

'Problem?' asked a man in a striped suit and trilby.

'I need to get the parcels down to the far door.'

'Not to worry,' said a young serviceman. 'We can pass them over everyone's heads. Give 'em here.'

'Wait,' said Dot. 'Let me fetch the rest. Is there room to put these down here for now?'

Somehow or other, room was made and Dot headed back the way she had come to collect the rest of the consignment. She didn't tell Mr Bonner what she was going to do. What he didn't know wouldn't hurt him.

She returned to where the young serviceman was ready to assist.

In spite of his youth, he had a parade-ground voice. 'Parcels coming overhead, folks. Pass them along to the door, please.'

Nerves fluttered in Dot's tummy. What if it went horribly wrong? What if someone hid a parcel under their coat? Too late to worry about that now. Her parcels were already on their way and all she could do was count them. Then she squeezed her way through to the door.

The familiar chuffing sound ceased, which meant the train was moving alongside the platform and coming to a halt. You weren't supposed to open the doors before the train stopped because it set a bad example to the passengers, but today Dot was the first to fling her door open and jump down, taking a few running steps to catch her balance. She ran to the door where the parcels were, almost bowling over the porter who was waiting to open the door and receive them.

Dot helped him load them onto his trolley, counting them under her breath. All present and correct. What a relief – or was she bad-minded for fearing otherwise? Most folk were good-hearted. That had always been her experience.

Climbing aboard, she returned to the guard's van and if she said 'Wigan Wallgate' once on her way, she said it twenty times. Everyone worried about getting off at the wrong place these days. The ones who were staying on until Manchester Victoria were the lucky ones. No mistakes for them.

Arriving at Victoria, Dot was grateful to the colleague who had brought along a flatbed trolley for the last lot of parcels to be unloaded. Once she had disposed of these, she could finish for the day – and only an hour late. She waited for the passengers to disappear along the platform and through the barrier before she followed, pushing the trolley slowly to get it moving at a steady pace. At the other end of the platform, the ticket collector waved. Mr Thirkle! A painful tingle shot up the back of Dot's neck and across her cheeks. How could he show her up like that? If she hadn't been in charge of a heavy trolley, she would have pretended not to see.

She looked again – and it was Persephone. How ridiculous to have 'seen' Mr Thirkle – and what an injustice she had done him by imagining he might behave in such an overtly friendly manner. Not that their friendship was a secret as such. But, well, it wasn't normal for a man and a married woman to be friends and it wasn't something you shouted from the rooftops. Not that she was ashamed, mind. Absolutely not. She valued Mr Thirkle's company. He was a real gentleman and he listened, really listened, to what she said. It grieved her to think he went home to an empty house. If ever a man deserved to be cared for by a loving wife, Mr Thirkle was that man, but his wife had passed away years ago.

He was lanky and Persephone was tall and slender, and they both wore ticket-collector uniforms, so that must be why her eyes had played tricks on her. There the resemblance well and truly ended, however. Persephone was a beauty from her golden hair all the way down to her toes, while Mr Thirkle had what you might call a lived-in face, with sunken cheeks and a beaky nose that stood out all the more because he didn't have much of a chin. Ah, but he had kind brown eyes. There was a lot to be said for having kind eyes.

'Evening, Mrs Green,' sang out Persephone. The young girls in their group called her and Cordelia by their proper titles when they were in earshot of anybody else. Persephone opened the barrier for her to push her laden trolley through.

'Thank you,' Dot called, eyes to the fore as she made her way between the people on the concourse. Some were talking to one another, some were gazing at the platform numbers, others were checking the little cardboard tickets in their hands, and all were apparently oblivious to the oncoming trolley that could deliver a hefty whack if Dot didn't steer it carefully.

Before she reached the parcels office, Persephone came hurrying after her.

'I say, are you about to finish for the day?' Persephone might have a posh background but you couldn't fault the girl for her friendliness. 'I've just finished my shift. I know how frightfully busy you are these days, what with Christmas coming up, but could I tempt you to ten minutes in the buffet? I haven't seen you to speak to in yonks.'

'I'd love to, but I'm ever so late. The train was delayed and I need to get home.' Then she had second thoughts. 'Well, why not? Ten minutes won't make any odds – but only ten minutes, mind. I must see to these parcels first, though.'

'I'll go and nab us a table.'

There was something pleasing about having her company sought by one of the youngsters. Dot headed for the parcels office to wind up her day's work, then made her way to the corner of the concourse where the first-class restaurant, the grill room, the buffet and the bookshop all clustered, their outer walls covered in tiles of the softest yellow.

Soon she was sitting opposite Persephone, both of them wearing coats over their uniforms, Persephone's a gorgeous deep-blue wool with fur collar and cuffs, Dot's – she smiled wryly – an ancient overcoat that still had wear in it.

'It's grand to take the weight off my feet.' All of a sudden, Dot's feet were swollen and aching.

'Long day?'

'I've had worse. How are you, love?'

Persephone tilted her head to one side, pressing her lips together as if in thought, though her eyes were smiling. 'Can I tell you my news? I'm going to have an article published in *Vera's Voice*. That's my ambition, you know, to be a journalist.'

'I remember. How exciting.'

'It is, isn't it? I'm feeling jolly pleased with myself.'

'What's it about, this article?'

'Christmas in wartime and the importance of maintaining family traditions so as to keep spirits up. I took church bells as my starting point. It was Joan who gave me the idea, actually. She pointed out that bells were rung all over the country last Christmas Day, but from now on they'll only ring in the event of invasion. That made me realise that it makes the other traditions all the more essential.'

'I get *Vera's Voice*,' said Dot, 'so I'll look out for your piece. You wait until I show all the neighbours and say "She's my friend." They'll be ever so impressed. I like what you said about the church bells.'

'So did *Vera's Voice*. I've submitted several articles to them before, but this is the first they've accepted. I got a letter saying they found my church bells idea poignant without being sentimental and that it's important to recognise readers' feelings of sadness and reflection at the same time as encouraging them to make the best of the situation.'

*Make the best of the situation*. Talk about an understatement.

But that was what they were all doing, wasn't it? Making the best of it. Going to work, including doing overtime; caring for home and family; getting by within the constraints of rationing and shortages; stubbing their toes in the blackout; surviving the air raids and emerging from the shelters when the all-clear sounded, chilled and exhausted and not knowing whether the house was still standing or if they would be joining the shocked, hollow-eyed folks at the rest centres, queuing up because a few hours ago they'd had homes and clothes and furniture and food in the pantry and now they had kissed goodbye to the lot.

There had been several raids at the start of December, including one on the evening of the first, which wasn't exactly how you wanted Stir-Up Sunday to end. There were more raids the following Wednesday and Thursday, including two daytime ones. After that, there had been no more raids from Thursday afternoon until breakfast-time the following Wednesday. Looking back, it seemed like a holiday – except, of course, that at the time they'd had no way of knowing how long the respite was going to last. It might have come to an abrupt end at any moment, for all they knew.

As it was, Dot had spent the weekend running around like a blue-arsed fly, getting Christmas sorted before Jerry could make a return visit. She had finished her Christmas shopping – well, almost. Cordelia had said she and her husband were giving war bonds as presents this year and Dot was sure that many of these patriotic gifts would be exchanged, but that wasn't what she wanted her Christmas to be like. She had already sent her boys their presents – shaving sticks, packs of cards, soap and face flannels, and a Ronson lighter each. Most important of all was a long letter to each of them in which she had blathered on about home and the neighbours and her job and the children, mainly the children, filling her pages with any and all details, no matter how silly or insignificant, knowing how much those snippets would mean.

She had splurged on tickets for all the family to see Tommy Trinder in *Cinderella* at the Opera House. For Jimmy she got a model ship to build, for Jenny a compendium of games, and a jigsaw each. She also bought Enid Blyton's *Mr Galliano's Circus* and *The Secret Island*, deliberately choosing books they could share, and, unable to resist the title, *The Naughtiest Girl in the School*.

The air raids started up again on Wednesday morning, followed by another that night, and as for that Thursday . . .

'Honest to God!' Dot exclaimed when the siren released its blood-curdling wail for the fifth time – the fifth! – since one o'clock that morning. Now it was half seven in the evening, with ten minutes still to go on *Howdy Folks!* on the Home Service. 'Hasn't that ruddy Hitler got owt better to do? You can tell he's not in charge of making mince pies.'

Not making mince pies, no, but he was dead set on making mincemeat of Britain's towns and cities, ports and factories. Why couldn't he bugger off and leave them in peace for a while? It was a week and a half to Christmas, for pity's sake. Aye, but that was the point, wasn't it? He had no pity, no common decency. Power-mad, that was Hitler. Well, he'd picked on the wrong country this time.

Reg put on his tin hat, fastened his silver ARP badge to the lapel of his overcoat and slid his ARP armband up the sleeve before slinging his gas-mask case over his shoulder. Dot saw him off.

She was proud of him for his ARP work. Not shoulders-back, heart-swelling proud, like she had been during the emotional days of Dunkirk when old remembered feelings had stormed her unsuspecting heart and made her love him again . . . for a time. Not that overwhelming kind of pride, but a steady, dignified pride that her husband was doing his bit.

She locked the front door behind him. Would she still have a front door come the morning? She fetched the air-raid box. Actually, she had two air-raid boxes now, because she took her Christmas things into the shelter with her an' all: a cardboard box containing the presents, her tin of mince pies, the pudding in its basin, a bottle of sherry and, stupid as it might sound, the fairy off the top of the tree.

Jerry could blow up her house if he wanted and there was nowt she could do to stop him, but he wasn't going to blow up her Christmas.

# Chapter Five

'But we went to church this morning,' Jimmy complained. 'Why do we have to go again?'

'Because it's special,' said Dot. She didn't want to come down hard on him. Goodness knew; he needed a firm hand, but this time she wanted him to understand and accept. She wanted him to feel the same way she felt. 'Because it's Christmas.'

'Christmas isn't until Wednesday.'

'Don't answer back,' said Reg.

'And stop your whining,' added Sheila, blowing out smoke in an irritated stream.

In her heart of hearts, Dot blamed Sheila for the way Jimmy so often had the grown-ups tearing their hair out. He wasn't a defiant boy and he didn't go looking for trouble. It was just that, with his high spirits, he ended up causing more trouble than a dozen puppies behind a sausage counter.

But what else could you expect? Sheila the Slattern wasn't just a lackadaisical housewife; she was an offhand mother an' all. She ought to keep Jimmy busy, set more rules and generally pay him more mind. Yes, all kids played out in the street, but Sheila behaved as if the road outside was some kind of babysitter.

Dot put her hands on Jimmy's thin shoulders and looked into his blue eyes, Harry's eyes, though Harry

47

had never been as much of a monkey as James Henry Green. Beneath her fingers, Jimmy's shoulders stiffened, then slumped in the manner of getting it over with. Oh, Jimmy.

'Christmas isn't just Christmas Day, love. It's Christmas now. You must have done advent at school. Christmas isn't just about opening a stocking on Christmas Day.'

Yes, it is, said Jimmy's expression.

'And it's even more special in wartime.'

She gazed into her grandson's face, freckled even in the depths of winter, all the things she couldn't say to him crowding her mind. Her heart was swollen to bursting with love and longing and fear for his dad and his uncle. All those air-raid deaths; all those bereaved families. Mothers who were separated from their children for the second Christmas running. Church bells all over the kingdom silenced until invasion or victory. Invasion or victory: the only two possible outcomes.

You couldn't say any of that to a child.

'Church is boring,' piped up Jenny, 'but this isn't ordinary church. It's a carol service. It's to get you in the mood for Christmas.'

It was as good an explanation as any. Jimmy shrugged and squirmed free. Dot wanted to pull him back for a hug, but she made her hands fall away.

'I couldn't have put it better myself.' She smiled at her granddaughter. 'Look at you in your smart winter coat with its velvet lapels and your beret, your hair spilling over your shoulders. Eh, you look like an angel.'

'A Christmas angel.' Pammy eyed her daughter complacently. She looked pretty swish herself in her rust-coloured tweed jacket and skirt, her brimless hat showing off her tight blonde waves.

'Some men have grandchildren,' said Reg, 'but I've got

48

a Christmas angel and a three-hundred-and-sixty-five-days-a-year monkey.'

'Three hundred and sixty-six in a leap year,' said Jenny.

That was all the encouragement Jimmy needed. Curling his arms, he thrust his fingers towards his armpits and started making chimpanzee noises. Those *Tarzan* films had a lot to answer for.

And so did Reg.

'Now see what you've done,' Dot hissed under her breath. 'He's not exactly in the right frame of mind for church, is he?' Raising her voice cheerfully, she called, 'Are we all set? Jimmy, fetch your cap.'

'Calm down an' all.' Sheila sucked in one final time and stubbed out her ciggy. 'I don't want you showing me up in church.'

They set off through the dark streets, winter's darkness made more intense by the wartime blackout, with their tissue-dimmed torches to guide them.

'Let's pretend our torches are candles,' said Jenny.

Jimmy held his high in the air like the Olympic flame. Several adult hands immediately reached out to swipe the muted beam downwards.

'You can't do that in front of Grandpa.' Dot tried to soften the moment. 'You mustn't show any light when there's an ARP warden about.'

'Or when there isn't,' Pammy added. 'I meant to tell you, Mother. I bought a couple of tins of corned beef. I thought they'd do us for tea on Boxing Day.'

'You'd think,' Sheila muttered, 'that the daughter of a master butcher would have access to summat more interesting than corned beef.'

'I'll have you know that my father treats all his customers the same and that includes family. He's not one of those sly shopkeepers with a list of favourites.'

Dot cut in swiftly before Sheila could retaliate.

'Thanks, Pammy. It's not as though the mock turkey is going to stretch very far.'

'It's not as though anything is going to stretch very far,' replied Pammy, 'now that the meat ration has been reduced by fourpence a week per adult. You'd think they'd have left it at two and tuppence until after Christmas.'

'What are you talking about?' Jenny asked.

'We're just saying that the government has given everyone a Christmas present,' Dot improvised.

Jimmy perked up. 'What, Nan?'

'They've doubled the tea ration to four ounces and put up sugar an' all.'

Jimmy slumped. 'Call that a Christmas present . . .'

Dot feigned surprise. 'Don't tell me you aren't keen on tea, our Jimmy. Well! And your mum told me specially that she'd asked Father Christmas to put tea in your stocking.'

'She never!' Jimmy exclaimed. 'And there's no such thing as Father Christmas.'

'Isn't there? First I've heard of it.'

The step to the church porch had a white line painted along its edge. White lines were painted everywhere these days – kerbs, steps, station platforms, you name it – but it still didn't stop the occasional twisted ankle. You could be walking along, minding your own business, and you'd hear a sudden swear word and you'd know that some poor blighter had come a cropper.

One of the churchwardens was at the front door. He'd left it ajar for the family to slip into the porch, then pulled it to behind them before another warden admitted them into the church. Dot stopped. She stood still and . . . breathed. Just breathed. This was what it was all about. Peace. Soft voices. Candlelight.

'Come on, Ma,' said Sheila. 'There's room for all of us over here.'

'You go on.'

Please let Archie and Harry experience some moments of this tranquillity over what would be for them a very unfestive season. Sadness washed over Dot, but there was strength within the sorrow. She would not crumble. None of them would. Christmas was a time for hope.

Joining her family, she sat in the wooden pew, the others shuffling along to make room. She placed her handbag on the floor, letting the murmurs of the congregation soothe her. The door at the side of the altar opened and everyone respectfully got to their feet.

In the candlelight, carols were interspersed with readings telling the story of that first Christmas long ago. Dot was close to tears more than once. What was that word Persephone had used? Poignant. She sniffed discreetly.

After sitting for another reading, everyone was about to rise for the next carol when they were asked to stay put and sing 'Silent Night' sitting down. At the end there came a few moments of silence and peace that Dot fervently hoped had reached inside the heart of every person present.

And then the siren commenced its wailing.

With the first rising notes of the siren, an alert jangle of fear took root inside Mabel's chest. She held on tighter to Harry's arm as she looked around for Alison and Paul. The four of them had left the Midland Hotel, where they had met for drinks and mince pies, and were now walking around the curved edge of Central Library, heading towards Albert Square.

Already the drone of aircraft engines could be heard and was growing louder. It sounded right overhead.

'Where's the nearest public shelter?' asked Harry. 'Or should we go back to the hotel and use their cellar?'

A prolonged screech tore through the darkness and an almighty boom pounded the earth. This was it. They were going to die. A great *whoosh* of air rushed straight at them, a solid wall of movement. Mabel was wrenched from Harry and lifted clean off her feet. She couldn't breathe. Her lungs were inside out. Then she was flung against a wall. Dear heaven, was it going to collapse on them? Vibrations clattered through her bones. But it wasn't this building that had been hit. It was that one way over there, on the diagonally opposite corner of Albert Square. Flames glared, then boiled upwards into the sky. How could it happen so quickly? Please don't let Jerry have dropped gas bombs. She didn't think she could keep her hands steady enough to pull on her gas mask.

A figure hunkered down in front of her. Harry.

'Are you all right? Can you get up?'

He helped her to her feet. A swooping sensation in her head suggested her thoughts had been left behind, rather like when you went up in a lift and your tummy felt odd for a moment. But this was no time to be a damsel in distress.

'I'm fine.' She turned to Alison. 'What's that on your cheek? Is it—'

'Nothing. A graze. Where's my torch?'

'I think the torches are gone for good,' said Paul.

Somewhere behind them there was another loud crump – and another. The sound crammed Mabel's ears, stunning her.

'They're lighting up the sky to show the way for more bombers,' said Paul.

'It's going to be a bad one,' said Harry.

'I must get to the Town Hall,' said Paul. 'They're going

to need telephone engineers if the lines are affected – which they will be.' He looked at Harry. 'Can I leave Alison with you?'

'We don't need taking care of.' Calm descended on Mabel. 'We're going to help. We're trained first-aiders.'

'You'd better come to the Town Hall as well, then,' said Paul.

'You aren't exactly dressed for it,' said Harry.

'I'd have worn my tin hat if I'd known,' said Mabel. 'Let's report for duty.'

Joan's bicycle wobbled as she made a hash of jumping off when she reached St Cuthbert's. It wasn't her night to be on duty and, anyway, duty started later than this, but the school gates were already standing open. Stowing her bicycle, she headed for the school hall, hurrying alongside her first-aid colleagues. It seemed pretty much everyone had turned out, wrenched from their warm firesides by the siren's warning. That was what had happened to Joan and Letitia. Gran had made a token effort to persuade them both into the Anderson shelter in the back garden, but they had all known that the girls wouldn't be diverted from performing their duty. Neither would Gran have been impressed if they had. With brief goodbyes, the two girls had set off for different destinations. Members of the same family weren't permitted to work in the same first-aid groups.

Mr Wilson, who ran the first-aid depot based at St Cuthbert's, was grim-faced. A few chairs had been set out, but most of the first-aiders stood about to listen, some with arms calmly folded, others bouncing slightly on their toes, ready for the off. He stood at the front, not moving but bristling with energy.

'The middle of town is taking a hammering. Albert

Square has been hit, but the Town Hall is still standing. The Royal Exchange is on fire. The same goes for Victoria—'

Joan's pulse raced so fast it tripped over itself, scattering the next few beats all over the place. Oh no – not Victoria Station.

'—Buildings, near the Cathedral,' finished Mr Wilson. 'There is a danger of collapse onto Deansgate. Also, a nearby gas main is alight. Things are pretty bad, but we're here to do what is required of us. Thank you all for turning out without being asked. Make sure your first-aid kits are ready.'

Joan checked her rucksack, forcing herself to concentrate. That was the trouble with doing something so frequently. You ended up doing it automatically. Something told her that tonight of all nights was not the time to make a mistake. Metal bottle for water – yes. She would fill that in a minute. Triangular bandages – six. Dressings – six of each size. Splints – four. And six labels, so that, where necessary, casualties could have an I for internal bleeding, F for fracture, or whatever, attached to them to make it a mite easier, a mite quicker, for the hospital staff to treat them.

She glanced round. There was no sign of Mabel. Wait, wasn't this the evening she was meeting up with Alison and their chaps in town? Please let them be safe.

More news arrived. Fires were blazing across Manchester and Salford – Stretford too. Joan bit the inside of her cheek, forcing herself to betray no fear or anxiety. Bob's family lived in Stretford. Had he legged it straight for his first-aid depot, just as she and Letitia had? Was he safe? And the rest of the Hubbles? She forced the thoughts down beneath a coating of calm, fixing her attention on what Mr Wilson said next.

'A fire bomb landed in the Cathedral Yard, but that has

been extinguished. There are fires in buildings along Market Street, and I don't know any details, but something dreadful has happened in Eccles.'

'We shouldn't be sitting around in here,' Mr Bambrook insisted, getting to his feet. He was one of those people who argued with everything.

'I understand how you feel,' said Mr Wilson, 'but, as you are well aware, we have to be here in case of local incidents. All current incidents are being attended to.'

'Ah, but are they?' demanded Mr Bambrook. 'I heard that most of our firemen and fire trucks were over in Liverpool, helping clear up after their last raid.'

'And as we speak, fire crews from all over the north-west will be heading our way to help us,' said Mr Wilson.

'It won't be just proper fire crews neither,' declared a voice from the back. 'You can bet that all the local residents will be doing their bit an' all.'

'What I want to know—' Mr Bambrook persisted, only to be drowned out by cries of 'Pipe down!' and 'Put a sock in it.'

The racket outside was building – the heavy drone of aircraft engines, the brittle bursts of fire as the ack-ack batteries opened up, and the explosions, some more distant but others sounding horribly close, as the deadly bombs landed. Were they finding their targets? And just what were the targets? Had the bomb in the Cathedral Yard arrived there by accident or by design?

Not knowing was hard. Waiting for the call was harder still. You didn't want the call to come, because it meant that your local area, your own home, was under attack. The places, the people you saw every day of your life. But with everything that was going on, all those enemy aircraft overhead, all those explosions, how could here, how could the local area, how could home not be affected?

# Chapter Six

Inside the Town Hall, they soon heard that Paul had been correct. There had been two bombs right at the start, aimed with devilish precision: the one that had landed in the corner of Albert Square, the blast from which had lifted them off their feet, and then another by the Cathedral. Together, those two flares of fire had shown the way for the rest of the attacking planes and now, from skies criss-crossed with searchlight beams and packed with the sound of aircraft engines and anti-aircraft fire, bombs and incendiaries were dropping in wave after merciless wave.

Mabel and Alison were assigned to different first-aid parties. The Town Hall girls were manning the telephones that were ringing like crazy with what could only be reports of bombs from all over Manchester. One of them took a moment to ask Mabel her shoe size before ripping off her own shoes and flinging them in her direction with the words, 'You'd better not cop it tonight. I need those back.'

Mabel kicked her brown and cream leather peep-toe slingbacks under a table and jammed her feet into the sensible brogues. A rucksack was thrust towards her, together with an instruction from the B Group leader, Mr Davis, to 'Stay close. Don't wander off on your own.'

A man with a clipboard ran partway up a staircase, calling for attention. Everyone looked up at him.

'C Group – round to St Peter's Square. Corner of Oxford Street. BDA factory is on fire.' His eyes scanned those below him, settling on Mr Davis. 'B Group – head to Piccadilly. There could be casualties in the shelters in Piccadilly Gardens. You must also help the ARP wardens get people out of the shelters under the warehouses. Those buildings are full of textiles and paper products, all highly flammable. It isn't safe to take shelter there, even in the basements.'

Mabel followed the rest of B Group out of the Town Hall into a world of glowing red light and flashes of exploding shells, of rumbling engines and sharp bursts of AA fire, of searchlights streaming into the sky, pinpointing aircraft.

They joined the policemen and civilians who were racing from one incendiary to the next along the road and the pavements, trying to snuff them out. Mabel's feet crunched through shattered glass. Thank goodness for the sturdy brogues. A van appeared from round a corner, pulling an Auxiliary Fire Service pump behind it. Mabel's heart leaped. This was what they needed. Half a dozen men tumbled out of the van, heading for the pump. Then there was a massive clap of noise, a vast shudder through the air – and the van and the AFS pump were mangled, the half-dozen men lying strewn around, and was that a lone leg over there?

'You – do what you can.' Mr Davis pointed at one of his followers, then to what until moments previously had been the AFS crew. To the others, he said, 'Leave it behind. Whatever you see, leave it behind. Concentrate on what's ahead. And there'll be plenty of that, believe you me.'

This was nothing like Mabel had experienced before. As a first-aider, she was one of the people whose job it was to work through the air raids, helping others, being sent to those dangerous places where bombs had done their worst, where buildings were in imminent danger of crashing to the ground and desperate folk were trapped, injured, dying . . . She had seen all that, lived through it. Heck, she had even driven through it, the motor bouncing over piles of fallen bricks and dipping into cracks and miniature craters, flames pouring out of the road itself from ruptured gas mains, while she concentrated on getting her fellow first-aiders to their next call or taking her patients to the closest hospital.

Even that had not prepared her for this. Was this how it had been in London every night? Was this what Liverpool had lived through time after time? Now it was Manchester's turn, and she might not be a Manchester girl by birth, but tonight, with the streets of the city centre quaking beneath the ferocity of the falling explosives and the smell of smoke crowding her lungs and stinging her eyes, by God, tonight she was Mancunian through and through, now and for evermore.

She was Mabel Bradshaw and she was Manchester.

'Assistance is needed in Hulme,' Mr Wilson announced. 'They're taking a bit of a battering over that way, so we've been told to send a couple of our motors.'

'But that leaves us with just one for our own area.' Trust Mr Bambrook to object.

'If Withington was in flames, you'd be glad enough for help from Hulme,' was the crisp response.

A minute later, Joan was in the back seat with rucksacks and blankets stuffed all around her, bumping along the street in the direction of Wilmslow Road. Mr Wilson had said that masses of incendiaries had fallen in the vicinity of St George's Park, plus at least three high-explosive bombs. Those HEs could do appalling damage.

'You can expect the nearby streets to be badly damaged. With luck, the first fire crews should be arriving from outside the city any time now.'

'My God.' In the front seat, Mr Carstairs leaned forwards, tilting his head up. 'Look at that sky.'

Behind him, Joan squirmed into a better position, then froze. The sky was red. Not black, streaked with the pearly-white of searchlight beams, but red.

'The middle of town's on fire,' said Mr Carstairs. 'Those buggers have set town ablaze.'

Joan slumped back in shock. Town – the word Mancunians used for their beloved city centre. Her hands fisted and her muscles tightened. She was ready to spring from the motor so that she could do her duty. As they approached Hulme, Mr Brannock slowed the vehicle outside an ARP post and Mr Carstairs jumped out to confer with a couple of ARP men. Then Mr Carstairs got back in.

'Erskine Street. People have been trapped inside a public shelter by a bomb blast. Goodness knows what we'll find.'

It took a few extra minutes to get there because of having to divert past the end of a road filled with the rubble of what used to be houses. The instant the car came to a halt, Joan scrambled out, pulling the rucksacks behind her and handing them out. Work was already going on to clear the way into the shelter.

'The people inside must be terrified,' Joan said to Mr Brannock. 'Let's hope they can hear the rescue work.'

Her group joined the human chain lifting away lumps of rubble. Some of the pieces all but tore her shoulders out of their sockets, but she was determined to maintain her place in the line.

Shortly after nine o'clock, the trapped people began to emerge. Joan and the others stood close by, ready to lead the injured away, but there were no casualties, just a seemingly endless stream of people stumbling out into the night.

'I thought this shelter was for two hundred,' said an ARP man. 'There's at least double that come out.'

Joan shivered. If the bomb had landed in a different place, the death toll would have been appalling. As it was, everyone, aside from the babes in arms, walked out on their own two feet.

Mr Brannock had been speaking with an ARP warden. Now he came towards the first-aid group. 'There's a first-aid centre near here. We'll see if they need us. If they can manage without, we'll head back into Withington.'

Instinct told Joan they should head the other way, into town. That was where they were needed most, but their first-aid depot was relying on them to return as soon as they were able – and what if they didn't and the people of Withington died as a result?

They gradually made their way back to base, diverting around fractured water mains and mounds of rubble, stopping to give help in bomb-blasted streets.

'We've got to go back now,' said Mr Carstairs. 'We've run out of supplies.'

Whoever had imagined that six of everything and four splints per first-aider would be sufficient? That person clearly had never pictured damage on this scale.

Back at St Cuthbert's, there was barely time to restock their rucksacks. Joan's hand hovered over the stacks of supplies. Should she take more than six? But if she did and then there wasn't enough for someone else . . .

'The roads both sides of Fog Lane Park,' said Mr Wilson. 'Parkville Road and Fog Lane. Houses damaged. A bomb landed in Parkville earlier on and a rescue team is already there. Incendiaries have since landed in both roads and we have reports of injuries. Brannock, drop Miss Foster and Mr Carstairs on Parkville, then drive round to Fog Lane. Get gone.'

On Parkville Road, residents were out in force, using buckets of water, earth and sand and a couple of stirrup pumps to put out fires while the rescue crew worked at removing rubble from the site of what had once been a pair of semi-detached houses.

'First aid?' An ARP warden approached Joan and Mr Carstairs. 'There's a lady with serious injuries at number a hundred and two and we think there's a boy trapped underneath all that.' With a jerk of his chin, he indicated the pancaked houses.

'I'll see to the serious injury,' said Mr Carstairs and hurried off with the warden, leaving Joan to attend to the walking wounded.

'Joan! Oh, Joan, is that you?'

'Dot!' Joan spun round, hiding her shock, or trying to, at the sight of Dot looking gaunt and ragged with fear. 'Is this where you live?'

'Nay, we live up Heathside Lane, but –' Dot clapped a hand on top of her head as if her hat might blow away, '– we were in church for carols and the siren went off and you know what it's like, you sit there for a moment. Then everyone was hurrying to get out of the church, and holding children's hands and calling to family to stay together, and trying to stay calm, though all we could hear was the enemy planes. We got outside and the folk who lived nearest said the rest of us could go into their shelters with them. I was with our Pammy and our Jenny in a shelter somewhere up yon, and Sheila and Jimmy went off with the mum of Jimmy's friend from school who's still evacuated. And then . . . Oh, heavens . . .'

Joan put her arm round her friend. 'What happened? Are Jimmy and Sheila all right?' That was what you said. Not 'Are they dead?' but 'Are they all right?'

'Oh, that boy – nothing ever stops him. Him and Sheila

61

went down to the Andy behind the house with Jimmy's friend's mum and grown-up sister, and they were all inside and about to shut the door when someone said "Where's the dog?" and quick as lightning Jimmy darted out and back into the house – and that was when the bomb landed.' Dot turned and gazed at the wrecked buildings across the road. 'My little lad's underneath all that lot. Oh, Joan. He doesn't deserve that.'

'No one deserves that. Have they heard any sounds from under the rubble?'

'No, nothing, not yet.'

Fear sent chills rippling through Joan, but she mustn't let it show. She had to be strong for Dot. 'Where's your husband?'

Dot started to point, but her hand was wobbly and she pulled it back, clutching it with her other hand. 'With the rescuers.'

'They'll find him,' said Joan. 'They won't stop until they do. You shouldn't be on your feet. You should sit down and save your strength.'

'Nay, I couldn't sit down. I have to keep moving. I'll go mad else. You get on with your job, love. I'm all right.'

She wasn't all right, but nothing Joan could say or do would make her all right. Only one thing would do that. Please let that child be alive.

Mr Carstairs appeared at her side and a moment later Mr Brannock came hurrying along the road.

'Have you got casualties?' Mr Brannock asked.

'A Mrs Trowell. I've done what I can, but she needs to go to hospital.'

'I've got a Mr and Mrs Hall in Fog Lane, both with serious injuries. The ambulance is taking them to Christie Hospital. I'll ask if there's space for your casualty as well. Then we must get back to the depot.'

'May I stay here?' Joan asked. 'There's a little boy under that rubble. There ought to be a first-aider here when he's dug out.'

'Very well, but come back to St Cuthbert's immediately afterwards.'

Joan made herself useful. She still had a few minor injuries to treat and she helped fill buckets of water, because you never knew whether the water supply would be cut off. A dark-haired young woman stood over the road from the rubble, one arm clamped around her waist, the fingers of her other hand putting cigarette after cigarette to her lips. She must smell like a tobacco factory. Dot went to stand beside her. She must be Jimmy's mum – Sheila.

The rescuers worked on, lifting away rubble with infinite care. Dot edged closer, probably unable to help herself, just needing to be close to her grandson. That was real maternal feeling for you. Not like Estelle, who'd found a new boyfriend and couldn't leave her old life behind fast enough. Joan might end up under a heap of rubble one of these days and Estelle would neither know nor care.

Having run out of small jobs, Joan did the one thing that was left for her to do. She went to stand with Dot, not saying anything, just being there, standing firm.

The men moving the rubble took a moment's break, easing their backs and rolling their shoulders.

'Eh, I'll need a stiff drink after this,' said one, quickly followed by, 'I'm sorry, Green. You know I didn't mean owt by it.'

That thin man must be Dot's husband. He said, 'Don't worry. We could all do with a pint of best bitter after this.'

And then it happened. From nowhere, from somewhere under the ground, a small voice piped up.

'Me an' all, Grandpa. Can I have a shandy?'

# Chapter Seven

Just before half past six on Monday morning, the all-clear sounded. The raid was over. It had lasted for twelve hours. Twelve hours! Dot's bones were still humming from the effect of hour upon hour of noise and hubbub and the heavy vibration that pulsated through the ground, telling you that another bomb had found its mark and another family had copped it. Dot's heart beat harder. After a twelve-hour onslaught, goodness knows how many folk had departed this life, how many more lay in hospital now with crushed limbs or shattered bones or with bits missing.

But their Jimmy was safe.

A whole house had dropped on his head, but Jimmy was safe, with not so much as a broken fingernail to show for it. Covered in dust from head to toe, he had been plucked from what might so easily have been his grave, and wouldn't you know it, he'd had a big grin on his face.

Dot and Sheila had rushed to him, but all he cared about was the ruddy dog that he had dived into the house to save. The dog, too, had been lifted out uninjured.

A pitiless twelve-hour attack. Hundreds of bombs. People dead, people dying, people injured beyond repair. Buildings smashed into the ground. The sky over the centre of Manchester red with fire. In amongst all that, Jimmy Green had been buried alive and had lived to tell the tale. As far as he was concerned, the worst bit was being subjected to a thorough wash from head to toe to get rid of the dust that caked him.

Much as Dot ached to stay close to her family that Monday morning, she had to go to work. So did everyone else. Through the battered streets, people in overcoats and hats headed for the bus stops. Yes, even today the buses were running.

'Morning, all,' called the bus conductor, addressing the queue before letting anybody on. 'Move right down the bus, please. Make room for as many as you can.'

The bus made slower progress than usual, edging round heaps of rubble and taking short detours to avoid craters in the road. Some places were untouched, others had taken heavy damage. It was impossible not to gawp out of the window. Dot poured a thousand blessings on the good fortune that had spared their Jimmy last night.

As the bus rumbled up Oxford Road, conversation died.

'We'll have to drop you off in a minute, because we can't get any further,' called the conductor. 'Brace yourselves for a shock. Acres of ground around Albert Square have been flattened.'

The bus pulled in at a bus stop as if it was an ordinary day. Dot waited for the standing passengers to file out first, then she rose and slid into the aisle, moving slowly down the bus with everyone else. The conductor was standing on the pavement. He gave her his hand to help her down.

'Thank you,' she said. 'And thank you for turning out to do your job.'

'Aye, well, make the most of my smiling face, because with luck you won't be seeing it again. As soon as my shift is over, I'm off to join up – and just let them try to tell me I'm too old.'

'Good luck,' Dot told him. She turned to face the way she had to go across the middle of town. As she did so, a tremor ran through her and she had to gasp for air.

She was gazing at the smoking ruins of the city centre. There were mountains of rubble where there were meant to be buildings. The buildings that were still upright had not a window left intact; a roof was missing here, a frontage missing there. Dot tottered forwards, then got a grip on herself. She mustn't be overcome by the emotion of the moment. She had to get to work and do her job and help keep the railways running.

Where the Free Trade Hall used to be was a great gaping emptiness in front of a curved wall with interior arches – well, they weren't interior any more, and the emptiness wasn't empty, either. It was a mess of bricks and rubble, wood and metal. Dot groaned, not out loud, but deep inside herself. She had never been to the Free Trade Hall. She wasn't one for Hallé Orchestra concerts – Stanley Holloway at the Palace was more her line – but in a vague sort of way, she knew what the Free Trade Hall stood for. She knew it was to do with the common man standing up for what was right. The common woman an' all. Hadn't Christabel Pankhurst hung a 'Votes For Women' banner over the balcony during a political meeting in the Free Trade Hall?

And now the building was gone.

She had better get gone an' all. She had to get to work and she was buggered if she was going to be late because of Herr Hitler. ARP wardens escorted civilians, helping them over and around the heaps of rubble. The air was thick with dust. Emergency-service bells rang in the distance. Overhead, a parachute was caught on tram wires.

An ARP johnny caught her looking at it.

'An aerial mine,' he told her. 'Now watch your feet for this next bit.'

Rounding the corner, she stepped straight into several inches of water that covered the whole street, hosepipes

66

slithering around inside it. Firemen sprayed water onto smouldering buildings, the stench of burning reaching down Dot's throat in spite of her tightly clamped lips.

'Oy! You, lad!' called the ARP warden as a youngster came running past. 'What are you up to?'

The boy hardly stopped. He waved a packet in the air. 'My mam's given me a leek-and-potato pie to bring to my dad. He's on one of the rescue teams.'

'Off you go then,' said the warden, but he was speaking to thin air – thin air? No, thick, dust-clogged air.

'I'll be all right on my own now, thank you,' said Dot. 'I've only got to get to Victoria Station.'

'Mind how you go.'

Treading with care, her heart torn to shreds by the destruction all around her, she went on her way. Nearly there now. She rounded the corner – and stopped dead. Victoria Station – oh, dear heaven.

Dot broke into a run.

'Thanks,' said the Town Hall girl who had lent Mabel her sensible shoes last night. 'I wasn't sure I'd see those again. It's been a rough night.'

'Pretty rough,' Mabel agreed. 'Have you seen the girl I came here with, by any chance?'

'Do you know which group she was put into?'

'C.'

'Hang on a mo.' The girl left her desk and disappeared into an office behind her. She returned a minute later with a smile on her face. 'C Group all reported back safe and sound. Are you going home now?'

'Work,' said Mabel.

'Why don't you come to the Ladies with me? You can freshen up and do your hair and use my lipstick. We all need to put on our best faces this morning.'

A couple of minutes later, leaning forward in front of the long mirror above the line of white basins, Mabel tugged ineffectually at her hair, suppressing a squeal.

'It's rock solid with brick dust.'

'It'll be fine after a good wash,' said her companion.

Mabel cracked a smile – literally. The layer of grime coating her skin had to be forced to let the smile through. 'Either that or the water will set it like cement. I may need to have my head shaved.'

'That's what I like to hear.' A middle-aged lady emerged from a cubicle. 'There's nothing like a bit of banter to start off the day. Miss Porter here will help you get cleaned up and I'll send along Miss Bennett with her cosmetics bag. She takes off all her make-up in her dinner hour and puts on fresh for the afternoon. I'm sure she won't mind sparing you a bit. After that, get along to the canteen and have some breakfast.'

'Breakfast?' Had she heard correctly? Manchester had taken a hammering that had lasted all evening and all night – and breakfast was still being served?

'Don't worry that you're taking food out of the mouths of bombed-out families. The rest centres are equipped with food, washing facilities, blankets, spare clothes and good old cups of tea. The Parks Department has even supplied deckchairs to the rest centre in Cheetham Hill Road.'

Sleeping bags, blankets, Thermos flasks and siren suits – that was what Pops had donated to the rest centres in Liverpool. Every city, every town, every port had to be prepared at all times, and not just every city but all its suburbs. Being prepared didn't just mean having air-raid shelters and fire crews and ARP wardens. It meant having the wherewithal in place to cope with the tragic aftermath – temporary shelter, meals, clothing, bedding . . . mortuaries.

Warmly thanking Miss Porter and Miss Bennett when she parted company with them a short while later, Mabel was heading downstairs when her heart leaped for joy almost before she consciously realised why. Harry! Harry's voice. She took the rest of the stairs at a run. At the bottom, he was already turning round. Seeing her, he opened his arms and she hurtled straight into them.

'Oh, Harry.'

'I know, I know.' His voice was a rumble in her hair. 'I'm so relieved to see you. Are you all right?' Without letting her go, he pushed her gently from him, his brown eyes raking her face and up and down her body. 'Are you hurt?'

'I'm fine, honestly.'

And she was. However exhausted she might have been a few minutes ago, that was forgotten now. In Harry's presence, her smile couldn't be contained. His hands resting lightly on her shoulders sent fireworks tingling through her. The expression in his eyes changed, deepened. Mabel stopped breathing. He lowered his head, pausing partway – giving her a chance to be modest? To recollect where they were? To turn her face aside?

Not flaming likely. Almost before she knew what she was doing, her hands had lifted to his cheeks. His face was smothered in dirt, but all she could feel was his morning stubble. This was what he felt like first thing in the morning. She pictured turning over in bed and reaching out.

She locked her gaze on his, in his, as she drew his face down to hers. His eyes fluttered shut as his forehead rested on hers, his breath warming her face. Then, in a series of tiny nudges, his nose moved hers and she lifted her face a little more. His lips sought hers, brushing them before settling on them. Mabel melted against him, accepting his kiss, returning it, clinging on, asking for more.

Harry's arms tightened around her, almost scooping her off the floor, his embrace increasing in demand and Mabel sinking in willingly. When Harry gradually ended the kiss, Mabel at first snuggled closer, but Harry, breathing heavily, withdrew his face from hers. Mabel pressed her lips together, tasting him, and blinked her way back to consciousness.

'I think we've provided enough of a floor show,' Harry murmured, easing her away from him.

Warmth seeped across Mabel's cheeks, but her embarrassment was superficial. She was still lost in the wonder of the moment. After the horror, desperation and sheer hard graft of the night, it was still possible for happiness to endure. This was what people meant about living for the moment – and boy, what a moment!

'I have to get back to Burtonwood,' said Harry.

'Breakfast first?' she said. 'They're serving it in the canteen.'

'No time,' said Harry. 'Duty calls. The lines in and out of Manchester are ropy at best for the time being. As soon as I get to Warrington, I'll send a telegram to your parents to reassure them you're safe.'

'Thank you. They'll appreciate that.'

'I'd do anything for you.' Harry leaned towards her. Another kiss? No, a murmur in her ear. 'Stay safe. I need you.'

'I need you too,' said Mabel.

Mabel stood transfixed by the sight of the Cathedral. It hadn't caught fire, but it had sustained heavy damage. The roof was still there, but there were no windows, no doors. Everything inside had been picked up by the blasts and dumped in heaps. Woodwork was shattered; the high altar had vanished beneath rubble; and yet the

statue of Sir Humphrey Chetham looked as if it had survived intact.

'The roof was lifted clean off and then dumped back on
again,' someone close by said.

Could such damaged beauty be restored? Was what
remained sturdy enough? All those years of history and
devotion – blasted away overnight. In the early morning,
too: one of the final bombs of the raid had landed here.

With an effort, Mabel forced her heavy limbs to take
her to Victoria Station. As it came into sight, the cords in
her throat tightened. The curved canopy beneath which
the station sheltered had been reduced to a skeleton of
girders. Rubble, girders, wood – a massive pile stretched
across the ground, but the way the tin-hatted rescue crew
talked to one another showed Mabel, even from a distance, that there were no bodies to be dug out. Well, that
was something.

'It happened about five o'clock this morning, I gather.'
Bernice had appeared at Mabel's side.

'Was anyone killed?'

'No, though there were some injuries. Four people were
stretchered away. Mind you, this is nowt compared to the
neighbours.'

The neighbours? Oh yes, Exchange Station.

'They're going to be closed for a fortnight, so I was told,'
said Bernice. 'Come on. Time to get to work.'

Inside, Victoria Station was surprisingly normal, if you
ignored the damage. People were queuing at the ticket-
office windows or asking questions of the staff, who were
patiently giving out information or pointing the way.
Repairs were under way – already! Mabel drew in a deep
breath of satisfaction. Nothing was going to stop the
railways from running to the best of their ability, regardless of the circumstances. Even so, there was nothing

extraordinary about what was happening here. All over the country, any factory, any office, any school or hospital that had been hit would be exactly the same, getting repairs under way while the staff carried on as best they could. Shops, their windows blown out, with notices outside saying MORE OPEN THAN USUAL. Office staff trundling filing cabinets and chairs halfway across town to their temporary new premises. Classes of children decamping into church halls.

'We'll be taking the train out to where we're working today,' said Bernice. 'You'll need something on your head to help keep you warm.'

Mabel realised she was hatless. When had she and her hat parted company? Probably when she and the others were caught in that blast. 'My mother would be appalled,' she said. 'Outdoors without a hat? Disgraceful!'

'I've got a spare headscarf in my knapsack that you can borrow,' said Bernice, which made Mabel realise she had turned out for work without her knapsack of essentials: thick gloves, hand lotion, a sandwich, a bottle of cold tea and – that vital article for any girl who didn't have the luxury of working indoors, where facilities were provided – toilet paper.

'Look at you in your posh coat and your heels.' Bernice tapped the corner of her mouth with a forefinger. 'You remind me of someone who wasn't exactly prepared for her first day packing ballast back in the spring.'

Mabel laughed. 'I can't think what you mean.' Was this what the lady at the Town Hall had meant about a bit of banter? Was this the way everybody was going to get through? By having a laugh and a joke?

Bernice laughed too. 'Don't fret. We'll look after you. There's Joan.' She raised her voice. 'Joan! Over here, lovey.'

Joan came hurrying over, dressed in her porter's

uniform of jacket and skirt with a peaked cap on top of her brown hair, which was caught up tidily in the snood she always wore. She looked thin and tired, but then so did everybody this morning.

'Mrs Hubble,' said Joan. 'Is the family all right?'

'Bob and the girls all came home safe this morning.'

Joan's shoulders dropped in obvious relief. Mabel slid an arm around her and gave her a quick squeeze.

'I heard Stretford had it bad,' said Mabel, deliberately not using Bernice's first name in front of Joan. To Joan, Bob's mum was Mrs Hubble, as was right and proper.

'Aye, we did, love, but our road escaped. The house is still standing and that's more than can be said for a lot of houses this morning. Eh, but our Bob and Petal – well, let's just say I'm glad I didn't know at the time what they were up to. It's bad enough having a son out there, doing his duty, but when your girls are out there an' all . . .'

'What did they do?' asked Joan.

'Nay, lass, don't fret. Bob's fine and so is Petal. But a landmine fell on the police station in East Union Street. It killed six bobbies and cut off communications between there and the ambulance and rescue depots and the Town Hall in Albert Square. So what was anyone to do? Information still needed to go to and fro, so Petal and Bob and others volunteered to be messengers and they set off on their bicycles. Petal's conchie was one of the first to volunteer.'

'I'm glad Bob and Petal got home safely,' said Mabel.

'And Maureen and Glad?' Joan asked.

'They came home safe too,' said Bernice, 'but it was a bad night. We could see the fires. The middle of Manchester was lit up so bright that my husband swore he could read the newspaper from all that distance away. Here come Bette and Lou.' Bernice pressed Joan's arm. 'You take care, my love. Remember, as far as us Hubbles are concerned, you're part of our family.'

As Bernice made a move to go, Mabel said, 'I'll catch up with you. I won't be a moment.' To Joan she said, 'Petal's conchie?'

'The chap she used to go out with. He's a conscientious objector.'

'Are you free later on? Could we meet in the buffet, just the two of us?' Oh, the thrill of confiding in her friend about that kiss inside the Town Hall.

But Joan shook her head. 'I'm sorry, but I want to get home as quick as I can tonight. Letitia hadn't come home from her first-aid duty before I had to come to work, so I want to get back and see her.'

'Of course you do.'

'Was it something important?' Joan asked.

'Nothing that won't keep.' And it would be all the more delicious for having been hugged to herself for a while.

Thinking about it, it was probably a good thing, really, that Joan wasn't available. Mabel needed to get home and speak to Mrs Grayson. More than speak to her. Lay down the law.

# Chapter Eight

Mabel opened the parlour door. Mrs Grayson sat in her armchair, up to her ears in the usual knit one, purl one. She looked up.

'Oh, there you are. You're safe.'

Had Mrs Grayson been worried about her? But not worried enough to search the streets, or do the rounds of the hospitals, or gaze with terrified eyes at the first lists of last night's casualties.

'I've put together a cottage pie. It won't take long to heat through.'

Reaching the end of a row, Mrs Grayson folded her work and, placing her hands on the arms of her chair, started to push herself up.

Mabel stepped in front of her and gently pushed her back. 'Never mind that now. We have to talk.'

Mrs Grayson looked startled. 'What about?'

'Where did you spend last night?'

'Under the stairs, of course, as I always do.'

'You do realise how bad it was?'

'I'm not deaf, you know. I heard everything. And Mrs Hannon from up the road popped in earlier to make sure I was all right and she was telling me about it.'

'Did Mrs Hannon spend the night in her Andy?'

'Where else? What a ridiculous question.'

'You do know that Jerry will be back again tonight, don't you?' asked Mabel. 'As far as they're concerned, Manchester is half flattened and the people are on their knees with exhaustion. They'll come back tonight and finish what they started.'

'I know. Lord Haw-Haw's been on the wireless, gloating – dreadful man!'

'Never mind that traitor,' Mabel said quietly. 'What I want to know is where will you be when it all kicks off?'

'You know the answer to that.' Mrs Grayson's face took on a pinched expression. 'And I don't appreciate these questions from my lodger, and a slip of a girl at that.'

Mabel belatedly realised she had folded her arms. She slid them free of one another and sat down opposite her landlady, leaning forwards a little, wanting to show her concern.

'If what you've heard about last night came from Mrs Hannon, who picked it up second-hand while she was out shopping, then let me tell you first-hand what it was like in town.'

'You were in town?'

'With friends at the Midland Hotel. We'd just left there when it started and we stayed overnight to do what we could.' Mabel shut her eyes. When she opened them again, it wasn't Mrs Grayson's parlour she was seeing. 'Everywhere you looked, in every direction, incendiaries were burning and people were silhouetted against the flames – and that was just on the ground. There were fires everywhere – up above, flames pouring out of empty windows. There was glass underfoot and bricks and rubble and hosepipes. Even the buildings that weren't on fire were hot to the touch. There were rats too.'

'Rats?'

'Streaming out of the warehouses in Piccadilly, trying to find safety. At one point, it looked like the road picked itself up and ran away, but it was the rats. At the beginning of the raid, you could hear every explosion; you could hear the aircraft engines and the ack-ack guns; but by the end, you couldn't hear any of that. It was all drowned out by the roar of the flames. The only way you knew the raid was still in progress was when the ground shook beneath your feet, as if it was going to split open and swallow you.'

Mabel's heart thudded. She tried to quell the tiny trembles that passed through her. She focused her mind on the job she had set herself, to keep her landlady safe.

'That's the first-hand truth of it, and it's coming again tonight. A huge amount of the city centre is in ruins, and what isn't in ruins now will be by breakfast-time.'

'But that's in town, not out here.'

'It happened out here too,' Mabel exclaimed. 'It happened all over. Salford's been clobbered; Stretford's been clobbered; Swinton, Pendlebury, Altrincham, Sale – Hulme. You could spit from here to Hulme. My friend Mrs Green – she lives in Withington – her grandson was buried alive.'

Mrs Grayson lifted a hand to her throat. Beneath her knitted cardigan was a plain white blouse with a Peter Pan collar. She wore a cameo brooch in the centre.

'Is he . . . ?' she asked.

'He's fine,' said Mabel. 'They pulled him out alive.'

'Thank heavens for that.'

'The point is,' Mabel persisted, 'it's not just town that's at risk.' It still didn't feel quite right calling the city centre 'town', but that was what the locals called it. 'Everywhere is. The whole of Manchester and Salford, all the suburbs, everywhere. Shall I tell you about last night in the suburbs, things I heard at work today? There was a Christmas party going on in a house in Eccles. The people were all first-aiders. The house took a direct hit and the rescuers and first-aiders who were sent to help had to dig out the bodies of people they knew personally and had worked alongside. Public shelters have been demolished; schools have been hit. You know Manchester High's new premises that opened in September? Wrecked. Whalley Range High took a hit as well. An oil bomb that came down by parachute destroyed the Royal Infirmary's main staircase. But no matter what happened, in all the hospitals, emergency operations carried on as normal. I don't know which hospital it was, but the boys from Manchester Grammar acted as stretcher-bearers. And the blast from an HE bomb lifted a motor car clean off the road and dumped it through a bedroom window – and that was on Yew Tree Road, which isn't far from here. So don't tell me you're going to be safe in the cupboard under the stairs.'

Mrs Grayson's hands gripped the arms of her chair. 'Mrs Hannon told me about some chaps from further along Nell Lane who used a handpump to put out a fire in the road. Then they moved on to the next fire, and the next, and the next. They ended up t'other side of town, somewhere on Cheetham Hill Road. They carried the pump all that way.'

Mabel let the ensuing silence fill the moment.

Then she said quietly, 'As soon as I've had my cottage pie, I'm going to get ready and report for duty, but I shan't leave you to sit under the stairs. Next door have said any number of times that you can go into their Andy and that's what you're going to do. You're going to spend tonight in the Warners' shelter.'

Mrs Grayson rubbed the palms of her hands down her skirt. 'I know you're right, Miss Bradshaw, but . . .' She lowered her voice to a whisper. 'But I can't leave the house.'

'You have to.'

'You don't understand. Do you think I want to stop indoors the whole time? Do you think I choose to?'

Mabel managed not to say 'Yes'.

'It's because . . . it's because I can't go out. I simply *can't*.'

As Joan bowled into the house through the back door, calling, 'I'm home,' a fragrant, cheesy, faintly mustardy aroma enveloped her.

Gran burst into the kitchen. 'Oh, it's you.'

'I called.'

'I didn't hear properly. I thought it might be Letitia.'

'Isn't she home from work yet? What shift is she on today? Gran, is that macaroni cheese I can smell?' That wasn't wartime fare. Her taste buds were turning somersaults in anticipation. 'When was the last time we had that?'

'Letitia hasn't come home yet.'

'Yes, you said.'

'I mean, she hasn't come home from last night.'

Joan felt a faint quiver inside. 'She hasn't come home from last night?'

'There's no need to repeat it,' said Gran.

'But . . .' She fought to understand. 'Even in town, all the fires were put out by midday and Letitia's depot is in Didsbury. There's still rescue work going on, but . . .'

Gran removed her apron from the hook, tying the bow expertly behind her back. She opened the oven door and the smell of baked cheese poured out, rich and piquant and ever so slightly not quite right.

'Have you overcooked it?' Joan asked.

'If you mean "Is it burnt?", say so,' Gran snapped. She fetched a gusty sigh. 'I put a plate over the top to keep in the moisture, but that was ages ago.'

Putting on the oven gloves, she lifted out the dish and placed it on the top of the oven, removing the plate from the top of it. In spite of having dried out somewhat, the macaroni cheese still looked delicious, all golden and orange.

'Gran, did you use all our cheese and butter?'

'Cheese isn't on ration.'

'I know, but—'

'It's not your job to run the house – or to criticise.'

'I'm not. I'm just asking.' She hesitated, but it had to be said. 'That isn't enough for three.'

'It's not meant to be. It's for Letitia.'

'You used all our butter and cheese on one meal for Letitia?'

'Hark at the voice of jealousy. Why shouldn't Letitia have something special? She's been out on duty for hours longer than you. When it got to dinner time, I thought, that poor child, she'll be ravenous when she gets in, so I set to and prepared her a macaroni cheese. I didn't know I was going to be taken to task by the voice of jealousy.'

'I'm not jealous.'

Gran frowned. 'I was sure she'd be home for her dinner. I've been keeping it warm ever since.'

'She must have gone straight from Didsbury to work in Trafford Park.'

'The bits of Trafford Park that are still standing,' Gran muttered. 'If I put this dish inside a bigger one with water in it and a dinner plate over the top, that should stop it drying out any more.'

'Gran—'

'I'll do your meal in a minute. Honestly, fancy begrudging your own sister a treat.'

'I don't.'

Gran wasn't listening. She bent in front of the cupboard in search of a bigger dish, standing up sharply when there was a knock at the front door.

'There she is now, too tired to come round the back.'

'I'll go,' said Joan.

But Gran had already whipped off her apron. Joan followed her down the dark hallway to hang up her coat and hat. With a rattle of brass curtain rings, Gran pulled back the floor-length blackout curtain that hung in front of the door because of the circular stained-glass window in the door's top half. Steven had put up the curtain pole for them.

Gran opened the door onto a rush of chilly air. Joan popped her hat on the shelf.

'Yes?' said Gran. 'Can I help you?'

A man's voice. Joan, with her back to the doorway, knew that voice from somewhere, but couldn't place it. She turned round.

'Mr Haslett!'

'Ah – Miss Foster.' He addressed Gran. 'My name is Haslett, as Miss Foster just said, and I'm the area coordinator for the local first-aid depots. This gentleman is Mr Chisholm from one of the depots in Didsbury. May I enquire, madam, if you are Mrs Foster, the grandmother and guardian of Miss Letitia Foster?'

'I am.' Gran spoke as if this was rather a grand thing to be.

'Is Letitia all right?' Joan demanded. Was there time for a hospital visit before she went on duty?

'Mrs Foster,' said Mr Haslett, 'might we come in, please?'

# Chapter Nine

Leaving her chair, Mabel picked up the padded pouffe from beside the hearth. Whatever it really looked like, there was no knowing, as it was one of the many items that had received the knitting treatment, courtesy of Mrs Grayson's busy hands. She had made a knitted cover in a zigzag pattern, adding some knitted flowers around the edge. Placing the pouffe in front of her landlady, Mabel perched on it and took Mrs Grayson's hands in her own.

'Tell me,' she said.

Mrs Grayson looked away. 'You wouldn't understand.'

'I certainly won't if you don't at least try to explain. Please, Mrs Grayson.'

Mrs Grayson sucked in a deep breath. Then she huffed the breath out, but she didn't speak.

Mabel tried again. 'Why can't you leave the house? "Can't" is different to "won't". All this time, I thought you wouldn't. I thought you chose not to.'

'You thought I was crackers, I bet.'

The clock ticked on the mantelpiece. It took all Mabel's willpower not to check the time. She couldn't afford to hang about here, but it was essential not to make Mrs Grayson feel rushed.

'Well, you're right. I am,' said Mrs Grayson. 'Gaga, off my trolley, round the bend.' Her eyes shone with tears, but they didn't spill over. Instead, she gave a bitter laugh. 'Who in their right mind can't set foot outside their own house?'

82

Letting go of Mrs Grayson's hands, Mabel added a touch of briskness to her tone as she said, 'All right, then. Tell me what sent you off your trolley.'

Mrs Grayson blinked. Her shoulders moved as if she was about to surge to her feet, pushing Mabel out of the way, but then she stayed still. She didn't slump; she sat up straight, but perhaps something inside her had slumped.

'I didn't do it on purpose. I didn't wake up one morning and say, "That's it. I'm never going out again." It just . . . happened. Not all at once, but gradually, almost of its own accord. It was nothing to do with me. I didn't choose it.' With a flash of fire, she added, 'There have been times when I wanted to tear down these four walls with my bare hands.' The fire vanished, replaced by resignation. 'Except that I couldn't tear them down, could I, because if I did, I'd be outside.'

'You still haven't explained why.' Mabel clasped her hands around her knees. Maybe if she looked ready to hear a story, Mrs Grayson would oblige.

'I had a baby nearly twenty years ago. I didn't marry young and I was what you might call an older mother. I was quite dreadfully ill while I was—' Mrs Grayson stopped. 'It's not the sort of thing you tell a young unmarried girl.'

Crikey, what was she going to say? 'I'm a trained firstaider,' Mabel said stoutly. 'I've probably read about it in books, and if I haven't, I should be told anyway. You never know what you'll come up against in an air raid.'

The change in Mrs Grayson was remarkable. She looked ready to settle in for a good gossip.

'I had a frightful time while I was expecting my happy event. You're supposed to put on weight, eating for two, you know, but I was losing weight hand over fist because I couldn't keep anything down, and my head felt as if it was going to explode. High blood pressure, the doctor said. They don't call it "pressure" for nothing. It was red-hot, right inside the top of my skull, and I could feel it pushing upwards in time with my pulse. Sometimes it was so painful I literally couldn't stand up.'

'Heavens,' Mabel murmured.

'And then the birth.'

Mabel braced herself for gore, but Mrs Grayson recollected herself in time.

'Anyway, my baby, my son, was ill and they told me he wouldn't live. The midwife said it wasn't even worth giving him a name, except that he had to have one for the birth certificate. She'd had to visit me a lot during my pregnancy and we'd had plenty of chats, so she knew I was rather keen on Rudolph Valentino. She said, "You can call him Rudolph Valentino Grayson, if you like, because it's not as though he'll live to be burdened with it." He lasted three days. I'd started to tell myself that the doctor and the midwife were wrong and that he was going to be all right, but he had a convulsion and slipped away. I used to worry that the shortness of his life was my fault for having been so ill while he was on the way.'

'Surely not,' Mabel breathed.

'Well, I'll never know, because I didn't dare ask. I didn't attend his funeral. Everyone said I wasn't well enough. My mother-in-law said it wasn't as though it was a real funeral anyway, since he hadn't lived long enough for anyone to be able to deliver a eulogy.'

'How cruel.'

'She had a way with words. Afterwards, when it was too late, I wished, oh, how I wished that I'd gone.' Mrs Grayson gazed straight into Mabel's eyes, as if willing her to understand. 'That would have made it a real funeral, wouldn't it? The grieving mother clutching her hanky.

And then, you see, because I hadn't gone, it was difficult to go anywhere else. What sort of mother can miss her baby's funeral and then go gallivanting round the shops?'

'Was that when you stopped going out?' Mabel asked softly.

'I told you: it didn't happen all in one go. I didn't even know it was happening. We'd always had my parents-in-law round for Sunday dinner, but my mother-in-law said it was too much work for me when I wasn't feeling up to it and that they would pop round after church and my husband could walk home with them and she would do the Sunday joint.'

'Leaving you behind?'

Mrs Grayson's shoulders lifted in a shrug. 'I know I should have said that this was my husband's home and he ought to eat his Sunday dinner here, but then I wondered how much of a home it was when I had taken to sending notes to the butcher and the grocer instead of doing my own shopping. It was a surprise when I worked out how long it was since I last went out. I thought it had been a matter of weeks, but when I looked back, it had been several months. Then my parents-in-law started calling before church and taking Benjy with them to the service and he didn't come home until teatime. I felt . . . inadequate, and I used to be such a sunny, confident girl when I was young. Then my parents-in-law died within a few months of one another and I had a stern talk with myself and decided that now was the moment when I had to get to grips with myself and live normally again. Only I couldn't. I was too frightened.'

'Frightened of what?'

'Have you ever climbed to the top of a church tower? Or stood on the edge of a cliff, with your toes curling up inside your shoes, trying to hang on? You know that feeling when your tummy plummets and your mind swoops and you're scared of falling? That's how I feel when I walk along the hallway and open my front door. It's how I feel when I have to open the door and pay the milklady. That's why I can't leave the house. I don't want to be stuck in here, but I am, because that front door is the edge of a cliff.'

Mabel almost wished she had never started this. She was out of her depth, without a clue what to do for the best. But in good conscience, she couldn't leave Mrs Grayson here to spend the night in the cupboard under the stairs.

Floundering for the right thing to say, she settled on, 'But you use the outside lavatory.'

'I can manage that. I take a deep breath and walk down the garden and my heart's pounding like a mad thing when I get back, but . . . well, I can manage that.'

'Then that's how we'll do it.' Mabel stood up. No time like the present. 'I'll go next door and fetch Mrs Warner. While I'm gone, you get together all the stuff you take with you under the stairs.'

'No . . .' breathed Mrs Grayson.

'Yes. Mrs Warner and I will each take an arm and hold on tight and the three of us will go out the back door. You can do that. You do it every day. You can especially do it with us guiding you. It's only a few feet to the back gate.' It was more like twenty, but she wasn't about to say that. 'Then just a few paces along the entry, in through Mrs Warner's gate and into the Andy. I know it'll be hard, but we'll be with you every step of the way. We'll sing "It's a Long Way to Tipperary" if it helps. Wait – how about this?' She started to sing. '*It's a short way to Mrs Warner's, it's a short way to go . . .*'

That made Mrs Grayson smile in spite of herself. But she still maintained, 'I can't. You don't know what it's like.'

'Yes, I do. We've all experienced that mad feeling that we might fall. And that's how you feel at the thought of walking through your own front door. Well, I'm not asking you to go through the front door. We're going out the back, to the end of the garden, which is somewhere you go every day, and then we're going a little further. We'll do it together, you, me and Mrs Warner. What d'you say? Will you try?'

# Chapter Ten

Joan clicked off the hall light, moving through the darkness to swish aside the front door's blackout curtain and open the door to let Mr Haslett and Mr Chisholm leave the house. She stood aside, holding the door, her hand on its narrow edge. The edge was solid and straight. So was she. She had to be, on the inside as well as the outside. If she let go for a single moment, she would crumple in a heap and might never get up again.

The men walked past her, transferring their hats from their hands to their heads. They had fiddled with their hats all through the visit, holding the brims, turning them round and round.

'Thank you for coming,' Joan said politely. *Thank you!* Why was she thanking them, after what they had said?

Mr Haslett paused and turned to her. 'Once again, I'm very sorry.'

He and Mr Chisholm departed. Joan remained where she was, rooted to the spot, the door wide open. Cold air flooded in, but who cared? She had been chilled to the bone long before the air touched her. She would never feel warm again.

She stirred herself and shut the door. It was unexpectedly heavy. No, it wasn't. It was her arms that were heavy, her hands, her whole body. Her thoughts were so heavy she couldn't quite manage to think them. She pulled the curtain across. The curtain rings rattled.

Her fingers reached for the light switch, but fell away

before they got there. Why have light when there was nothing you wanted to see? She returned to the parlour.

Gran sat in her armchair beside the fire, which was burning merrily. She had built it up while the men were here. Mr Chisholm had stood by, looking stricken. Mr Haslett had delivered the news – no, he hadn't. He'd started to, but Gran interrupted. 'You must be cold, coming out on an evening like this,' she'd said. She had used the small brass shovel to place a few pieces of coal on the fire. The interruption had lasted a matter of moments, but for those moments Mr Haslett's words went unspoken, and while they were unspoken they weren't real. It hadn't happened. The world was the way it was meant to be.

But not any longer.

Joan closed the door behind her and sat down. She and Gran stared at one another. Joan gripped the sides of her chair. Her breathing was shallow, tiny gasps of disbelief . . . except it wasn't really disbelief, was it? After everything she had seen last night and heard today, all those tales of tragedy and courage, she couldn't really disbelieve, could she? She couldn't really deny it. Not deep down.

'Well.' Gran's voice was brusque. She pushed herself to her feet. For a moment, it looked as if she might sway, but she didn't.

Joan followed her to the kitchen. Gran seized the oven gloves, wrenched open the oven door and removed the large dish with the smaller dish of macaroni cheese inside it. She banged it onto the top of the oven and took off the plate, releasing the tangy aroma into the air. Then she picked up the smaller dish one-handed, releasing her other hand from the gloves to open the cutlery drawer and snatch a fork. This she stuck into the macaroni cheese before pushing Joan aside so she could get to the back door.

'What are you doing?' Joan asked.

'Switch off the light.' Gran turned the big old key that lived in the lock and flung the door open. Cold and darkness poured in. Gran stepped down into their side passage, reaching to unfasten the side gate.

'Gran! It's pitch-black. Where are you going?'

Gran barrelled through the gate. Joan followed, stumbling on the path, but there was no stopping Gran. She marched down the front path to the garden gate as if it was broad daylight and she was late for church, opening the gate so briskly that it didn't have time to squeak. Joan hurried after her as she bustled along the pavement.

Rounding the corner, Joan found Gran at the pig bin, the heavy-duty, galvanised metal bin that all the housewives scraped their vegetable peelings and food waste into, to be collected and taken away on the back of a truck to be processed into pig food.

'Gran, you aren't going—'

Gran swung round. 'Give me one good reason why not.'

'You . . . you can't waste good food.'

'This was for Letitia. She isn't going to have it, is she?'

Seizing hold of the handle on the circular lid, Gran flung it aside, releasing the stench from within. The lid had barely struck the pavement with a sharp crash before Gran began using the fork to scrape the macaroni cheese into the bin.

And then the dreaded wail of the siren sounded in the darkness.

Mabel arrived at St Cuthbert's just after six o'clock, speeded on her way by the memory of yesterday's raid starting just after six thirty. As she entered the school hall, it was buzzing with activity. When the first-aid group had initially been stationed here, they'd had the premises to themselves, but now other services were based there as well. Tonight, all the first-aiders were here, not just the ones who were officially on duty that night. Some ARP wardens were deep in conversation with Mr Wilson. A couple of chaps whom Mabel knew to be electricians sat together, smoking. Their job would be to help make damaged houses safe. The gas men must be here somewhere too, as well as the heavy-rescue chaps.

Mr Carstairs was seated with one leg across his other knee, the *Manchester Evening News* held up in front of him as he read the inside pages. MANCHESTER BLITZ: MANY BUILDINGS FIRED shouted the front-page headline, while above it were the words: *Bombs Shower on City: Shelterers Trapped in Wreckage.* As if that wasn't enough to convey the horror, a second, smaller headline beneath the principal one proclaimed TWO RAIDERS BELIEVED DOWN IN NORTH-WEST: VIVID FLASH – SILENCE.

Mabel went to Mr Wilson's deputy, Mr Varney, to report her arrival.

'Isn't Joan here yet?'

Mr Varney glanced at her. 'Joan?'

'Miss Foster.'

'Ah.' Mr Varney looked away. 'Miss Foster won't be joining us tonight. Excuse me.'

An ARP man was pinning notices to the board. Along with other first-aiders, Mabel clustered round. They were the lists of last night's damaged areas, with information about roads that were best avoided by motor cars, and – something that sent shivers through Mabel – a note detailing the public air-raid shelters that had been hit and were, in the tactful words of the person who had compiled the information, no longer in use – Gibson's, Cornbrook and St George's. Mercifully, it was just the three. Imagine following instructions and taking shelter in the officially designated place, only for that place to be bombed.

'Gibson's shelter – that's on Erskine Street,' said a fellow beside her. 'Packed to the rafters, but everyone got out alive.'

'Not all the poor beggars at Cornbrook were so lucky,' replied another man. 'But St George's Park shelter was empty at the time, I gather – and just as well. A direct hit.'

Mabel wriggled out of the group. The clock on the wall said quarter past six. Fifteen minutes to go. She took a few deep breaths to quell the butterflies and checked the contents of her rucksack.

Twenty past six. Mr Wilson had finished talking to the ARP wardens and they were leaving the building.

'Your attention, please,' Mr Wilson called and the first-aiders crossed the school hall towards him. He referred to his clipboard. 'We had a bad time last night and we're expecting more of the same tonight, but this time we're better prepared. Last night, our own fire and rescue services were depleted because we'd sent assistance to Liverpool. During the night, assistance came to Manchester from as far afield as Middlesbrough, Nottingham and Birmingham. Extra policemen were drafted in too, but there have been no concerns regarding law and order. And of course, our own fire and rescue teams have now returned from Merseyside. We can all expect another busy night.'

Mr Wilson read out the lists of first-aid parties, some of which were different because of the addition of some first-aiders who had been attached to a mobile unit that had taken a direct hit last night. Those who had been inside the van had perished and those who remained had been assigned to St Cuthbert's. It was a chilling thought. Luck or fate – you could call it what you liked. After spending last night digging out the remains of their comrades from the mangled vehicle, the ones remaining now had to face another night performing their duties in the face of more unspeakable danger.

It had just turned half past six. Mabel listened expectantly. Were other ears also pricking up? Or was she being stupid, expecting a six-thirtyish raid just because that was what had happened yesterday? In any event, nothing happened. Mabel tried to swallow, but her mouth had gone dry. This waiting was taxing. But it was infinitely better than what would follow.

Shortly after seven, the siren sounded.

The motor car couldn't get any further because of debris in the road. Mabel and the others climbed out, dragging their rucksacks after them. The night sky was crammed with the sounds of aircraft engines and repeated bursts of ack-ack fire. There were lights too, the eerie beauty of parachute flares drifting slowly downwards and the flare of fires, golden, red and orange, leaping up. Mabel ran round the corner just as the windowless shell of a house shifted, as if shrugging its shoulders before it crumpled into a vast heap that threw dirt and noise upwards and outwards all around it. Mabel, spying rescue workers further along the road, veered as far away as possible from the newly collapsed building, holding her breath so the dust couldn't invade her lungs.

'First aid!' she called as she approached the rescuers.

Several of them stood in a tight circle, talking to one another. One of them looked over his shoulder.

'Good. We may need you.' He finished conferring with the other men and walked towards her as the rest of the group split apart in a decisive way that said everyone had a job to do.

'There's a lady trapped inside – Mrs Benson. We've got to get to her quickly because she's in the kitchen and the kitchen fire is ablaze. Make sure your tin helmet is securely fastened. I need you to be ready to treat her for burns, although with any luck, all she'll have is a few scrapes.'

Mabel looked round for a window or a door, but at ground level there was only rubble.

'How do we get in?' she asked.

'Through the roof. I've got some blokes up there, making a hole. Then the team will be lowered in. That includes you,' he added. 'Shouldn't be long now. My name's Jones. What's yours?'

'Bradshaw.'

While she waited, Mabel tended a couple of walking wounded.

'It's time,' said Mr Jones.

A ladder was positioned against the heap of rubble that had once been the house, the top of the ladder sticking up above the edge of the roof. Two men stood at its base, each with a foot on the bottom rung and their hands clamped around the uprights, holding it steady as Mr Jones went up, another rescuer reaching out to help him onto the roof.

Ensuring her rucksack was firmly fastened to her back, Mabel took her turn in climbing up the ladder. Before she reached the top, there was a sort of spasm on the roof and tiles plunged downwards. 'Hold on!' roared voices from below as she instinctively began to let go of the ladder to protect her head. She tightened her grip, shrinking her neck into her shoulders as the tiles flew past.

She started up again. As she came to the edge of the roof, hands reached out and grasped her arms.

'Don't try to stand up straight,' ordered Mr Jones. 'Lean forwards towards the upwards slope of the roof.'

'Here.' Another man, further up the roof, stretched out his hand to her. 'You're nearly there.'

Mabel's hand disappeared inside his large paw as he hauled her further up.

'Sit there. Don't move,' he ordered.

From here, the red glow in the sky above the city centre was plain to see. Mabel focused her attention on the men beside a hole in the roof. Mr Jones tested a knot that made a loop in a length of thick rope. He slipped it over his head and under his arms, then sat on the edge of the hole. Two others lifted the rope and positioned themselves. Mr Jones edged forwards. There was a jolt as he dropped and the others took the strain, before easing him down. Moments later, they relaxed and pulled up the empty rope.

'Your turn,' one of the men said to Mabel.

Tightening the strap on her tin helmet, she looped the rope around herself and crept forwards to sit at the edge of the hole. Taking a breath, she eased herself over the side – a plunging sensation – and then the rope went taut, sending a jolt through her body before she was lowered to the uneven surface below.

'Careful where you put your feet,' warned Mr Jones. 'This is what's left of the upstairs floor. The kitchen is underneath us at the back. It shouldn't be too difficult to get through.'

Another man was already digging his way through. He leaned right down, putting his face to the hole he had made, then straightening up to shout, 'Kitchen.'

Once the whole rescue team was on the upstairs floor, the hole was made larger. Mabel joined the human chain that lifted away pieces of timber and plaster, and was it her imagination or was it getting hotter in here? No, it wasn't her imagination. Thanks to the damage done to the chimney, the kitchen fire was blasting out heat.

Mr Jones peered down through the hole. 'I can see her. She'll need digging out. She's too close to that fire for comfort. We'll need sheets of asbestos to protect her. Send word up.'

One of the others stood beneath the hole in the roof to shout the instructions. While they awaited the asbestos, they kept making the hole down to the kitchen larger and called reassurance to the trapped woman.

Mr Jones leaned back and told Mabel, 'Call up for a stretcher and straps as well, just in case.'

When she had done that, it was time to descend into the kitchen, most of which – walls, furniture, bits of ceiling – seemed to be on the floor, leaving a cramped and devilishly hot space for them to dig out Mrs Benson, who was conscious, though the heat had got to her and was making her gasp and her eyes flicker.

Mabel and two of the men placed themselves between her and the fireplace, holding up the sheets of asbestos to protect her while the rescue effort went on. Thank goodness for the thick gloves she'd brought in her rucksack. Without them, the flames would have taken the skin off the backs of her hands.

Sweat poured down Mabel's brow and into her eyes, but she held firm. However uncomfortable this was for her, it was nothing compared to what poor Mrs Benson was going through, trapped and petrified as well as being half roasted. At last she was dug free and Mabel was able to examine her. She had both a broken collarbone and a broken arm, as well as a nasty gash all the way down her leg. Despite her pain, she wouldn't let Mabel look at her leg until the men had turned away. Mabel tended her patient, then wrote the label that would expedite matters when she arrived at the hospital.

'We'll haul you back up to the roof while we strap Mrs Benson to the stretcher,' said Mr Jones. 'She won't be far behind you.'

Mabel felt as if her shoulders would be ripped apart as the rope pulled her up. As she emerged onto the roof, tiles shifted beneath her feet.

'Careful, miss.' A hand grabbed her by the arm. 'We don't want the roof caving in and spoiling our rescue.'

Mabel slithered towards the ladder, which another rescuer held steady at the top. Not letting herself think about it, she swung herself onto it and began to climb down.

No sooner had she reached the bottom and been helped over the rubble onto the pavement than Mr Brannock, who drove their first-aid motor, came hurrying over to her. Accustomed to balancing on something that might shift beneath her feet at any moment, Mabel stumbled as she tried to regain her land legs.

'There you are, Miss Bradshaw. There has been an explosion a few streets away. You and I will go in the motor.'

Mabel threw one last look over her shoulder to see Mrs Benson being lifted into an ambulance. It was a wrench to leave her patient, but she had done all she could for her and she must move on. She and Mr Brannock ran to where the motor was parked. Mabel jumped into the front passenger seat, catching a look of surprise on Mr Brannock's face. Did he think females should sit in the back? Well, if he didn't want her choosing her own seat, he shouldn't have left the vehicle unlocked. Not locking the car behind you when you left it was an offence.

Mr Brannock started the engine and turned the car round, clipping the kerb in the process. 'If we head this way, we can go under the railway bridge and it'll be quicker.'

Mabel peered upwards through the windscreen. Searchlights stretched skywards, searching, searching, then capturing enemy planes for the ack-ack guns to target. By contrast, with its single headlamp fitted with a slit mask, the motor had to keep to a pace that felt agonisingly slow.

'The bridge is up ahead,' said Mr Brannock, 'then it's the second or third road on the right.'

The sound of the engine grew louder. Was the motor having problems? No, the sound came from outside, a persistent and deadly thrumming.

'There's a plane overhead,' Mabel exclaimed. 'Stop the car!'

'We can shelter under the bridge.'

'There's no time.'

The whining of the falling bomb filled Mabel's ears. Was this it? Was she going to die because a stupid man thought he had time to drive under the bridge when it was blatantly obvious that he hadn't? Mr Brannock lost his nerve – or possibly saw sense – at the last moment, because he stamped on the brake. Mabel yanked open the door and threw herself out, her body scraping across the pavement. She didn't waste time getting upright, just scrambled on all fours into a narrow passage between two sets of terraced houses, curling up in a ball and jamming her fingers in her ears. Not that that prevented her from hearing the explosion, the noise of which filled her body and coursed through her bloodstream. At the same time, she was thrown to the other side of the passage. Her shoulder struck the brick wall and a dull pain spread down her back and along her collarbone. It was easier to comprehend what had happened to her than it was to focus on the wider event. Easier – but wrong. She was a trained first-aider. She had her duty.

She tried to stand, but her legs gave way and she collapsed in a heap. Clenching her jaw, she had another go and hauled herself up, her hands clawing at the brickwork. Even though her ears were humming, she could have sworn she could make out the tiny grazing sound of gloves against brick.

She staggered into the road, expecting to see a whopping great crater, burst water pipes, probably the fronts taken off the nearest houses. Instead, there was nothing. No change.

Yes, there was. Down the road, the railway bridge had been hit.

Limbs that moments previously had barely been able to hold her upright were now energised as Mabel pelted along the street. Someone was puffing behind her. As she neared the bridge, her steps faltered as she made out the large vehicle underneath, then she picked up speed again.

There was a hole all the way through the structure of the bridge. Beneath it was a bus. She could see it was a bus because a slice of the back end was still more or less intact and recognisable. Its height was still there, as were a couple of upstairs windows above the rear platform with the pole you held on to when getting on or off – or, if you were a kid, that you swung round, leaping to the ground before the bus had quite reached a standstill. The rest of the vehicle had crumpled to almost nothing. The front wheels were there, with a bit of a hump on top where the engine had been, but between that and the morsel standing up at the back . . . Who would have thought a bus would be so fragile, so easily destroyed?

Mabel plunged forwards, but a hand on her arm held her back as Mr Brannock caught up with her.

'Steady on. We need to take this slowly.'

'But there might be people on board,' said Mabel. Then she stopped, her heart delivering a dull thud. How could anybody have survived that? She delved in her pocket for her torch. She had to look. She had to try. It was amazing what people could survive. Just look at Dot's grandson. A whole house had dropped on top of him and he was as fit as a fiddle.

'We need to take our time,' said Mr Brannock, 'so as not to disrupt the site and make things worse.'

As they edged forward, skirting the side of the demolished vehicle, there were no bodies to be seen. Mabel almost buckled in relief.

Running footsteps made them both turn round and step in the way of a man who was racing towards them, his uniform showing he was either the driver or the conductor. His peaked cap had blown off during his mad dash. He came to a halt, bending over, hands on knees, head hanging down. At first it looked like he must have run out of puff, but then, as he reared upwards, mouth twisted, eyes staring, Mabel realised it was shock that had doubled him over. He lurched forwards, but Mr Brannock held him back.

'Pull yourself together,' said Mr Brannock. 'There's nothing you can do.'

'I drove under there to keep it safe.' The driver tried to pull free, but shock rendered him unable to break away from the arms restraining him.

'Be grateful there was nobody on board,' said Mabel.

The driver's wild gaze swung in her direction. 'But there was. A young couple – they stayed on. All lovey-dovey, they were. The other passengers got off. There's a public shelter back there.' He made a vague waving motion with his arm. 'And . . . and the conductress, the clippie, she stayed on. One of us had to. It's in the regulations. You can't leave the bus unattended. I . . . I pulled rank. I'm the driver.' He made another lunge in the direction of the mangled bus. 'We've got to get them out. We've got to get them to hospital.'

Mr Brannock hung on. 'Help will be here in a minute. Look, here come some ARP chappies. There's nothing you can do. Best if you don't look, eh?'

'But I can help. I can help dig 'em out.'

'Let the rescuers do their job, sir. This young lady will take you back to the shelter and see if anyone has a flask of tea.'

'Yes, come along.' Mabel tugged the driver's arm to get him moving. 'Show me where it is.'

'This way.' The driver's voice sounded dull and distant. 'They don't let them in the men's dining room, you know.'

'I'm sorry?'

'The clippies. They're not allowed in the proper dining room.' The driver looked back over his shoulder, but didn't try to return to his mangled vehicle.

It was the shock talking. Mabel delivered him back to the shelter, where kind hands received him and offers of sustenance were called out from all sides. Questions, too. Everyone wanted to know what had happened.

Mabel left them to it and returned to the bridge, where the ARP men were gingerly climbing through the wrecked bus. Mr Brannock came to meet her.

'There's no sign of the three people. Blown to smithereens, I imagine, but the vehicle has to be checked thoroughly. You can do that.'

'Me?' Mabel squeaked.

'Yes, while I go to the incident we were supposed to attend. The ARP men need to be elsewhere too, if there's no one here to rescue and no imminent danger of the bridge falling down.'

'You mean I have to check the inside of what's left of the bus for . . .'

'Body parts, yes. Walk back to the car with me and fetch your rucksack. You'll need it in case you find anything.'

# Chapter Eleven

Before her shift started, Dot stood staring at the destruction. On the first night, Victoria Station had been among the final buildings to be damaged, at around five in the morning, and last night it had been the same, with Victoria being severely damaged after an aerial mine exploded next to its premises a few minutes after midnight. The raid had finished not long afterwards, though the shorter raid had not meant an easier night for Manchester as strong winds had swept the fires along and buildings that last night had escaped attack were now ablaze, part of a wall of fire. The explosions that now reached her ears weren't bombs, but controlled blasts designed to bring down unharmed buildings so that the fire couldn't reach them and spread even further. Dot's chest filled with the heat of unshed tears. How much would be left when the fires were finally extinguished? And would there be another attack to face tonight?

She had been thrilled to pieces last week when she had been put down for an early shift on Christmas Eve. She had planned how she would rush home afterwards and peel tomorrow's veg and get out the posh sherry glasses. Instead, here she was, gazing at some of the damage sustained by the station last night, and Christmas seemed a million miles away.

A copper had lost his life and she had heard that eleven folk had been injured, though she didn't know how badly. The bomb had thrown huge quantities of rubble and other debris at the station. Fires had started and it had taken six hours to get them under control. Six hours! The stench of smoke still hung in the air. As for the damage – oh, if she could get her hands on Jerry, by crikey, she'd give him what for. Platforms 12 all the way to 17 were out of use.

Shock and distress pinned her to the spot. She was on the concourse, looking down at the double-width platform that served two lines, one on each side. From the gantry, a sign hung down, straddling the middle, declaring 14 PLATFORM 15, to show passengers on which side to stand. The tall metal columns were still erect, the fancy metalwork at the top of each one branching outwards to support the long metal beams that helped hold the over-arching canopy. The lights still hung on their long chains, most of the lampshades intact. But the platforms were a mess of debris – glass, timber, metal. And above, the graceful arch of the canopy was a skeleton of metal joists, empty of the glass that had protected the station from the elements. A group of men in overcoats and tin helmets huddled together, locked in conversation. Every now and again, one of them turned and pointed and the others craned their necks before returning to their huddle.

Hearing voices, Dot glanced round. Several business-men were looking down the platform. She glanced away so they wouldn't think she was earwigging.

'They're saying that if anyone within twenty-odd miles of Manchester was unsure of exactly where the city was, they're sure now, because the sky was bright red all night.'

'I heard it's the worst fire since the Great Fire of London.'

She felt a flare of anger. Call this flamin' Christmas. Two nights of relentless bombardment. But the folk of Manchester were carrying on as normally as they could, with dignity and determination – aye, and with courage an' all, like the patients at the Eye Hospital who had tunnelled through a two-foot wall to rescue a doctor, and those nurses at the Royal Infirmary who had faced fire and smoke to tackle an incendiary that had fallen down the chimney, endangering everyone in their ward.

That was one of the good things about working for the railways. You met staff and passengers from all over and you heard good news from all over an' all. But the other side of the coin was that you heard the tragic news from all over as well, like in Hulme, where a dozen or more folk were killed when a pub copped it while they were celebrating a wedding, and workmen who were striving to save a damaged viaduct perished, along with their workhorses, when the whole bally structure came crashing down.

'Mind out, love. 'Scuse me.' A man appeared beside Dot, armed with a folding camera. Its battered leather case hung from his shoulder, the strap tangling with that of his gas-mask box.

Dot stepped aside. 'Will that be in the papers?' she asked as he took his photograph.

He tilted his head from side to side in a sort of shoulder-free shrug. 'Not likely. It won't get past the censor. But it'll be seen one day . . . I hope.'

'It ought to be seen,' said Dot. 'People should know about this.'

'I agree,' came another voice and Dot's heart warmed at the sight of her friend, Mr Thirkle. 'But not just yet. We've a war to win and we can't afford for people to be downhearted. How are you, Mrs Green? And your family?'

'We're all in one piece and our houses are still standing, so we're better off than a lot of folk. Our Jimmy had a miraculous escape. He went to rescue a dog and the house collapsed on top of them, but neither of them is any the worse for it.'

'Trust your Jimmy.'

'And yourself, Mr Thirkle? I can see you're all right, but what about your daughter? And your house?'

'All's well, though as you say, you can't help but be aware of everyone who's homeless or injured or who's lost loved ones.'

'And all the destruction,' said Dot.

'They've had to set up a new control system in the cellars for the trains.' Mr Thirkle looked along platforms 14 and 15. 'It could have been worse. We still have platforms one to eleven.'

Dot smiled. 'Looking on the bright side?' What a dear man he was.

'It's a duty in wartime, but I like to think I do it anyroad.'

Dot wanted to tell him how much she appreciated his kindly common sense and gentle manner, but she didn't. You couldn't say summat like that to a man you weren't married to.

'If you'll excuse me,' said Mr Thirkle, 'I must get on.'

'Aye, I must an' all.'

Dot gave him a farewell nod and turned on her heel. The concourse was quieter than usual, not because it wasn't busy, but because people were shocked and exhausted, though that didn't rob them of their resolute air. Seeing more than a couple of male heads turn in the same direction, Dot smiled to herself, hardly needing to glance the same way to know what, or rather who, had caught their attention so thoroughly. Persephone, bound to be. She looked round – yes, there was Persephone, dressed as a ticket collector, but making the uniform look like something that could be worn under the twinkling chandeliers of a ballroom. With her slender figure, honey-gold hair and violet eyes, she was a real bobby-dazzler.

Persephone hurried her way, asking, 'Dot – your family? Is everyone all right?'

'Yes, thank you.'

'I'm so pleased. I can't stop – I must get to my ticket barrier.'

But as she started to walk away, another voice called her to a halt.

'Persephone! Don't disappear. Dot. I need a word with both of you.'

It was Mabel, ready for a day on the permanent way in her wool overcoat, her knapsack and gas-mask box over her shoulder. She looked shattered, poor love. She must have spent all last night on first-aid duty. But it was more than that. There was something restless and jumpy about her. She came to a halt in front of them. Her gaze shifted and her mouth moved as if she was about to speak, but no words came out.

Dot's heartbeat slowed down. 'What is it, lovey?'

'I . . .' Mabel covered her mouth with her gloved hand. Then she took her hand away and stood taller. 'I have some bad news. It's Letitia – you know, Joan's sister.'

'What about her?' Dot didn't really need to ask. She knew straight away. At the same time, she did need to ask, just in case the news was something else, something . . . not so final.

'Not last night, as in this night just gone, but the previous night, she went out on duty and she didn't come home. Joan told me about it this time yesterday. Then last night Joan didn't come on duty and I assumed she'd been posted to another depot to help out, but . . . she stayed at home because she'd just heard that Letitia . . . Mr Wilson and Mr

Varney, who run the St Cuthbert's depot, knew about it before I went on duty yesterday, but they didn't tell me until my shift ended.'

'Are you saying that Letitia is dead?' Dot posed the question gently. She had to hear Mabel confirm it, just to be sure there was no mistake.

'Oh, Dot.' Mabel's eyes were dark as coal in her shocked face. 'Poor Joan and her gran.'

'You needn't imagine for one moment I'll agree to that.' Gran's voice started off strident, but cracked mid-sentence, descending into a hoarse whisper. 'My girl . . . my Letitia . . . Never.'

'I'm so sorry, Mrs Foster.' Mrs O'Leary from up the road rubbed her hands down the front of her skirt. 'I thought you should know, that's all.'

It was left to Joan to say, 'Thank you, Mrs O'Leary. You did right. But—'

'Never!' Gran exclaimed. 'My Letitia, part of a mass burial service? I'm not having it. She'll have her own funeral. She deserves that, at least.'

'Doesn't everyone?' Mrs O'Leary said quietly. 'But with so many dead . . .'

So many dead. So many that the Bishop of Manchester was going to preside over a mass burial service in Southern Cemetery on Saturday, and there was to be one on the north side of Manchester, too. Letitia was one of many, one of several hundred, but, under this roof, she was the one, the precious single one, that mattered. The knot in Joan's stomach tightened.

'If you don't mind, Mrs O'Leary,' said Gran, 'we're . . . we're expecting Letitia to be brought home any time now. In fact, when you knocked . . .'

'Yes, yes, of course.' Mrs O'Leary came to her feet. 'You have my deepest sympathies, Mrs Foster – and you too, Joan. I'll say a prayer for the repose of Letitia's soul.'

'Thank you.' Gran's voice was clipped. She didn't move.

Joan stood up to see Mrs O'Leary to the door, stretching the sides of her mouth into what passed for a smile as she expressed her thanks, watching politely until Mrs O'Leary had closed their gate before she shut the door. What now?

Letitia was gone. Beautiful, clever Letitia.

*'I'm enjoying the war.'* That was what she had said. Enjoying it! *'When this war is over, I want to be able to say, "I helped win it," not "I spent it changing nappies and wiping snotty noses." I know there's more to motherhood than that, and I've every intention of loving my children to distraction, but they're not here yet and I am.'*

Now Letitia wasn't here and her children never would be either. Joan pressed her hand over her mouth to hold in a cry. She stumbled towards the parlour, pausing to straighten her back before she entered. Gran hadn't moved. Her hands were curved like claws over the arms of her chair. Her gaze was unfocused, the lines in her face more deeply gouged.

Joan struggled to find words, but what was there to say? She knew only too well that there was no comfort to be had. Mrs O'Leary had said something about Letitia doing her duty and no doubt when the letters of condolence started arriving, they would say the same. Good God, hadn't Gran, writing to Lizzie's mum, said that very thing?

There was a knock on the door, as if the person outside was knocking as quietly as possible while still hoping to be heard. An ache ballooned at the back of Joan's throat. Gran moved her hand, eyes suddenly huge and filled with pain. Joan had to save her from doing this. Fighting dizziness, she returned to the front door, fingers clammy as they turned the knob on the lock. She didn't want to do this, she didn't want it to be happening, but she swung the door open.

Steven was outside. He wasn't in his police uniform, but he held himself as if on duty.

'They're here.' His face had lost all its colour. 'The undertakers have brought her home.'

Joan's heart gave an almighty clunk, as if it might never beat again. She nodded, her breaths emerging in shallow little bursts. Beyond the garden gate was – no, she couldn't look.

'Are you ready?' Steven asked. 'The room, I mean.'

Joan tried to say, 'Yes.' She tried to say, 'She's going on the dining table,' but no words came, which was just as well because 'She's going on the dining table' sounded unbearably crass. But the undertakers must hear those words all the time, because where else could you lay a coffin?

A coffin. Oh, Letitia. She couldn't believe it, couldn't take it in.

Steven nodded, his gaze sliding away from hers. He turned away and walked to the gate, stepping onto the pavement to speak to a man dressed in black. Joan's fingers flexed. She wanted to slam the door and keep them outside. If she stopped them coming in, it might not be true. Instead, she walked down the hallway and opened the door to the dining room.

Leaving it open, she walked into the parlour. Gran was on her feet. She had a strength of character that made her seem taller than she was, but not today. Today the burden of her shock and grief had crushed her shoulders.

Joan went to her. They grabbed one another's hands and almost staggered out of the parlour, getting no further than the hallway before movement at the front door stopped them in their tracks. Joan's insides turned to mush as Letitia's coffin was brought inside. Steven led the way. Gran squeezed Joan's hand so hard it seemed her knuckles might crumble to dust. The men carried the coffin into the back parlour. Flinging aside Joan's hand, Gran followed them.

'Carefully, please,' murmured the undertaker as the coffin was manoeuvred onto the table.

Joan's mouth was bone dry. She tried to swallow but a desperate lump stuck in her throat.

'Mrs Foster,' said the undertaker, 'may I extend my deepest sympathies.'

'Take off the lid,' said Gran.

'Madam—'

'I want the box open.'

The man's eyes shifted. He glanced at Steven and then back at Gran. Joan's skin tingled. Might it be a mistake after all? It wasn't as though Letitia had been identified by family. Perhaps it wasn't her inside that box. Perhaps they would take the lid off and it would be somebody else. *Oh yes, oh please, yes.* Joan held herself utterly still, poised on the brink of . . . of . . .

'Madam, may I recommend that the coffin remains closed?'

'I said I want it open.'

'Mrs Foster.' Steven stepped forward. 'Please take the gentleman's advice.'

Gran seemed to study the floor. Then she took a step backwards, granting the men permission to depart. Steven followed them to the front door. Voices murmured. Then the door clicked shut.

Steven reappeared. 'I'm sure you want some time alone. I'll come back later, if I may.'

'You're not going anywhere,' said Gran. 'Joan, fetch the screwdriver.'

Joan went to the kitchen drawer where they kept their small collection of tools. Her hand shook as she retrieved the screwdriver. She returned to the back parlour, every part of her skin tingling.

Gran looked at Steven. 'Go on, then.'

'Mrs Foster—'

'If you don't do it, I will.'

Steven's voice was gentle. 'I'll do it, but please wait in the other room. Let me remove the lid and . . . and take a look, so that I can tell you . . .'

Tell them . . . that it wasn't Letitia after all? That it was a case of mistaken identity; that Letitia was still out there somewhere, in hospital, unconscious?

Gran froze. Then she nodded. She left the room. Joan followed. Gran's back was rigid. How could she manage that? Joan felt as if her whole body was on the verge of collapsing. The door shut behind them.

Gran stopped in the hallway and Joan bumped into her. Gran evidently wasn't moving another step, which meant Joan couldn't either. She couldn't leave Gran standing here alone. Her ears strained for the sound of screws turning, but all she could hear was the rushing of her blood.

The door opened. Steven came out, closing it behind him. And Joan knew. Well, she had known all along, really and truly. Letitia's first-aid boss wouldn't have made a mistake. But just for a few moments, the possibility of its not being Letitia had been dangled in front of her. For those few precious moments, she had had a small reprieve from the unbearable truth.

Steven's face was set in grim lines. He blinked away the anguish in his eyes.

Oh, heavens, it must be bad. If he didn't want them to see her, it must be bad.

'I need handkerchiefs,' he said.

'Why?' Gran demanded.

'Please, just bring them. Several.'

Gran stayed stock-still. Joan forced her legs to move. She trailed up the stairs, her mind spinning as she fetched handkerchiefs from her drawer and Gran's, but not from Letitia's. Next thing she knew, she was downstairs once more, though she didn't remember descending the staircase.

'Thank you.' Steven took the handkerchiefs from her.

He slipped into the back parlour, closing the door. Joan and Gran looked at one another. The door opened again. This time, it stayed open.

Steven stood in the doorway. He drew a deep breath. 'She looks . . . Letitia looks as beautiful as ever. Not a mark on her face. But . . .' He made a helpless gesture and stood aside before Gran could bowl him over.

Joan followed her in. Gran went straight to the coffin and looked inside. She made a lurching movement as if about to utter a cry, but all that emerged was a loud, shuddering breath. Slowly, Joan took her position at Gran's side.

Letitia – oh, Letitia. Steven was right. She was beautiful, her face unblemished. Why had Steven put the hankies round her face like that? Then she realised. They were filling in the gaps where . . . where . . .

They were hiding, or rather trying to hide, the fact that although Letitia's face was unmarked, the back of her head was no longer there.

# Chapter Twelve

You had to make the best of it, didn't you, for the sake of the children, if nowt else. Even so, Christmas in the Green household wasn't the light-hearted affair Dot had put her heart and soul into preparing. Yes, they had Pammy's fancy electric fairy lights on the tree, and yes, the mock turkey was better than expected and the children didn't ask any awkward questions, but everything was underpinned by sadness. Switching on the wireless when they came in from church and hearing a programme of Christmas wishes from evacuated children to their families nearly flattened Dot. Her heart broke for all those separated families and she had to fold her arms tightly to stop herself smothering her grandchildren in an enormous hug. How lucky their family was to have their children here with them. Yet what sort of parents and grandparents were they to have exposed their beloved children to two nights of all-out blitz?

They had all survived in spite of what Jimmy cheerfully called his brush with death, and their houses, all three of them, were intact, which made the Greens a darned sight more fortunate than hundreds of other Mancunian families, not to mention the hospitals, churches and schools, factories, offices and shops that had been damaged.

And then, much closer to home and far too soon after losing Lizzie, there was Letitia. Dot had never met her, but Mabel, Alison and Persephone all had. They had gone to the pictures together; they had gone dancing.

Letitia's funeral was going to be held on Friday, the day before the mass burial in Southern Cemetery for the victims of the blitz.

That morning, Dot and Cordelia met on the pavement outside the church in Chorlton.

'Poor Joan and Mrs Foster,' said Dot. 'What sort of Christmas must they have had?'

'Mrs Cooper, too,' said Cordelia. 'Her first Christmas without Lizzie.'

'This time last year, she and Lizzie had their first Christmas without Lizzie's dad. Mr Cooper was one of the first people to be run over in the blackout.'

'It sometimes seems that tragedy haunts certain families,' said Cordelia. 'Joan has lost her sister now as well as her parents.'

Dot brightened at the sight of Alison coming towards them, looking smart in her hat with its upturned brim and her wool overcoat with the large collar and padded shoulders. She wore a black armband. Just about everybody Dot had seen since the blitz was wearing one of those, as they all showed their respect for the dead.

'We're pleased to see you, Alison – aren't we, Cordelia?' Dot greeted her. 'It's good to have one of you youngsters here.'

'Mabel and Persephone couldn't get the time off,' said Alison.

'What about Colette?' asked Cordelia. 'Does she even know?'

Dot pressed her lips together, feeling guilty. It was easy to forget Colette because they saw so little of her, but she was still one of their group. Dot felt strongly about that. She tried not to be a mother hen when she was at work, but Colette's shyness and her quiet way of speaking brought out Dot's protective streak.

The group around them on the pavement was getting

larger. Neighbours of the Fosters, presumably, and colleagues of Letitia from the munitions at Trafford Park. For some, this wouldn't be the only funeral they attended following the blitz.

'Here comes Colette,' said Cordelia.

Colette was wrapped in a wool coat with a beige and brown checked pattern. The dainty pockets and double-breasted front suggested it was a few years old, although, Dot acknowledged with a smile, it was practically brand spanking new compared to her own coat. The softly nipped-in waist and gentle flare of the garment's lower half were certainly flattering to Colette's figure.

'Oh.' Colette stopped a few feet away, the smile dropping from her face. 'I knew I should have worn a black armband. I was going to, but Tony said it wasn't right, seeing as I'd never met Letitia.'

'We were concerned that you might not have heard,' said Cordelia.

'Persephone sought me out,' Colette answered. 'I was determined to come because of not being able to attend Lizzie's funeral— Oh!' She stopped speaking, a blush fluttering across her pretty face.

Along with Alison and Cordelia, Dot looked round, following Colette's embarrassed gaze, and found Mrs Cooper, Lizzie's mum, hovering close by.

'Mrs Cooper, how good of you to be here.' Trust Cordelia to rise to the occasion. 'It can't be easy for you to face this so soon after . . .'

Mrs Cooper was a little bird of a creature whose clothes were well worn but spotlessly clean – the sort of woman Dot's dear mam had held in high regard as being 'clean poor'. When you came from the background Dot's family did, you knew the difference between clean poor and dirt poor and made your judgements accordingly.

'I wanted to come,' said Mrs Cooper. Losing her daughter had added depth to the lines in her face. 'Mrs Foster came to my Lizzie's funeral, you know, and Lizzie was ever so fond of Letitia – well, of all of you. Sorry, hark at me, blathering on.' She addressed Alison. 'You've come a fair way this morning. I remember Lizzie saying you live north of town.'

'I set off straight after breakfast,' said Alison. 'I didn't know what the buses would be like.'

How mundane, talking about buses, but that was what it came down to, wasn't it? No matter what terrible events unfolded, ordinary everyday life had to carry on as best it could.

'I think we should go inside,' said Cordelia.

The five of them went in. The organist was playing softly. Leading the way, Cordelia stopped halfway up the aisle and they all sidestepped into a pew. There weren't many folk in front of them. Presumably, family members would fill the space after the coffin arrived.

Presently, the vicar appeared and everyone rose as he walked down the aisle to meet the funeral procession at the door. Not that 'procession' seemed the right word. It was just the coffin followed by Mrs Foster and Joan. Dot's heart all but cracked open. No other family? She knew the girls were orphans, but even so. It made Letitia's death even worse.

She gave Mrs Cooper a discreet nudge. 'D'you think we should move forwards? They look so alone up at the front.'

It was Cordelia who answered. 'We can't move now.'

The pall-bearers settled the coffin. One of them was in a policeman's uniform. He must be the boyfriend. What a task to have to perform for the girl you loved.

The opening hymn was 'The Lord is My Shepherd'. Dot

drew a deep breath and sang loudly. Not that her voice was owt special, but it felt important to fill the gaping space between her and the Fosters. It was all she could do to support them.

'Is it shallow of me to be glad the station buffet is still intact?' asked Mabel. 'It makes me feel that, in spite of everything, our group is continuing as normal.'

Aye – and there was an awful lot of 'everything'. So much so that it was barely possible to comprehend it. You had to think of it a bit at a time or else your mind was swamped. Dot lifted her chin. She wouldn't buckle under. None of them would.

There was massive disruption to the railways. The damage to Victoria Station alone was having a knock-on effect all over Lancashire, Derbyshire and Yorkshire, and that was before you took Manchester's other stations into account. Bus services now terminated outside town, leaving passengers to end their journeys on foot through the ruined remains of their beloved city centre. Tram services were restricted where overhead wires had been brought down. Hundreds of buildings of all kinds had to be, at best, made safe; at worst, rebuilt.

And the death toll. Hundreds in hospital. Two mass burials.

Yet Manchester was carrying on. On Upper Brook Street, William Arnold's, which had built pieces for motor cars before the war and now constructed parts for aeroplanes, after losing their roof on the first night of the blitz had simply dragged a tarpaulin into place as a temporary covering and got on with their work. The railway girls' very own LMS Railway Company had loaned railway carriages to Trafford Park to billet all those workers involved in the massive clear-up operation. And goodness alone knew how many cups of tea had been provided by kindly neighbours and WVS ladies.

Now, after work on the Monday between Christmas and New Year, Dot and the others were in the station buffet, crowded round a table that was barely big enough to hold their cups and saucers. She looked round at the friends who meant so much to her – Cordelia, Mabel, Alison, Persephone – and, for a wonder, Colette was here too. Joan was back at work today, apparently, but it was understandable that she was keeping herself to herself. When she was ready to venture back into the buffet, she would be welcomed with warmth and compassion. And if she stayed away too long, Dot would go and give her a nudge in the buffet's direction.

'It's not shallow,' Cordelia said to Mabel. 'We all need to cling to normality at a time like this.'

'I'm glad to see you here,' Dot told Colette.

'I wish I could come more often, but you know how it is,' said Colette. 'After attending Letitia's funeral, it seemed important to be here this evening, just for a short while.' She glanced at the clock on the wall, then looked embarrassed when she realised Dot had noticed.

Dot turned to Persephone. 'I saw your article in *Vera's Voice.*'

Persephone looked troubled. 'I feel rather wretched about that article, actually.'

'What was it about?' asked Alison.

'Christmas traditions providing hope. It seems naive now.'

'You weren't to know what was going to happen,' Mabel pointed out.

'I know, but I feel like a prize idiot.'

Alison's shoulders twitched impatiently. 'If the worst thing that happens to you in this war is that you write an article that turns out to be badly timed, then you'll have got off more lightly than the four or five thousand people in Manchester who are currently homeless and relying on friends and neighbours and the rest centres.'

There was a short silence, not because of what Alison had said but because of the sharp way she had said it. A faint flush brushed Persephone's cheekbones.

'Your parents must have missed having you at home with them this Christmas,' said Colette.

'I expect so,' said Persephone, 'but it's a long way to Sussex and train journeys take for ever these days. Anyway, I kept busy. On Christmas Day, Miss Brown let me have the Bentley to help deliver Christmas dinners to the rest centres. The people at the Cooperative Society in Winsford stayed up all night to prepare hundreds upon hundreds of hotpots, meat pies and sultana puddings so that the bombed-out people in the rest centres could have a Christmas dinner. And the Winsford people weren't the only ones.'

'Eh, folk are good,' said Dot, her heart warming.

'They are,' Persephone agreed. 'Most people are simply splendid when it comes down to it.'

'And I suppose you're going to write about it in your next article, are you?' There was a gleam in Alison's eye. 'I suppose that's why you did it, wasn't it? Not out of the goodness of your heart.'

'On the contrary,' said Cordelia in that cool voice that made her sound so knowledgeable, 'I'm sure that's precisely why Persephone did it, and if she happens to write about it – well, why not? It's just the sort of hopeful story that people appreciate these days. I shouldn't be at all surprised to see something of the kind on the Pathé news.'

Colour rose in Alison's cheeks, but the awkwardness of the moment was dispelled when a pretty blonde girl in a cherry-red hat wound her way between the tables and chairs and arrived beside their table. The girl looked back over her shoulder and waved, calling 'I've found her,' then she turned to speak to Alison. 'I told Mummy you'd be in here.'

Alison glanced round the table. 'This is my sister, Lydia.'

'Pleased to meet you,' Lydia said with a smile before speaking to Alison again. 'Mummy's been in the Town Hall at a WVS meeting about sorting out everyone who's been bombed out and I thought the three of us could go home together.'

As Alison picked up her gas-mask case and handbag and departed, Dot wasn't altogether sorry to see her go. Evidently she wasn't the only one.

'Well!' said Mabel. 'What's got into her? Are you all right, Persephone? Not upset?'

'It takes more than that,' said Persephone.

Colette leaned forward, saying quietly, 'I don't want to sound like a gossip, but I think maybe Alison is the one who's upset. We work in the same office and three of the girls came back to work after Christmas flashing engagement rings.'

'I see,' said Cordelia. 'And that young man of Alison's hasn't popped the question, I take it?'

'One of the girls in the office asked Alison straight out if she was engaged – not being snide or anything; I think she honestly expected Alison to say yes – but Alison said Paul wouldn't have felt it right to propose in the aftermath of the dreadful hammering we took before Christmas. She made out that she was perfectly happy with his decision, but she's been rather quiet ever since.'

'I don't see why the blitz should stop anyone proposing,' said Mabel. 'I'd have thought it would make it all the more important to go down on one knee.'

'If Alison's boyfriend hasn't proposed, that's a shame,' said Cordelia, 'but she's got no business taking it out on Persephone.'

Dot held back from joining in with the conversation. Alison had confided in her a few months back and Dot knew how desperate the poor girl was to get Paul's ring on her finger, but with both families and presumably all the neighbours waiting with bated breath, he was finding it difficult to pick a moment that felt truly special and intimate. Meanwhile, Alison was surrounded by girls flinging themselves into engagements and marriages the way folk did in wartime.

Colette stood up. 'My husband's here.' She picked up her things. 'I might not see you again for a while, but I shall think about you all the time.'

She hurried across to where her handsome husband was waiting, holding the door open.

Dot pushed back her chair and got to her feet. 'I need to go an' all or I'll have a riot on my hands.'

'What's for tea tonight?' asked Mabel with a grin.

'Corned beef hash. Our Pammy got a couple of tins of corned beef before Christmas, but what with one thing and another, they never got opened. We've got her and Sheila and the children round tonight, so it's as good a time as any to use them.'

However tough the past week had been for Manchester and its inhabitants, Dot was grateful to have her family around her and her own four walls to go home to. It was as much as anyone could hope for at present. She felt blessed and determined to take nowt for granted. Serving up a tasty meal at a crowded table was her idea of bliss.

But her feelings of gratitude scattered to the winds pretty soon. At home, she prepared the corned beef hash. Afterwards, while she was clearing away, the children started arguing about whose turn it was to see to the waste collection.

'It's my turn,' said Jimmy.

'No, it isn't. Anyway, you never take the paper labels off properly.' Jenny hung on to the tins. 'You rip them to pieces. Paper has to be saved as well as tin.'

'You can't boss me about.'

Jimmy made a grab, but Dot got there first, magicking the tins away before the children could fight over them.

'You can do one each. That's fair.' Her glance fell on a small mark on the label of one of the tins, sending her hot and cold all over. 'Actually, I'll sort this out. You two, go and work on the jigsaw.'

'But Mummy said to help you,' whined Jenny even as the door swung shut behind their Jimmy.

'Go on, chick,' replied Dot. 'I can manage.'

When Jenny had vanished, she looked at the label again.

A cross, drawn in pencil.

A cross that she herself had drawn last March on her very first day working for the railways. She and Joan had been taken to a church hall in a Scammell Mechanical Horse, driven by a railway delivery man called Mr Hope. The floor and tables in the church hall had been piled high with tinned goods – corned beef, soup, fruit, condensed milk, tins of biscuits and more. She had been allocated the job of counting out certain numbers of each variety of tin. So as not to lose track, she had pencilled a small cross on the label of every tenth one. Then she, Joan and Mr Hope had ferried sack barrows of crates full of tinned foods out to the Scammell and loaded up the trailer attached to the back, covering the crates with a tarpaulin. Then they had driven to a disused railway shed – it was called a shed, which had put Dot in mind of the little garden sheds you saw on the allotments, but this was a whopping great building. The three of them had unloaded their delivery and headed back to the church hall for another one.

How many folk could say they had helped set up a food dump in a secret location to be used in the event of invasion? And now here was one of those tins, with her mark on it. There was no doubt in her mind. She turned the other tin round. There wasn't a cross on it, but it had been only every tenth one that she had marked. So it might or might not be from the food dump.

But the first tin, the one with the cross, was definitely from the food dump.

Somebody had stolen it and sold it. If they had taken this tin, how many more had they stolen and sold?

# Chapter Thirteen

## Sunday afternoon, 12 January 1941

The all-clear had sounded about an hour ago. Joan brushed grime from her cheek. The raid had begun at just gone midnight and had lasted until nearly one in the afternoon. By the time Joan was signed off from duty, it was three o'clock.

Welcome to 1941. New Year's Day had brought snow and a raid that had clobbered Gorton and Withington. Burton Road in Withington had had it bad. The public air-raid shelter near the Old House pub had received a direct hit that had killed everybody inside, including a couple of ARP wardens. Since then, it had been one raid after another, some short, admittedly, but the one last Thursday had been the heaviest since those two dreadful nights before Christmas – the 'Christmas Blitz', they were being called.

Now, after being on duty since yesterday teatime, Joan was cycling home to Chorlton, though what she wanted – needed – to do was head straight to Southern Cemetery to visit Letitia's grave. She could have gone to the cemetery on her way, but she had to get home so Gran would know she was safe.

Anger at being kept from Letitia flashed through her with an intensity that made her insides judder, as if she had cycled over a hole in the road. She braked and stepped off her bicycle. What with work, air raids and first-aid duty, she hardly had time to visit Letitia, even though Letitia's grave was the one place that called out to her.

Dear Letitia, the best sister ever. Unselfconsciously beautiful. Brainy without being show-offy about it. As a family, the Fosters had gone without in order to pay for the uniform, books and hockey stick Letitia required for grammar school. Some sisters would have lorded it over their younger, less clever siblings, but not Letitia. She had even tried to stop Gran lording it over Joan on her behalf.

Gran's favourite.

The grammar-school-educated granddaughter. The granddaughter who resembled Daddy. The granddaughter who was the only person in the world who could talk Gran round when she was in a snit.

If one granddaughter had to have the back of her head blown off, would Gran have preferred it not to be Letitia?

*Don't think like that.*

Joan focused on the scene in front of her. Time was – and that made it sound like a hundred years ago, when really it was last summer and autumn – when you could look at bomb damage and say, 'Oh yes, that happened on such-and-such a night.' But not now. Now, there had been so many raids, they were largely indistinguishable.

The road was strewn with planks of wood and piles of rubble. On one side of the road the buildings were still upright, though there wasn't a windowpane to be seen. On the opposite side was a shop with no roof and no windows in between two demolished buildings, each a mass of timber and bricks, a chimney stack sitting atop one heap.

This was what the world looked like now. Well, no, not all of it. You could go from a scene such as this to another road that might be just around the corner and had escaped unscathed – for now.

Climbing back onto her bike, she pedalled home.

Gran was adamant that Joan should change out of her first-aid togs before going to visit Letitia's grave. Gran detested trousers. Some people called them slacks, as if they weren't really trousers, which gave Gran something to sneer at. 'Slacks for slack girls' was her opinion.

'There isn't time.' Joan glanced through the window. Not that you could see clearly, as Gran favoured net curtains that were almost as thick as a lacy tablecloth. Even so, she could tell the day was already closing in.

'There is always time to dress appropriately,' sniffed Gran. 'Unless, of course, you don't think Letitia is worth dressing nicely for.'

The jibe stabbed Joan's heart and she had to catch her breath. Oh, the temptation to retaliate, to express her hurt, but she clamped her lips together and darted upstairs.

As she opened the wardrobe, her hand flew to her chest in shock.

She ran onto the landing and leaned over the bannister rail.

'Gran! Where are Letitia's clothes?'

No answer.

'Gran!'

She clattered downstairs and into the parlour. Gran was sitting in her armchair beside the fireplace, with Daddy's photograph in her hands. Seeing Daddy's photo brought Joan up short, but she couldn't afford to back down.

'Didn't you hear me calling?'

'I hold conversations with people who are in the same room. I don't bellow up the stairs.'

'Where are they?' asked Joan.

'Where are what?'

Had she *really* not heard Joan calling from upstairs?

'Letitia's clothes.' Joan kept her voice steady, with no hint of accusation. 'They've gone from the wardrobe.'

'I've put them in the boxroom. I'm going to donate them to the WVS for the rest centres. There are so many people in need, and there are some good clothes there.'

Joan was well aware of that. She had made most of them.

Gran gazed at the studio portrait in her hands.

Joan was finally forced to say, 'I would have liked them for myself.'

'Why? Haven't you got enough clothes?'

Her muscles tensed beneath her skin. 'They're Letitia's and I'd like to have them.'

'Well, you can't. You think I could bear to see you cavorting about in Letitia's dresses? They're going, and that's that.'

Joan forced herself not to be distracted by that word *cavorting*. 'If you have to send them away, why not wait just a little longer?'

'What for? It won't change anything. It won't bring her back.' Gran gazed at Daddy's picture and Joan felt a thud of shock at the anguish in her face. 'When someone's gone, they're gone. Hanging on to a few dresses won't make any odds.'

Joan pedalled furiously along Barlow Moor Road, desperate to get to Southern Cemetery in time to have a reasonable spell with Letitia. Would Gran realise what she had done? It had been cowardly to go behind Gran's back, but she couldn't stand by and let all Letitia's belongings slip out of her life. She had silently helped herself to some of Letitia's things, including a few items of clothing, a good coat and a piece of material that had been left over from a dress she had made for Letitia and which would be enough to make something small – a bolero jacket or a pyjama case. Would using Letitia's fabric make her feel closer to her? Joan had sneaked out to the Anderson, where they kept suitcases packed ready for a swift getaway in the event of invasion. Emptying out her own belongings from the one she had shared with Letitia, she had stuffed these other things of Letitia's inside and knelt hard on the lid to force it to fasten.

Now, cycling through the cemetery entrance, she jumped off her bicycle. She pushed her bike along the quiet paths between the rows of headstones of varying sizes and styles, some simple, some frankly Gothic. It was a chilly afternoon and there was mist in the air. Her heart slumped in disappointment as she spied people at a grave close by Letitia's. She wanted to be alone. From here, they were so close to Letitia's plot that it almost looked as if they were visiting Letitia. Wait – yes, they *were* at Letitia's graveside.

Bob! In that instant, Joan recognised his tall figure and square shoulders and her heart warmed. The exhaustion of the long night and morning on duty, and the upset of Gran's determination to be rid of Letitia's clothes, fell away. Here was Bob – his family, too, or a couple of them. Petal. Mrs Hubble. How kind. But they were a kind family. The Hubbles' house was filled with warmth of a type she had never experienced in her own home. Gran thought that feelings were something you kept to yourself, but the Hubbles had no qualms about showing their affection for one another and Joan felt privileged to have been accepted into their ranks.

Petal saw her, which made Bob and his mother turn

and look, and Joan had to grip her handlebars, because otherwise she might have thrown her bike to the ground and run along the path straight into Mrs Hubble's arms.

Bob strode towards her. He slid an arm around her shoulders and kissed her cheek before he took charge of the bicycle.

'I was sure you'd want to come here today, it being Sunday, but with some of the rescues still going on after last night's raid, I thought I'd come, so that . . .' His voice faded away, as if he wasn't sure what words to use.

'So that Letitia wouldn't be alone.' Joan's heart swelled. Before Christmas, she had intended to tell Bob that she loved him. Of course, that hadn't happened, but now every reason why he was important to her came storming into her heart, filling her with reassurance and gratitude and, yes, with hope. 'Thank you. Your mum's here too – and Petal. You're all so good.'

'When I said where I was off to and why, they insisted on coming with me.'

Oh, what a family. Did they have any idea how lucky they were?

Mrs Hubble and Petal came over to her.

'Did Bob explain why we came?' asked Mrs Hubble. 'You don't mind?'

'Of course not. It's such a kind thing to do. Thank you.'

Petal squeezed Joan's arm. 'I know nothing will ever make up for losing Letitia, but don't forget you've still got me, Glad and Maureen wanting to be your sisters.'

'We don't want to butt in,' said Mrs Hubble. 'We'll leave you on your own, if you like.'

To her own surprise, Joan said, 'Not yet.'

# Chapter Fourteen

The familiar rhythmic sound filled the misty air as the handsome locomotive passed by, adding to the mist by puffing great clouds from its funnel. Mabel and her fellow lengthmen, Bernice, Bette and Louise, stood well to the side even though the train was travelling on one of the tracks furthest away. Bernice, as the foreman of their gang, refused to take any chances where personal safety was concerned.

'I swear it comes of being a mum,' she had told Mabel. 'When I was walking out with my Den, we took his younger brother and his mates to the boating lake and they were larking about, jumping from boat to boat like nobody's business, and me and Den never turned a hair. A couple of years later, with a baby in my arms, I was amazed at how cavalier I'd been with the safety of other people's children.'

Mabel leaned on her crowbar. She never tired of seeing the trains go past. Those dark red coaches were filled with passengers relying on the railways to get them from A to B, and the railways relied on hundreds upon hundreds of hard-working members of staff to make sure that it happened with as little upheaval as possible in these uncertain days. Being a lengthman was jolly hard work, but Mabel had a strong sense of being part of the process, even more so since Manchester had suffered so badly in the air raids before Christmas.

She stamped her feet to warm them.

'Snow,' she said as it crunched under her feet. 'That's all we need.'

Bernice laughed, her breath describing white curls in the crisp air. 'It's better than pouring rain.'

'At least we're near a gangers' hut all week,' said Bette, 'so we'll have a chance to thaw out.'

'And so say all of us.' Mabel hefted her crowbar shoulder-high in pretend triumph.

Not that there was anything luxurious about the gangers' huts. Usually they were built from railway sleepers, but there would be a fire inside and there was always a supply of coal. And if the hut wasn't luxurious, then the treat of a steaming cup of tea certainly was, compared to the flasks of cold tea they had to make do with if they weren't close enough to a hut that day.

'Are you seeing your Harry again soon?' Bette asked when they were sitting crowded in a corner of the hut, munching their sandwiches. Bette tucked a stray wisp of copper-coloured hair back inside her turban. Like the others, she had taken off her coat and, despite her thick jumper and trousers, there was no disguising her curvaceous figure.

The mention of Harry's name was all it took to send excitement frothing inside Mabel. She nodded. 'This weekend. We're spending the afternoon together and then going to the pictures in the evening.'

'The pictures? Good idea,' said Bernice. 'A bit of escape is what we all need at the moment.'

Escape? That was the last thing Mabel needed. Yes, they could all do with a let-up from the air raids, but sinking into the fantasy world of a film wasn't high on Mabel's agenda. She had quite enough of her own personal fantasies to keep her occupied, thanks very much. Fearing that colour was rising in her cheeks, she stuck her nose in her mug.

She couldn't wait to see Harry again. They hadn't seen one another since their brief meeting the morning after the first night of the Christmas Blitz. Her heartbeat drummed inside her chest at the memory of that kiss they had shared in full view of anybody who happened to be in the Town Hall foyer. Talk about tearing up the etiquette book. She wasn't sure if she could ever look Mumsy in the eye again.

After they'd finished their sandwiches, they walked back to that day's section of the permanent way and set to, using pickaxes or crowbars to lift the edges of the sleepers so that displaced ballast could be packed back underneath. When their day came to an end, they caught the train back to Victoria, squeezing inside amongst the passengers.

Everyone crammed in the corridor lurched in the same direction and then righted themselves as the train pulled out. It took only twenty minutes to get to Victoria and if it was an uncomfortable twenty minutes, Mabel didn't care. It was a decidedly warm twenty minutes, and after a working day spent outdoors in January, that was a luxury.

The familiar *chuff chuff* of the locomotive ceased as the train ran beside the long platform at Victoria Station. The brakes gave off their shrill squeal. Doors banged against the sides of the coaches as they were thrown open by passengers, even before the clunk sounded when the train came to a standstill. Mabel and her gang climbed down, but just as they were setting off along the platform, Mabel spied Dot's familiar figure at the open doors of the guard's van. Outside, an elderly porter, obviously brought out of retirement for the duration, had positioned a flatbed trolley for the boxes and parcels to be unloaded.

'I'll see you tomorrow,' Mabel told her workmates and

went to help with the unloading of the parcels, but Dot shook her head.

'Kind of you, but best not. Mr Bonner wouldn't be pleased.' Dot rolled her eyes. 'I'd never hear the end of it if he thought I wasn't pulling my weight.'

So Mabel had to stand by while Dot and the elderly porter transferred the parcels – and, as Dot had once explained, a parcel meant anything at all that the railway transported, from a book wrapped in brown paper to a whopping great cabin trunk.

There might be significant damage elsewhere within the station, but this platform looked reassuringly normal with its sea of passengers heading purposefully towards the concourse, tickets at the ready, the lamps shaded to stop the lights shining upwards and the familiar notices advising: *If your journey is REALLY necessary and you can choose your times, travel between 10 & 4* and *Heavy parcels cause delay.*

'Good day?' Mabel asked when the parcels had been unloaded.

'So-so. The usual hold-ups because of Victoria being damaged and freight taking priority,' said Dot, adjusting her peaked cap, which had slipped forwards. 'Have you seen Joan?'

'Only on first-aid duty. She's . . .' Mabel struggled for the right word, '. . . focused.'

'And of course, you can't really ask how she is when you might both be rushing off to deal with an emergency any moment.'

'She's keeping herself to herself.'

Dot pressed her lips together. 'I think it's time to draw her back into the fold. She needs support.'

'She might not want it yet,' said Mabel. 'Presumably she feels better on her own at present.'

Dot dealt her a shrewd look. 'Oh aye? How much better were you when you were coping on your own?'

Mabel had to concede that Dot had a point. Her own grief and guilt over Althea had propelled her into the labour exchange in her home town with the demand, 'I don't care what war work I do or where I do it – as long as it isn't here.' It sounded dramatic now, but at the time it had felt like her one hope for not going stark staring mad. Once she had achieved her aim of leaving home, grief had kept her from making friends in her new environment, since, with the responsibility for Althea's death weighing down her spirit, she had neither wanted closeness nor considered herself worthy of it.

So Joan's retreat into herself hadn't struck Mabel as unusual or undesirable. If anything, she had regarded it as normal. But she herself had benefited from the friendship and support of the other railway girls once she had let down her barriers. Now she couldn't imagine her life without her friends.

She couldn't bear to imagine Joan's life without them either.

'Are you clocking off after this trolley has been unloaded?' she asked Dot. 'Good. After that, we'll go and find Joan.'

Wrapped up in her warm coat, with her felt hat on her head, her gas-mask box over her shoulder, her wicker basket over one arm and her handbag over the other, Dot took a few small steps as the queue, which stood two or three wide across the pavement, shuffled forwards. Queuing was time-consuming and often frustrating, but it was a good source of chat. Northerners were always happy to pass the time of day, and the food queues certainly gave them plenty of opportunity.

'The joys of shopping in wartime!' said Mrs Finch, juggling her shopping basket and gas-mask case so that she could adjust her headscarf. She lived opposite Fog Lane Park and her daughter, after spending her youth being no better than she should be, was now a stout married mother of six.

'At least we've had a few days without that blinking siren going off,' said Mrs Whittaker from Cotton Lane. She was a widow from the last war and had single-handedly brought up her two boys, only to watch them march off to this new war.

'Aye,' Dot joined in. 'I'd almost forgotten what a full night's sleep was.'

'You're sleeping through? I keep on waking up. Still,' Mrs Whittaker added, as if remembering that complaining wasn't the done thing, 'it's good to have a breather from the air raids.'

An old woman whose ankle-length black skirt hung lower than her coat stopped beside them. 'What are you queuing for?'

It was a common question. You saw a queue and hoped for something worthwhile when you reached the front. Some folk joined queues without even knowing what they were for. You just assumed that if all those others were queuing, there must be a good reason.

'Tinned fruit, love,' said Dot.

'I never thought I'd be queuing for food again,' said the old woman. 'We had enough of that in the last war, though it got better after rationing was started. When they brought in rationing at the outset this time round, I thought, that's good. At least we won't have queues for food. Huh! Fat lot I knew.'

'Aye, and in this cold weather an' all,' said Mrs Mulgrew, who lived round the corner from Dot.

There were murmurs about this being proper brass-monkey weather.

'At least there's plenty of us here, so we can huddle together for warmth,' said a voice behind Dot, and Dot turned to give Miss Rooney an approving glance. It was essential to look on the bright side, even in a joke, and it was a wonder that Miss Rooney had retained any ability to do so when you thought of how that nowty old mother of hers had put the mockers on her attempt at an engagement so as to keep her at home waiting on the old bag, hand and foot.

'Did you hear about that Mr Webb from Yew Tree Road?' asked Mrs Mulgrew. 'Him and his missus took in a couple of office girls as lodgers last summer. The girls had been sent here to work in the Food Office. Anyroad, the girls found themselves another billet that was more to their liking, and you'll never guess what.'

'What?' asked several voices as more women turned round to listen.

'Mr Webb only went on claiming his billeting allowance, didn't he? He was took away by the police and he's up before the magistrate tomorrow.'

'He'll get a hefty fine for that,' said Mrs Finch, 'and quite right an' all.'

'A fine?' repeated Mrs Whittaker. 'He'll get sent to prison, more like.'

'It's wicked, making money out of wartime,' said Mrs Mulgrew and everyone in hearing distance agreed, including Dot.

Later, at home, putting away her shopping, having spent a disproportionate amount of her morning off queuing, she took the label from the corned beef tin out of the kitchen drawer. With the air-raid sirens going off every five minutes, she had pushed the matter to the back of her mind, but now, after a few days of being left alone by Jerry, it was time to do summat about it.

Reg was an ARP warden. She would tell him and let him take the credit. That would be a wifely thing to do, wouldn't it? Also, as an ARP warden, he would be more likely to be listened to than she would.

She would tell him tonight. He wasn't on duty and would be at home when she got in from work. He would probably rather be down the pub, but their Jimmy was staying with them tonight and one of Dot's rules was that the children weren't to be left in the house at night on their own.

'Pity you didn't think of that before you took on this flaming job,' Reg had groused the first time she'd pointed out to him that her shift work meant he wouldn't be able to knock back a pint, but she had stood firm.

Talking to Reg wasn't the only item on Dot's agenda. That afternoon Joan was due to return to her place at the railway girls' table in the buffet and Dot reckoned she had time to fly in for ten minutes. She was determined to be there to support her young friend.

When Dot and Mabel had gently persuaded Joan to return to their ranks, she had insisted they tell the others not to say anything about Letitia.

'If anyone is kind to me, I'll weep buckets,' she said.

Now, as Dot hurried to the buffet after her shift, she almost bumped into Joan in the doorway.

'It's good to have you back, love. Pardon my language, but I've been dashing about like a blue-arsed fly today.' She launched into a lively anecdote that lasted for the duration of their time in the queue and when they approached the table, cups and saucers in their hands, she said brightly, 'Look who I found. Shove up, Alison, and make room for a little 'un. Last time I saw you, you were due to go to the pictures. Did you see *The Philadelphia Story*? I've got a soft spot for Cary Grant, but don't tell my Reg I said so.'

'I prefer Jimmy Stewart myself,' said Alison and, as easy as that, a conversation got going that Joan could join in with or not, as she pleased. She looked like she was listening – or was she simply going through the motions? That would be understandable.

All at once Joan covered her mouth with her steepled fingers. Around the table, the conversation faltered as they all looked at her with concern.

Her eyes were bright with tears. 'I'm sorry. You're all being so kind by not mentioning Letitia, which is what I asked for, but . . .'

'But you've changed your mind?' Mabel asked as Joan's words dried up.

'I don't know. I honestly don't know. I just want to say thank you. You're all trying to do the right thing, but I've realised there isn't a right thing. I just have to get on with it.'

'As long as you realise you don't have to do it on your own,' Dot said. 'We all care about you.'

'I know.' Pushing back her chair, Joan stood up. 'Excuse me. I have to go.'

As she left, the rest exchanged looks.

'Poor Joan,' said Alison. 'She's finding it hard. I must admit the first thing I did after I heard about Letitia was hug Lydia.'

'We have to make sure she carries on coming to the buffet,' said Cordelia. 'That's as much as we can do for now. We'll help her through it.'

Dot got up. 'I must get back on duty.'

Her stint in the buffet, as short as it had been, had left her feeling wrung out, so goodness alone knew how poor

Joan must be feeling. At least Joan was going home now. Home was the best place to be when things were hard. Dot had always set great store by having her family around her.

Later, heading home in the pitch-darkness, she was cold and tired. How much longer would this respite from air raids last? Manchester and its people needed time to heal, to think, to accept what had happened, but the chances of having very long to do that were so small as to be not worth considering.

Opening the door, she squeezed inside through the smallest gap she could. Reg had left the hall light off, but there was still the danger of a sliver of light creeping down the hallway from the kitchen to break the blackout.

Reg was at the kitchen table, with his newspaper in front of him.

'There you are,' he said, barely glancing up. 'I'm ready for my Ovaltine.'

There was no point in trying to get his attention before he had his bedtime drink in front of him. Dot made the drinks and sat at the table.

'Reg, I need to tell you summat.'

'Oh aye?' He didn't look up from his paper.

'In your capacity as ARP warden.'

That got his attention. 'What is it? One of the neighbours showing a light?'

'You remember that corned beef hash we had the other day?'

He looked at her as if she was mad. 'You want to talk about what we had for tea?'

'Our Pammy bought two tins before Christmas and she left them here because we were going to have corned beef on Boxing Day, only we didn't because of the Christmas Blitz and everything. Anyroad, when I opened the tins, I saw that one had a little cross pencilled on the label. The thing is, I put that cross there last spring.'

'What on earth are you on about?'

'I'm not supposed to tell anybody this, because it's a war secret, but on my first day on the railways I helped take a load of tinned food to a secret place. I had to count the tins and I pencilled a cross on every tenth one to make it easier. The cross on the corned beef tin that Pammy bought was one of my crosses. Somebody stole from a secret food dump. It needs investigating.'

'Investigating? Do you realise what you've done? Served up the evidence for your family's tea, that's what. You daft bat. We've eaten stolen goods.'

Dot blinked. 'I never thought of it like that.'

'Well, think of it now. And think of our Pammy an' all. She bought the stolen goods.'

'But she wasn't to know—' Dot began.

'You know that and I know that, but the powers that be might decide to make an example of her. Is that what you want? Saints alive, Dot, how could you be so flaming stupid?'

# Chapter Fifteen

Having unloaded her flatbed trolley at the parcels office, Dot checked the list of parcels assigned to her next train. She loaded her trolley once more and parked it in the waiting bay before taking her break. She could have gone into the station mess, but she often preferred to have a private few minutes sitting on one of the platforms. Even after nearly a year, she still wasn't used to the remarks that some of her male colleagues persisted in voicing, pretending to address one another, but making sure that the women nearby would overhear. Some men just couldn't accept that women could do these jobs as well as they themselves could. If Dot could have gone home to a husband who worshipped the ground she walked on, the way Colette's husband did, she could have shaken off her colleagues' derogatory remarks without a second thought. As it was, Reg had been doing her down in front of the family for years, and having to put up with more of the same at work was no fun.

Besides, it was pleasant to spend a few minutes on her own. She seemed to have spent her whole life as part of a crowd. She had grown up one of eleven surviving children, in a cottage that wasn't much more than a hovel, and although she'd had just two children herself, she lived in a community in which all the neighbours exchanged news – yes, all right, gossiped over the garden fence, down the shops and outside church. On top of that, she now spent her working life in trains crammed with passengers, being asked the same questions over and over, so a short spell on her own was a treat.

Besides, when she sat on the platform, sometimes Mr Thirkle sat with her.

Not that there was owt untoward in that and you'd have to be a dirty-minded so-and-so to think there was. He was good company, that was all. Kind. Sympathetic. A quiet, civil man who thought before he spoke and treated her with the utmost respect. She found his company . . . well, soothing, if that didn't make her sound barmy. Soothing and interesting. And he made her feel good about herself, because he listened to her, really listened, as if what she said mattered.

She headed for the platform, noticing that Persephone was on duty at the barrier. Dot smiled at the reactions of the passengers when they caught their first sight of the beautiful ticket collector, some men gazing in instant adoration, others pretending not to sneak a second glance in case their wives noticed. Women weren't immune either. An elderly lady's face softened: was she remembering her own youthful beauty? A girl in her twenties gazed in open admiration while her friend scowled with unrestrained envy.

Mr Thirkle appeared by Dot's side. 'She's a pretty girl, that Miss Trehearn-Hobbs.'

'Pretty? A beauty, more like.'

'And with a pleasant manner,' said Mr Thirkle, which made Dot feel like a proud parent. 'Are you going to have a sit-down, Mrs Green?'

'Yes, I am. If it's your break an' all, you're welcome to join me.'

'I'm here to start my late shift,' said Mr Thirkle, 'but I have ten minutes before I'm due to relieve Miss Trehearn-Hobbs.'

Smiling at Persephone, they walked onto the platform. There was a bench just inside the ticket barrier, too far from the train to be used by passengers. Presumably it was there so that people waiting to meet somebody off the next train could take the weight off their feet.

'If you don't mind my saying so, Mrs Green, I think you have something on your mind. I noticed your expression out there on the concourse and you looked troubled.'

Trust him to notice. Dot tried to laugh it off. 'You just caught me wishing I'd had Persephone's looks when I was a girl.'

'It was before you caught sight of her. If you'd prefer me to mind my own business, say so. I don't wish to speak out of turn.'

'You could never speak out of turn, Mr Thirkle. You're a gentleman. And you're right. I do feel troubled.' She told him about Mr Webb from Yew Tree Road.

'I've heard of that,' said Mr Thirkle. 'The swindle, I mean, not this Mr Webb in particular. It's called the billeting lark.'

Dot sniffed. 'That makes it sound like a game.'

'I know, and that's the last thing it is. It's the same with the bomb lark, where folk fraudulently apply for financial assistance at rest centres after an air raid.'

'It's wicked. Making money out of the war is plain wicked.'

'It is, and it's enough to trouble any right-minded citizen, but I think it's something more specific that's got to you.'

Dot glanced down at her hands. Should she confide? Reg had instructed her to forget it. That was Reg all over. He was happy to leave all the day-to-day stuff to her, but the moment anything important happened, he became the lord and master. Typical man.

143

'Something has happened that's put me in a bad position. If I tell you, it'd put you in a bad position an' all.'

'If there's one thing I know about you, Mrs Green, it's that you are a lady of integrity. If you find yourself in a bad position, I refuse to believe it's through any fault of your own.'

'Thank you.' Now if only Reg had said summat like that . . .

'You know what they say. A trouble shared . . .'

'. . . is a trouble halved,' she finished. What a good friend he was. Without mentioning the food dump, she explained, 'My daughter-in-law bought two tins of corned beef and I know for a fact that one of them was what you might call government property. I don't want to get my family into trouble, but if I do nowt, the thief will get away with it and probably do more thieving an' all.'

'Do you know where your daughter-in-law bought the tins?'

'From her usual grocer.'

'That's good,' said Mr Thirkle. 'If she'd bought them off a market stall, the powers that be might challenge her for not asking questions about it.'

'You think she wouldn't get into trouble, then?'

'It's not for me to say. You do hear tales of snoops from the Food Office who encourage shopkeepers to sell goods over and above the ration and then take them to court for it, and occasionally you hear of real customers being taken to court for purchasing more than they should. But if your daughter-in-law bought the tins in good faith in a shop, it's difficult to see how anybody could blame her.'

'Ah,' said Dot. 'It wasn't exactly in good faith. You see, this chap keeps stuff under the counter to oblige his regular customers.'

'And that's where the corned beef was? It's becoming

common practice for shopkeepers to keep unrationed goods aside for their loyal customers. I'm no expert, but I don't see how anybody could say that compromises your daughter-in-law's good faith.'

'But it would take only one person to say, "It came from under the counter, so she should have guessed." That's the trouble. "Under the counter" has more than one meaning.' Dot fetched a sigh that seemed to drag itself all the way up from the soles of her shoes. 'I've been worried sick about getting our Pammy into trouble, but how can I stand by and do nowt when I know there's a thief? There's summat else an' all. I fed the whole family, the kids included, and my husband says we've benefited from a crime and eaten the evidence, only we haven't – eaten the evidence, I mean.'

'You mean the evidence was on the tin itself. Of course it was. Where else could it be?'

'I've still got the label, but . . .' Dot's fingers squeezed into fists. 'There's more to it than I've said, but I can't tell you.'

The corners of Mr Thirkle's mouth pulled downwards in a thoughtful way. 'Careless talk costs lives, you mean?'

'Well, not lives in this case, but it is important.' Actually, now she thought about it, it might cost lives. If the food dump was depleted, and then the tinned goods were needed . . . 'Anyroad, you can see why I'm in a bit of a state.'

'I sympathise, though sympathy isn't what you're in need of, is it? You need practical help. I have an idea. Are you working this Saturday?'

'No.'

'Me neither. Let's see if we can do something about your problem, shall we?'

In the last letter she'd written to Harry, Mabel had suggested he pick her up from Mrs Grayson's house. She had never let him near the place before, but ever since the Christmas Blitz she had been regularly assisting Mrs Grayson to go round to Mrs Warner's Anderson shelter and this had, if not quite brought down the wall Mabel had built between them, certainly put substantial cracks in it. It would feel churlish now not to let Mrs Grayson meet Harry. To her surprise, she found herself looking forward to it.

When Harry arrived that afternoon, handsome in air force blue, she took his hand and led him into the parlour, where, with perfect manners, he didn't so much as glance her way as his gaze took in the masses of knitting that festooned the room – the lampshades covered in knit-and-purl diamonds, the baby cable stitches covering the waste-paper basket, the flowerpot covers of Irish-moss stitch, the doilies in fern-lace stitch. He didn't blink even when he saw, most hideous of all, the upright wooden chair hidden beneath a cable-stitched cover.

Harry shook Mrs Grayson's hand and engaged in a spot of small talk before he looked around the room and said, 'I see you enjoy knitting, Mrs Grayson. Does it take up a lot of your time?'

Having her knitting admired by a handsome man in uniform clearly made Mrs Grayson's day. She actually blushed with delight. Mabel smiled, glad to have been instrumental in bringing a moment's pleasure into her landlady's restricted life.

Presently, Mrs Grayson excused the pair of them and Harry helped Mabel with her coat. Checking in the mirror hanging on the hall wall as she positioned her brimless fur hat and fluffed up a few of her dark brown curls, Mabel couldn't help noticing the glow that being with Harry had given her complexion.

She pulled on her gloves and swung her gas-mask box

over her shoulder, opening her handbag to make sure her torch was inside. Then she turned to Harry with a smile.

'Shall we?'

He opened the door with a flourish and she stepped outside. It was another cold, grey day, or at least it probably seemed that way to other people. Even without her high-quality coat with its fur collar, Mabel was quite sure she wouldn't have felt the chill. She was too happy and excited.

'Do you think Mrs Grayson approved of me?' Harry asked.

'I'm sure she did. Congratulations on not letting your eyes pop out of your head at the sight of the wool palace.'

'You mentioned it in your letters. Even so, it did rather take my breath away.'

'I think you've got an admirer for life.'

'I'd sooner have you than Mrs Grayson any day.' Harry offered her his arm. 'Which way shall we go?'

'You said I could choose the film, so I narrowed it down to the Rivoli or La Scala. I chose the Rivoli, so let's walk along to Chorlton.'

'It's good to see you again.' Harry passed his free hand across his body to squeeze the hand Mabel had tucked into the crook of his elbow. 'I've been worried about you, with all the air raids, especially after seeing for myself how brave you were that night before Christmas.'

'I didn't do anything above and beyond what anyone else did. In fact, I did a lot less than some.'

'Maybe, but I don't have a vested interest in the others. It's you I care about.'

They left Nell Lane behind, turning the corner onto Mauldeth Road, with Chorlton Park on the other side of the road. The school in its grounds had been hit during the Christmas Blitz.

'A sad sight,' Harry commented.

'There's sadness wherever you look. Had we been going to La Scala, we'd have gone past the back of Southern Cemetery, which is where the mass burial was held. A bugler played the Last Post and I stood there with tears streaming down my face. And I didn't even know anyone who had died. That is, I did know a girl who was killed, but she had a separate burial on her own. I don't know if I was weeping for her or . . . I don't know what I was weeping for.'

Stopping, Harry turned towards Mabel. She lifted her face to receive his steady gaze. How dark his eyes were, how full of concern and . . . something more? Her breath hitched in her chest.

'I want to take you in my arms and hold you and keep you safe,' said Harry. 'If we weren't standing here in broad daylight . . .'

'It didn't stop you that morning in the Town Hall.'

'Don't tempt me.' Securing her hand inside his elbow, Harry started walking again. 'May I ask you a question? Am I your first boyfriend? It's difficult to believe a beautiful girl like you hasn't had men queuing up.'

'Flatterer.' But her heart thumped.

'Am I the first?'

'Am I your first girlfriend?'

'Ah, turning the question back onto me.' Harry laughed. 'Yes and no. I've taken girls out and until a few weeks ago, when I spotted a certain young lady laid up in a hospital bed, I'd have said those others were girlfriends, but I wouldn't call them that now. I liked them and enjoyed their company, but I know now there was never anything serious in it. I think that qualifies you as my first girlfriend.'

Mabel ducked her head, not from embarrassment or any kind of discomfort, but to hide how fluttery and breathless his words made her feel. Her delight was squashed, though, by Harry's next words.

'I've come clean with you, so now it's your turn. Am I your first boyfriend?'

'Yes. I mean no. Yes.'

'Yes, no, yes?' There was amusement in Harry's voice, but curiosity too. 'Is that the equivalent of my reasoning about you compared to other girls?'

It would be so easy to say yes, but somehow she couldn't dismiss Gil as easily as that. Harry's previous girlfriends might have been casual relationships rather than the real thing, but Gil – Gil . . .

'Something like that,' she murmured.

'I apologise if I've embarrassed you.'

'You haven't – honestly. But . . .' Her chin dipped, not out of modesty this time, but from pure embarrassment. Her face was impossibly hot.

Harry took her across the road and through the park gates to the trees. Once more, he stopped, but this time he had to take her by the shoulders and turn her to him.

'Allow me to apologise properly.'

He kissed her. In spite of the delicious feelings that swamped her, Mabel pulled away.

'This is a bit public.'

'It's less public than the Town Hall foyer.' Harry glanced round at the trees. 'Should I apologise again?'

'No.' She tried to laugh it off, then decided on the truth. She might have dodged the truth about Gil, but she wasn't going to dance around the edges of this.

'Everyone's feelings seem to be heightened these days. That's the nature of wartime, I suppose.' Hence the soaring number of marriages, she thought, but didn't say. She mustn't sound as if she was hinting. 'And my emotions are as heightened as anyone's. It's impossible not to be affected. We live on a knife-edge. Will there be a raid tonight? Does one of those bombs have my name on it? Think of everything we've seen – all the destruction. I spent a large part of the second night of the Christmas Blitz searching through the remains of a bus, looking for body parts. And in amongst all of this,' she gazed up at him, 'there's you, the cheeky blighter who was there every time I turned round in hospital and who followed me home to the wilds of Lancashire.' She placed her hands on his upper arms, giving him a tiny shake. 'There's you, Harry Knatchbull. And . . . it's scary.'

'Scary? That's the last thing I expected you to say.'

She couldn't look him in the eye. She stared fixedly at the front of his coat. His brass buttons were polished to a high shine.

'I know it's part of the way things are at the moment. People are flinging themselves into relationships left, right and centre. I've become far too fond of you far too quickly. My feelings are running riot and – and I'm frightened of losing control.'

There was a long silence. At last she looked up and found his gaze locked on her. Had he been waiting for her to look at him?

'It's very simple,' he said softly. 'I'll never do anything to hurt you, so you hand over control to me.'

The grocer's was busy, but thriving busy, not queue-up-for-half-an-hour busy, when Dot walked in, followed by Pammy. Bringing Pammy was part of the plan. Dot didn't like to use her daughter-in-law, but it was the only way. She had been into Lowell's before, but Mr Lowell wasn't her regular grocer and she needed Pammy to wheedle some under-the-counter goods out of him.

The shop had wooden counters on three sides, with

shelves behind, all the way up to the ceiling. This side of the counter were two ladder-backed wooden chairs for customers. The sawdust, fresh on the floor that morning, was well and truly flattened by now, this being mid-afternoon.

Dot and Pammy took their turn behind a woman in a smart overcoat, a dainty eye veil hanging from her hat. When it was their turn, they stepped up to the counter and exchanged greetings with Mr Lowell's assistant, a man who was old enough to be the grocer's father. Too poor to retire, presumably. Life was hard on some folk.

Pammy made a few purchases, the old boy creaking up and down his stepladder to reach Campbell's soup and a bottle of HP Sauce from the upper shelves.

Dot's gaze raked its way round the shop. Those tins of condensed milk over there – did any have her pencilled crosses on them? And what about the tinned pilchards and peas and baked beans? A sense of something not far from defeat washed through her. There were so many tins here and she had marked only every tenth one of those that had passed through her hands. What were the chances of being served a marked tin – even supposing any of these tins had come from the food dump? Not that she necessarily needed a marked tin. All she needed was a tin of corned beef from under Lowell's counter. If it had her cross on it, all the better, but if it didn't, she would remove its label and take both it and the marked label from her Christmas tin to the police and tell her story about the food dump, as if this was the very first time she had seen a marked tin – as if Pammy was nowt to do with it and no evidence had been eaten.

Behind her, the little brass bell dinged as the door opened. She glanced round, looking away again immediately as Mr Thirkle walked in. They had agreed that he would wait outside and enter the shop when he spotted her and Pammy at the counter. Knowing he was here, supporting her in her endeavour to do the right and honourable thing, straightened Dot's spine and focused her thoughts.

She peered round the shelves with what she hoped was an innocent look on her face. 'I can't see any corned beef. What a shame. It was Lowell's that you got it from before, wasn't it, Pammy?'

'Yes.' Did Pammy actually flutter her eyelashes at the old boy? 'Mr Lowell kindly let me have some, because of being a regular customer.'

As if by magic, Mr Lowell himself appeared in front of them, even as he was saying goodbye to the lady with the eye veil.

'Afternoon, Mrs Green,' he greeted Pammy. 'Did I hear you mention corned beef?'

'It was my mother-in-law who mentioned it,' said Pammy.

Dot's heart beat faster. Was this the moment?

'I'm sorry,' said Mr Lowell. 'I can't oblige today.'

'Never mind,' said Pammy.

'Are you sure?' Dot hardly knew what she was saying, only that she had to say something. This was their one chance to get Mr Lowell to hand over stolen goods in front of Mr Thirkle as an independent witness. She leaned forward confidentially and dropped her voice. 'My daughter-in-law said that you had some set aside for regular customers.'

'Aye. Before Christmas I did put some goods to one side so that I could supply my regulars with all their wants, it being a special time of year.' Mr Lowell waved his hand around to indicate his shelves. 'But as you can see, we're fairly well stocked at present, so there's no need to set anything aside.'

Was there a challenge in the look he gave her? Was there summat in her face that warned him to be on his guard? There was nowt for it but to back down.

'Thanks, anyroad,' said Dot.

Pammy paid, putting her shopping in her bag while she waited for her change to be counted into her hand. As they left the shop, she pushed up her coat sleeve and rolled down the edge of her glove to look at her wristwatch.

'I have to fetch Jenny.'

'Aye, you get along, love. Here, give me your shopping. I'll take it home and you can collect it later.'

When Pammy disappeared round the corner, Mr Thirkle presented himself at Dot's side and raised his hat politely. Two acquaintances bumping into one another in the street. Dot didn't know whether to feel thrilled at the subterfuge or ashamed of herself.

'That got us precisely nowhere,' she said.

'There's so much that is unknown,' said Mr Thirkle. 'Was the stolen corned beef under the counter because it was stolen or because Mr Lowell wanted only his best customers to have it? Does he even know it was stolen?'

'Don't,' said Dot. 'If he doesn't know, and I was prepared to get you to report him, then that's as bad as me wanting to keep my family out of it.'

'Would you rather forget about it?'

Dot sighed, wishing she could say yes. But she couldn't. Someone had stolen from the food dump – could still be doing so on a regular basis, for all she knew. She couldn't let it continue. Even if it had happened just the once, that person deserved to pay the penalty.

'Stealing is always wrong,' she said, 'but it's extra wrong in wartime.'

'Perhaps we've been looking at this the wrong way,' Mr Thirkle suggested. 'We've thought of it in terms of how it came into your family's possession. Maybe we should think about who could have got their hands on it in the first place.' He looked at her. 'I'm sorry not to be able to help further, but you did say you couldn't give me any information and I respect that.'

Oh heck. Maybe she should report it to the police and be done with it. But there might be consequences. What if it ended up before an overzealous magistrate who liked to penalise customers who had unwittingly bought stolen goods? Or who came down hard on her for feeding stolen goods to her family? She couldn't risk that.

She looked at her friend. Yes, her friend. Mr Thirkle didn't have a handsome face by any stretch of the imagination, but he had a kind and honest face and that was far more important.

'Mr Thirkle, if you'll help me get to the bottom of this, I'll tell you the rest.'

'I'll assist in any way I can.'

'Right, then. On my first day on the railways, me and a couple of others had the job of delivering tinned food-stuffs to a – have you heard of food dumps? They're big collections of food, secretly stored in places like old barns, only this one was in a disused railway shed. You know how big some of them buildings are. Anyroad, I had the job of counting the tins and I marked every tenth one with a cross, so as to avoid mistakes. Then, before Christmas, our Pammy comes home with a couple of tins of corned beef and, lo and behold, one of them has my cross on it.'

Mr Thirkle nodded slowly. 'I see.'

'D'you remember when you realised the evidence must be on the tin itself? Aye, well, you were right.'

'Mrs Green, please don't take offence, but I have to ask. This is one cross on one tin. Are you sure you aren't overreacting?'

Dot pulled her shoulders back. 'Aye, it's just the one cross, but it's my cross and I know summat wrong is going on.' Was he going to change his mind about helping her? 'You daft bat,' said Reg's voice in her head.

'Well then,' replied Mr Thirkle, 'that's good enough for me.'

As Mabel and Harry walked down the stairs of the Rivoli after seeing *Rebecca*, they were surrounded by many other couples, some of the men in uniform, others in civvies. Mabel lifted her chin, proud to be on Harry's arm, not just because he was Harry Knatchbull, her very own cheeky blighter, but because he was in uniform. She would never say so, but she felt sorry for Joan and Alison, whose boyfriends were a railway signalman and a telephone engineer.

They paused in the foyer to fasten their coats and fish out their torches before heading into the blackout.

'I'm glad we got through the film without the air-raid warning flashing up on the screen,' said Harry. 'I know most people stay put and carry on watching the film, but I'm not sure I could do that with you beside me. I'd want to take you to safety.'

Mabel laughed. 'You'd have had a job on your hands trying to get me out of *Rebecca*.'

'Enjoy it?'

'Loved it.'

She must have, because otherwise she would have spent the whole evening dreaming about Harry and their relationship. She was smitten. Simple as that. Smitten – and amazed at being smitten. Yes, she still felt guilty about what had happened to Althea, still remembered how she had spent so long feeling she didn't deserve to lead a happy, normal life, but even so – smitten. Gil was on the edge of her thoughts, too, after Harry's question earlier on. Harry was different to Gil. Gil had been serious. Not that he had lacked a sense of humour, but he had been a serious, staunch sort of chap. Harry, on the other hand, was a laugh a minute when he was in the mood. He was fun and she loved being swept along – loved being smitten.

There was an exclamation somewhere close by, followed by a yell of laughter. Somebody had obviously walked into a pillar box or a telegraph pole. It happened all the time in the blackout.

'Are you warm enough?' asked Harry.

'Yes, thanks.'

'Warm enough to slow down so I can take my time walking you home?'

'I'm not sure,' Mabel teased. 'Let's try it and see.'

Harry stopped.

'I wasn't thinking of going quite that slowly,' said Mabel.

'There's something I want to say. It ought to be said by candlelight after an evening of dancing, but here we are and I have to say it. You're very important to me, Mabel – more important than I can say. I know lots of couples are dashing into engagements and marriages because of this being wartime. That bothers me because it might make me seem as if I'm carried away by the situation. I want you to know I mean this from the bottom of my heart. You're the girl for me. I don't want to push you into anything you're not ready for, but might I be the right man for you?'

# Chapter Sixteen

'You didn't get the Christmas engagement you were hoping for,' Mabel said to Alison, 'but we're coming to the end of January, so Valentine's Day isn't far off. Maybe you'll have a Valentine's proposal.'

Alison perked up, as she always did when there was the chance to talk about her relationship with Paul. Joan didn't say anything. She just listened. The three of them were in the buffet after work. Nothing would bring Letitia back, but there was a certain . . . not comfort, exactly, but an easing of the pain to be had from being with her friends. They cared about her and that answered a need she carried deep inside, so she gravitated towards them, wanting, needing to be with the friends her heart knew she could rely on.

Besides, it was – for a short time – a distraction from her terrible loss.

'A Valentine's Day proposal would be lovely, obviously,' said Alison. 'I'm sure there'll be plenty of Valentine's Day engagements, but I've told you what Paul's like. He wants it to be a surprise and it'll hardly be that on Valentine's Day, will it?'

'It will if you tell yourself it isn't going to happen,' laughed Mabel. 'Perhaps you should have made use of last year's leap year and done the proposing yourself.'

Alison screwed up her nose. 'I'd never do something like that. Fancy having to propose! It would be humiliating.'

'Humiliating is a strong word,' said Mabel.

'What would you say when all your friends asked if he went down on one knee?' Alison retorted. 'I'd rather wait and have it done properly. Any decent girl would.'

It was odd, in a way, listening to the conversations of her fellow railway girls; odd to be reminded that in the real world, ordinary things mattered – Dot talking about the queue at the shops, Mabel wanting to go to the pictures, Cordelia extolling the virtues of cod liver oil or sharing something her daughter Emily had said in a letter from boarding school. Missing Letitia every minute of the day, and throughout the long hours of the night, would Joan ever care about such things again? People talked so glibly about life going on. And it did. It had to, she knew that, but . . .

But.

There was a massive hole in Joan's life and in her heart, where Letitia used to be. The house felt empty too. She had always known that Letitia was the glue that held their little family together, but it had taken Letitia's permanent absence to show her, with the force of a hammer blow, how true this was. Letitia was the favourite. Joan was just . . . Joan. The extra granddaughter in the shadow of the special favourite. She had never minded. Or rather, there had been times when she had hated Gran for preferring Letitia, but she had never been jealous of her sister.

When Alison left to catch her bus, Mabel switched seats, placing herself beside Joan.

'I've got a few minutes more, if you have. How's your grandmother getting on?'

Joan's heart lurched. The angry starkness of Gran's grief frightened her. She didn't know what to do about it, didn't know how to help.

A few days ago, Steven had come to see them, armed

158

with a ceramic bowl with three hyacinths, pure white and smelling delicious. His dad, who had grown them over the winter, had given them to Steven for Letitia's grave, but Steven had had another idea.

'I thought you might like to have them, Mrs Foster.' His gaze included Joan in the thoughtful gesture. 'I thought that Letitia would rather you had them in the house to enjoy.'

'Thank you,' said Gran. 'How kind.'

'They smell heavenly,' Joan had said.

Later, when she returned to the parlour after showing Steven out, Gran wasn't there – and neither were the hyacinths. Gran must have popped upstairs to put them in her bedroom.

But then came the sound of water running in the kitchen, and when Gran walked into the parlour, she was carrying the ceramic bowl, which was now empty and freshly washed. She thrust it at Joan, whose hands fumbled in shock.

'Where are the hyacinths?'

'In the compost, where they deserve to be. What good are flowers compared to what we've lost?'

Joan could never tell anyone else that. Her shoulders drooped with shame at the thought of it. And she still had to face Steven with appreciative lies when she handed back the bowl after an appropriate amount of time. How long did hyacinths last, anyway?

'Gran's in the depths of misery,' she told Mabel now. 'I don't mean she's in floods of tears all the time, nothing like that. In fact, I don't think she's shed a single tear. She gets up and gets dressed every morning and cleans the house and does the shopping and the cooking. She does everything she's always done.'

'It must be very hard for her,' Mabel murmured.

Joan glanced at her. It took a true friend to start a conversation about the effects of grief. Maybe it was her own experience of blaming herself for her best friend's death that had given Mabel the courage to tackle a subject that most people shied away from.

'She's lost so much. She lost Daddy, her son and only child, and now she's lost Letitia. But she isn't the sort to cave in and feel sorry for herself. She carries on as normal – except that it isn't really normal, is it? She's always been a strict person, but now she's sterner than ever.'

'It's her way of getting through it,' said Mabel, 'but her sternness, as you call it, must be hard on you.'

Emotion swooped over Joan in a wave in which grief and fear were so deeply entwined that every nerve end tingled, sending tiny, sharp-edged vibrations skittering through her. Shaking her head, she held up her hands, palms towards Mabel.

'I'm sorry.' Mabel backed down at once. 'Let's talk about something else.'

Joan pushed her chair backwards, its legs scraping across the floor. 'I must get home.' She started to gather up her things, but then stopped. 'I'm the one who's sorry. People treat bereavement as such a private thing and they never say a word to you about your loss, but you brought it up and I appreciate it, I honestly do, because the last thing I want is for Letitia never to be spoken of again, but . . .'

'But it's too soon,' Mabel said softly. 'I understand. I just want you to know that I'm here.'

Joan caught Mabel's hand and squeezed her fingers. 'I know. All of you are here. All of us railway girls, looking after one another.'

'Goodness, you'll have me blubbing in a minute,' said Mabel. 'I'll see you later at St Cuthbert's.'

Joan didn't say so, but she had put her name down for extra shifts. Was it mean of her to find it easier to be away from Gran? The atmosphere in the house was one of pure misery, but not the kind of misery where two people wept together and cuddled each other. She would have stayed at home if it had been that kind of misery. But Gran wasn't a weeper and she certainly wasn't a cuddler and Joan was rather afraid that she herself was both.

Joan hoped that nobody knew. How could they? She hadn't told anyone, so she should be safe. It was just an ordinary day as far as everyone else was concerned. She threw herself into her work, determination making her quicker than usual as she pushed her sack barrow around, no matter how heavy it was.

There was going to be a get-together in the buffet that evening. Should she skip it? A voice inside her said it wouldn't be right to go, but another voice said she needed her friends more than ever – even if she wasn't prepared to tell them the reason.

At the end of her shift, she gathered her belongings and headed for the station's cluster of interior buildings, their outer walls tiled in pale yellow with a line of wooden panelling above, on which the names of the rooms were written in mosaic lettering. Was it wrong to be grateful that these rooms hadn't been damaged when the station received its direct hit? It would certainly have been a lot better in terms of railway travel if the buffet and bookshop had been blown to pieces and the platforms had survived. But being able to meet up with her friends in the buffet gave her a sense of continuity that she was very much in need of at present.

She made sure her coat was fastened over her porter's uniform and her cap was in her bag. She was wearing her shallow-crowned, narrow-brimmed felt hat. She scanned the room as she walked in. The others were already there – all of them. It didn't often happen that they were all present. Colette was there too – and that almost never happened. Joan experienced a little flutter of pleasure. This was exactly what she needed.

She queued for her cup of tea and carried it across the room to where her friends had pushed two tables together to accommodate them all. Smiles and greetings were exchanged and the others asked about her day. If she hadn't known better, she might have thought they were making her the centre of attention.

Colette glanced round at the clock on the far wall.

'Will your husband be along to collect you soon?' Cordelia asked.

A faint flush highlighted Colette's cheeks. 'I explained that I needed more time today.'

'Put your foot down for once, did you?' asked Alison.

The flush deepened to a definite blush. 'Not at all.'

'Anyroad,' said Dot, 'I for one can't stop much longer, so I think the time has come, girls, if you're ready.'

'Ready for what?' Joan asked, bewildered.

'I saw Miss Emery a couple of weeks ago,' said Cordelia.

Joan sat forward, pleased at the prospect of hearing news of the assistant welfare supervisor, to whom they all owed such a debt of gratitude.

'In fact,' Cordelia continued, 'she sought me out and gave me a piece of information that she thought we as a group might wish to be aware of.'

'Have you quite finished speechifying?' Dot demanded. To Joan, she said, 'What Cordelia means is that we know it's your birthday, chick.'

'We know how hard it must be for you,' said Mabel. 'We

162

knew you wouldn't want us to make a fuss, so we've simply each got you a card.'

The others opened their handbags and a pile of cards appeared on the table in front of Joan. Tears welled. Her heart thumped.

'You don't have to open them now,' said Alison.

Yes, she did. As she opened the top one, Joan steeled herself for the birthday greeting inside, but Mabel had written, *Thank you for being my first-aid partner. I feel more confident with you by my side.*

Startled, Joan met Mabel's steady gaze. 'Thank you,' she whispered.

Dot had written: *As a fellow porter, I have seen how hard you work. Lizzie would be proud to know her old job is in such good hands.*

Alison's words were: *Paul and I will save you and Bob a place on the dance floor.*

Cordelia's was a bit like reading a school report. *You are a sensible girl with backbone – just what the country needs these days.*

From Persephone: *Thanks for giving me the idea of the church bells. Because of you, I sold my very first article.*

Joan picked up the last card. What could Colette have to say? They barely knew one another. But as she read it, she had a moment of shame.

*I can't come to the group very often, but you always make me feel welcome when I do. Thank you.*

Persephone handed her another card. 'This is from Mrs Cooper.'

Joan fumbled as she opened it. How kind of Lizzie's mum.

*You are a dear girl, Joan, and any friend of my Lizzie will always find a welcome in my house.*

With the cards spread out in front of her filled with

such caring messages, Joan felt overwhelmed. She caught the anxious glances passing between the others. Were they expecting her to burst into tears? Was she about to?

No, as it turned out. Yes, there were some tears – and not just hers – but what she felt more than anything else was the simple, honest-to-goodness rightness of being here with her friends.

'Thank you,' she said. 'Thank you all. But how did you . . . ?'

'We have our ways.' Dot waggled her eyebrows roguishly.

'Cordelia couldn't write anything in our notebook,' said Alison, 'because you would have seen it, so she wrote us all a letter.'

'We've been passing it around secretly,' said Mabel, 'like mischievous schoolgirls.'

'And Persephone went to see Mrs Cooper,' added Cordelia.

Joan felt a smile building up as the day's tension slipped out of her muscles.

Dot pressed her hand. 'I hope we haven't upset you.'

'Not a bit,' said Joan. 'It was naughty of you to go behind my back, but it was such a thoughtful thing to do. I've been dreading today and you've got together and turned it into something good.'

'We were worried about making you feel worse,' said Alison.

'Safe.' Joan looked around the table. 'That's how you've made me feel. Safe.'

Was it mean not to want to show her birthday cards to Gran? Joan didn't want to be ungracious, but would the woman who had chucked away the kind gift of a bowl of hyacinths have any qualms about spoiling the gestures of friendship from the other railway girls? Gran seemed bent on spoiling everything these days. Grief took people in different ways, but did it have to make Gran so angry? Joan was treading on eggshells at home and it shouldn't be like that. When two family members were mourning the loss of a third, shouldn't they stick together and do all they could to bolster one another's spirits?

Nevertheless, she showed Gran her cards. How could she not? It would be insufferably rude not to, and Gran wasn't the sort to tolerate bad manners. Joan imagined not showing them and Gran finding out and asking, 'Would Daddy be proud of you for keeping them from me?'

*Would Daddy be proud of you?* It was the question that Gran had used all their lives to make her and Letitia toe the line. Oh, how they longed to make Daddy proud! He was long since dead and neither of them remembered him, but they still wanted him to be proud of them.

Gran read the cards in silence. Joan fingered her collar. Might this be the moment when Gran softened? She had softened for Letitia, but then Letitia had always known what to say. Mind you, even when Letitia hadn't said the right thing, when she had stood up to Gran, like she had over the matter of their being allowed to wear fashionable skirt lengths, Gran had swallowed it. Letitia could get away with plenty where Gran was concerned.

When Joan couldn't bear it any longer, she forced a smile. 'Wasn't it kind of them?'

Gran huffed out an almost snort, then seemed to change her mind. 'Yes. Yes, it was. This isn't an easy day for either of us.'

Was it too hard for Gran to celebrate Joan's birthday? Was her head crammed so full of Letitia's twenty-first birthday this coming Saturday that there was no room left for Joan's special day?

Or was it more than that – worse than that? Would it have been easier for Gran if she could have spent today consoling Letitia on what would have been Joan's birthday?

'You'd better go and tidy yourself before Bob arrives,' said Gran.

Upstairs, Joan changed out of her uniform and hung it up. She put on a skirt and her white blouse patterned with tiny forget-me-nots, over which she put the dark blue knitted cardigan that was her birthday present from Gran. Carefully, she removed her snood and shook out her hair, twiddling the waves with her fingers to fluff them up. She and Letitia had sworn a solemn oath not to get killed with their rollers in.

She picked up their shared bottle of lily-of-the-valley scent and took out the stopper, holding the dainty glass bottle close to her nose as she inhaled. Gran had said they had to make this bottle last until the war was over.

Now she had to make it last for the rest of her life.

Noises downstairs said Bob had arrived. Joan went down. He stood up as she entered the parlour. No matter how concerned or serious he looked, nothing could diminish the boyishness of his features. Warmth filled Joan's heart. What would she do without him?

Bob brushed her cheek with a kiss. Letitia used to walk into Steven's gentle embrace here in this room, in front of Gran, but that was more than Joan and Bob would have felt comfortable doing.

When she sat down, Bob picked up a couple of parcels from the table. One was flat and wrapped in brown paper, the other in creased Christmas paper, small enough to sit in the palm of her hand.

'These are for you for your birthday.'

She noticed he didn't say 'Happy birthday'. The railway girls hadn't said it either.

'The big one is from my parents and my sisters,' Bob added.

'Oh aye?' It was the first flicker of interest Gran had shown. In her old-fashioned world, a gift from a young man's family was as good as a proposal.

'I'll be honest,' said Bob. 'These were meant to be your Christmas presents, but . . .'

Joan opened the large parcel, handling the wrapping carefully. You couldn't waste anything these days. A folded length of soft wool jersey in rich chestnut brown immediately made a dress pop into her mind – and yes, it had a boat neck, elbow-length sleeves, an A-line skirt with a bit of a swirl.

'It's lovely,' she said. 'I'll write a thank-you note.'

'The other one is from me,' said Bob.

It was a necklace – an oval locket.

'Oh aye?' said Letitia's voice in Joan's memory. 'Preparing to cast my necklace asunder, are you?'

'It opens,' said Bob.

Obediently, Joan fiddled with the tiny catch. The locket was empty.

'You might want to put a picture of Letitia inside,' Bob said quietly.

'Yes.' But Joan knew Gran would never let her cut up a precious picture of Letitia.

Putting her hands behind her neck, she unfastened the clasp on the silver necklace that had been Letitia's gift to her on her sixteenth birthday, slipping it into her pocket before Gran could identify it and possibly say something that would take the gloss off the moment. She bent her head for Bob to put the locket on her.

'Thank you. I love it.'

Why hadn't she agreed to let Bob take her out, as he had offered? Because she had thought how horrid it would be for Gran to be stuck indoors all alone today, the first birthday they'd had to face since losing Letitia. It was difficult not to think of it as a sort of dry run for Letitia's twenty-first birthday in just three days.

With the BBC Orchestra playing on the Home Service in the background, Joan and Bob played a few hands of whist while Gran worked at her knitting. At the end of the concert, they listened to the news together.

Joan picked up the *Radio Times*, which had a photograph of the Duchess of Kent in uniform on the cover. She flicked through to find today's programmes. In other people's houses, they folded the pages over so that the current day was always on show, but not under Mrs Beryl Foster's roof.

'There's a play on in a while that looks interesting.' Joan glanced through the description. 'It starts with a murder and then goes back in time to show what happened to lead up to it.'

Gran held out her hand for the magazine. 'It doesn't end until half past ten.'

Bob took the hint, getting to his feet soon afterwards.

Joan saw him out, pushing aside the door curtain and following him outside onto the step, pulling the door shut behind her. He was on the path and she was on the step, the extra few inches bringing her to a height that proved to be very snuggly as Bob put his arms around her.

'I'm sorry we had to stay in,' she said. 'I couldn't leave Gran, not today.'

'I know.' He murmured the words into her hair.

'Thank you for my locket.'

'It turned out to be an appropriate gift in a way I never

imagined when I chose it.' Bob hesitated. 'I was in two minds as to whether I should give it to you.'

'Why?'

'In case it hurt you.'

'Hurt me? To carry a picture of Letitia with me? Never.' Gratitude washed through Joan. 'You're always so considerate. That means the world to me.'

'I hope there's more to it than liking me because I'm considerate.' There was a smile in Bob's voice.

'Of course, you daft thing.' She swatted his chest with one hand. 'It's because you've got such a lovely family as well.'

'Oh well, as long as it's not just me being considerate.'

'There might be something else too.' She pretended to think about it. 'Something like this . . .'

She slid her arms around Bob's neck, drawing his face down to hers, excitement wriggling through her as she brushed her lips against the warmth of his mouth.

'Oh yes, I remember that,' Bob murmured. He rubbed his nose against hers, nudging her face upwards to make her lips more accessible. The kiss was butterfly light and her breathing quickened as Bob lifted his face away. Then she caught the back of his head in the palms of her hands and pulled him down again, their kiss this time deep and lasting.

Bob gave a shaky laugh when it ended.

'I love you, Bob Hubble,' Joan whispered. Surprise shimmered through her, lighting her up on the inside. She hadn't known she was going to say that. She had been thinking it for some time, but she hadn't planned to say it tonight.

Another kiss was his reply before he said, 'I love you too, Joan Foster.'

'I – I was going to tell you at Christmas.'

He held her tighter, his cheek pressing into her hair. 'I'll always look after you. I know how much you miss Letitia. I'll help you through this difficult time. Just remember that I love you. My folks do too.'

How right it felt. How safe. Bob loved her and his family had accepted her as one of their own. In the terrible darkness of her loss, it was something to cling to, something to give her hope.

# Chapter Seventeen

On her way into Victoria Station to start her day's work, Dot paused beside the station's beautiful war memorial. It filled an entire wall. The top half was made up of tiles laid out to depict a map of the old Lancashire and Yorkshire Railway, which Victoria Station had belonged to at the time of the Great War. Indeed, at the curved end of the station's handsome exterior, beneath the clock face, the words LANCASHIRE & YORKSHIRE RAILWAY were literally set in stone to this day. Beneath the tiled map was a long row of seven bronze panels, listing the names of those railway men who had enlisted to fight for King and country and had given their lives.

*This tablet is erected to perpetuate the memory of the men . . .*

So many men. Well over a thousand. At one end of the names was a panel showing St George on horseback, slaying the dragon. At the other end stood St Michael the Archangel with his foot on the neck of the fallen Lucifer.

Dot's gaze ran across the memorial, absorbing the beauty and the sadness. All those lost lives. All those shattered families. And now they were in the middle of another war and there were more shattered families.

'Good morning, Mrs Green.' Mr Thirkle appeared. His quiet voice was dear to her. He sometimes spent a few moments here by the memorial and she liked him for it. He was such a good man. It was a shame he was a widower. If any man deserved to be looked after by a loving wife, it was Mr Thirkle. 'Stopping to pay your respects, I see.'

'Yes,' said Dot. 'If I was in any doubt as to the importance of getting to the bottom of this tinned-food business, this,' and she waved a hand to encompass the memorial wall, 'is why I have to do it – the last war and the war we're fighting now. Everyone should be pulling together and doing the right thing. It's wicked that there are folk doing the dirty on the rest of us.'

'I agree,' said Mr Thirkle. She could feel him looking at her. 'I hope you don't regret taking me into your confidence about the food dump.'

She turned to face him. 'I may have blabbed a war secret, but I did it out of honourable intentions.'

'I won't let you down.'

'I know you won't. Neither of us will let our country down.' Dot laughed. 'Hark at me, making the big wartime speech. We have to decide what to do.'

'We must talk about the people who know about the food dump and that will take time. Meeting up in our break wouldn't be sufficient. Might I suggest we meet after work? Or do you need to hurry home?'

Did she need to hurry home? Of course she did. She was permanently in a hurry, rushing round the house with her duster, rushing to work, rushing to the shops. Even when she was standing still, she was in a rush – hurrying to get the vegetables peeled so she could put them in a pan of water ready for later, hurrying to get the ironing finished, hurrying to get the kettle on so everyone could have a cup of tea.

But this was another job that needed doing and Dot Green had never been one to shirk her duty.

'Fine,' she said. 'What time do you finish?'

They compared notes and found they were due to clock

off at the same time. It was too good a chance to miss. Inside her head, Dot threw all today's jobs in the air and caught them in a different order.

'Where should we meet?' asked Mr Thirkle. 'In the station mess?'

'No. I don't go in there often. What about in the buffet? If we can get a corner table, we can talk privately.'

All day, as she ferried parcels up and down the train, answered passengers' questions and helped them get their luggage off the train, Dot thought about the people she and Mr Thirkle should discuss. It wouldn't be easy. It was all very well to think about folk she barely knew, but two of them she counted as her friends. What would they think if they knew she was having bad thoughts about them? Not that she was, not really, but it wouldn't be fair to leave their names out when she talked to Mr Thirkle.

When she walked into the buffet, all wrapped up so that no passengers would be aware of a member of staff supping tea in public, she spotted Mr Thirkle at a corner table.

'I wasn't expecting you ladies this evening,' said Mrs Jessop, who was on duty behind the counter, as Dot got out her purse to pay for her cup of tea.

'We aren't meeting today,' said Dot, 'but we'll be here tomorrow.'

As she crossed the room to join Mr Thirkle, he politely stood up.

'I would have got your tea for you,' he said.

'No need.' Dot wanted to get down to business right away. 'I've worked out who knows about the . . .' she dropped her voice to a whisper, '. . . food dump. Three of us made the deliveries: myself, Joan Foster, who is one of the porters, and a man I haven't seen since called Mr Hope.'

Mr Thirkle nodded. 'I know him. He's a delivery driver. When you unload parcels here in Victoria that you've collected along your route, Mr Hope is one of the men who deliver the ones that are addressed to places in Manchester.'

'Have you known him a long time?'

'Donkey's years.'

'When we arrived at the railway shed to unload, another girl I know was there – Mabel Bradshaw. She's a lengthman and her gang was with her. Let me see if I can get their names right. There's Bernice Hubble – who, incidentally, is the mother of Joan Foster's boyfriend – and the other two are called Bette and Louise, but I don't know owt about them. Where do we start?'

'With the ones we know about.'

'The ones I know are Joan and Mabel,' Dot said promptly, 'and we can discount them right away. They aren't thieves. Mabel is, shall we say, rather well heeled and wouldn't need any extra money, and Joan was strictly brought up. Besides,' she added, a pang searing through her, 'her sister died in the Christmas Blitz.'

'You mean,' Mr Thirkle suggested gently, 'she can't be a thief because she's endured a bereavement?'

'Of course not. But I know her – and I know Mabel. They're good girls.'

'Likewise, Mr Hope is a good man,' Mr Thirkle replied. 'I'm sorry, Mrs Green, but we aren't going to get far if we assume the people we like are innocent.'

The back of Dot's throat tightened. However hard it was to acknowledge it, it was true.

'So how do we narrow it down?' she asked.

'I can think of one way.' Mr Thirkle took a sip of his tea and Dot noted that he sipped silently. Reg was inclined to slurp. 'Did the lengthmen see the food?'

Dot's brows tugged together as she pictured the scene. 'No. It was covered by tarpaulin. The girls appeared just as we drove up.'

Mr Thirkle leaned forwards. 'If they didn't know about the food, then none of them could have stolen it, could they?'

Dot went hot and cold. 'That leaves Joan and Mr Hope – and me, I suppose. I can't believe for a minute it was Joan, but I imagine you can't believe it of Mr Hope either.' Her sigh felt heavy. By, it was a nasty business.

'The lengthmen might not have seen the tins,' Mr Thirkle said slowly, 'but they might have been curious – or one of them might have been.'

Dot grabbed at the suggestion with both hands. Not that she wanted one of Mabel's fellow lengthmen to be the guilty party, but – oh heck.

'What we have to do next,' said Mr Thirkle, 'is see for ourselves if they could have gained access to the railway shed at a later time.'

Alighting from the train that had brought her and the rest of her gang, as well as a couple of all-male gangs, back to Victoria Station, Mabel stamped her feet on the platform and rubbed her gloved hands up and down her arms.

'Though why I should still be chilled, I can't imagine,' she laughed, 'after that journey. Talk about sardines in a tin.'

'Not so much standing room only,' said Bette, 'as squeezing room only.'

'Barely room to breathe only,' Louise added.

'At least you're skinny, Lou,' said Bernice. 'I'm off to the buffet for a hot cuppa before I go home, if anyone wants to come. But first – the Ladies!'

There were no staff toilets for the women, so the female

railway employees, whose numbers were increasing all the time, had to make do with the public lavatories used by lady passengers. One bright spark had had the idea of hanging an Out of Order sign on one of the doors, so there was always a vacant cubicle for railway women to use. And to avoid having to pay a penny every time, the girls used a bent nail to manoeuvre the penny-in-the-slot lock on the door, a gem of an idea that Dot had imported from Southport Station.

On their way from the Ladies to the buffet, as Mabel, Bernice, Bette and Louise made their way through the crowds of passengers, Mabel said, 'I'll sit with you to start with, but I hope you won't mind if I join my friends when they arrive.'

'Oh!' said Bette. 'Abandoning us for something better?'

'How else am I to keep you in your place?' Mabel retorted.

The buffet was busy, but they found a table and settled down to chat, Mabel keeping one eye on the door.

'Excuse me,' she said when Dot walked in. 'There's one of my friends.'

With a chorus of 'Have a good time tonight' ringing in her ears, she bagged a table that a couple were just leaving and waited for Dot to join her.

'That's your gang, isn't it?' Dot peered across the buffet, not taking a seat. 'You didn't have to leave them. We can go and sit with them until the others come.'

'They'll be gone in a minute,' said Mabel.

Dot sat down. 'What are they like?'

'Who?'

'The others in your gang.' Dot made it sound almost jokey. 'You know what us backstreet women are like, always ready for a gossip.'

Mabel smoothed her brow before she could frown. If

there was one thing she knew for certain about Dot Green, it was that she wasn't a gossip. Mabel felt uncomfortable and she was glad when Cordelia walked in, tall and elegant in a belted coat with cuffed sleeves, leather shoes with fan-shaped tongues, and a hat with an asymmetric crown. Nobody seeing Cordelia arriving at the station in the morning, or going home at the end of the day, would imagine for a single moment that her job as a lampwoman involved removing, cleaning and putting back the signal lights on the permanent way and the side- and tail lights on the wagons. She would arrive looking like the perfect lady on her way to meet her friends for bridge, got changed to do her job and then changed back into the perfect lady at the end of her day's work.

Cordelia's arrival was swiftly followed by Joan's. Then Alison joined them, which meant they were just waiting for Persephone, since Colette, as usual, wouldn't be joining them.

'What plans do you girls have for tonight?' Cordelia asked. 'I hope young things like you aren't staying at home on a Friday night. Good heavens, I think we can safely say Persephone will be going out tonight.'

With the rest of them, Mabel turned to look. Persephone was standing behind a group of lads in uniform in the queue at the counter. Her caramel-coloured coat with its oversized collar was unfastened, its unbuckled belt dangling, revealing a pale sea-green evening dress of silk chiffon. It was high-waisted, with a fitted bodice that flared into a floor-length skirt, from beneath which peeped evening shoes in a deeper sea-green that matched her small handbag. But it wasn't just her clothes that put everyone else in the shade. It was her slender figure, her golden-blonde hair and those lovely violet eyes combined with her friendly smile.

The soldiers in front of Persephone had noticed the stunner behind them and, with much laughter and bowing, were insisting upon putting her in front of them in the queue. Persephone smiled and said something that caused more laughter as she accepted the courtesy.

When she brought her cup of tea to the table, even before she could sit down, the questions and comments started.

Persephone smiled. 'My brother's friend is taking me out. He's booked an early table for dinner before we go to the theatre – hence the gown. And before you ask, Forbes regards me as a kid sister.'

'Forbes?' asked Alison. 'Is that his first name?'

'How the other half live, eh,' said Dot.

'Here he comes now,' said Persephone.

Once more, they all turned. The delicate skin around Mabel's eyes stretched as her eyes widened at the sight of the army officer, his peaked cap tucked beneath his arm, making his way towards them. He had the easy, confident bearing of an athlete. His mid-brown hair was cut in the regulation short back and sides, his eyebrows a darker shade of brown above smoky-grey eyes. His nose was straight, his face narrower than Harry's, his jawline less square but just as compelling.

He stopped by their table. Were all the other girls in the buffet grinding their teeth with jealousy?

'Ladies.' He inclined his head politely, then grinned at Persephone. 'Percy, old thing. Splendid to see you after all this time.'

'Percy?' Cordelia exclaimed. 'You can't call her that.'

'She doesn't mind – do you, Percy? It's an old nickname, ma'am.'

'It's not a question of whether Persephone minds,' Cordelia replied, her cool voice taking on an edge of sharpness. 'Percy was a nickname given to conscientious objectors in the last war. Anyone of an age to remember that would take offence at hearing it applied to this patriotic girl, who is working hard to do her bit. Kindly don't use the name again, young man.'

'Put like that, of course I won't,' Forbes agreed. 'I apologise for any offence.' He had the same innate good manners as Persephone. He looked at her. 'We ought to make a move, old thing.'

'Let me introduce you first.' Persephone looked round the table, doing something that Mumsy's etiquette book referred to as 'gathering eyes', which was what the lady of the house did at the end of a posh dinner party when it was time for the ladies to retire and leave the gentlemen to pass the port. 'May I present Captain Forbes Winterton. Forbes, these ladies are my colleagues, but, more importantly, they are my friends: Mrs Masters and Mrs Green, Miss Foster, Miss Bradshaw and Miss Lambert.'

'My pleasure, ladies,' said Forbes, and Mabel was aware she wasn't alone in breathing a little sigh. 'And now, Percy – I beg your pardon – Persephone, we ought to go. Please excuse us, ladies.'

'Would someone drink my tea for me?' asked Persephone. 'Mustn't waste it.'

Was it Mabel's imagination or did the volume in the buffet drop as Persephone and Forbes made their way out? They certainly turned heads.

'What a handsome chap,' said Dot, 'and so well mannered.'

Cordelia chuckled. 'It's a good thing you three young ones have boyfriends or you'd probably all have fallen head over heels.'

'Persephone isn't the only one going out tonight,' said Mabel. 'I'm seeing Harry – and no,' she added with a laugh, as Cordelia and Dot pretended to look for his arrival through the buffet door, 'he's not picking me up from here.'

'That's a shame,' said Dot. 'I'd like to see the famous Harry.'

'The infamous cheeky blighter,' said Joan.

Mabel leaned forward. 'May I ask you something, all of you? To do with Harry and me.'

'Ask away,' said Alison.

'I hope there isn't a problem,' said Cordelia.

'Not at all. Everything's fine. In fact, almost too fine.' She bit her lip. Was this going to make sense? 'I'm happy.'

'That's good,' said Joan.

'I'm extremely happy.'

'Even better,' said Dot.

'Only if Harry feels the same,' said Cordelia.

'What I'm really asking is,' said Mabel, 'is there such a thing as falling in love with love? You know, like in the Rodgers and Hammerstein song.' Or maybe the others didn't know the song. Mabel knew it because a friend of her parents had brought back a copy of the sheet music from America. She looked round at the attentive expressions on her friends' faces. 'After my friend Althea died, I convinced myself that I didn't deserve to have anything good happen to me, but you all helped me to see that while I'll never cease to regret what happened to her, it isn't wrong for me to . . . to . . .'

'To have a life of your own,' Dot finished.

'It's more than "not wrong". It's right,' said Cordelia.

Mabel filled with what felt like an inner glow. 'Thank you. But am I simply being swept away by the sheer relief of having moved on from feeling guilty?'

'Do you mean,' said Alison, 'you fear your feelings for Harry might not be real?'

'I'm glad and grateful to have found such happiness,' said Mabel. 'I'm rather overwhelmed by it, to tell you the truth.'

Dot reached for Mabel's hand and pressed it warmly. 'The way I see it, love, is this. Your grief and unhappiness were real enough, weren't they?'

Mabel nodded. She couldn't speak. Her throat felt thick.

'Then why can't this happiness be real an' all?'

'Dot is right,' said Cordelia. 'If your happiness feels overwhelming, that could be because you spent such a long, dark time struggling with grief and guilt.'

'You've gone from one extreme to the other,' said Joan.

'I think that makes it official,' said Alison. 'The railway girls are united in telling you to get on with your romance – aren't we?'

As the others agreed, Mabel laughed. She felt like hugging them all. What a fool she had been to have denied herself this support for most of last year. Nothing would ever replace the special closeness she had shared with Althea, but what she had instead with her fellow railway girls was deeply satisfying and sustaining.

She was buoyed up as she went home and got ready for her evening out, putting on her mauve wool-jersey dress, teaming it with her art deco amethyst and crystal beads and matching earrings that had been her twenty-first-birthday gift from Althea's parents.

'You look nice,' said Mrs Grayson when she went downstairs. 'That's my favourite of your dresses.'

'Harry's seen me in it before – more than once. Maybe it's time for a quick trip home to raid my wardrobe.'

'There are plenty of girls who have just the one good dress and consider themselves lucky.'

'Am I being shallow? I want to dress my best for Harry.'

'What girl doesn't want to look her best for her beau?'

'Talking of appearances,' said Mabel. Would Mrs Grayson mind? There was one way to find out. 'Wouldn't you like a change from wearing your hair in a bun? Now that you've been outside, would you like to go to the hairdresser? I'll come with you.'

Mrs Grayson paled. 'I couldn't possibly. Just because I've been to next door's shelter – and you've no idea how hard it is each time . . .'

'But it's a bit easier each time, isn't it?' Mabel coaxed. 'Just the tiniest bit. It all adds up.'

'Anyroad, I couldn't get as far as the hairdresser.'

'I thought you might say that, so here's another suggestion. What if I arranged for the hairdresser to come here?' The front-door knocker rat-tatted. 'There's Harry.' Mabel got to her feet. 'Think about it.'

She let Harry in and they spent a few minutes with Mrs Grayson. Harry produced a tub of Bournville cocoa and presented it to Mrs Grayson with a flourish.

'Mabel tells me what a wonder you are in the kitchen. I thought you might use this to knock up a chocolate pudding or two.'

As she and Harry got up to leave, Mabel felt an unexpected impulse to drop a kiss on her landlady's cheek, though she didn't act on it. How surprising that her attitude towards Mrs Grayson should have changed – developed – so much.

'It was kind of you to bring the cocoa,' she told Harry as they walked along the road.

'It's a well-known fact that the way to a young lady's heart is via her landlady's cooking pot.'

Mabel pretended to swat him. 'Cheeky blighter.'

'That's me. The one and only.'

'Yes. The one and only.' Mabel stopped walking and turned to him, right there on Nell Lane. 'The last time we saw one another, you asked me a question. Do you remember?' She would die if he didn't. But of course he would.

She gazed into his face. The sight of his dark eyes and generous mouth made her heart do a little flip, while his broad forehead, straight nose and sweep of square chin filled her with pride.

'I asked,' said Harry, 'if you thought I might be the right man for you.'

Mabel went from feeling fluttery and breathless to feeling calm and steady. This was right. This was what she wanted.

'Are you ready to answer the question?' Harry asked.

'Are you the man for me, Harry Knatchbull?' Mabel leaned closer. 'I think that you are, to quote a certain cheeky blighter, the one and only.'

# Chapter Eighteen

The thing about grief was that you thought it couldn't get any worse, but then it did. The prospect of having to get through Letitia's twenty-first birthday twisted Joan's heart inside out. Should she have volunteered to do a day's overtime? But she couldn't abandon Gran today of all days.

They went to Southern Cemetery. The undertaker had said it would be several months before they could erect a headstone. They had to wait for the earth to settle. Would it be easier on their hearts when there was a headstone? Or would it set the final seal on Letitia's absence?

Gran stood at the foot of the grave, staring down, her expression unmoving but raw with pain. Was she sobbing deep inside? Joan ached to put her arms around her, but nothing in Gran's upright stance invited it. The last time they had visited Letitia there had been a couple of girls at a nearby grave weeping freely on one another's shoulders, and Gran had muttered something about making a show of yourself in public. The trouble was that Gran didn't give way to tears in private either. If only she would, they could cry together. As it was, Joan felt it would be weak of her to cry.

Would crying together help them heal?

Did Gran *want* to heal?

Ridiculous thoughts – unhelpful. It was far too soon to think of healing.

When they got home, the day stretched ahead, unutterably bleak.

Gran picked up the photograph of Daddy.

'It's a shame we haven't got a studio portrait of Letitia,' said Joan.

'I booked one, to be taken this afternoon. Letitia on her twenty-first birthday, to stand beside the picture of Daddy.'

Don't say it. Don't say it. *Do you want a studio portrait of me on my twenty-first?*

Gran replaced Daddy's photograph. Joan looked across at it, imagining a picture of Letitia standing beside it. Two generations of Fosters.

'I wish we had more photographs of her,' said Joan. 'Let's look through them and choose the best one.'

'I don't know—'

'Please. It won't take long.'

No, it wouldn't. The Fosters didn't possess a camera. Their only photographs were those taken by the kind of photographer who had a booth on the pier and took snaps of holidaymakers as they walked past, and the next day you went back to look at the display to see if your picture was there.

Joan went into the back parlour and opened the sideboard drawer where Gran kept a stout envelope containing their few family snaps – and that really was all they were: snaps. An elderly widow with two children to bring up didn't have money to throw around on posh photographs.

A handful of pictures. A few of Letitia and Joan together at various ages, two or three of them with Gran.

'Not one of Letitia on her own,' said Joan.

'I could have told you that,' said Gran.

'This is the best – the most recent.' She was going to see this through if it killed her. 'The three of us walking along Southport pier in '39. Do you remember what a blazing hot summer it was? And we nearly didn't go, because what if war was declared while we were away?' *Come on, Gran. Say something. Make a conversation out of it.* 'And Letitia said, "Don't be daft. If war is declared, we'll come straight home." Do you remember?'

'Of course I remember. I'm not senile.'

Joan persevered. 'Should we buy a frame for this one?'

'I have to cancel the appointment at the photographer's.'

'You what? You mean they're expecting Letitia to turn up today?'

'There's no call to use that tone of voice. I'll walk round and tell them.'

'I'll do it,' Joan said at once. 'You don't have to.'

'I'm perfectly capable of telling the photographer the appointment has to be cancelled.'

'Would you like me to come with you?' she offered.

'I told you. I'm perfectly capable. What's the matter with you today?'

And that was that. End of.

Joan expected Gran to set off immediately, but she didn't. She disappeared into the kitchen, where she banged about, crashing saucepans together and sorting noisily through the cutlery drawer, as she started to prepare the dinner.

The hot vegetable cake was normally one of Joan's favourites, but today it was all she could do to swallow it. Only her determination not to waste good food and to support Gran by behaving normally enabled her to eat it. Then, when she had forced down the final morsel, Gran put her own knife and fork together on the plate, leaving her own portion half finished.

'I'll add it to the cheese pudding for tea,' she said.

Did she have any idea how bad that made Joan feel? Did eating all her own meal make her seem uncaring, as if she wasn't grieving?

Refusing help, Gran washed up, then put on her coat, hat and gloves and picked up her handbag and gas-mask box.

'I could come with you,' Joan offered again.

'No need.'

'What time was Letitia's appointment?'

'Two o'clock. I wanted her to spend all morning looking forward to it.'

'Two!' Joan exclaimed. 'It's twenty-to now.'

'I'm aware of that. Unless you intend to keep me here talking, I'll arrive at two on the dot.'

Joan snapped her mouth shut. The poor photographer. It would have been an awkward enough moment for him if Gran had cancelled because of bereavement a while ago, but for her to arrive at the time of Letitia's appointment to announce her death was something Joan wasn't prepared to dwell on. It was as if Gran wanted to make everything as hard for herself as she could – and for other people too.

Gran had been gone five minutes when Steven arrived. Would the hyacinths he had given them have finished flowering by now, if Gran had kept them? Could she return the ceramic bowl to him without a blush? Life was hard enough without Gran creating extra difficulties.

Steven was thinner in the face now. Joan could understand that. Grief had sliced a few pounds off her frame too.

'I hope it's all right for me to turn up unannounced.' On the doorstep, Steven gave a light shrug of his shoulders, his mouth in a sort of upside-down smile. 'It's a difficult day.'

'You're always welcome,' Joan assured him. 'Come in. Gran's just popped out.'

The sky was a brilliant blue. Joan led the way into the parlour. Until her eyes adjusted, the room seemed extra dingy in comparison to the dazzling day outside. The net curtains didn't so much cover the windows as smother them, turning the day's brightness to a sombre sepia in a room of well-worn but spotlessly clean furnishings. A clock ticked soberly on the mantelpiece. It was a staid room, a stern room – like Gran. A frisson ran through Joan. Lord, how was she to face life without Letitia?

'Actually,' said Steven, waiting for Joan to take a seat on the small sofa before he sat in one of the armchairs, 'I'm pleased to see you on your own. I've called round and seen your gran a few times and we've had long conversations.'

'Have they helped?'

'They did at first, but I've realised that Mrs Foster talks about Letitia as if she was perfect, which, of course, she was in my eyes – or rather, she was perfect in my heart. But she had her faults – don't we all? And I don't want to talk about her as if she was some kind of angel.'

'Gran's so unhappy, so angry. She obviously finds it easier to talk to you than to me.'

Steven hesitated before he said, 'Maybe because Letitia was her favourite.'

'You saw that?'

'Letitia talked about it sometimes. She didn't want to be the special one. She said it wasn't fair on you. Why should she be special just because she'd been blessed with your father's good looks and a few extra brain cells?'

'Gran sets great store by passing the scholarship.'

'Letitia always said how generous you were. You might have been jealous, but never were. She loved you for that.'

'It was probably good for both of us that Gran thought so highly of her. We both benefited from Letitia's talking

Gran round about things like fashionable skirt lengths. I remember the day she got Gran to agree to that. They were arguing because Gran insists on having all the family papers in her handbag – you know, birth certificates and what have you – and Letitia said they ought to go in the air-raid box, but Gran wouldn't give them up. But she did say we could stop wearing those ridiculously long skirts. Looking back, I wonder if Letitia really meant it about the family papers or whether she used that as leverage to get Gran to agree about the hems.'

'She was the kindest person, but when she latched on to something, she wouldn't stop until she got it.' Steven hesitated. 'May I show you something? Today was going to be the day when – when I asked Letitia to marry me. I had it all planned.'

A flare of surprise burst inside Joan. She hadn't seen this coming. What would Letitia's response have been?

*'Steven would get engaged like a shot, I'm sure, but I don't want to.'*

Letitia had been too committed to the highly responsible munitions job she loved and was so proud of to risk losing it through finding herself pregnant, thanks to a wartime marriage. Letitia had loved Steven, but she hadn't wanted to tie herself down.

'May I show you the ring?'

'You bought a ring?'

'Ages ago. I saw it in the jeweller's window and knew it was the one.'

Steven flicked up the pocket flap of his jacket and delved in his pocket, bringing out a small ring box. Leaving the armchair, he moved across and sat on the sofa, almost as if about to propose to Joan. Her heart gave a thud. When push came to shove, would Letitia have turned him down? Or would she have made him agree to a long engagement? That would have been hard, given the way so many couples were getting married at the drop of a hat.

Steven opened the box and held it up to show her an oval-shaped diamond that managed to twinkle in spite of the gloom in Gran's parlour.

'Oh,' Joan breathed, 'it's beautiful.'

She reached towards it at the same time as Steven handed her the box. Their fingertips brushed and a jolt of consciousness surged through Joan's body, bringing every single nerve ending vividly to life.

Although she was determined to see this through, Dot couldn't help feeling shocked at herself. It was Saturday afternoon and she ought to be with her family or cleaning the house or doing the shopping or possibly baking a cake or finding something new to do with fish, courtesy of *The Stork Wartime Cookery Book*. That was what housewives did with their Saturday afternoons, not go traipsing off with men they weren't married to, to solve wartime crimes.

'It's further than I expected,' she said apologetically. 'Either that or I've brought you the wrong way.'

'No, you haven't,' said Mr Thirkle. 'We're walking parallel to the permanent way, so we'll come to the right shed eventually.'

'Aye, eventually. I thought it wouldn't be far, because I remember Mabel walked to where she and her gang were working the first few days she was a lengthman.'

Mr Thirkle chuckled. 'We'll get there, never fear.'

'How will I know which shed?' asked Dot. 'We've passed several.'

'They all had railway tracks running into them. Yours didn't, did it?'

'No, it didn't, so at least we know we haven't passed it yet, even if we have walked halfway to Southport.' She laughed, feeling brighter. 'What would you normally be doing on your Saturday afternoon off?'

'Our Edie had some jobs lined up for me.'

'Oh, I'm sorry if I've dragged you away from your domestic responsibilities.'

'No matter. I can oil those hinges and fix the shelf this evening. With her Vic away fighting, it's left to her old dad to sort things out. She likes jobs to be done promptly, does my Edie. She reckons you can't feel truly comfortable in a house if you know there's things that need doing.'

Reg might learn a thing or two off Edie, thought Dot, although she didn't say so. 'Was her mum the same?'

'Oh aye, that's where our Edie gets it from. A lot like her mum, she is. My wife liked everything to be just so.'

'I can understand that.' The strap on her gas-mask box slipped. She shoved it back onto her shoulder. 'So you have two homes to take care of, your own and your daughter's.' It was good to think of him keeping busy. She didn't like the thought of him spending long, quiet evenings all alone.

Mr Thirkle pointed. 'When you drove here, did Mr Hope turn the Scammell off the road onto a cinder track?'

Dot floundered about inside her memory. 'I think so.'

'Then that shed over yon could be what we're after.'

The wide cinder track crackled and crunched underfoot. It wound around a curve, and up ahead was a railway shed. No, not a shed, *the* shed. It was brick-built and, had a length of railway track led into it, could easily have housed a locomotive. At this end was a wide, arched doorway, with a pair of wooden doors that a lorry could drive through.

'Is this it?' asked Mr Thirkle.

'Definitely. I recognise it.'

Daft as it sounded, Dot trembled as they walked closer. Each door possessed a large circular handle. A thick chain wound through both of them, fastening the doors. A large padlock held the chains securely.

Dot lifted part of the chain, releasing a cascade of metallic clinks. 'No one could have got in this way – unless they had a key, and no one on our list would have one.' She smiled, relieved.

'Didn't you tell me that some bigwigs came along while you were unloading the tins? They might have access to a key, depending on who they were.'

'Nay, important men like that wouldn't be in the thieving lark.'

'Why not?' Mr Thirkle asked.

'You're right.' Dot frowned. 'Why should toffs be exempt from suspicion? Why is it easier to blame a lower-class person? I'm lower class and honest with it.'

'It's because if someone is upper class, you look up to them,' said Mr Thirkle. 'Let me see if I can find out from Mr Hope who the men were. He might know.'

'Will there be another way in?' asked Dot.

'Unlikely.'

'We should check, just the same. We've come all this way.'

'Halfway to Southport.' Mr Thirkle smiled his soft smile. He had such a kind face.

They turned the corner and walked the length of the building. It wasn't an easy walk. There was no path. The ground was bumpy and their way was interrupted by bushes and piles of old sleepers. It wasn't possible to see inside. The windows were too high off the ground, and even if they hadn't been, they were thick with grime.

The rhythmic sound of a train coming along the permanent way made them look round.

'I think we should hide,' said Mr Thirkle. 'We can't afford for someone to report seeing people poking about outside railway property.'

There was a tall shrub with waving branches, which spared them the indignity of ducking behind a bush. The train came closer, great clouds of steam thrusting up into the air as the locomotive passed by, drawing its line of deep-red liveried coaches behind it.

Once it was gone, they carried on. At the end of the building, they went round the corner to find that the back wall was solid brick – no windows, no door. They walked to the far end to turn the corner and walk back up the other side – and stopped dead at the sight of a small, brick-built add-on sticking out of the building, undoubtedly an outside lavatory. Its door was sagging badly. Its upper hinge had dropped and the door had rotted away at the bottom. Mr Thirkle took a torch from his pocket. Dot could have kicked herself for not being similarly prepared.

Mr Thirkle peered round the door. 'A privy.'

Dot waved her hand in front of her face. 'It's a bit whiffy.'

'It must have been put here for the lengthmen, lampmen and so forth out on the permanent way. It's not what we're looking for, anyroad.'

What with the slack door and Mr Thirkle in front of her, it wasn't easy to see in, but Dot caught a glimpse. 'Shine your torch over there.'

Mr Thirkle did so, revealing an inner door.

'Not just for the lengthmen,' said Dot. 'For the men inside the shed an' all.'

Mr Thirkle heaved the wonky door further open and the sour smell wafted out.

'Wait here,' he said.

Not likely. 'It's only a pong. You've obviously never changed the nappy of a baby with diarrhoea.'

They squeezed inside and tried the door. It didn't budge. Locked? Or stiff? Mr Thirkle put his shoulder to it and shoved. It moved a jot and then the hinges groaned and the door swung open enough for them to pass through one at a time into an atmosphere that felt as though they were breathing dust. In the vast, murky interior, Dot sensed as much as saw the high ceiling and the shapes of wheels and lengths of metal, piles of bricks and huge springs, even one of those flatbed things with a sort of see-saw on it that you moved up and down to make the contraption travel along the permanent way.

'On our way out, I'll put a matchstick in the door as we close it,' said Mr Thirkle. 'If the door is opened again, the matchstick will fall down.'

'And that'll show if this is the route the thief has been using to get into the building,' said Dot. 'Good idea.'

'Mind your step,' said Mr Thirkle as they walked cautiously through the gloom. He stopped and unpicked the tissue from the lens of his torch. He shone it around, its tiny beam picking out details here and there in the cobwebby dimness – and Dot tingled all over at the sight, along the wall furthest from the permanent way, of the piles of foodstuffs that had been arranged there by Joan, Mr Hope and herself nearly a year ago.

How could this have happened? The slightest brush of Steven's fingertips against her own was all it had taken for Joan's old feelings for him to come thundering back and take possession of her. She stared at him, then pulled her gaze away so he couldn't see what was in her eyes. Did he know, did he sense, had he seen what had just happened to her? Her chin dropped onto her chest in shame. She had successfully kept her secret for so long before she met Bob. Was it to be revealed now?

Those same fingertips that had grazed hers now touched her chin, sending weakness through her body. She ought to drag herself away from him, but, whether she wanted it or not, her face lifted under his guidance and she met his gaze.

'Joan ...' It was a whisper. Steven's eyes clouded beneath a frown.

As he made to draw back from her, Joan's hand darted up to touch his cheek. Steven rested his forehead against hers, sending an anguished tingling cascading through her. At one time, she had dreamed of this, and been ashamed to dream of it. She had never wanted to steal her sister's boyfriend, and yet she had dreamed.

Steven's lips feathered the tiniest of kisses across her face before brushing her lips. Emotion rose within her as her face tilted, her lips yearning towards his. Steven's mouth brushed hers, once, twice, then settled softly into position, his lips moving slightly, slowly, with no sugges-tion of demand, yet a response surged up inside her as if he had hauled it up from the pit of her belly. She turned her head a fraction, pressing closer to him – just as he pulled away, clearing his throat, not looking at her. He swallowed, his breath coming swiftly, as did her own.

Standing up, he stepped away from the sofa.

'I'm sorry, Joan. I can only apologise.'

She got to her feet. Her legs were unsteady, but some-how they held her up.

'Don't apologise,' she said. 'It wasn't just you.'

Steven wouldn't look at her. Did she want him to? He picked up the ring and its box, stuffing the ring into the velvet slot, and the box in his pocket.

'I shouldn't have come,' he said.

'It's a hard day for both of us.'

At last Steven looked at her. He appeared dazed. A lump clogged Joan's throat as remorse coursed through her. Was that how Steven felt too?

'I'd better go,' he said.

He left the room, stumbling against the edge of the sofa and muttering something, an apology presumably. Joan followed him, her limbs forcing their way through air that felt thick with shock and shame.

When Steven pulled open the front door, he looked back. A flush of colour across his cheekbones made him look vulnerable.

'I apologise for my conduct. As you said, this is a hard day.'

Joan nodded. No words would form. Her eyes stung with tears that lent a silvered edge to Steven's shape in the doorway. He stood there, seemed about to speak again, then turned away. She pushed the door shut, practically falling against the wall for support, but this was no time for weakness. She had just made the most almighty twit of herself and there was no consolation in the knowledge that Steven had done the same – except that he hadn't, had he? He had acted on a mad impulse, but for her there was the memory of those old feelings that had once been very real. How could she – they – have betrayed Letitia like this?

She placed the flat of her hand against the door. When she had let Steven in, she had had no idea of what was going to happen. Now she had shut him out for ever. He could never return. She never wanted to see him again.

The knock on the door reverberated through her hand, sending tiny vibrations up her arm and into her chest . . .

into her heart. Not allowing herself to think, she pulled the door open, feeling no sense of surprise when Steven walked inside. She didn't resist when he took her in his arms, kicking the door shut behind him, and pushed her against the wall as he started to kiss her.

# Chapter Nineteen

It was too good an opportunity to miss. Dot was meant to go straight home after her shift, but the sight of Bernice Hubble entering the station buffet sent her beetling in pursuit. As long as Mrs Hubble wasn't meeting somebody, this was Dot's chance to pump her for information.

Dot joined her at the back of the queue.

'Eh, it's Mrs Hubble, isn't it?' she said as if she had just this moment realised.

Mrs Hubble looked round. 'Evening, Mrs Green. How are you?'

They exchanged pleasantries. Not that there was anything very pleasant in discussing the war.

'Fire-watching is going to be a legal duty for men from sixteen to sixty, according to my Den,' said Mrs Hubble. 'He reckons it's because of the terrible fires we had in the Christmas Blitz.'

Talking to Bernice Hubble, Dot felt a sense of familiarity. They were two of a kind. Two ordinary housewives who loved their children more than anything in the world and who worked hard at their wartime jobs and then went home and started work all over again, this time with mops, irons and vegetable peelers. All of a sudden, Dot couldn't meet Mrs Hubble's eyes as shame speared her at the thought of how she intended to manipulate this decent woman.

'Your lad is Joan's boyfriend, isn't he? Now there's a lovely lass if ever there was one. Such a shame about her sister.'

'It doesn't bear thinking about. That poor girl. She would have turned twenty-one at the weekend, according to our Bob. He had to work all weekend and he felt wretched about not being with Joan.'

'It sounds like you've fetched up a good lad.'

There was a pause in the conversation while they bought their tea and found a table.

'I like to think of Joan being looked after,' said Dot. 'She deserves it.'

'Between you, me and the gatepost, I think she could do with a spot of coddling. I get the impression that her grandmother is a strict sort. Uncompromising.'

But Dot wasn't here to discuss Joan. 'Mabel's another likeable girl. No airs and graces, for all that she's from money. Who else do you have in your group?'

'Gang,' said Mrs Hubble. 'It's called a gang. Bette and Louise are the other two.'

'I've heard Mabel mention the names. What are they like?'

'They're decent girls.'

'I'm sure they are,' said Dot. How could she steer Mrs Hubble in the right direction? 'What I meant was, you're an ordinary body, like me, and there's Mabel whose dad owns a factory. When she first mentioned it, I thought he must be the manager, and that would have been posh enough, but no, he owns it.'

'There's all sorts of folk being thrown together these days.'

'Aye. That's why I wondered about this Bette and Louise.' She shrugged. 'Just making conversation.'

Mrs Hubble laughed. 'Put it this way. I don't think Mabel's mother would welcome them into her best parlour.'

'I bet she doesn't even have a parlour,' said Dot. 'She

probably has one of them fancy drawing rooms, like in *Gone With the Wind*.'

'Bette and Lou wouldn't be rubbing shoulders with Clark Gable. They'd be wearing frilly aprons and serving drinks – same as us.'

'Doing the washing-up, more like,' said Dot.

'I expect Bette has washed a few glasses in her time. She used to be a barmaid.'

'Oh aye?' Dot's nose for impropriety sprang into action.

'She looks a bit brassy. Wiggles her hips when she walks, you know the kind of thing. But she's a grafter, I'll give her that. Full make-up and a crowbar, that's our Bette.'

An ex-barmaid with watch-me hips. Did she have a taste for the good life?

'She was the wrong side of thirty and feeling a bit long in the tooth for pub work when the war started. She was glad to sign up for railway work,' said Mrs Hubble. 'I'm not talking behind her back. She'd tell you the same herself.'

Did Bette's good-time wiggle lose its appeal once men clapped eyes on a face that wasn't as youthful as it had once been? And what did the future hold for her when the war ended? Was she pinching tins from the food dump to sell so she could build up a nest egg?

'What about the other girl?' Dot deliberately didn't use Louise's name. It sounded more casual that way.

'There's not much money in that family. Lou's job on the railway has made all the difference.' Mrs Hubble drained her cup and pushed back her chair. 'I needed that. I was gasping. It's been nice talking to you. Evening, Mrs Green.'

Dot would have appreciated more details about Louise's home situation, but the snippet Mrs Hubble had supplied was enough to suggest that Louise had reason to pilfer from the food dump. Heat tingled beneath Dot's skin as shame squeezed her bones. What sort of person was she to be thinking about others in this way? She didn't know the first thing about Bette and Louise, yet here she was, sitting in judgement on them. As a backstreet lass born and bred, she'd never been backwards at coming forwards with an opinion on the behaviour of others, but even so.

Would Mr Thirkle glean anything useful from Mr Hope? Might it be easier for him, given that the two of them had known one another a long time, or would that make it trickier? For a decent fellow like Mr Thirkle, it would make it distasteful. Distasteful. Aye, that was the word.

She didn't have to wait long to find out. The next day, Mr Thirkle snatched a word with her when he opened the gate beside his ticket barrier for her to manoeuvre her trolley onto the concourse.

'I've spoken to Mr Hope.'

'And I've found out a bit about the other lengthmen girls.'

A swift comparison of shifts showed the impossibility of finding even five minutes to talk.

'I'm on duty all weekend,' said Mr Thirkle, 'so I've got tomorrow off. I could meet you after you finish.'

Dot thought quickly. It was one thing for them to chat in their breaktime, quite another for Mr Thirkle to be spotted by colleagues coming in on his day off to speak to her. It wouldn't do at all. Not that there was anything untoward going on, but it just wouldn't do.

'There's a little place by my bus stop where we can get a cuppa,' said Dot. 'It's called the Worker Bee. Could you meet me there?'

Later, she hurried to the buffet. She was meant to meet

up with her friends tomorrow, but seeing Mr Thirkle was important.

'May I have our notebook, please?' she asked the girl behind the counter.

In it, she wrote: *Sorry, can't come. Dot x*

Alison, Persephone and Mabel would all be there, so it wasn't as though she was leaving a single person stranded. Even so, she felt guilty the next day as she hurried off. She didn't like breaking arrangements. She had brought up her boys not to do so.

It was raining hard and Dot didn't have an umbrella. Doing her best not to slosh through any puddles, she still managed to step in one and the water seeped through to her foot.

Mr Thirkle was waiting for her in the Worker Bee café. The place was busy and his table was in the window.

'It was the only one left,' he apologised. 'Sit down, Mrs Green, and I'll fetch tea.'

Raindrops streamed down the window. It was a miserable day, but the evenings were starting to get longer, which always made Dot feel better as long as the coming spring didn't herald invasion.

Mr Thirkle set down the tray and took his seat, leaving Dot to be mother.

'I know I should feel glad that we're perhaps taking a step forward in our investigation,' she said, 'but it feels tacky to be talking about folk behind their backs.'

'It's the only way, unfortunately.'

Dot told him what she had gleaned about Bette and Louise, without mentioning Bette's wiggle. It wouldn't be decorous to mention that.

'So they both might have reason to feel tempted,' she finished. 'Mind you, they might say the same about me. Our house isn't exactly overflowing with money.'

'You're a fair-minded lady, Mrs Green.'

'Did you find out anything from Mr Hope?'

'It wasn't easy. I could hardly say, "Who were the important men who came to the secret food store I'm not supposed to know about?" It would have been a lot easier if I could.'

'It's a pity I never asked at the time who they were.'

'One of them must have been a man from the ministry. I might have found out who the other one was. I started a conversation about the different kinds of war work folk are doing. I don't mean paid jobs, such as you and your friends are doing for the railway, but voluntary work, like the Auxiliary Fire Service and the ARP.'

'And first-aiders,' Dot added, thinking of her young friends.

'I said there must be a huge need for people to organise all these groups and that men who are high up in the railway service would very likely have the right kinds of skills.'

'That was a good idea.'

'That remains to be seen. I'd taken the trouble to find out the names of railway managers who also organise heavy-rescue services at an area level and I threw them into the conversation. Mr Hope mentioned a couple of names in reply. One of them, I've since discovered, works for the Home Guard, so let's discount him, at least for now.'

'And the other?' asked Dot.

'A Mr Samuels. Now I'll tell you something he was involved in at the beginning of the war. When the museums and art galleries in London were being packed up and sent away for safe keeping, tons of foodstuffs were dispersed from the Port of London warehouses into the provinces.'

'And this Mr Samuels helped organise that?' She felt a

rush of excitement, but remembered to keep her voice down. Loose lips and all that. 'So he could be the bigwig who came to the food dump.'

'It's possible.'

'It's more than possible.' In her heart, Dot was exonerating the other railway girls and heaping the blame at the feet of Mr Samuels.

'I daresay, but we don't know for certain, and won't unless . . .' Mr Thirkle's voice faded.

Dot leaned forwards. 'Unless what?'

'Unless we can arrange for you to identify him.'

She fell back in her seat. 'I don't know about that.'

'I can't think of any other way. Can you?'

No, she couldn't. She fiddled with her teaspoon. Eh, it was a shabby business. This Mr Samuels might be a law-abiding citizen and here she was, thinking bad thoughts about him. It was the same with Bette and Louise. And if they were suspects, then Bernice Hubble should be an' all, as should Joan and Mabel, though suspecting those two felt downright bizarre.

Dot chewed the inside of her cheek. 'I don't mind telling you, Mr Thirkle, that I don't like thinking bad thoughts about other folk. I'm a great believer that what goes around comes around. The way you treat others will always find its way back to you. If we're doing wrong by poking about in other people's lives, what if it comes back to haunt us?'

Did she look as if she was walking around in a daze? It certainly felt like it. But if others noticed, presumably they would put it down to her bereavement. Joan shuddered. That made it sound as if she was hiding behind Letitia's death. Maybe she was. How could this have happened? That one spark – no, it had been more than a spark, a lot more. That huge surge of attraction between her and

Steven had turned her world upside down. How could her heart hammer with excitement, how could every single nerve end sing, when she was meant to be in the depths of grief for her sister?

And of all the men to fall in love with, it had to be Steven. But then, how could it have been anyone else? He had been her first love; a secret love, loaded with shame, but her first love nevertheless. The only secret she had kept from Letitia.

And now she was keeping a secret from the whole world – including Bob. Oh, Bob. Only a matter of days ago, she had told him she loved him – and it was true, something she had been nursing close to her heart for some time. She had intended to tell him at Christmas, but that had been long ago, before the Christmas Blitz, before everyone's lives had changed for ever.

On her birthday, she had stood on the doorstep and kissed him.

'I love you, Bob Hubble,' she had whispered.

'I love you too, Joan Foster,' he had replied.

A declaration of love that had been full of piercing sweetness amid the strain and sorrow of her first birthday without her sister.

Then, just three days later, she had been engulfed by desire for another man, for Steven, for Letitia's boyfriend, the man she had ached for before she met Bob. When he had pushed his way back into the house and started kissing her, she had melted under his touch and was sure she would have slithered to the floor if the wall behind her hadn't held her up.

Since then, she had existed in a haze of shock, elation and desperate shame. Being in love should have meant many things, but the one thing it shouldn't was secrecy. Secret love affairs were for the unfaithful, the adulterers.

The adulteresses.

Estelle.

Dear heaven, had she turned out to be a copy of her mother? Gran would skin her alive.

It was what she had lived in fear of all her life: being like Estelle. It had been bad enough when she had hankered after Steven before she met Bob. The wretched secret she had kept from Letitia now seemed trifling. It was nothing compared to this – to seeing Steven on the sly, with Letitia barely cold in her grave.

And what of Bob? A wild picture formed in her mind of her and Steven being found out, and Bob fading away through unhappiness. You could die of a broken heart. Look at Daddy.

It wasn't as though she had stopped loving Bob. Could you love two men at once? She was so confused, she couldn't think straight. Or was she too ashamed to think straight?

Was this how it had been with Estelle? Had she still loved Daddy while she was in the throes of a passionate relationship with her lover? Joan had never felt an ounce of sympathy for her runaway mother, but now the thought that Estelle, like herself, might have genuinely loved two men at once opened her eyes to new possibilities.

Gran would skin her alive for that, too.

Bob was on a stint of working nights, so she couldn't see him, which was a relief, but it perversely also gave her an urgent need to be with him, in the hope that she could be restored to sanity.

Did she want sanity to be restored? Her feelings for Steven were more fervent than anything she had experienced before. Her flesh ached with an intense awareness of herself. It was odd to look at her reflection and see her usual self. No, not quite usual. Her eyes were warm with an inner glow and her skin was radiant. Ha! Radiant on the outside, but dark as pitch on the inside.

Steven wanted them to meet up on Saturday evening.

'I can't,' said Joan. 'I'm going to the pictures with Bob. It was arranged ages ago.' Yes, when they had wondered how they were supposed to get through the long sequence of night shifts without seeing one another.

Steven didn't actually utter the words 'Tell him you can't go,' but she sensed them loud and clear.

'Don't mind me,' said Steven, his features relaxing into a smile. 'I'd keep you all to myself if I could. Are you going to tell Bob about us?'

'Have you told anyone? Have you told your parents?'

'Of course not. They'd be shocked. It's too soon.'

'But you want me to tell Bob?'

'You have to admit, it is different. He's your boyfriend. He deserves to know you've met someone else.'

Joan's scalp prickled as unease roused inside her. 'We can't tell anybody. They wouldn't understand. Imagine if Gran knew.'

'I know.' Steven took her in his arms and held her close. 'It has to stay a secret. But you can end things with Bob without telling him why.'

Joan wriggled away a fraction without actually pushing free, so she could press her fingers to his lips.

'Hush, please. Stop. Everything is so confused. Let's just enjoy this hour we've got together.'

*Enjoy?* That was a laugh. How could she enjoy being with Steven when she carried the burden of so much guilt? Yet, when he started kissing her, she did enjoy it; oh, how she enjoyed it.

Joan sat frozen in her seat in the cinema, boggling at the knowledge that one week ago today she had fallen in love with Steven again. She cried during the film – not *at* the film, just during it – but it was a weepy, so plenty of other girls were dabbing their eyes as well, so that was all right.

After the national anthem, Bob tenderly dried her cheeks with his hanky.

'Don't worry. My mum always sends me out with a clean one.'

How kind he was. He cherished her, something she had never experienced until she met him. How could she have looked at another man? Bob was perfect for her and she loved and appreciated being part of his family.

After a restless night, she got ready for church the next morning, putting on the double-breasted overcoat she had made when she was sixteen and Gran had finally let her stop wearing the old gabardine she'd had for school.

'Do you mind going to church on your own?' she asked Gran. 'I'd like to go and see Letitia.'

Gran jabbed in a massive hatpin and faced her. 'What about church?'

'I'll go to the evening service.'

But when she reached Southern Cemetery, her feet dragged as she walked the familiar paths. As much as she loved and missed her sister, she couldn't face her, not after betraying her memory with Steven. She sat on a bench, huddling inside her coat against the damp, chilly morning.

'Joan.'

Steven was standing beside the bench.

'Are you on your way to see Letitia?' Joan asked.

'I'm here to see you.'

'How did you know I'd be here instead of at church?' Was the emotional bond between them so strong that it had drawn him unerringly to her?

'Mrs Foster told me. I was loitering around near your road like a lovesick boy, hoping to catch a glimpse of the girl of his dreams.' He sat down beside her. 'Have you seen Letitia yet?'

'No. I couldn't go. Not now that you and I . . .'

'I'm sorry you feel that way. It must be hard for you. It must hurt you.'

'Nothing like as much as it would hurt Letitia if she knew.'

'Maybe,' said Steven, 'or maybe she'd be pleased that two people she loved had got together.'

'Not this soon. She died just before Christmas and it was the first of February yesterday. What does that say about us?'

Steven reached for her hand, his gloved fingers winding around hers. 'It says how lucky we are to have found one another.'

A black-clad couple came along the path. Joan withdrew her hand from Steven's under the pretext of checking her hat. When the lady and gentleman had gone past and were out of earshot, she rose to her feet.

'No, don't get up.' She looked down into Steven's face. 'I'm sorry, Steven. I can't continue like this. It's too difficult. I can't bear the thought of all the people we'd be hurting.'

'Joan—'

'It should never have happened. We should never have let it happen.'

Steven stood up. He was tall. You had to be tall, to be a policeman.

'As I recall,' he said, looking into her eyes and rendering it impossible for her to look away, 'we couldn't stop it.'

# Chapter Twenty

Mabel's hands were so cold that, although she managed to open her purse, she couldn't extract the necessary coppers. Behind the buffet counter, Mrs Jessop took pity on her.

'Give it here, love, and I'll do it.' Mrs Jessop removed the coins, holding them out on the flat of her hand for Mabel to see. 'Come round this side of the counter and wrap your hands round the hot-water urn. That'll warm 'em up. Keep your gloves on, mind, or you'll burn yourself.'

'Thanks, Mrs Jessop. You're an angel.'

Mabel placed her hands around the metal urn. At first, she couldn't feel anything, then warmth started to seep through.

Alison appeared at the counter. 'I'll take your tea for you. We're sitting over there.' She nodded towards the far corner.

'Don't bank on my joining you,' said Mabel. 'This urn is the new love of my life.'

'Far be it from me to come between you and your beloved,' said Mrs Jessop, 'but I've got a queue of folk here gasping for a cuppa and I need to fill my teapot.'

Mabel unpeeled her hands from the source of heat and headed for the table where her friends were. Colette was with them. What a nice surprise.

'Here comes Frozen Freda,' said Dot.

'This weather is shocking,' said Alison. 'When it isn't

210

snowing, it's raining, and when it isn't raining, the wind is jolly cold.'

'At least bad weather keeps Jerry at bay,' said Cordelia.

'It's extraordinary how quickly power and transport have been restored since Christmas,' said Colette.

'But all the rebuilding will have to wait,' said Cordelia.

Mabel smiled at Colette. 'It's good to see you here.'

'It's more than that,' said Dot. 'It's a treat to have your company.'

Colette went pink. 'How are you all?' Then her glance landed on Joan. 'I'm sorry. I didn't mean to be insensitive.'

'That's all right,' said Joan. She looked rather drawn, but what else would you expect? A pang of her old grief for Althea pierced Mabel, followed by an ache of compassion for Joan's unhappiness.

When Colette's husband appeared in the doorway across the room, she gathered up her handbag and gas-mask box.

Alison sighed dreamily. 'Paul would love to be able to collect me from work.'

'Excuse me.' Colette tucked her chair under the table.

'You don't want to miss your bus,' said Dot.

Joan stood up. 'I must go too.'

Colette waited for her and they wound their way between the tables.

'Poor Joan,' said Alison. 'I know Bob has been working nights, so they've not seen much of one another. When their shifts coincide again and they can spend more time together, perhaps being with him will help her.'

Mabel was about to agree, then said something else instead. 'I was about to say that being with Harry helped me overcome my unhappiness about Althea, and it did, of course, but what helped me the most was all of you.' She looked round the table. 'Being friends with you, letting my guard down, confiding my troubles: that was what brought me out of my dark time.'

'Now it's up to us to see Joan through her dark time,' said Dot.

Mabel agreed wholeheartedly. 'I want to give Joan what all of you gave me.'

She thought about it as she went home on the bus. Maybe it was time to encourage Joan to have an evening at the pictures with her friends. She knew Joan had been to the flicks with Bob, so it wouldn't be as if she was suggesting something different and impossible. After that, she would gauge the best time to get Joan to return to the dance floor. That wouldn't be easy, as Joan had always gone dancing with Letitia, but that made it all the more important that she should have her friends there to keep an eye on her when she tried it.

The bus was packed; it was that time of day. At the next stop, more got on than got off and Mabel gave up her seat to an old lady in a headscarf. She was glad to have reached a decision regarding Joan. After spending last year focusing almost exclusively on her own problems, it was good to put others first. She smiled to herself. She had arranged for the hairdresser to call at Mrs Grayson's this afternoon, so she was looking forward to seeing her landlady with an elegant new hairstyle in place of her ancient bun.

Walking from the bus stop to the house, she practised a few compliments in her head, but as she approached, the front door flew open.

'Oh, Miss Bradshaw! There you are.'

Mabel took the final steps at a run. 'What is it?'

'Something terrible has happened. I've lost my home. We're being thrown out.'

*

Mrs Grayson was so agitated that it took some time to get her not just to sit down, but to stay put. With a sense of déjà vu, Mabel perched on the pouffe at her landlady's feet, just as she had when Mrs Grayson had confided the tale of how she'd come to be housebound. On that occasion, Mabel had positioned herself thus to encourage Mrs Grayson to open up. This time, it was more with a view to barricading her in her armchair so she couldn't leap up and pace the floor.

'Tell me what this is about.' Mabel made an effort to keep her voice steady even though alarm had tightened her muscles.

Mrs Grayson huffed out a breath. 'The door knocker went and I thought it was the hairdresser, so I opened the door with a smile on my face, only it was – my husband.'

'Your husband! I thought he was— I thought you were a widow.'

'That's what everyone thinks who doesn't know any better. The neighbours all know different and I imagine it happened long enough ago that they've stopped talking about it.' Until this point, Mrs Grayson's gaze had been everywhere except on Mabel, but now she looked directly at her. 'I take it Mrs Mitchell didn't tell you.'

'She never breathed a word,' Mabel murmured, picturing Pops's Cousin Harriet, who had found her these digs.

'She knows the meaning of discretion.' Mrs Grayson clamped her lips together and blinked furiously, dabbing at her nose with her hanky.

It was horrid to be indelicate, but if Mrs Grayson had clammed up, then a prod was called for.

'Mr Grayson arrived unexpectedly—'

'Unexpectedly!' Mrs Grayson exclaimed. 'You can say that again. When I saw him standing there, it felt as though my tummy had dropped out of my body and fallen through the floor.'

'What did he want?'

'I told you. To throw me out.'

'He can't do that. This is your home.'

'He says he can. He pays the rent and it's his name on the rent book. When he left me for that floozy, he said he'd keep a roof over my head if I promised not to be difficult. What choice did I have? I needed my home. I hadn't set foot outside in years.'

'Why does he want you to leave now?'

'So he and his floozy can move in. They were bombed out in the Christmas Blitz and so were Floozy's sister and her children, and the whole lot of them descended on Floozy's mother, and they've all been there ever since. Benjy says he can't stand it a moment longer and he wants his house back.'

'That's outrageous,' Mabel declared. 'You must go to the Citizens Advice Bureau and ask for help.'

Mrs Grayson shuddered elaborately. It was a real shudder, too, not a theatrical one, as was proved by the way the colour drained from her face.

'I couldn't . . .' she began.

Mabel clasped her landlady's hands. 'You've been so brave about going next door to the air-raid shelter. This would mean going further, but I'd be by your side. Mrs Warner would come too, if we asked. You could walk in the middle.'

Mrs Grayson wrenched her hands free, tangling her fingers together, her mouth twisting in distress. 'No, I couldn't. You don't understand.'

'I do appreciate how hard it would be for you.'

'I don't mean that. I mean – oh, the shame of it.'

'There's no shame in going to the Citizens Advice.'

'Well! You're keen to wash my dirty linen in public, aren't you!' Mrs Grayson burst out. 'Do you imagine I want folk to know? The only reason I'm telling you is because you live here and I've got no choice but to tell you. I remember the . . .' she shut her eyes, '. . . the shame and the indignity. And the *fear.*' Her voice dropped to a whisper. 'Wives are reliant on their husbands. For your husband to leave you is . . . Never mind the shame, it's terrifying. How shall you cope on your own? What shall you do for money? And everyone will know that you're a failure as a wife.'

'Please don't call yourself a failure. I'm sure you did your best.'

'My best? Clinging to the house and never going out? When Benjy left me, some of the neighbours said I'd brought it on myself. Mrs Warner told me that.'

Mrs Warner would have done better to keep her trap shut. But all Mabel said was, 'I'd offer to go to the Citizens Advice for you, but I don't think they'd discuss it with me since I'm not family.'

Mrs Grayson sniffed and gulped back tears. 'You need to pack your things and find somewhere else. Could you go back to Darley Court?'

'Don't fret about me. What about you?'

'Benjy said I'd have to apply for help at a rest centre. He wants to move back in on Saturday afternoon next week, the fifteenth. I've got to be out of here by midday. He said he was doing me a favour, allowing me that long.'

Mabel's nails bit into her palms as anger stormed through her. 'The brute!'

But it was no use being vexed. She needed to keep a clear head. Of one thing she was certain.

'You're not going to face this on your own, Mrs Grayson.'

'But what can you do?'

'On my own, not much, I don't suppose.' In spite of crouching on the pouffe, she stretched her back and sat up straight. 'But I have the best friends you can imagine and we agreed we'd always help and support one another. Give me permission to tell them and we'll see what we can come up with between us.'

It was another cold day out on the permanent way, but Mabel had her indignation to keep her warm. How dare Mr Grayson treat Mrs Grayson this way? Before joining Bette, Louise and Bernice on the platform to catch the train out to where they would be working today, she had dived into the buffet to snatch a quick look at the note-book. The group was due to meet that evening and she wanted to see who would be there. Good, all of them, except for Colette. That was what this problem needed – a discussion with sensible, caring friends.

At the end of the day, when she was so anxious to return to Victoria, the train her gang was on was held up and she was the last one to arrive at the buffet.

'I thought I was never going to get here.' She put down her cup of tea and drew out a chair. She hadn't even bothered to get changed in the Ladies and beneath her overcoat was still in her cord trousers and thick woolly.

Dot laughed. 'Did you think we'd all sup our tea and clear off before you arrived?' She looked at the clock. 'Mind you, I do have to be off in a few minutes.'

'Then do you all mind if I say my piece now?' Mabel looked round at her friends. 'I apologise if I'm butting in on your conversation, but this is important and I don't want Dot to miss it.'

'Go ahead,' said Cordelia. 'We're all ears.'

'It's about my landlady, Mrs Grayson. I've mentioned her before, and how she's confined to the house.'

There were a few murmurs, mixing interest, sympathy and, yes, impatience at Mrs Grayson's strange way of life, but the murmurs were over too quickly for Mabel to assign the different reactions to the faces around her.

She explained about Mr Grayson's return and his demand that his wife should hand back the house on Saturday of next week.

'So she has only until a week tomorrow to find another home and move?' said Joan. 'That's horrible.'

'That's why I want to discuss it,' said Mabel. 'I need help. I need ideas.'

'For yourself and where you'll live?' said Alison.

'No – for Mrs Grayson. I can sort myself out, but poor Mrs Grayson can't go traipsing around looking for lodgings, can she? Even if she didn't have the housebound problem, she's so ashamed, she can barely hold her head up.'

Persephone looked at Cordelia. 'Can her husband throw her out of the house she's occupied for years?'

'I don't know why you're all looking at me,' said Cordelia. 'Being the wife of a solicitor doesn't endow me with legal knowledge.'

'It's his name on the rent book,' said Mabel. 'And before you suggest it, I tried to get her to go to the Citizens Advice Bureau, but she won't hear of it. Even supposing she managed to walk there, she couldn't bear to tell a stranger her problem – and it would be a hundred times harder if the volunteer turned out to be someone she knew. She only told me because I'm being thrown out as well.'

Alison pursed her lips. 'But she must go to the Citizens Advice.'

'Listen, love,' said Dot. 'It's no use saying she must do this or she must do that, if she's honestly not capable. It is what it is. She can't sort it out, so we'll have to sort it out for her. That's what you were hoping for, wasn't it, Mabel?'

Tension flowed out of Mabel's body as relief warmed her. 'Thank you, Dot. That's exactly it. I thought that between us . . .'

'Then you thought right,' Dot declared. 'Could one of us go to the Citizens Advice for her?'

'Not without being family,' said Cordelia.

'We might have more luck at one of the rest centres if we went on her behalf,' Alison suggested.

'Rest centres are there to help families who have been bombed out,' said Joan. 'Mrs Grayson's house is still standing.'

'The rest-centre volunteers wouldn't involve themselves in the Graysons' marital dispute,' said Cordelia.

'Then we need to come up with an idea ourselves,' said Dot. 'Somewhere for her to go.'

'And Mabel,' Alison added.

'Perhaps Miss Brown would invite Mrs Grayson to Darley Court,' suggested Persephone. 'You as well, Mabel, natch.'

Mabel smiled. How right she had been to turn to her fellow railway girls. They had agreed to support one another way back on their first day and here they were, putting that promise into action.

'I don't think I could return to Darley Court.' She looked straight at Persephone, whose presence there had been one of the reasons she had left in the first place, her other reason being that she had craved an ordinary life among ordinary people. 'I've already left there once and I know I wouldn't wish to stay there for the duration.'

'So if you went back now,' said Persephone, 'you'd only have to leave a second time.'

'Which would be staggeringly rude,' finished Mabel. 'But if Miss Brown were to invite Mrs Grayson . . .'

'Don't be daft,' said Dot. 'You can't take an ordinary

body like Mrs Grayson to a place like that and expect her to fit in.'

'Then what are we to do?' asked Persephone.

Dot smiled. 'I've got a much better idea.'

Although she would have liked to stop longer in the buffet with her friends, Dot had to get away sharpish.

'Time to get the tea on the table?' asked Alison, voicing what the rest were probably thinking.

Dot fiddled with her handbag and gas-mask box to avoid answering, lowering her face as guilt shot through her, though she wasn't intending to do owt wrong. In fact, she was doing summat that was very much right. Not that that made her feel better about lying to her mates. Just because she hadn't uttered a word didn't mean she hadn't lied. You could tell a whopping great lie without even opening your mouth.

What would they think of her if they knew she was going to meet up with Mr Thirkle in the hope of finding out who was committing a war crime? What if they knew that she had been under instructions from her conspirator that very morning to keep an eye out for a certain Mr Samuels, who was due to visit Victoria Station to view the repairs that were under way following the damage done in the blitz?

Eh, put like that, it made her sound like someone from the Secret Service instead of plain old Dot Green, trying to do the right thing.

Mr Thirkle was waiting for her in the Worker Bee café.

Dot didn't want another cup of tea, but you could hardly go into a café without having something and she didn't want to spoil her appetite with a bun. She sat with her drink in front of her, taking an occasional sip and wondering if her bladder would hold out.

219

'Did you see Mr Samuels this morning?' Mr Thirkle asked, leaning forward slightly so they could converse quietly.

'Aye, I did. It was him all right, the man from the food dump.'

'So he's now officially a suspect,' said Mr Thirkle. 'The gentleman with him was probably from the Invasion Committee, so we can discount him as he probably wasn't a local man.'

'That's a reasonable assumption,' said Dot.

'It was my morning off yesterday and I walked back to the railway shed. The matchstick I fixed in the door between the privy and the shed wasn't there. It was on the floor.'

'So we were right. That's the way the thief gets in, and no doubt he's done more thieving.' Dot felt like pounding her fists on the table. 'It's downright wicked, that's what it is. Stealing from the food dump is stealing from the whole of the local population.' But her anger subsided, anxiety creeping in to take its place. 'I should have gone to the police at the outset, shouldn't I?'

'Don't lose sight of why you didn't. You were worried about getting your daughter-in-law in trouble, even though she couldn't have known the goods were stolen.' Mr Thirkle smiled tentatively. 'And you were worried about getting into trouble for eating the evidence.'

An answering smile tugged at the corners of Dot's mouth. 'When the war's over, that bit might be funny.' She sat up straight. 'But this is here and now and there's nowt funny about it.'

'Do you want to go to the police now? We have more to tell them. There's the evidence of the matchstick – though I fear they'd say we had no business investigating and should have gone to them at the beginning.'

'And that puts me in even more trouble – and this time, you're included.'

'There's one piece of good news,' said Mr Thirkle. 'We can rule out Charlie Hope. He's been off work with a broken arm since just after we went to the shed, so he couldn't possibly have stolen anything since then.'

'I'm pleased. I know you think highly of him.'

'And now you're worried because the chances have increased against the ladies you very much want to be innocent.'

'I want to say I hope it's this Mr Samuels, but I don't want it to be him either. I'd hate someone high up in the railways to be responsible for such a thing. It would give the whole company a bad name. But it has to be one of them, doesn't it? Mr Samuels must have a good income, but maybe he's greedy for more. If I say that he's greedy for more, then I have to say the same about Mabel, because she's from a well-heeled family. Eh, it's a nasty business, isn't it?'

'It is,' Mr Thirkle agreed, 'and it's harder on you than it is on me, because my friend has been ruled out.'

Something inside Dot slumped. What had she got herself into?

# Chapter Twenty-One

Joan's spirits lifted as she cycled away from home. Sometimes she felt guilty about that, but mostly what she experienced was a dull acceptance. Home wasn't home any more. The only time she felt at home was in the Hubbles' house. There, she had only to walk through the door and the warm atmosphere settled around her, making her one of the family. She felt special and ordinary, both at the same time.

Not that there had been much opportunity in recent weeks for going over to Stretford to be with the Hubbles, what with her work and first-aid shifts being at odds with Bob's so much of the time.

'Come any time you like, love,' Mr Hubble had told her. 'You don't have to wait for Bob to be here.'

For any member of the family to have spoken those words would have touched her, but to hear them from Mr Hubble had made her feel like running a lap of honour. For as long as she could remember, she had yearned for Daddy, for his love, companionship and approval, and now here was a loving father who had accepted her as one of his own.

Much as she loved being with the Hubbles, it was probably just as well that she hadn't seen much of them. What would those dear people think if they knew of her ill-fated fling with Steven? They would be outraged and distraught that she had betrayed their beloved son and brother, and rightly so. How could she have done it? What had come over her? Bob was everything that was kind and generous, and the Hubbles were, in her eyes, the perfect family. How could she have placed all that in jeopardy?

But that was behind her now. A lapse, that was all it had been. A mad moment, born of grief.

Except that it had been longer than a mere moment.

She pushed hard on the pedals as she cycled through the early-evening streets, realising she was pedalling harder, faster, as if she could outdistance uncomfortable thoughts. It was time to stop thinking about all that. She had told Steven it was over and that had been the right thing to do.

When she arrived at St Cuthbert's School, she spotted Mabel's bike as she stowed her own in the rack. She walked into the school hall, where Mabel hailed her from across the room.

'Lend a hand, will you? We've received new supplies of bandages and so forth that need putting away.'

They counted the items, checking them against the supplies list.

'Wasn't it clever of Dot to think of asking Lizzie's mum to take in Mrs Grayson?' said Mabel. 'I'd never have thought of that.'

'I hope she won't mind being asked.'

'Maybe she'd enjoy the company, though it wouldn't make up for Lizzie, of course,' said Mabel. 'It must be hard on her, living on her own after having a family.'

Joan nodded, but beneath the semblance of agreement was the certainty that living in the same house as another person didn't necessarily reduce the loneliness or the despair. Look at her and Gran.

The evening drew out. It had been ages since the last raid – a couple of weeks before Letitia's birthday.

'We mustn't become complacent,' Mr Wilson reminded everyone in his nightly pep talk.

Towards midnight, the telephone bell rang and the atmosphere tightened. Everyone sat up straighter – first-aiders, ARP wardens, heavy rescue, the gas and electricity men. Shouldn't the air-raid warning have gone off?

The second hand dragged its way round the dial once, twice, before Mr Wilson appeared and the room stilled, all eyes turning his way.

'It's a call for heavy rescue. It's not on our patch. You have to go to Chorlton. Here's the address, lads.'

'What about their own heavy rescue?'

'Mechanical fault, unfortunately, so the job's been given to us. A copper was chasing a burglar who ran into a bomb-damaged building. The ceiling collapsed, trapping them both. It's your job to get them out. A couple of first-aiders will go with you. And while it isn't our job to differentiate between victims in an incident, no one will blame you if you give priority to Constable Arnold.'

Ice froze Joan's insides. 'Constable Arnold?' The words were hardly more than a breath. She cleared her throat. 'Constable Steven Arnold?' But even those words didn't carry.

It was Mabel, beside her, who raised her hand and addressed Mr Wilson.

'Excuse me, Mr Wilson, but would that be Constable Steven Arnold?'

'I couldn't say, Miss Bradshaw. Why? Do you know a policeman by that name?'

'Is it Letitia's Steven?' Mabel whispered to Joan. 'I don't know his surname.'

Joan nodded. This was overwhelming. She wanted to sink to the floor in a corner and hug her knees.

'Oh, Joan. What a blow.'

This was no time for feebleness. She drew herself up in readiness. 'I have to go to him.'

'Best leave it to someone else,' Mabel murmured.

'I'm going and I don't care what anybody says.'

Mabel bit her lip. 'Let me speak to Mr Wilson. Promise me you won't run off on your own.' She disappeared for a minute or two, then hurried back. 'Mr Wilson says we can go. I've sworn that knowing Steven won't in any way compromise our professionalism.'

Joan nodded. She had never felt more alert or focused in her life.

'Righty-ho.' Mabel nodded too. 'Let's see what we can do to help Letitia's Steven.'

The whole of the front of the building was missing. It was a large place, of a size that suggested a warehouse. The sides and back walls were there and so was the roof, but it looked like a dolls' house with the hinged front opened up. In front of the building, what used to be the façade and windows was now a vast heap of rubble. Joan and Mabel stood at a distance, as directed by Mr Shanley, the man in charge of the heavy-rescue team. It was all Joan could do to keep still. Her feet were itching to get moving, but she had to wait to be allowed in. It seemed ages since the men had gone inside.

'They'll find him,' said Mabel. She didn't add, 'He'll be all right.' They were trained not to say things like that, so as not to give false hope.

A couple of men emerged from the building, one of them Mr Shanley. He came over to them.

'We have to make the place safe as we proceed. If we see a casualty, you can come in, assuming it's safe enough and on the strict understanding that you'll vacate the place immediately if you are told to.'

'Of course,' Mabel agreed.

'Good. It might not happen like that, but I need you to

know who's boss.' Mr Shanley called to a bobby nearby. 'Constable! Could you escort these young ladies further away, please.'

It was Toby Collins, Steven's friend, whom Letitia and Steven had tried to get Joan to go out with. There was a smear of blood on his cheek and deep grazes on his hands.

'Hello, Joan,' said Toby. 'I tried to get in there and help Steven, but he's trapped underneath—'

Mabel interrupted. 'Let us clean up those cuts for you.'

Toby made an attempt at a refusal, but Mabel didn't listen.

'Sit down over here and I'll sort you out. The sooner you give in gracefully, the sooner you can get back on duty.'

Joan left them to it. She shrugged her rucksack onto her back and put on her tin hat so that she was ready. Then she fixed her attention on the building, in the same way that next door's cat fixed its penetrating gaze on the door when it wanted to be let in.

Eventually, Mr Shanley reappeared, brushing his gloved hands together and creating a cloud of dust. Joan stepped forward, so that when he said one of them could come into the building with him, she was already on her way.

'Tread carefully and stay behind me,' said Mr Shanley. 'I'll use my torch to guide you. You concentrate on staying upright. There's rubble everywhere and it isn't stable. It won't help anyone if you come a cropper.'

In spite of every instinct urging her to move forwards as fast as she could to get to Steven's side, Joan slowed down, not least because what was beneath her feet was shifting as she walked, threatening to snap her ankle or pitch her flat on her face. The air was musty and thick. Her lungs would be coated at this rate. Around her, the building creaked and groaned.

'Don't be alarmed by the noises,' said Mr Shanley. 'You should be safe enough if you stay where I say. He's over there.'

In the torch's beam, Joan moved ahead, almost taking a plunge as some lengths of wood shifted and resettled. Her eyes and mouth were dry, thanks to the stale atmosphere filled with dust, but her skin was tingling with anticipation as she approached Steven – except it wasn't Steven. It was a stranger lying there, slumped across a rubble heap. Shock rippled through her. She hadn't given the burglar a thought and now she was obliged to tend to his injuries. A swift examination told her the fellow had broken his arm and was drifting in and out of consciousness.

'He'll need a stretcher,' she told Mr Shanley.

'Stretcher here,' Mr Shanley called over his shoulder. 'I'll send for your colleague as well.' He retraced his steps.

A minute later, Mabel appeared at Joan's side.

'You see to this one,' Joan said at once. 'I'm going further in.'

'You don't have permission,' Mabel hissed. 'It might not be safe.'

Flicking on her torch, Joan eased her way further across the area, managing not to exclaim when the wood and rubble changed shape beneath her weight and she tilted sharply sideways. Shining her torch into the space beyond, she made out a half-buried body. Panic clutched at her throat and she gasped, then had to ward off a fit of coughing as she inhaled a dollop of murky air.

'I can see him,' she called to Mabel and she edged further forwards.

Behind her, Mabel called to Mr Shanley. 'Miss Foster

can see Constable Arnold. He's in the room beyond. She wants to go to him.'

'Tell her to wait,' Mr Shanley called back.

Shuffling sounds came from behind Joan, then Mabel's hand caught her arm.

Joan turned to look her in the face. 'I've lost so much already.'

'I know you have, and so has your grandmother. Just imagine if the worst happened and she lost you too. You're not going through there before it's safe to do so, even if I have to bop you on the head and drag you out of here.'

Joan knew she had to give in, even though she longed to crawl across the debris to Steven's side. She helped Mabel strap the burglar to the stretcher, then they picked him up and stumbled across to where Mr Shanley and an ambulance man took over.

'Follow us,' ordered Mr Shanley and Mabel grabbed Joan's arm.

Outside, the night air hit Joan with a blast of welcome freshness, but it only made her more worried for Steven, trapped under rubble with only filthy air to breathe.

The burglar's stretcher was manoeuvred into the back of the ambulance.

'Not that he deserves it,' remarked one of the heavy-rescue men.

'We'll hang on for you to bring the copper out,' said the ambulance man.

Mr Shanley and his team, followed by the ambulance crew, headed back inside the building. Joan and Mabel weren't required any more, but Joan wasn't having that. She went in after them, with Mabel stumbling behind her. Heading further into the building, the air was dense with a fog of plaster particles. The beam from Joan's torch, restrained by layers of tissue, was wholly inadequate, but even when she ripped off the tissue, the full beam wasn't much better, just a haze of light.

'What the ruddy— What do you two think you're up to?' Mr Shanley demanded. 'Lord preserve us from silly girls who can't follow orders.'

'It's easier for us to get through that gap than for you,' Joan said quickly. 'Please let us help.'

'At least let us go and check Constable Arnold, so we can see if he's all right,' said Mabel.

There was a tense silence, then Mr Shanley snapped his assent.

Joan slid through the gap.

'Take your time,' warned Mabel.

She was right. Haste could set the rubble shifting and they were so close to Steven now. He was face down, motionless, pinned in position by a thick beam that lay diagonally across him, partly on his legs, partly on his back. With a shaking hand, Joan reached out to take his pulse, her muscles turning to putty from sheer relief as she felt the tiny movement beneath his skin.

'Right, ladies,' came the voice of one of the ambulance men, 'time to let us take over. Move aside, please.'

With some stumbling that made Joan want to shriek at them to be careful, the men got themselves into position to raise the beam.

'You two girls, out – now,' ordered Mr Shanley. 'When we stretcher him outside, we can't have you fussing about, getting in our way.'

Mabel pulled Joan outside. Joan's feelings were at war. She needed to be at Steven's side, helping with the rescue, but she had seen too many air raids, too many dangerous rescues, to attempt to force the issue. The best thing she could do for Steven right now was let the rescuers do their job.

As he was carried out, she broke free from Mabel's grasp and ran towards the stretcher, only for Mabel to dart after her and pull her away. They clung to one another as Steven's stretcher was loaded into the back of the ambulance.

Brushing off Mabel's hands, Joan hurried forwards again.

'Can I come with him to the hospital – please? I know him.'

'Family, are you?' asked one of the ambulance men.

'No. I'm a friend.'

Mabel's arm snaked around Joan's shoulders. 'Please, if there's room inside. Constable Arnold – Steven – is . . . was Miss Foster's sister's boyfriend.'

'Then you'd best get home and comfort your sister, miss,' the man advised Joan.

'You don't understand,' Mabel insisted. 'Letitia – Miss Foster's sister – was killed in the blitz. Please,' she added.

'That's rough on you,' said the man. 'Hop in, then.'

'Go on.' Mabel gave Joan a push. 'I'll tell them back at St Cuthbert's. I hope Steven's—'

The ambulance doors slammed shut on Mabel's kind words. Joan squeezed into a corner by the burglar's head, prevented from being nearer to Steven by the ambulance man, who, swaying with the movement of the vehicle, was leaning over Steven.

Letitia's boyfriend.

Not any more.

Joan's boyfriend now.

At the end of her shift, at six o'clock on Saturday morning, Mabel paused in the act of taking her bicycle from the rack. Joan's bike was a couple of places further along. Joan hadn't returned from the hospital. How serious were Steven's injuries? Poor Joan – no wonder she had been in such a state. First Letitia, and now the possibility of losing Steven, which must have brought her grief for Letitia storming back as powerfully as if Letitia had copped it yesterday.

Mabel's breath bottled up inside her chest from sheer gratitude at having Harry. After the long-drawn-out misery of losing Althea, she had found fresh happiness, and in spite of the night's worries, she experienced a floaty feeling of hopefulness. She smiled at herself. Floaty? That was probably tiredness.

'You look miles away,' said one of the other first-aid girls, lifting her own bicycle out of the rack.

'Just wondering what to do with Joan's bike. I'll leave it here for now and sort it out later. I'm not at work today.'

She cycled home. Should she tell Mrs Grayson about Dot's inspired idea of asking Mrs Cooper to offer her a home? Or was that jumping the gun? Mabel unlocked the front door and crept in. Sometimes, when you had been up all night, it was easy to forget that you were arriving home at an early hour.

She shut the door, then a chill passed through her at an unexpected sound from somewhere close by. A burglar? Or did she have burglars on the brain, after last night? Turning, senses primed, she realised the sound had come from – no, it couldn't have.

The sound had come from the cupboard under the staircase. Mice? Mabel clicked her tongue impatiently. Jolly loud mice.

She knew without looking what, or rather whom, she would find when she opened the door and her heart sank at the thought of poor Mrs Grayson reverting to her old ways, but she made sure she exhibited nothing but compassion and concern as she gently drew her trembling landlady out from the cupboard and into the hall.

'What is it? Has something happened?'

'Oh, Miss Bradshaw,' whispered Mrs Grayson. Her hands were clammy inside Mabel's own. 'Oh, Miss Bradshaw.'

# Chapter Twenty-Two

Who the heck was that knocking at the door at this time of the morning?

'Go down and answer it, Reg,' Dot said.

'Can't you do it?'

'I've still got my rollers in.'

As Reg grumbled his way down the stairs, Dot unwound her rollers at top speed and combed her hair.

'It's for you,' Reg called up.

'Who is it?' she called back, but he didn't answer.

With a huff of annoyance, she ran downstairs to the hallway, where Reg had left the front door ajar before retreating to the kitchen. Dot pulled the door open.

'Mabel! What are you doing here?' Her insides sank. 'What's happened?'

'Don't be alarmed. Everyone's fine.'

'Come in, lass, and I'll put the kettle on. Park yourself in there.' She pushed open the parlour door and ushered Mabel inside. 'Have you just come off first-aid duty? Have you had breakfast?'

'Yes, and no, but please don't prepare me anything. I couldn't impose. I'm here to ask you about Mrs Cooper.'

'At this time of the morning? You sit yourself down and I'll make us a cup of tea and then you can tell me all about it.'

Reg wasn't best pleased at being told he would have to wait for his breakfast. On the other hand, he didn't leap up from his place at the table to prepare summat for

233

himself, so presumably he wasn't about to expire from hunger.

Dot took two teas into the parlour.

'Now, chick, what's this about?'

'I got home from first aid to find Mrs Grayson in a right old state. Mr Grayson turned up last night and he wants her out of the house today.'

'Today?' Dot exclaimed. 'He can't do that. It can't be legal – and if it is legal, it certainly isn't moral. What changed his mind?'

'Apparently, he and his, um, lady friend can't stand living a moment longer in cramped conditions with all her family. Mrs Grayson doesn't want to put up a fight. She doesn't believe she has a case and she doesn't want the publicity.'

'Nay, love, it's not her fault. Mind you, when did that ever stop a woman feeling the shame of a situation?'

'That's why I asked about Mrs Cooper. Did you call round yesterday evening?'

'I'm afraid not.' She had been too busy sitting in the Worker Bee café, plotting against a thief. Eh, when had life become so complicated?

Mabel's shoulders slumped. 'What now? It's one thing to drop in on Mrs Cooper this weekend and ask if she could possibly take in a house guest starting next weekend, but we can hardly turn up this morning and say, "Would you mind? And by the way, she has to move in today, because her husband's a rat."'

'Why not?' Dot sat up straight. 'This is wartime and folk have to put up with all sorts, aye, and pull together an' all. Let me get my husband and our Jimmy's breakfast sorted, then I'll pop round to Mrs Cooper's. She'll take it on the chin, just you wait and see. My generation has already lived through one of these wars, remember.'

'You're a brick, Dot. I'll cycle to Darley Court and see if Miss Brown will let us borrow the Bentley.'

'Aye, you do that, love,' Dot replied wryly, 'and when I've seen Mrs Cooper, I'll see the rag-and-bone man and ask if he'll give us a lend of his horse and cart.'

Mabel laughed. She was such a pretty girl. Last year, her good looks had been dampened by grief, but now her brown eyes glowed in her heart-shaped face. She had lovely cheekbones and an abundance of dark brown hair, but, most important of all, she had a warm heart.

'I don't suppose you know Cordelia's address, do you?' asked Mabel. 'It would be good to have her involved.'

'As a matter of fact, I do.' Dot lifted her chin. 'We exchanged addresses last summer.'

'Really? Have you been to her house? I imagine it's rather nice.'

'I've never been there and she's never been here. But summat happened, never mind what, and it made proper friends out of us, and we exchanged addresses. It's what friends do.'

'It's a pity Alison lives such a long way away,' said Mabel. 'She'll be sorry next week that she wasn't involved. What about Colette?'

'I don't know where she lives, only that it's in Seymour Grove.'

'Seymour Grove?' Mabel looked startled. 'I had no idea. That's near enough that she could come to the pictures with the rest of us, or she and Mr Naylor could come dancing.'

'I think those two are well and truly wrapped up in their own little world,' said Dot. 'But you could let Joan know what's happening.'

Mabel touched a hand to her throat. 'Oh, you don't know yet. Steven – Letitia's boyfriend – he's a policeman and . . . well, the short version is that he was injured last night and Joan went to hospital with him. I ought to call at her house and see if there's any news, but that will have to wait until later. Mrs Grayson gets top priority.' She delved inside her pocket and produced a pencil and a scrap of paper. 'Here's the telephone number for Darley Court.' She scribbled it down. 'Is there a telephone box near Mrs Cooper's?'

'I couldn't say, but there's a booth in the paper shop on the way there. I'll telephone from there and let you know what Mrs Cooper says.'

Mrs Cooper said yes. No fuss, no bother, no faffing about. Dot was filled with affection for her, this poor woman who had lost her husband in a motor accident in the early days of the blackout and then her beloved daughter in an air raid. She was thin and faded and probably didn't know whether she was coming or going, what with losing her Lizzie, but Dot knew a fighter when she saw one, a good working-class body who hauled herself to her feet and carried on, no matter what.

Mrs Cooper didn't just say yes. She said, 'Of course she must come here, the poor dear. Fancy her husband waltzing off with another woman and then demanding his house back. She must be beside herself.'

'Before you say yes,' said Dot, although it seemed a bit late for that now, 'I ought to explain that Mrs Grayson is a bit of an oddity. She doesn't set foot outdoors, except to spend a penny. But young Mabel has got her to use next door's Anderson shelter, though she has to be escorted there.'

'So she does go out a bit, then.'

'A little bit,' said Dot. 'A very little bit.'

She held her breath. Would Mrs Cooper change her mind?

'Then it would be dreadfully hard for her to find accommodation if she doesn't come to me. Go and get her packed up, Mrs Green, and she can have . . .' Mrs Cooper's voice caught in her throat. She pressed her lips together into a crinkly line, then gave her shoulders a tiny shake and hoisted her chin. 'I never thought I'd hear myself say this, but she can have my Lizzie's room.'

It should have been a sad occasion, shouldn't it? Packing up Mrs Grayson's belongings for her to be moved from the house that was more than a home to her – more like a cocoon to keep her safe from the world outside; it ought to have had them all creeping about, their voices barely above a whisper. And it might have been like that had Mrs Grayson been in charge, but with Dot and Cordelia in their different ways injecting a healthy dose of common sense into the proceedings, it was a lot more bearable, taking on an air that was fuss-free and busy. Cordelia had arrived with a pair of suitcases and Dot had magicked up some cardboard boxes.

'I know I shouldn't say it,' Mabel murmured to Dot, 'but I'm rather enjoying this. It's because we're mucking in together.'

'I take it from the squeals of those lads outside that Persephone has arrived in that posh motor car of Miss Brown's,' said Dot.

They went out to greet Persephone. Cousin Harriet got out of the Bentley too.

Mabel went to give her a kiss. 'How good of you to come. Let me introduce you to my friends.'

'Me and Amanda Grayson have been friends for many

a year. Miss Brown wanted me to tell her that she would have offered her the gatehouse at Darley Court, only she handed it over to the land girls last month. But she has sent a hamper.'

'Yummy,' grinned Mabel.

'Not for you, missy.' Cousin Harriet swatted at her arm. 'It's for Mrs Grayson to give to the lady who's taking her in.'

Cordelia helped Mrs Grayson pack her clothes while Mabel and Persephone wrapped her ornaments in newspaper and packed them inside pillowcases.

'What about the furniture?' asked Cousin Harriet when Cordelia and Mrs Grayson came downstairs.

'It was all paid for by Benjy,' said Mrs Grayson.

'Then we'd better leave it behind,' said Cordelia. 'Besides, Mrs Cooper has her own. There wouldn't be room.'

'I'm taking my baking things,' said Mrs Grayson. 'I don't care who paid for them. Floozy isn't getting her hands on my mixing bowl.'

'Darned right she isn't,' said Mabel. 'You work magic with that mixing bowl.'

'Perhaps you could take just one or two smaller bits of furniture,' suggested Dot, glancing from Mrs Grayson to Cordelia. 'Mr Grayson wouldn't begrudge you that, surely, and it'd be good for you to have your favourite pieces around you.'

'That little table by my armchair,' Mrs Grayson said, 'and the pouffe.'

Persephone picked up the pouffe, exchanging glances with Mabel and widening her eyes in amusement at the sight of the knitted cover.

'I can't leave all my knitting behind,' said Mrs Grayson.

'I'm sorry,' said Cordelia, 'but you can't expect Mrs Cooper to adorn her home the way you have adorned yours. And where would you store it all?'

Mabel had a flash of inspiration. 'Besides, Floozy will loathe it. It might be Mr Grayson's name on the rent book, but you're the one who has stamped your own style on the place.'

Persephone carried the pouffe outside, only to come hurrying back in with it still in her arms.

'I hate to say it, but I think Mr Grayson and Floozy might be arriving. There's a horse and cart coming along the road and the cart's piled high.'

Mrs Grayson let out a long groan.

'They can't,' Cordelia declared. 'It's far too soon. They're not supposed to be here before midday and it's only just gone eleven.'

Mrs Grayson went to the window. 'It's them.'

Dot slipped an arm around her and gave her a squeeze. 'Don't you fret, love. You're among friends.'

'Leave it to us, Mrs Grayson,' said Cordelia. 'We'll send them away.'

'Me and Mrs Masters have done this kind of thing before,' said Dot. 'We're a team. If her hoity-toity voice and her long words don't get rid of them . . .'

'. . . then a spot of plain speaking from Mrs Green certainly will,' Cordelia finished. She raised an eyebrow at Dot. 'Shall we?'

Arm in arm, they left the parlour. Mabel and Persephone jockeyed for position at the window. On the cart's bench seat, beside the driver, sat Mr Grayson, a portly fellow in a checked suit and a pork-pie hat. Beside him, showing enough thigh that she was in danger of giving the neighbours a glimpse of stocking top, Floozy clutched her coat around her, tossing her shoulders inside the huge fur-trimmed collar. She had a pouty red mouth and her face looked unnaturally pale beside dark hair that hadn't a strand of grey in it and would have looked a lot more natural if it had. She wore a jaunty little hat with cherries bobbing on the front.

'I would say she looks like a barmaid,' Mabel remarked, 'but I work with a former barmaid and she looks like a lady compared to this.'

Persephone didn't mince her words. 'She looks like a tart.'

'She *is* a tart,' said Mrs Grayson. 'She stole my husband and now she's stolen my home.'

The three of them watched as words were exchanged outside. Mr Grayson glared towards the window, but he helped Floozy down, treating everyone to a flash of her suspenders, and they walked off, noses in the air, leaving the cart in the care of the driver.

Dot and Cordelia came back inside. If Mabel was expecting the same jokey high spirits as the two had shown before they went out to confront the interlopers, there was no sign of them now. Of course not. They would both realise how hard this was for Mrs Grayson.

'Let's finish as quickly as we can,' said Cordelia.

Mabel was still by the window. Catching a movement outside, she turned to look.

'Harry! Harry's here.'

She ran outside to greet him, quickly explaining what was going on. He went upstairs and brought down suit-cases and cardboard boxes and carried them out to the Bentley.

'Lord, here comes another horse and cart,' said Persephone.

Dot batted her forehead. 'That's my fault. I didn't know how much stuff would need moving, and I didn't know whether Miss Brown could spare her motor, so I asked our local rag-and-bone man to pop along.'

'Not to worry,' said Harry. 'I'll send him on his way.'

Mabel noticed that he tipped the fellow generously and she smothered a grin of pride. This was the right sort of man to have, one who took everything in his stride and wasn't afraid to put his hand in his pocket.

'Mabel, don't forget to pack your own things,' said Cordelia.

'Already done.'

Cordelia looked around. 'It's nearly time to go. Where's Mrs Grayson?'

Mabel found her sitting on the top stair. She squeezed in beside her. Dot came up as well and settled a few steps lower, twisting round to look up at them.

Mrs Grayson's eyes shone with tears. Her chin trembled. 'Look at me. What a duffer.'

'Eh, love, what is it?' asked Dot. 'Has it all got on top of you? Your home being packed up all around you, and his lordship pitching up early.'

'It's not that – well, it is, of course.' Mrs Grayson pressed a shaking hand to her face. 'You've all been so kind to help me when you don't know me from Adam.'

'Our Mabel reckoned you needed a spot of help,' said Dot, 'and that's good enough for us.'

'You've got me all packed and ready to leave, but . . . I can't.'

Mabel slid an arm around her shoulders. 'Yes, you can. It's no different to going to the Warners' Andy.'

'But it is. It's going out the front and I haven't done that since I don't remember when, *and* getting in a motor car and whooshing through the streets to I don't know where.'

'I'll tell you where,' said Dot. 'To the kindest lady you can imagine. She's opening her home to a stranger. Now isn't that worth making an effort for?'

'I know it is,' said Mrs Grayson. 'I just . . .'

'There's two ways of doing this,' Dot announced. 'We

can get Persephone to park the motor right outside and we can have the door open ready for you to get straight in without faffing about on the pavement, then you, me and Mabel can march outside together, holding on as tight as if we've all had one port and lemon too many, and we'll bundle you into that there motor. How does that sound?'

'What's the other way?' asked Mabel.

'We get your Harry to carry Mrs Grayson out. That'd give the neighbours summat to remember you by, Mrs Grayson.'

A small spurt of laughter was the reply. Mabel took advantage of it to heave Mrs Grayson to her feet. Dot called down the stairs to Persephone to move the motor directly outside and to Cordelia to open the car door. Then the three of them went downstairs, Mabel and Dot taking their positions either side of Mrs Grayson.

They stood just inside the front door while the motor was prepared, but when Mabel and Dot made to step forwards, Mrs Grayson didn't budge.

'I know it's hard,' Mabel whispered. 'Close your eyes if you have to. We won't let go.'

Mrs Grayson took a tentative step, then took a huge breath and more or less plunged through the door. Mabel and Dot walked her to the motor and helped her in. Tears were streaming down the poor lady's face.

Dot leaned into the motor. 'Well done, love. Persephone will take you straight to Mrs Cooper's. The rest of us will finish in the house and see you round there.'

'But—' Mrs Grayson began.

'Persephone will introduce you,' said Dot, closing the door.

They waved the motor off and went back inside.

'Where shall you go, Mabel?' Cordelia asked. 'Have you made arrangements?'

'Actually, I've been too busy worrying about Mrs Grayson.'

'Come back to Darley Court,' said Persephone. 'I know you said you'd rather not, but this is an emergency.'

'I can get your old room ready in no time,' added Cousin Harriet.

Mabel was touched, but she shook her head. 'I wouldn't want to stay there long-term, and I'd feel rotten if I left a second time.'

'I could squeeze you in,' said Dot, 'just to tide you over. You could have our spare room and Jimmy could sleep on the sofa when he stops the night. He'd love that.'

'Bless you, but I couldn't pinch your grandson's bedroom.'

'Joan's?' Dot said doubtfully.

They all looked at one another.

'Not so soon after her bereavement,' said Cordelia.

'Mrs Cooper's house is no bigger than a musical box,' said Persephone.

'Don't worry,' said Mabel. 'I can nip up to Hunts Bank and look at the noticeboard. You often see postcards with rooms to rent.'

'There's no need for that,' said Cordelia. 'You shall come home with me.'

# Chapter Twenty-Three

'You're not allowed in, I'm afraid. It's two at a time and Constable Arnold's parents are at his bedside just now.' The nurse, in her crisp apron and cuffs and starched cap, gave Joan a sympathetic smile. 'Are you his girlfriend?'

If she said yes, would the nurse bend the rules? But if the nurse then announced in front of Steven's parents . . .

'No. Can you tell me how he is today, please?'

'I'm not at liberty to give out information. Are you family?'

'No.'

'Then Sister wouldn't tell you anything either.'

It was all Joan could do not to throw up her hands in frustration. She smiled politely. 'Thanks anyway.' She turned to go, her feet like lead. After a couple of steps, she swung round again. 'You couldn't possibly tell him I came, could you?'

'You're quite right, young lady,' said a new voice as an older nurse stopped beside her, her larger headdress declaring her to be a sister. 'Nurse could not tell him. Kindly refrain from wasting her time. Our visiting rules are in place for a reason. I suggest you come back this evening.'

Joan wouldn't be able to do that because she was going to Bob's for Sunday tea and would be expected to stay into the evening, chatting with his family and playing cards. The back of her neck prickled. Going to Bob's for tea – when the place she most wanted, needed, to be was at Steven's bedside.

'How is he?' Gran asked when she arrived home.

'I wasn't allowed in. His parents were there.'

'If he's up to having visitors, that's a good sign.'

Later, at the Hubbles' house, Bob's mum said, 'You look peaky, love. Are you all right?'

'She must be tired,' said Maureen. 'She was on duty last night, weren't you, Joan?'

'Don't they have anywhere for you to grab a bit of shut-eye when it's quiet?' asked Glad.

'There are a few cots,' said Joan.

She ought to keep her mouth shut. She ought not to mention Steven's name in front of these dear people who had welcomed her into their hearts. Yet somehow it came tumbling out, the tale of the call-out and the heavy-rescue team and of Steven being pinned beneath a fallen beam, and the Hubbles said all the right things, expressing concern and sorrow, denouncing the burglar and praising Steven, and, oh heavens, sympathising with her, poor Joan, for the shock she must have suffered at something bad happening to Letitia's boyfriend.

'How is he?' they wanted to know and she had to explain about not being let in to see him.

'Do they have evening visiting?' Mr Hubble asked, taking his pipe from his mouth. 'Bob, you have to take Joan to evening visiting. She must be worried sick, poor lass.'

'I expect he'll have family there again.' Joan's pulse ricocheted about. She had to grab hold of the situation before control slipped away completely. 'You're very kind, but there's no need.'

Lord, what a rat she was. What had happened to her? She had believed that the attraction that had thundered between her and Steven on Letitia's birthday had occurred because of the heightened emotion of the day, and having later determined to send him on his way, she had settled back into her cosy relationship with Bob and his family, only for her feelings for Steven to come storming back again last night.

She felt even worse when Mrs Hubble said she looked tired and that Bob should take her home earlier than normal. When she got there, it felt like a punishment when Gran told her Steven's parents had come round earlier.

'How is he?' she demanded.

'He'll do.' This was what Gran always said about anybody who wasn't at death's door.

'What did they say?'

'That he'll be fine.'

Tears of relief sprang into Joan's eyes, but she couldn't let them spill over. 'That's good. What injuries does he have?'

Gran drew in her chin. 'I didn't ask. It isn't polite to ask about people's bodies. But they did say he'd be coming home tomorrow.'

Tomorrow!

Energised, Joan stayed awake for much of the night, her mind crowded with daydreams.

The next day passed by in a haze and when she clocked off, she dashed to catch the earlier bus, her heart thumping all the way to Steven's house, and not simply because she was in a hurry.

Mrs Arnold let her in. 'This is a surprise, but I know someone who'll be pleased to see you.'

Joan followed her into the parlour. The walls were the colour of wet sand. There was a blue-tiled fireplace, a glass-fronted cabinet for ornaments and a matching three-piece suite. It made a big difference to a house, having not one but two men's wages coming in.

Steven was lying on the wood-framed sofa, propped up by cushions. His face lit up when he saw her and Joan's heart drummed in response, but he had another visitor – Toby Collins, in uniform, his helmet on the floor at his feet. He rose politely, sinking down again when Mrs Arnold offered Joan a seat. Toby was precisely where she wanted to be, in the chair closest to Steven. Instead, she had to make do with the other armchair.

Steven's face was pale and the purple bruising beside his eye and all down the side of his face made him look even paler, but his eyes were as warm as ever when his gaze met hers. His lower half was covered by a blanket, but his striped pyjama jacket was on show, its top button not quite as high as the dip between his collarbones. The garment looked thicker than it should, suggesting the presence of bandages underneath.

'Toby's been telling me about the rescue,' said Steven.

'It was a team effort,' she replied. Did he know she'd had a hand in it?

'I'm grateful to everyone who was involved.'

Was he grateful to her? Did he know she had insisted upon accompanying him to hospital? Did he know she was the one who had given his details to the nurse as if, almost as if, she and he belonged together?

'I'd best be off.' Toby picked up his helmet and stood up. 'Thanks for the tea, Mrs Arnold.'

'I'll see you out,' she replied.

The moment it was just the two of them, Joan moved to Toby's vacated place. 'How are you?'

'A bit battered, but I'm all right. I have to rest for a day or two, and when I return to work I'll be stuck behind a desk at first.'

'I'm so relieved.'

'So am I.' Steven's smile pushed against the bruise, causing him to flinch, but he didn't stop smiling.

Mrs Arnold walked in.

'Would you make Joan some tea, please, Mum?' Steven asked. Was he getting rid of his mother on purpose?

As the door shut, Joan said, 'I went with you to the hospital.' She couldn't keep it in a moment longer.

'I know. Toby told me. I'm glad you were part of the rescue crew.'

'I didn't go to hospital because I was part of the crew.'

'I'm hoping you did it because you cared . . . because you care.'

She nodded.

When the air-raid warning sounded a few minutes after seven on Wednesday morning, Joan's first thought, even before she grabbed her stuff and headed for the Andy, was to wonder whether she and Steven would be able to meet that evening. Her first thought? Her first feeling, more like; a white spear of dread that they would be kept apart by the Luftwaffe.

But she and Gran hardly had time to settle themselves in the shelter before the all-clear sounded and they, along with their neighbours and everyone else all over Manchester, resumed their normal lives.

Normal? Desperate to see her sister's boyfriend – that was normal? Actually, now she considered it, it was. That old hopeless yearning she had felt for Steven for such a long time until she met Bob, that had once been her normal life. A distressing way of life, but, for her, it had been normal.

And here she was again, longing to see Steven, only he was no longer unattainable.

That evening, they met accidentally on purpose in Chorlton Park and fell in step beside one another. Did Steven's hand itch to catch hold of hers, the way hers did for his? She had a mad urge to reach up and soothe his bruised face with her fingertips. Steven walked with a slight limp.

'I hope that's only temporary,' she said.

'It is. Thank you for worrying about me.'

'This feels strange, doesn't it?' Joan asked in a low voice.

'How so?'

'Being together in public.'

Steven laughed and then groaned and touched his ribs. 'If by that you mean it's a mixture of the marvellously exciting because we're in one another's company, and the deeply frustrating because all I want is to hold you in my arms but I mustn't lay a finger on you, then, yes, it is.'

'Do you . . . do you feel you should ask for Letitia's forgiveness?'

Steven stopped walking. Was he about to put his arms around her? A thrill of anticipation mingled with fear made her shiver, but Steven simply lit a cigarette, briefly offering her one before popping the packet back into his pocket. The offer was a polite gesture, nothing more . . . wasn't it? Did he remember that she had never got the hang of smoking?

Steven fixed his gaze, not on her, but on some unspecified place in the middle distance. He blew out a stream of smoke.

'I like to think that Letitia would . . .'

*Please don't say she'd be happy for us.*

'. . . that she'd understand.'

*Understand?* If Joan had been killed and Letitia had done the dirty on Steven with Bob, would that have been understandable?

Oh, Bob . . .

'This is way too public,' said Steven, even though the park wasn't exactly heaving with people. He ground his

249

cigarette beneath his heel. 'We need to be properly on our own. Let's walk among the trees. I want to kiss you.'

Was it unromantic to be given notice of a kiss? Or extra romantic because it was exciting and forbidden? Laughing, they picked up their pace, clasping hands as they left the path and ducked into the trees that clustered along the sloping bank where Chorlton Brook slid on its way below.

Stopping, Steven turned her towards him. She looked up into his face. He was so handsome. She had always thought what good-looking children he and Letitia would have.

Steven brushed the side of her face with the backs of his fingers. Her eyes fluttered shut as her face pressed against his feather-light touch. His knuckles lifted her chin and his mouth covered hers. He tasted of tobacco and fresh air. Her arms snaked around him and clung, but he surfaced from the kiss for long enough to murmur, 'Bruises,' before his mouth took possession of hers once more.

When the kiss ended, Joan kept her eyes closed until her heart calmed. 'When the telephone call came through to the first-aid depot about your being trapped in the bombed-out building, I was terrified I might have lost you for ever.'

'Not a chance,' Steven murmured.

Moving to stand beside him, Joan slipped her hand into his and began to walk. The ground was bumpy with tree roots spreading out.

'You were my first love.'

Steven frowned. 'What about Bob?' He stopped, but Joan didn't, so he had to keep walking too. 'If he's just a casual boyfriend, that must make it easier for you to drop him.'

Her face jerked up to look at him. 'I'm surprised you're so offhand about it.'

'I just meant it'll be easier on you, less painful.' Steven paused. 'I imagine it'll be hard for Bob, though.'

'I just told you that you were my first love and here we are talking about Bob.'

'Go on, then. Tell me more about being the first man you've loved.' There was a smile in Steven's voice. 'I'd enjoy hearing about that.'

'You don't understand. I don't mean now. I mean when you were going out with Letitia.'

That stopped him in his tracks – literally. Joan carried on walking, tugging at his hand to bring him with her. She spoke in a consciously light-hearted tone.

'Yes, I was in love with my sister's boyfriend. I was mad about him. And I was almost mad with guilt because of my sister. There. Now you know.'

'I had no idea.'

'Good,' she said crisply. 'You weren't meant to. I couldn't have borne it if you'd guessed. Or if Letitia had.'

Steven stopped again. This time, she stopped with him. He placed his hands on her shoulders and looked into her eyes. 'I'm honoured to think you loved me back then, even if it did cause you pain. But can't you see? You loved me when I was with Letitia. Now she's gone and we've found one another. This was meant to be – *we* are meant to be.'

Were they? Was this what her life had been building up to?

Had their shared grief for Letitia dragged them together artificially or was Steven really her one true love?

Joan worked harder than ever. She had always done her best in her portering job, not just because she was proud to have a wartime post, but also to honour the memory of dear Lizzie. When she'd been a clerk, Joan had wished with all her heart for a 'proper' railway job. Wasn't there a saying about being careful what you wished for?

She had been in Lizzie's job for five months now and mostly had ceased to feel guilty. It was strange what you could get used to. Unsettling. Sometimes she felt guilty for not feeling guilty.

Now she had something else to eat her up with guilt, which was why she was throwing herself into her work with even more commitment, pushing her sack trolley around with a longer stride, which might not have been entirely ladylike in her uniform skirt. Some of the lady porters wore trousers and looked very smart, but Gran wouldn't hear of it for Joan.

As her working day ended, it was impossible to ignore the way her heart thumped. She was seeing Steven this evening and she couldn't wait to clock off and hurry home to get changed, but it was important to carry on as normal, which, today, meant meeting her friends in the buffet.

It was one of those times when they were all there – well, all but Colette. Today being what it was, the conversation naturally opened up with Dot asking who had received Valentine cards.

'I had one from Harry,' said Mabel, and Joan could tell she was sucking in her cheeks so as not to beam her head off.

'I had one from Bob,' said Joan. Actually, she had had two cards, but she couldn't say so. Thank heaven she had picked the cards off the doormat while Gran was in the kitchen.

'What about you?' Dot looked at Persephone. 'A lovely-looking girl like you must have them queuing round the block.'

'I wish!' laughed Persephone.

Dot smiled at Alison. 'I don't need to ask if you got a card. The only question is whether you'll get a proposal.'

'Paul has to work tonight.' Alison pulled a face. 'It's disappointing, but it does mean he can spring it on me another time when I'm least expecting it.'

Dot's glance encompassed Mabel and Joan. 'Are you seeing Harry and Bob tonight?'

'Unfortunately not,' said Mabel. 'Harry's on duty.'

'Same here,' said Joan, quickly adding, 'I wonder how Mrs Grayson is settling in with Lizzie's mum. Tomorrow it'll be a whole week.'

'I popped round to see them,' said Dot, 'and goodness me, what a wonderful smell of baking as I walked through the door!'

'Mrs Grayson is an excellent cook,' said Mabel.

'How are you settling in at Cordelia's?' Dot asked Mabel.

'Very well, thank you.' Mabel glanced at Cordelia. 'I've been made to feel most welcome.'

'I'm sure you won't mind, Mabel,' said Cordelia, 'if I say in front of everyone that I've had a letter from Mrs Mitchell.'

'From Cousin Harriet? What about?'

'Politely asking if she may come and see your new digs for herself, so she can write and inform your mother.'

Mabel's hands flew to her cheeks. 'I'm so sorry.'

Cordelia waved her apology aside. 'She says that since your parents sent you to stay at Darley Court, it's her responsibility to ensure you are, as she calls it, "properly situated". I can appreciate that. It's important to me that Emily is well cared for. I'm sure your parents worry about you, being away from home.'

'Even so.' Mabel shook her head, but laughed at the same time. 'I never realised Cousin Harriet's job was to spy on me.'

There was laughter around the table, then Dot turned to Joan.

'I know we've been concentrating on Mrs Grayson, Mrs Cooper and Mabel in recent days, but that doesn't mean we've forgotten about you, chick. It'll be a long time before you feel even close to normal again and we're all here to watch over you and help you whenever we can.'

'Hear, hear,' said Persephone.

And what was Joan doing to warrant such care? Carrying on with her sister's boyfriend, that's what.

# Chapter Twenty-Four

'I tell you,' Dot confided to Cordelia as they met for a swift cup of tea after working the early shift on Saturday, 'my heart bled last night for all those Valentine couples when the siren went off at – what time was it? Half seven?'

'About that.' Cordelia took a sip of her tea. 'But we'd hardly got settled in the shelter and started our game of whist when the all-clear sounded.'

Dot laughed. 'Well, it was good news for all those couples even if it spoiled your game of cards. It was a shame for our young lasses, not one of them seeing her boyfriend.'

Cordelia sighed. 'Alison had made such a palaver out of not expecting a proposal that I wonder if she was preparing the ground for when the proposal didn't happen. Poor girl. He really is keeping her dangling.'

'Or maybe he finally got his act together and surprised her by popping the question before he set off for work,' said Dot. 'Or maybe having to work last night was a big pretence and the two of them spent the whole evening together, all lovey-dovey, with Alison gazing at her ring as much as into her beloved's eyes.'

'You should take up writing romances for the story papers.'

'Can you blame me for wanting happy endings for everyone? I reckon Mabel might receive the first proposal.' Dot pressed her lips together. It would be hard on Alison if the others started getting engaged before she did.

'Mabel did seem rather smitten with her cheeky blighter last weekend when he mucked in with Mrs Grayson's move.'

'Eh, but wasn't that good of him? It showed what a decent sort he is. It's important to know these things before you take the plunge.'

'Goodness,' said Cordelia, 'you are keen to hear wedding bells, aren't you?'

'What's wrong with that? Mabel and Harry, Alison and Paul, Joan and Bob. Don't you think that getting engaged to Bob could be just the thing to lift Joan's spirits?'

'It would certainly give her and her grandmother something to pin their hopes on.'

'From everything I've heard, Bob sounds like what my old mam would have called reet good husband material, and he's in a reserved occupation an' all.'

'Which is more than can be said for most young men,' Cordelia agreed. 'And from what Joan says about his family, they sound like the in-laws from heaven.'

'Now who should be writing for the story papers?' grinned Dot.

'Touché. Did you get your daughters-in-law's Valentine's presents sorted out?'

'I helped our Jenny sew a heart-shaped pincushion for her mum, but it remains to be seen what Jimmy came up with for our Sheila. He refused point-blank to sew anything. Sewing is sissy and so are hearts. I told him to think about what his dad would want him to do to make Valentine's Day special for his mum.'

'Do you think he came up with a decent present?'

'I hope so, but you never know with that lad.'

They finished their tea, gathered up their belongings and left the buffet. As they walked past the long ticket office, with its beautiful wooden panelling that curved elegantly at either end and had a clock set into the top of the arched panel in the middle, Dot felt a sense of gratification, as she always did when she passed by.

'I can never walk past here without thinking of all the elbow grease that goes into keeping that wood polished.'

'It must be jolly hard work,' said Cordelia.

'Aye, but satisfying. I'm starting on my spring-cleaning this afternoon.'

'It's a bit early, isn't it?'

Did that mean that Cordelia's daily wouldn't be doing hers for a while yet?

'Maybe. Normally, I'd do it in March, but what with working full-time, I need to get going on it early.'

Aye, 'need' was the right word. Being a full-time worker was no excuse for a shabby house. She would get her brush box out this afternoon and give her brushes a wash. Sheila said it was old-fashioned to have a brush box in this day and age, but Sheila the Slattern wouldn't know a bannister brush from a wardrobe brush, or a laundry brush from a furniture brush. There was nowt old-fashioned about keeping your house spick and span when a high explosive going off would raise every particle of household dust in every street within a ten-minute walk.

Dot opened her front door into a quiet house. For once in her life, she was on her own indoors. Reg was out all day doing ARP training. Dot felt a rush of nostalgia for the clatter of Harry and Archie's footsteps on the stairs. How many times had she scolded them for running their grubby fingers along the wall as they ran up- and downstairs? How many times had she told them not to jump the last few steps?

'It's like having a pair of elephants in the house,' she had said a hundred times. 'Tell 'em, Reg.'

But he never did. 'Boys will be boys,' was all he said.

Now she would give anything to have them back again and they could make as much of a racket as they liked.

She cleaned out the fireplaces and took the ash pan to the dustbin. She'd had no time to do the fireplaces this morning when she had dragged herself out of bed at half past you-must-be-joking and it looked like Reg had simply built the new kitchen fire on top of the old one when he got up.

She was just going inside through the back door when there was the sound of a commotion in the entry that ran between the back gardens of Heathside Lane and those of Ashdene Lane. Her back gate was thrown open with sufficient force that it banged against the brick wall and Sheila came marching towards her, dragging Jimmy by his ear while he wriggled and yelped.

'Sheila! What's the matter?' Daft question. 'What's our Jimmy done this time?'

Sheila flung Jimmy aside, sending him flying towards the coal bunker.

'I'll tell you what he's done,' she flared. 'I've been with Rosa most of the day.'

'Rosa?' Dot wasn't keen on Rosa.

'Why shouldn't I see my friend if I want to? Anyroad, the point is I've come home to find half my furniture missing.'

'You what?' said Dot.

'It wasn't half,' said Jimmy.

'I thought we'd been burgled.'

'You've been burgled?' Dot repeated in alarm. 'Oh, Sheila.'

'No, we haven't been burgled,' Sheila snapped, 'but I thought we had. Are you going to stand in that doorway all afternoon or can we come in?'

Dot's eyebrows shot up her forehead at being spoken to in such a snippy way, and in front of one of the kids an' all, but she was more concerned about what the heck Sheila was on about. She backed through the scullery into the kitchen as Sheila made a grab for Jimmy, who evaded capture and darted indoors, putting the kitchen table between him and his mum.

'Please tell me our Jimmy never gave your furniture away to the rag-and-bone man.' Dot eyed her grandson, whose gaze fell away at the reminder of what had happened to his nan's saucepans last year.

'I didn't, Nan,' said Jimmy. 'You said I was never to do that again and I never have.'

'Then what happened?' asked Dot.

Sheila was busy with her fag. She exhaled a furious stream of smoke. 'I told you. I came home and loads of stuff was missing. This one,' and she dealt her son a glare, 'had only taken the whole lot to the park.'

'The park?' Dot repeated, baffled.

'And scattered it all over the grass in the half that hasn't been given over to growing veg.'

'It wasn't my idea,' he blurted.

'Oh aye?' said Sheila. 'Don't tell me. Henry Fawcett made you do it. Either that or it was in a *William* book.'

'It was Nan's idea. She said to.'

Dot's exclamation was echoed by Sheila.

'You did.' Jimmy turned earnestly to Dot. 'You said to do summat special for Mum for Valentine's Day. You said to do what Dad would want. Well, what he'd want is for me to keep Mum safe. I couldn't do it yesterday because of school, so I did it today instead.'

'Jimmy!' cried Sheila. 'You took the kitchen chairs, and the card table, and the drawers out of the sideboard, and the bedside cupboards, and heaven knows what besides, and scattered them all over Fog Lane Park. What the hell – heck, has that got to do with keeping me safe?'

Again, Jimmy looked at Dot. He was getting tearful now. 'It's what Nan said.'

'What's he on about?' Sheila demanded.

'I haven't the foggiest,' said Dot.

'But you *did* say!' Jimmy's voice was a desperate squeak. 'You said they've put old motor cars and slabs of concrete and other stuff into the fields so the Germans can't land their planes. You *said*.'

Dot's bemused frown loosened into slack astonishment. 'That was months ago – when they put me on the Leeds train.'

How pleasant and helpful that guard had been compared to the nowty Mr Bonner. He had liked a chat and he had explained to her about the variety of large objects in the fields. He had told her about Rule 55 an' all. Mr Emmet, that was his name. Nice fellow.

Sheila's eyes narrowed accusingly. 'D'you mean he got this mad idea from you?'

'Pipe down, Sheila. Let the lad tell us.'

Jimmy was exasperated now. 'You said I had to do summat for Mum for Valentine's Day. You said I had to do what Dad would want.'

'I meant a paper heart or a poem,' Dot said, 'not scattering the furniture far and wide so Jerry can't land.'

'But Dad would want her to stay safe,' Jimmy insisted. 'He'd want all of us to be safe.'

Shaking her head, Dot turned to Sheila. 'Is the furniture back indoors now?'

'Aye, but—'

'Then let it be. Jimmy did a barmy thing, but you can't fault him for wanting to do right by you.'

'Are you taking his side?'

'It isn't a question of sides, love. It's just our Jimmy being Jimmy. It could have been a lot worse. Be grateful it hasn't rained.'

Sheila tensed sharply, as if about to stamp her foot. 'I can't believe I'm hearing this. I haul him round here, thinking I'll get some support, and what do I get?' She drew a breath to answer her own question, but Dot forestalled her.

'I reckon Jimmy's learned his lesson – haven't you?' She gave him the evil eye.

He dropped his gaze. 'Yes, Nan. Sorry, Nan.'

'Don't tell me. Tell your mum.'

'Sorry, Mum.'

'Look at your mum when you say it,' said Dot, 'and say it like you mean it.'

Jimmy lifted his eyes. Oh, those blue eyes, just like his dad's.

'Sorry, Mum. I won't do it again.'

'Damn right you won't,' snapped Sheila.

'Language,' said Dot. 'Not in front of the children.'

Sheila narrowed her eyes in vexation. 'I shan't be doing owt in front of him for the rest of today. You can keep him, as far as I'm concerned. I'll fetch him back tomorrow.'

It was on the tip of Dot's tongue to say, 'You can't dump him here,' but how could she utter those words in front of Jimmy? Especially after his mum had made it clear he wasn't welcome at home.

Sheila was already outside the door. She looked back to say, 'I'm going to enjoy the rest of the day. I'm going to ask Rosa if she wants to go to the flicks this evening and I'm going to take my time getting ready *and* I'm going to use Jimmy's share of the bathwater as well as my own.'

She didn't actually say 'So there!' but she might as well have done. Dot stood with her hand on Jimmy's shoulder and they watched Sheila march past the Andy and bang the gate behind her.

'You did a wrong thing, Jimmy,' said Dot, 'but you did it for the right reasons.'

'Does that make it all right?'

'You saw how upset your mum is. Do you think she thinks it's all right?'

Jimmy shrugged.

Right reasons or not, he ought to be punished. 'I'm getting started on my spring-cleaning this afternoon. You can help.'

'*Nan*, housework is sissy. And boring. And girls' stuff. Can't you ask Jenny?'

'Jenny isn't the one in trouble.' With her hand clamped on his shoulder, she steered him across the kitchen and into the narrow hallway. 'Since I've got an extra pair of hands, I can get the furniture shifted and take up the carpet and give it a good beating.'

Jimmy perked up. 'I'm good at shifting furniture.'

So much for punishment. 'So I gather.'

The parlour carpet might be second-hand and the arrangement of the furniture might be a bit eccentric because of covering the worn patches, but it was still summat to be proud of. Dear old Mam had never had a carpet, just rag rugs. Aye, and they had been the real things an' all, made from rags, not from strips of decent material.

Between them, Dot and Jimmy moved the furniture, rolled up the carpet and manhandled it out of the house, hurling it over the washing line in the backyard. Dot thrust the carpet beater at Jimmy.

'Put your back into it, our Jimmy.'

The lad set to with a will. Where did all that dust come from? Anyone would think she never swept her carpet from one week to the next.

'Take that, Jerry!' yelled Jimmy. 'Drop your weapon! Handy hock!'

Leaving him to defeat the might of Hitler's army, Dot went to wash her parlour floor and her skirting boards, all the while composing the description of Jimmy's latest escapade to be included in her next letter to Harry. She would ham it up and make it funny – well, it was funny. Jimmy's antics often were, as long as you weren't on the receiving end.

When Reg came home, he wasn't best pleased to find Jimmy dusting the picture rails with the long-handled feather duster.

'You've never got the lad doing housework.'

'Actually, I think you'll find he's hunting for explosives.'

'I'm not having any grandson of mine doing women's work. Jimmy! Stop that this minute. I've got a cigarette card of a Hawker Hurricane for you.'

Dot made the tea, putting half her rissoles on Jimmy's plate and adding bread and marge to bulk up the meal a bit.

'How did it go?' she asked Reg.

He told her all about accurate reporting of the extent of bomb damage and repeated at length the discussion about assessing the need for help from the emergency and rescue services. He didn't ask about her day.

Afterwards, Dot washed up and settled down with her knitting. She couldn't pick up a ball of wool these days without thinking of Mrs Grayson. What had Floozy thought when she walked through the front door and found herself in woolly wonderland? Eh, Dot would have liked to be a fly on the wall for that.

At seven o'clock, she sent Jimmy upstairs to wash and change into his pyjamas. He stayed here so regularly that she had bought him pyjamas, a dressing gown and slippers. Then he was allowed to come back down again until eight o'clock. Jimmy lay on his tummy on the floor, reading an old *Beano* and looking as if butter wouldn't melt. He was always good as gold of an evening when he was here, in the hope that his nan would forget the time, even though she never did. Sheila was slapdash about bedtimes. Sometimes she let Jimmy stay up, but when it suited her, she packed him off pronto.

'It's nearly eight o'clock, Jimmy,' Dot said, giving him fair warning.

But at five to, the siren sounded. Jimmy sat up and looked at her.

'If they land in Fog Lane Park, don't say I didn't warn you.'

# Chapter Twenty-Five

Joan attended the nine o'clock service at church instead of her usual half-past ten, because she had a shift at Victoria Station starting at midday. Gran didn't like her working on Sundays, but couldn't say anything. Not that Gran needed words. She had a way of breathing in sharply through her nose that was highly eloquent.

Joan went to church proudly wearing her LMS uniform of jacket and skirt, though Gran had put her foot down over the matter of the peaked cap, insisting that Joan should wear a proper hat or it wouldn't be respectful. Positioning her shallow-crowned felt hat over her snood, Joan could almost hear Letitia's voice whispering something cheeky about the 'respectful hat'.

She didn't concentrate during the service. All she could think about was her tangled personal life. She ought to be mourning her sister, not dithering between two men. Thank goodness she was due at work today. Victoria felt like a safe place where she could set her problems aside. Or was that cowardly? She should be disappointed, not grateful, not to go to the Hubbles' for tea. Bob would be desperately hurt if he knew what was going on. So would his family. They cared about her. They trusted her.

It was a relief to get to work and keep busy. At half past two, she pushed her sack trolley across the concourse and onto the platform, ready to meet the train that was due in from Bradford, placing herself between a pair of benches and the stall that sold newspapers and tobacco. Further along, a porter with a flatbed trolley was already in position for parcels to be unloaded from the guard's van. Shortly after, the train's distinctive rhythmic sound could be heard, accompanied by regular puffs of white cloud. Both of these stopped as the train drew alongside the platform, heading towards the buffers at the far end, and there was a loud hiss from the top of the engine. The brakes shrieked and when the engine driver brought the train to a stop, there was a loud clunk, audible above the sound of doors banging open even before the train halted. Passengers alighted onto the platform and went on their way.

A gentleman called 'Porter,' swiftly followed by a confused-sounding 'Porter . . . ette.' Honestly!

Joan pushed her trolley towards him and the elderly lady by his side. 'Can I help you with your luggage, sir?'

The smile fell from her face and had to be forced back into position as she realised they had more baggage than you could shake a stick at: a trunk, two suitcases and a carpet bag. Joan 'walked' the trunk onto the metal plate at the foot of her trolley and swung the first suitcase on top, effectively filling the trolley. She balanced the other case on the top, where the trolley's handles and her own will-power would have to keep it in position, and wondered how to manage the carpet bag.

When a hand appeared and removed it, she assumed the gentleman was helping out. She glanced up to thank him – and there was Bob in his signalman's uniform. He placed the carpet bag on the platform, removed the two suitcases and placed the bag on top of the trunk. Then, with a suitcase in either hand, he gave the lady and gentleman a cheery smile.

'Taxi rank, is it, sir?'

'Left Luggage, if you please.'

Trust Bob. Was there ever anyone kinder? She must be mad to betray him.

'Thanks for helping,' she said when they parted company with their passengers.

'Pleasure,' said Bob. 'I hitched a ride back on the train at the end of my shift. I was hoping to see you, but didn't expect to be able to put you in my everlasting debt.'

She couldn't help laughing. 'I must get back to work.'

'What time is your break?'

'Half three.'

'I'll wait for you.'

'Don't be daft. That's a whole hour.'

'It's not being daft.' Bob struck a pose, clasping his hands to his heart. 'It's being devastated.'

Oh heck. 'I'll see you in the mess. Now I'd best get on. You know how it is, trains to meet, luggage to ferry.'

Her heart thumped as she went on her way. The hour half dragged, half flew. When she entered the mess, she saw that Bob had bagged a corner table. He came to his feet, pulled out a chair for her and then headed to the counter to get her a cup of tea and a bun.

'No expense spared,' he joked as he returned. 'Seriously, I'm glad to snatch a few minutes with you. I wish I hadn't had to work on Valentine's evening.'

'Someone had to. I thought about you in your signal box when the siren went off that evening and again yesterday evening.' She might be torn between Bob and another man, but she still hated the thought of the 'coffin', the metal cabinet made of boilerplate that was in effect the signalman's air-raid shelter. Its principal function was to protect him from flying glass, should the signal box's many windows be shattered.

'Were you on first-aid duty last night?' Bob asked.

'No, I was at home with Gran. The first time the siren

sounded, we hardly made it to the Andy before the all-clear sounded.'

'A bit different the second time, though.'

Yes, indeed. The second raid had started at half past eleven and dragged on for three hours.

'They reckon the raid would have been a lot worse,' said Bob, 'only the weather was in our favour. Anyway, we're here now, you and me.' His hands almost crossed the table towards her, then, with a self-conscious glance round, he withdrew them and smiled. 'Not the best venue for a courting couple.'

'It'll do,' said Joan.

'I've got a Valentine's present for you.'

She went hot and cold. Please, not an engagement ring.

But Bob produced, of all things, an old envelope. 'Sorry. I know it doesn't look like much. Open your hand.'

She obeyed and he shook a small piece of card onto her palm. No, not card, a piece of a photograph, the smiling face of a young lad.

'I thought you might like to put it in your locket. I'm sure you've already put in a picture of Letitia, but it's one of those double lockets where you can put a second picture in the back of the locket face.'

Joan stared down at the image of the boy. His hair was thick and dark, the fringe in need of a trim. It was unmistakably Bob. Same open features, same smile.

'You haven't changed.'

'I've always been a handsome devil.' Then, with a trace of uncertainty, he added, 'It was Dad's idea. I didn't like to give you a recent picture of myself. It seemed rather presumptuous. Then Dad had the idea of using an old snap. He said you could use it without feeling – well – committed.'

'It was your dad's idea?'

She had always wanted a dad. She and Letitia had Daddy, of course, but it wasn't the same as having a real father there with you, in the flesh, bringing you up and being proud of you.

She loved the Hubbles. How easy it would be to slip into the ranks of their family, how comfortable, how secure. In her mind, she couldn't seem to separate Bob from his loving, generous, fun-filled family. The Hubbles were the family she had always wanted.

Letitia's voice surfaced in her head.

'You're obviously so taken with Bob's family. Don't get me wrong. I think it's lovely. But is it Bob you're in love with, or the whole Hubble family?'

Well, which was it?

The oddest thing about living with Cordelia was calling her Mrs Masters. If it wasn't so weird, it would be hilarious. At work, she and Mabel called one another by their first names, but when they went home in the evening – home, the one place where you would expect familiarity – they changed to being Mrs Masters and Miss Bradshaw.

'I hope you shan't mind if we address one another formally,' Cordelia had said in that cool voice of hers. Not apologising, just stating the rules. 'My husband wouldn't understand.'

Well, no, having met him and lived beneath his roof, Mabel could appreciate that. No two ways about it, Mr Masters was stuffy. Cordelia called him Kenneth and that said it all, really. Not Ken, but Kenneth. Full names and formality. Everything in full and probably in triplicate, that was Mr Masters.

To her surprise, Mabel felt a twinge of nostalgia for her old room in Mrs Grayson's house. It had seemed pretty hideous at the time, with that knitted stuff all over the place, but Cordelia's guest room, for all its elegance, was . . . well . . . soulless. The whole house was like that. Beautiful, perfect, quietly costly. A place for everything, and everything in its place, but no sense of warmth.

Not that she felt unwelcome. On the contrary, Cordelia was a gracious and considerate hostess. Having offered Mabel hospitality, she had gone home, leaving Mabel to follow later. When Mabel arrived at Cordelia's house, she had found her room filled with attractive little touches – rose-scented soap in the soap dish, fluffy towels and a hot-water bottle on the bed, even a crystal bud vase with snowdrops in it.

'You'll find writing paper and envelopes in the dressing-table drawer,' said Cordelia, 'and would you like to borrow an alarm clock?'

It was as if her stay there had been planned for weeks, not pulled out of the hat that morning.

And yet . . .

Everything was so formal. Mumsy would adore it. It was her etiquette book come to life.

But for all Mumsy's insistence on social protocol, that had never stopped Pops dumping his elbows on the table or chucking two fingers of Scotch down his neck after a long day instead of sipping it, and it didn't stop Mabel flinging up the sash windows to lean out for deep breaths of sunshiny fresh air or dashing about and neglecting to cast a demure parting glance over her shoulder as she left a room. Even Mumsy was wont to leave her current novel lying around instead of returning it to its rightful position in the bookcase. Neither was she above slipping off her rhinestone-decorated evening shoes, popping her feet onto a tapestried footstool and waggling her stockinged toes in front of the fire.

One evening in the buffet, when it was just Mabel, Alison and Joan, Alison had leaned forward.

'What's Cordelia's house like?'

'Probably what you'd expect. Bay windows, plenty of space.'

'You've landed on your feet there,' said Alison, 'especially after living with mad Mrs Grayson.'

'Don't be unkind,' Joan had said.

'I'm not,' said Alison, unabashed. 'It's true. Mrs Grayson has bats in her belfry. Mabel has bagged herself a jolly good billet, if you ask me.'

Harry approved, too. He hadn't accompanied her when she moved in, but had turned up that evening to take her out.

'It's more in keeping with what you deserve. Mrs Grayson's a decent sort, but you've been brought up to better things than a house smothered in knitting, where you're expected to trail around doing the household shopping.'

'It wasn't that bad.'

'Yes, it was, and you know it.'

In the presence of Mabel's new landlord and landlady, Harry toned down his cheery charm and called Mr Masters 'sir'. Leaving the house to go to the pictures, Mabel giggled so much she stumbled on the garden path.

'What is it?' Harry's lips twitched as her laughter infected him. A chuckle bubbled forth.

'You,' she'd managed to say. 'You and your "sir". I'm surprised you didn't click your heels and salute.'

'I don't think he'd mind if I did. He's a bit of a stuffed shirt, isn't he?'

She had now been at Cordelia's house a week and a day. On Sunday afternoon, she dropped in on Mrs Grayson at Mrs Cooper's house.

'How kind of you to come,' said Mrs Cooper. 'I've been

trying to persuade Mrs Grayson to come for a breath of air, just to the corner and back, but I don't think I'm quite enough for her to hang on to.'

Mabel went straight to her old landlady's side. 'How about if you have me to hang on to as well?'

'You need to get used to walking to the public shelter,' said Mrs Cooper.

'I know,' said Mrs Grayson. 'I'm sorry to be a nuisance.'

Mrs Cooper bobbed down beside Mrs Grayson's chair and looked into her face. 'You're not a nuisance, love. Nobody's a nuisance that just needs a spot of help.'

'Chop-chop, ladies,' Mabel sang out. 'Get your coats.'

Two minutes later, they were in the narrow hallway, arms linked, with Mrs Grayson in the middle. Mabel opened the door and they emerged, crabwise, onto the pavement.

'All right, love?' Mrs Cooper asked. 'Best foot forward.'

Without giving Mrs Grayson a chance to retreat, they stepped out. Somehow or other, Mabel tripped and staggered. Her heart gave a lurch. Would the stumble destroy Mrs Grayson's confidence? But, to her amazement, Mrs Grayson let out a snort of laughter.

'You'll get us a bad name, you will, Miss Bradshaw, staggering about like you've been on the cooking sherry.'

'Oh, Mrs Grayson, you are a one!' Mrs Cooper exclaimed.

It wasn't especially funny, but all three of them dissolved into laughter. Boosted by a warm feeling of caring and comradeship, they almost got to the corner before Mrs Grayson's nerve went and she had to be helped home.

'There,' said Mabel as they reached Mrs Cooper's doorstep. 'That wasn't so bad, was it?'

'Actually,' Mrs Cooper said to Mrs Grayson, 'from what you've told me about yourself, I imagine it must have been terrifying, but you were very brave. Now that you're settled in here, we're going to go out a couple of times a day to get you used to going to the public shelter. I've took the liberty of telling a couple of the neighbours about your little problem and they're going to help us.'

Mrs Grayson's face had gone pasty-white, but she swallowed and nodded. 'I've got to learn to get there. I know that.'

Mabel squeezed her arm. 'Good for you.'

Lizzie's mum lived in a narrow terraced house with a front door that opened straight onto the street. She kept it spotlessly clean, but it was small and cramped and had very little to recommend it compared to Cordelia's house. And in thinking that, Mabel put her finger on the difference between the two. Cordelia and Kenneth Masters had a large and beautiful house, but Lizzie's lovely mum, in spite of her shattering bereavement, had a home.

Everyone had told her she had found a jolly splendid billet at Cordelia's house, and of course they were right, but could it be that Mrs Grayson had got a better one?

# Chapter Twenty-Six

It was simple to pop round and see Steven while he was recuperating. No one thought anything of it, not Steven's mum, not the neighbours. Why would they? She was as good as his sister, which made the deception easy to continue. Horribly easy.

And today, Monday, she had the excuse of asking about Steven's appointment with the doctor.

'How did it go?' She was confident there would have been no problems. Steven was still sore, but his bruises had all but faded away and he was in fine spirits. Mind you, that was partly down to her having returned to him.

'I'll be back at work on Wednesday.'

'Good for you.'

'I'll tell you something else that's good for me.'

'Oh yes? What's that?' She leaned forward, responding to the flirting.

'I happen to know a certain young lady whose day off is tomorrow.'

'Do you really? Who would that be?'

'Someone who, I hope, will spend it helping me make the most of my final day of freedom.'

'It can't be the entire day. I've got errands to run for Gran in the morning.'

'So if a breath of fresh air should take my fancy, and if I should happen to bump into you while you're out . . .'

Which was what happened accidentally on purpose the next morning. If anything, it must have appeared an awkward meeting because Joan, startled to see the joy in Steven's eyes and fearful that her own gaze was equally starry, could barely look at him for fear of their feelings being on show for all to see.

'Are you all right?' Steven asked as they fell in step. 'You're not having second thoughts?'

'I feel conspicuous.'

'Nobody knows about us. It's called hiding in plain sight.'

'I hate feeling like I'm sneaking around.'

'Does that mean you're ready to tell Bob? It'll be hard on him, but you have to put yourself first.'

'Don't.' Joan couldn't suppress a shiver. 'Just picturing it makes me feel guilty. I hate doing things on the sly, but I can't help myself. You and me – it's like being on a ride at the funfair, one of those roller-coaster rides that Gran would never let us go on because she said they were dangerous.'

'D'you mean now you're on, you can't get off?'

She lowered her voice. 'I've always been good little Joan, obeying the rules, and now . . .'

'And now you've gone to the bad?'

'Don't tease.'

'I'm not. I feel pretty much the same myself.'

'Really?' She longed for him to say more, needing the reassurance.

'I never thought I'd love anyone but Letitia. These feelings I have for you have knocked me for six.'

It had never occurred to Joan that Steven might be entertaining doubts and reservations. She had assumed he felt certain of what they were doing. Knowing he shared some of her uncertainty sent a chill through her. How stupid she was – how selfish. As if she alone was permitted to have doubts.

They went to the library, the cobbler's and to the stationer's for a bottle of Quink, then Steven walked her home.

Joan stopped at the gate. 'I'll see you later.'

'Aren't you going to ask me in? It'd be rude not to pay my respects to your gran.'

Rude not to come in? But coming in would be ... manipulative. Dishonest. Yet how could she not invite him in?

Gran wasn't at home. As they entered the house, shedding coats and hats, Joan's hands trembled as she hung things up in the hallway.

'She must still be at the shops,' she said, leading Steven into the parlour. 'I'm sent on errands to the ironmonger's and to the newsagent's to pay the papers, but Gran guards the food shopping with her life. She's probably thoroughly fed up in an hour-long queue. Shall I pop the kettle on?'

'No. Come and sit down. Let's talk.'

Taking her hand, Steven took her to the sofa and they sat down. A frisson passed through her. Did he feel it too? Did he remember, too, that time when they had sat here and he had shown her the engagement ring he had bought for Letitia?

'I want us to be together,' said Steven. 'I'm terrified you'll choose Bob or you'll decide against me because of Letitia. I can't bear to lose you, not now. I've already lost Letitia and you mean so much to me.'

He moved his face closer, hesitating, waiting for her to make a similar move. Joan's pulse raced as she tilted forward. They didn't use their hands, just leaned towards one another. Her heart swelled as lips brushed lips. Steven's mouth closed over hers, kissing gently, drawing a response from her, breaking away so he could murmur words she barely heard, though her heart heard them.

Another kiss, and another. At the same moment, they both shuffled across, their arms snaking around one another. Steven's body was lean and muscular. She sank against him, excitement radiating throughout her body. Reaching up, she pushed her fingers through his hair.

'What the ruddy hallelujah is going on here?'

Gran!

Crikey, Dot would be glad to get back to Victoria. It hadn't been the pleasantest of journeys, what with a crowded train and numerous delays. Mr Bonner was in a worse mood than usual, which had turned out to be because he had heard about a woman being appointed to the post of train guard.

At last they arrived, cruising into Victoria alongside the platform. Dot walked through the connecting section from the guard's van into the passenger coach, hanging back as the last few people descended onto the platform. Then she pulled the door closed, pushed the window right down and stood there, arms resting on top of the window, watching everyone streaming down the platform. This was a treat she sometimes allowed herself. She loved being on 'her' train, satisfied to have delivered all the parcels en route, watching the passengers disappear.

Ah well, no rest for the wicked. She returned to the guard's van, where Mr Bonner was unlocking the big double doors. Outside, one of the porters, Mr Weaver, was ready with a flatbed trolley. Mr Bonner opened the door to the wire cage in which all the parcels were stored for safe keeping. Then, leaving Dot and Mr Weaver to get on with unloading the parcels, he climbed down onto the platform and started up a conversation with the ticket inspector, breaking off to speak to some passengers, who seemed to be asking questions.

When all the parcels were out of the wire cage, Dot climbed down to assist Mr Weaver with arranging the trolley.

'Excuse me,' said a woman's voice behind her.

Dot turned round, always happy to help. The woman was thin-faced and in her thirties. Her overcoat had seen a few years of wear, as had her brown felt hat. Her hair was light brown, and there was summat pinched and tired about her skin, but her eyes were sharp. Dot knew all about being tired but having to keep on top of things.

'What can I do for you?' she asked.

'Are you Mrs Green?'

'That's me.'

'Mrs Dorothy Green?'

'Aye.' There was summat odd about this. 'Who wants to know?'

The younger woman looked her straight in the eye. 'Mrs Dorothy Green, *Mrs* – as in, you're a married woman?'

Dot tilted her head, confusion blundering through her. The fact that everyone else had turned round to listen didn't help.

'What's this about?' Dot asked.

'Mrs married-woman Dorothy Green – as in, *you're* the married woman who's chasing after my father?' The woman raised her eyebrows in a challenge. '*That* Mrs Dorothy Green?'

Joan had trouble breathing. She tried to speak, but no words would come.

Steven rose to his feet. 'Mrs Foster—'

'Don't you Mrs Foster me, you – you libertine!' Gran flared. Still in her coat and hat, she marched from the doorway into the room to confront them. 'How dare you

278

take advantage of Joan? And you, young lady, where's your self-respect?'

'He wasn't taking advantage.' Joan's hands were clammy, but she had to defend Steven. 'It – it was both of us.'

Steven tugged at his jacket, straightening his appearance. There was a slash of colour in his cheeks and his hair was askew where Joan had dragged her fingers through it. Who would have thought you could mess up a short back and sides?

'I appreciate that this comes as a shock to you, Mrs Foster,' said Steven.

'A shock? A bolt from the blue, more like. Letitia's ever-loving young man and the sister who was supposed to think the world of her. Disgusting! That's what it is – disgusting.'

'If you'll let me explain—' Steven began.

Gran stepped round him, shoving him aside, and bent over Joan, her chin thrust out, eyes glinting.

'You! Both of you, is it? Both of you?'

She nodded. 'Yes.' She wanted to speak confidently, but fear and shame had thickened her throat.

'Get out of my house and don't come back, Steven Arnold. I thought you were a decent sort, but you've deceived me and you've dishonoured Letitia's memory.'

'Mrs Foster, please—'

Gran's gaze bore into Joan as she continued to address Steven. 'I would say you've deceived Joan too, but by her own admission she's as morally loose as you are. She's a trollop and you're a scoundrel. Get out!'

Steven's head jerked back. He stared at Joan.

'It's all right,' she tried to reassure him through her own panic. She forced herself to her feet. Her body felt empty, as if everything had drained out of her. 'I'll see you out . . . *Oh!*'

The exclamation was wrenched out of her as she landed back on the sofa, courtesy of a sharp push from Gran, who now swung round to confront Steven. She jabbed him in the chest.

'Leave my house this instant, do you hear? Now!'

Gran's voice rose. Gran never raised her voice. Raised voices were for people who lacked self-control and Beryl Foster was always fully in control – of herself, her home, her granddaughters.

'Come with me, Joan,' said Steven, 'just while things calm down.'

Gran placed herself directly in front of him. Her voice was dangerously quiet. 'Either you leave my house this minute or I'll go to the police station and tell them I found Constable Arnold molesting my granddaughter.'

'Gran!' Joan exclaimed in horror. To Steven she said, 'I'll be all right.'

Steven rubbed the back of his neck worriedly, but he left. Gran neither moved nor spoke, her stillness holding Joan captive. She tried desperately to think of something to say, but her mind was filled with a white blanket of panic. At the sound of the front door shutting, Gran swelled as if about to explode.

'You slut! You *slut*! Just like your mother. God help us. Anything in trousers.'

'Gran! That's not fair.'

'Isn't it? Shall we ask Bob how fair he thinks it is?'

'Steven and I never intended any harm. It just happened.'

'Never intended any harm? Your sister is barely cold in her grave and you never meant any harm? What about *Letitia*?'

Gran's hand darted out and smacked Joan across her

face hard enough to snap her head sideways and wrench a gasp all the way up from her lungs.

'There! I never had the chance to do that to your mother. It's what she deserved and what you deserve as well. Tarts, the pair of you. Never mind the proprieties – never mind your responsibilities – never mind behaving like a decent human being with standards and morals. Who cares who you're letting down as long as you get your secret lustful pleasures? You're a slut, Joan Foster, like your mother was – and there's no place for you under my roof. You've got ten minutes to pack a bag and get out. Leave your key behind. You won't be needing it again.'

How she got through the remainder of the day, Dot did not know. She felt like hiding and never coming out again. For this to have happened at all was appalling, but for it to have happened in public, in front of colleagues, in front of passengers . . . The hairs on her arms and the back of her neck stood up. Mr Bonner and the other men wouldn't keep quiet about it. She would be the talk of the mess, and not just there, but the porters' office and Left Luggage and . . . oh, the whole flaming station. Probably Hunts Bank an' all.

And all because she had made friends with dear, kind Mr Thirkle.

That woman who had made a holy show of her for all to see was his daughter, his Edie. No wonder she had brown eyes. No wonder her face was thin. She was Mr Thirkle's lass.

'She's always been the apple of my eye,' Mr Thirkle had said about her.

'Mrs married-woman Dorothy Green,' Edie had proclaimed for the world and his wife to hear, 'as in, *you're* the married woman who's chasing after my father?'

Dot had spent the rest of the day trying to hide her face from everyone else. Oh, the shame.

But there was one thing she could do to help herself – well, she hoped it would help. For all she knew, her friends might think she had behaved like a hussy. It was one thing to promise to support one another, quite another to stand by a married woman who had been publicly accused of pursuing a man.

She clocked off and slipped away without calling her usual cheerful goodbye. Making her way along the busy concourse, she felt as if all those voices were tattling about her. She would never live this down.

Dot's heart pounded as she opened the buffet door. The warm atmosphere, with its hum of voices and the scent of tea and lardy cake, enveloped her, but instead of feeling welcome, today she felt distanced. She joined the queue, riveting her gaze on the tweed-clad back of the lady in front of her as she edged towards the counter. Finally, armed with her cup of tea, she headed for the table where Cordelia, Persephone and Alison were. At least it was a corner table, not one in the middle, where wagging ears might overhear.

'Good evening, Dot.' Cordelia frowned. 'You look pale. Are you quite well?'

'Pale?' Dot couldn't bring herself to look at her friends.

'I was going to say "shaken", but I didn't want to sound dramatic.'

Shaken. That was precisely the right word. Her insides were wobbling and she'd had to spend a penny a dozen times since the incident. A burning sensation lurked in the backs of her eyes. It wouldn't take much to tip her over the edge and make her bawl her eyes out.

Dot lifted her face and made herself look round at her friends. 'I take it none of you has heard.'

'Heard what?' Alison and Persephone asked at the same time.

Beneath the table, Dot clutched her fingers. 'I've got summat to tell you.' How stiff she sounded. But she had to be stiff or she would fall to pieces. 'The most awful thing happened today. Eh, I'm that ashamed.'

'What is it?' Cordelia asked. 'You can tell us.'

Aye, and what would their response be? What if the friends she relied on saw it from Edie's point of view?

'When my train got into Victoria this morning, I was nabbed by—' No, she needed to start before that. 'Do you know Mr Thirkle? He's a ticket collector.'

'Yes,' said Persephone. 'He's a sweet old duck.'

Cordelia and Alison shook their heads.

'Persephone's right,' said Dot. 'He's a true gentleman.' She wanted to praise him as he deserved, but had to hold back for fear of sounding too keen. 'Anyroad, him and me, we get on and we like to have a chat now and again.'

'Nothing wrong with that,' said Alison.

'I know, but . . . well, his daughter's took it bad. She was waiting when the train came in and – and she accused me of chasing after her dad.' Heat flared in her cheeks. 'There. Now you know.' There was silence round the table and Dot died a thousand deaths. 'Have you took against me? I can't blame you if you have. I grew up in the backstreets, where women are nowt if not judgemental. I know what my dear old mam would have said about a woman who'd had just such a thing said about her. No smoke without fire.'

Another silence, and then Cordelia spoke in her composed voice.

'That is certainly a popular saying, and there's another one about getting hold of the wrong end of the stick. There's no question in my mind that that's what Mr Thirkle's daughter has done.'

It was a good job Dot was sitting down or she might have buckled as her legs turned to water.

'Absolutely,' Persephone chimed in. 'We know you, Dot, and you're a respectable lady.'

Dot covered her mouth with her hand as gratitude filled her heart with warmth. Oh, her dear, lovely friends, how could she have doubted them for even a moment?

'Someone from my rank of life isn't supposed to be friends with someone from yours,' said Cordelia, 'but if this war, and being a railway worker, has taught me anything, it's that one shouldn't rely on class to determine who is a worthy friend. I realised last summer, Dot, that you and I have the same standards and I don't believe for one moment that you would ever let your standards slip.'

'Thank you,' said Dot. 'You've no idea how worried I was about telling you all.'

'I hope we've made you feel better,' said Alison.

'Ah,' said Cordelia. 'I don't think it's quite that simple, is it?' She looked at Dot.

'No. What Edie Thirkle-as-was said to me was said in public.'

'Never!' Persephone exclaimed.

'In front of Mr Bonner and Mr Weaver and Uncle Tom Cobley an' all. There were passengers there. What if they complain?'

'What if they do?' said Alison. 'Colleagues making conversation isn't a sackable offence. This is the daughter putting two and two together and making five.'

'Her father needs to have a stern word with her,' said Cordelia.

'But word gets round the station,' said Dot, 'and everyone will hear about Dot Green setting her sights on Mr Thirkle. Mr Bonner isn't going to keep his trap shut, believe you me.'

Cordelia released a slow breath. 'I hate to say it, but you'll have to ride the storm.'

'Is Miss Emery around?' asked Persephone. 'I know her work takes her all over the place, but if she's at Hunts Bank, perhaps she could defuse the situation.'

'Good idea,' said Alison.

'Chin up, Dot,' urged Persephone. 'You can't be the only one this is happening to. There must be railway men and women all over the country who have formed innocent friendships.'

'Aye, but how many of them have had family members yelling the odds at them? And . . . well, I need you to hear this from me and not from gossip. After she said her piece about me chasing her father, she said summat like, "You can't deny it. You've been seen in the Worker Bee." That's a café.'

'You mean you've met up outside work?' asked Persephone, and Dot didn't miss the swift glances that passed between the others.

'Aye, but it's not what it sounds like. We had a reason for meeting.' Cripes. She wanted to clear her name, but how could she without spilling all kinds of beans? 'And not because we were doing owt we shouldn't.' How defensive she sounded. Grouchy, even. Reet nowty, Mam would have said. Oh heck, and the others weren't saying owt. What were they thinking?

'Come on, Dot,' said Alison. 'We need more of an explanation than that.'

And that was the problem, because how could she tell her friends about the food dump? She had already stretched a point by telling Mr Thirkle. Aye, and look where that had got her. After being upset most of the day, Dot surprised herself by going all businesslike.

'I'm sorry to make a mystery of it, but there's a secret

involved, and not a mucky secret like Edie Thirkle-as-was thinks neither, but summat serious to do with the war effort. Me and Mr Thirkle are trying to find out summat before we go to the police.'

'Why not tell the police now?' asked Persephone.

'Just take it from me that I can't. I wish Joan was here. She might have an inkling what this is about. Or Mabel, though she doesn't know what Joan knows.'

'You're talking in riddles,' said Alison.

'Why Joan and Mabel?' asked Cordelia.

'Because they were there.'

'Where?' Three voices, one question.

Oh heck. If she didn't tell them, it might look like she didn't trust them. But this was a wartime secret.

'I wish I could confide in you, I really do. I've no idea what to do next, especially now that – well, now that I'll have to steer clear of Mr Thirkle.'

'I don't understand what this is about,' said Persephone, 'but it sounds serious. If you need help, Dot, you have to tell us. We aren't being nosy. We care about you and we want to help.'

Dot shook her head. It wasn't a way of saying no. It was pure confusion. She honestly didn't know what to do for the best.

'Here's someone who may be able to shed some light,' said Alison as Mabel appeared beside them and sat down. 'Mabel, we have a mystery to solve.'

Dot listened, shamefaced, as Cordelia quietly explained about Edie Thirkle-as-was.

'Oh, Dot.' Mabel was all concern.

'There's more,' said Persephone. She explained the rest – in so far as she could explain it.

'It's something you know about,' Alison told Mabel. 'What is it?'

'I haven't the foggiest.' Mabel looked bewildered.

'Dot said it was something serious to do with the war effort,' Cordelia prompted.

'Dot, why don't you just tell us,' said Alison, 'and save us all this floundering about?'

Mabel sat up straight. 'It's to do with that railway building on our first day, isn't it? That's why you said Joan and I were there. I'm right, aren't I?' She turned to the others. 'On our first day, my gang stopped near a big railway shed and who should come along in a Scammell Mechanical Horse but Dot and Joan. Nobody asked them at the time what they were doing, because we've all had it drummed into us not to ask busybody questions, but this is to do with whatever brought you to the shed – isn't it?'

All of them looked at Dot, not curiously or expectantly, but with concern on their faces.

'Come on, Dot,' said Mabel. 'I've worked it out, or started to. All you have to do is fill in a few gaps.'

Was it wrong to confide? *Be like Dad – keep Mum* said the posters. But Mabel was part-way there and she had nobody else to turn to. Her friends were trustworthy. They would help her.

Dot explained everything.

'So it has to be someone who knows about the food dump,' said Persephone.

'I hope you don't consider Joan a suspect,' said Mabel.

'Don't take it personally,' Cordelia advised, but Mabel still looked miffed.

'I don't believe for one moment that Joan would do such a thing,' said Dot, 'or you, Mabel.'

'Me?' Mabel squeaked.

'I know the pair of you and I know you'd never be involved in anything like that.'

287

'But if you didn't know us, we'd be suspects?' Mabel demanded.

'As Cordelia said, try not to take it personally,' said Persephone. 'It makes sense, you know. I imagine you've thought about Mabel's gang, haven't you, Dot?'

Mabel's mouth dropped open.

Cordelia touched Mabel's hand. 'It's a nasty business. Don't take it out on Dot. She's confided in us because she trusts us and we aren't going to let her down.'

'Believe me, love,' Dot told Mabel, 'you can't feel any worse about it than I do.'

'I hope telling us has eased the burden a little,' said Persephone. 'We'll help you.'

'Thank you.' It was all Dot could manage to say.

'And whatever trouble this Edie woman has caused,' said Cordelia, 'we'll see you through that too.'

# Chapter Twenty-Seven

Walking along Heathside Lane on her way home after what felt like the longest day of her life, Dot felt like a wrung-out dishcloth, but she had to pull herself together. She mustn't let her family see she was upset. Upset? Shaken to the core, more like.

As she drew nearer to home, she caught sight of a figure sitting on her doorstep. Instinct leaped to the fore, her eyes showing her what she expected to see – Jimmy! But no, it wasn't their Jimmy, it was Joan.

Dot picked up her pace.

'Joan, lovey, what are you doing here?'

Joan looked up at her with bewildered eyes. She had never looked younger. Then Dot saw the suitcase. She helped Joan to her feet, then slid her arms around her in a hug.

'There, chick. You come indoors with me and we'll see what's what.'

'I'm sorry to descend on you like this. I've been walking round and round. I didn't know where to go.'

'Well, you've ended up in the right place and that's what matters. In we go. Leave your case there – no, on second thoughts, I'll pop it in the parlour.'

That way it wouldn't be the first thing Reg saw when he walked in. The last thing they needed was him complaining about stuff being left lying around for him to trip over and who the ruddy heck did it belong to, anyroad?

Dot kept up a cheerful monologue while the tea brewed, but she had one eye on Joan and was alarmed by the girl's stricken expression, blue eyes dark with shock, skin pulled taut, her mouth a line of smothered distress where the pretty smile used to be.

Sitting at the table, Dot pushed Joan's tea towards her, taking a sip of her own in the hope it would prompt the child to follow suit. It didn't.

'Are you going to tell me what's happened?' she asked gently.

Joan let out a shaky breath. Her eyes filled and she blinked hard, scrabbling in her pocket for a hanky.

'Have a good blow,' Dot advised. 'The last time somebody pitched up on my doorstep with a suitcase, it was my grandson a couple of years back, only it wasn't a suitcase, it was a paper bag of pear drops and pieces of jigsaw, which apparently is all you need when you run away from home. Oh aye, and he had a folded-up comic sticking out of his back pocket an' all. You can't run away without the *Beano*.'

Joan gave her a watery smile.

'Do I take it from the suitcase that you've left home?'

A nod.

'You've never had a row with your grandmother and stormed out, have you?' Even as she suggested it, Dot rejected the idea. Joan was too sensible to march off in a huff and too polite to have a fight with her elders.

'No,' Joan whispered.

Aiming for a lighter tone, Dot said, 'I'm not a mind-reader, chick.' Catching the despair in Joan's face, she added, 'Is it because of summat you've done? I know how that feels. Let me tell you what happened to me today and then you might feel like telling me about your situation. Earlier today, I was collared in public and accused of chasing after a man.'

Joan's eyes widened.

'You see, I made friends with Mr Thirkle – you know, the ticket collector. I'll save the gory details for another time, but for now let's say that his daughter cottoned on to our friendship and decided to play merry heck with me in front of Mr Bonner and I don't know who else.'

'That's dreadful.'

'I've faced my share of ups and downs, but I've never known humiliation like it.' She wriggled her shoulders. 'I've gone all shivery just thinking about it. So that's been my day. Now tell me about yours.'

After a long pause, Joan spoke up. 'Letitia had a boyfriend called Steven. He and I both loved her, and we miss her so much, and it sort of threw us together.'

'And one thing led to another? Oh, Joan.'

'I stopped seeing him, but then there was an incident when I was on first-aid duty and he needed rescuing when part of a building collapsed. All I could think was, what if I lost him?'

'Does Bob know?'

'No one did until today.'

Dot pictured the suitcase in her parlour. 'Your gran found out.'

'She caught us together. Oh, Dot, it was awful. I know I shouldn't be creeping about, seeing Steven in secret. But Gran was . . .' her voice dropped to a whisper,'. . . so angry.' She covered her mouth with her hand.

A frown tugged at the space between Dot's eyebrows. 'Did she tell you to get out? I can understand her being shocked and upset, but to sling you out . . . Surely she'll have calmed down by now?'

Joan shook her head. 'No. There's – there's more to it than I've said.'

'More to it? You don't mean she caught you and this chap doing bedroom things, do you?'

Joan gasped. 'We were kissing, that's all.'

'Are you sure you can't go home?'

'Positive. I don't know how I ended up here. I've been trailing around in a daze all afternoon.' Joan started to get up. 'I need to look for a billet.'

'Sit down, lass, and let's put us heads together. You can stop here for a bit, if push comes to shove.'

'I couldn't put you out.'

'What are friends for? It would only be for a couple of nights, because we've got just the two bedrooms and one is for Jimmy when he stops here. Not that he'd mind kipping on the sofa, I'm sure. He'd think it a great adventure.'

'Thank you for not having a go at me about Steven.'

'I expect you feel bad enough without me letting rip at you. I can see how it happened. Anyone with a heart could understand that. If I give you a piece of advice, will you promise to think about it?'

Joan nodded.

'Talk to the girls in the buffet.'

'I couldn't.'

'Why not? You've told me and I haven't bitten your head off, have I? Besides, I'm not suggesting you do owt I haven't done myself. Before I found you sitting on my doorstep like a stray cat, I was in the buffet, explaining the whys and wherefores of me getting a public dressing-down from Edie Thirkle-as-was.'

'But that wasn't your fault. It was her getting her knickers in a twist.'

'The chances are that word will spread and there's more humiliation to come. Women always get the blame. Remember that business with you and Mr Clark. You hadn't put a foot wrong, but you'd have got the blame if word had got out; or if not the blame, you'd certainly have ended up with a reputation.'

Joan's mouth twisted in distaste.

'There are plenty of women who would have said about me, "What did you expect, getting chummy with a man?" But our friends didn't. They believed in me and that was the one good thing to happen today.'

'I'm pleased they took your side.'

'Give them the chance to take your side an' all. You're in a pickle and you need your friends standing by you. Promise me you'll consider it.'

Joan nodded, but did she mean it?

'Righty-ho, I'll climb down off my soapbox. While I've been rabbiting on, I've had an idea. Not that you aren't welcome here, but having my Reg and our girls asking nosy questions isn't the best situation for you to be in. You need somewhere quieter. I can't promise there'll be room for you, mind, but it's worth asking.'

'Where?'

'Where do you think? Mrs Cooper's, of course.'

Mrs Cooper's parlour was small and old-fashioned, with cupboard doors in the alcoves on either side of the fireplace, and knick-knacks on the mantelpiece. Mrs Grayson sat in one of the armchairs, her own table beside her and her pouffe with the zigzag-patterned knitted cover beside her feet.

'Mrs Grayson, I'm sorry to inconvenience you, but would you please excuse us? Me and Joan here need a word with Mrs Cooper, private like.' When Mrs Grayson had left the room, Dot asked Mrs Cooper, 'Have you got room for a little one? Let her tell you what she's done before you say yes.'

'I don't care what she's done. Joan was the first railway girl my Lizzie met. I remember her arriving back here after she'd sat her railway tests and saying she travelled home on the bus with a girl called Joan.'

'Even so,' said Dot, 'let her tell you before you adopt her and leave her all your worldly goods.'

'All my worldly goods? As if my bits and bobs are worth tuppence.'

'Go on, love,' Dot said to Joan in a straightforward way that was better suited to asking for a weather report than an embarrassing admission of having two boyfriends at once.

'Well, I won't say I'm not shocked,' said Mrs Cooper, 'but you aren't the first and you won't be the last.'

'You'll take her in, then?' asked Dot.

Mrs Cooper turned to Joan. 'I'm sorry to speak ill of your grandmother, but I don't think anyone has cause to turn their child out, no matter what, especially these days when every goodbye could be the last. You stop here with me and Mrs Grayson until Mrs Foster is ready to have you back. There isn't much room, mind, as the two bedrooms are spoken for, but I have a little boxroom.'

Mrs Cooper might be small and thin, but her scrawny frame, worn with work and grief, contained a massive heart and it was all Joan could do not to leap across the room and fling her arms around her. 'Thank you.'

'If you can make do with the settee tonight, I'll sort out the boxroom tomorrow as best I can. I haven't got a bed for it, but I've got a sleeping bag from when Lizzie went camping with the Guides.'

And, simple as that, Joan had a new home. Part of her was still reeling in shock at the bizarre turn that events had taken, but the other part was keenly aware of the friendship and care that had helped her in her time of need. That boosted her spirits and made her determined to tell Gran her new address the very next day.

When she arrived in Torbay Road, she rang the bell and waited, half hoping that Gran would be out. Gran's jaw-line set like granite at the sight of her.

'If you've come to beg me to take you back, you're wasting your time.'

Joan experienced a sudden coldness, but why was she taken aback? In Gran's view, she had behaved like Estelle, and Estelle was the lowest of the low.

'I've got my new address for you.' She held out a scrap of paper. 'I thought you should know where I am. Just in case.'

'In case what?'

Was Gran not going to accept her address? As Joan started to withdraw her hand, Gran reached out and took it. She stuffed it in her pocket.

'I suppose one of your modern young friends took pity on you,' said Gran. 'That Mabel, I expect. I always had reservations about her.'

'Actually, I'm staying with Mrs Cooper.'

'Mrs Cooper?' It wasn't often you could take Gran by surprise.

'Lizzie's mum.'

'I know who Mrs Cooper is, thank you. Duped her, then, have you?'

'Not at all. I – I told her the truth.'

'A likely story. Well, if you did, she's not the decent body I took her for.'

With that, Gran stepped back and shut the door.

Joan tried not to be hurt, but it was difficult. The main thing was to concentrate on the kindness she had received from Dot and Mrs Cooper.

The following day, Dot snatched a moment with her on the station concourse. 'Settled in all right, have you, chick?'

'Do you want to hear something strange? I feel I'm in a secure place, which is peculiar after I've been chucked out of my own home.'

It was true. After the stern, judgemental atmosphere in which she had grown up, the friendliness with which she had been received at Mrs Cooper's didn't simply make her feel welcome, it also came as a revelation. Mrs Cooper and Mrs Grayson were decent women with sound morals, but they didn't see other people's faults in the black-and-white way Gran did.

At first Joan feared that, because of the way Mr Grayson's floozy had put the mockers on Mrs Grayson's life, Mrs Grayson might take against her for having two boyfriends.

But Mrs Cooper simply poured another cup of tea and said, 'What your husband and his bit on the side did to you, Mrs Grayson, was a disgrace, but Joan is young and unmarried and you know what youngsters are like in wartime, with romance flying about all over the place. Besides, she's had a bereavement and folk do strange things when they've lost a dear one.'

'That's true. When my old neighbour Mrs Shaftesbury's husband died unexpectedly, she went off to live at the seaside six weeks later and spent the rest of her life regretting it, by all accounts.'

'Did she?' Joan rather liked the idea of living by the sea.

'Aye, Miss Foster. You need your friends and neighbours around you, folk that have known you all your life. The worst part, so she said in a letter to Mrs Warner, was that nobody in Abergele had known her William and she found that very hard to bear, but she could never afford to move back.'

'How sad.' Joan was thoughtful. 'I'm lucky to have people who knew Letitia. She was friends with Mabel, Alison and Persephone.'

'And Lizzie,' added Mrs Cooper.

'And Lizzie.' Joan felt again the pang of loss for dear Lizzie, who had been deservedly popular among the railway girls. While she lived under Mrs Cooper's roof, she must make a point of talking to Mrs Cooper about Lizzie.

'I thought I'd go mad after Lizzie died,' said Mrs Cooper, 'but having you two here has given me a reason to get up in the morning.' She smiled sadly at Joan. 'So, you see, love, we're all helping one another.'

It was horrid to think of Dot being shown up in public like that. Sympathy swelled up inside Mabel. She was enormously fond of Dot. How could she not be? The combination of devoted mother and grandmother and cheerful, hard-working railway worker was irresistible. Admirable, too.

But no matter how deep her regard for Dot ran, that didn't stop Mabel feeling outraged. Yes, outraged. How could Dot have Bette, Bernice and Louise on her list of suspects? What made it worse was that Dot had crossed off Mabel and Joan because of being friends with them. But she wasn't friends with the others and so she was happy to suspect them of committing a crime.

Well, Mabel didn't suspect Bette, Louise or Bernice – because she knew them well and they were her friends. Yes, her friends. When she had first known them, she had been happy to be pally, telling herself that it was important to be on good terms with her workmates. But now, with astounding clarity, she saw that they were her friends. She wasn't as close to them as she was to her buffet friends, but they were friends nonetheless and they would be appalled if they knew what one of them was suspected of.

As vexed as Mabel was, she had to keep it to herself and

not utter a word to her fellow lengthmen, even when, out on the permanent way, Bette insisted that they were near enough to the railway shed to use its WC.

'By the time we've walked there,' said Louise, 'we'll only get a ten-minute break.'

'I don't care,' Bette retorted. 'It's worth it not to have to go behind a bush.'

'Are you all right, Mabel?' Bernice nudged her. 'You're miles away.'

'Just thinking.' Just thinking about walking to the railway shed in Dot's story. Just thinking about her fellow gang members being suspects.

They reached the shed and took turns to use the lavatory. The door was ajar, as always. When it was her turn to go in, Mabel tested the inner door, putting her shoulder against it and shoving. It opened; not easily, but it opened. The hinges groaned in protest. Mabel went cold, but what had she expected?

She pulled the door closed and used the privy, taking some lavatory paper from her knapsack. When she emerged, squeezing her way round the door, she found Bette chuckling.

'Blimey, Mabel! What a noise! That's the worst case of gippy tummy I've ever heard.'

Embarrassment flooded Mabel's cheeks with heat. 'It wasn't me. It was that hinge on the outside door. I tried to shut it.'

She looked at her three friends. Did one of them know the sound had come not from the hinge on the outside door, but from the one on the inside? Might one of them be Dot's thief?

# Chapter Twenty-Eight

They were unendurable, all those smirks and the nudges that made her cheeks feel as if they were on fire, and the whispers that weren't quite behind her back. In some ways, Dot found it worse than being on the receiving end of Edie's ire. The constant drip-drip-drip of muffled scorn made her wish a hundred times a day that she could sink through the floor.

And Mr Bonner, drat him, made a point of ordering her to watch her p's and q's in the presence of men. 'Colleagues and passengers alike,' he said in a disapproving tone that made her long to offer a sharp retort, but that would only make things worse.

Worst of the lot, though, was that she needed to see Mr Thirkle, but she hadn't clapped eyes on him. Was he avoiding her? Had his Edie taken it upon herself to set him straight regarding Mrs married-woman Dorothy Green? Dot chewed the inside of her cheek. Or had Mr Thirkle himself requested that in future his duties should keep him well away from her?

Arriving back at Victoria after her final trip of the day, Dot unloaded her parcels onto the flatbed trolley and manoeuvred it down the platform – and there was Mr Thirkle at the barrier, opening the gates for her to pass through. Instead of feeling relieved to see him, she was filled with embarrassment at what he must think of her.

As she approached, he stepped forward. 'Mrs Green—' he began.

'I'll come back when I've seen to my parcels.'

She took the trolley to the office for everything to be sorted for the next stage of the various journeys. Was it her imagination or were her colleagues less keen to lend her a hand? Good grief, were the men backing off for fear of being pursued by a middle-aged maneater?

Afterwards, she hurried back to Mr Thirkle's ticket barrier, gritting her teeth as she was obliged to pass a group of porters and workmen.

'Aye aye. Off to see your fancy man, are you?'

'I wish my missus was that keen to see me.'

It was the most open anyone had been and shame rendered Dot almost light-headed, but she held her head high, which probably made her look even more of a brazen hussy as she marched on her way.

Mr Thirkle saw her coming.

She jumped in with both feet. 'I expect you've heard, though I don't know whether it'll have been from your Edie or the other blokes or both—'

'Mrs Green, I can't apologise enough.'

'You what?'

'Edie's neighbour spotted me in the Worker Bee with you and told her, and then Edie asked me, and she asked in such a pleasant way that I was glad to tell her about our friendship. I had no idea she was planning to come here and shout the place down.'

'It wasn't my finest moment,' said Dot.

'She's overprotective of her old dad, I'm afraid. If we'd been seen chatting inside the station, Edie wouldn't have thought twice. It was because we were elsewhere. She said it looked—'

'I can guess.'

'And, of course, I couldn't tell her why we were there, as a result of which you were subjected to a scene.'

Dot sighed. That food-dump business had a lot to answer for. When she got her hands on the thief, she would give him or her what for.

'Mrs Green,' said a displeased voice and here came Mr Bonner, having checked the train was empty before making his way to leave the platform, 'what have I said to you about minding your p's and q's in the presence of men?'

'Mr Bonner, sir,' said Mr Thirkle, 'Mrs Green was only—'

'I think we all know what she was only,' snapped Mr Bonner and stalked past them.

'I'd best get back to the parcels office,' said Dot. 'I'm sorry if you've had to put up with so-called clever remarks.'

In spite of Mr Bonner's nasty dig, she felt better for having cleared the air with Mr Thirkle. Fancy him feeling the need to apologise. Just when she had been about to grovel an' all. Knowing that he didn't consider she had done owt wrong sent a little boost of confidence swimming through her bloodstream.

It would be summat positive to tell her mates about in the buffet later.

But when she walked into the buffet, she looked across and there, sitting with Cordelia, Alison and Persephone, was Miss Emery. Dot went cold right to the centre of her being. She didn't bother queuing up for a cuppa, but went straight to the table.

'This is a pleasant surprise, Miss Emery.' She greeted the assistant welfare supervisor in her friendliest voice, as if this was a social call and nowt to do with the nastiness that had been going on – because Miss Emery might just have popped in to see how they were all getting on, mightn't she? She might not even have heard of Dot's problem. 'Come to join us for a cuppa, have you?'

'Not exactly, I'm afraid. I thought it might be less daunting for you if I saw you here than if I sent for you.'

'Take a seat, Dot,' said Cordelia.

'Unless you'd prefer us to talk in private,' said Miss Emery. 'You're entitled to that.'

'Nay, there's no call for that.' Dot sat down. Her legs felt wobbly, but she stiffened her spine. 'There's nowt you can say to me that can't be said in front of my friends.'

'Very well.' There was a subtle change in Miss Emery's expression from kindly to businesslike. 'I regret to inform you that a complaint has been lodged against you regarding your conduct, and you are required to attend a formal interview where the matter will be discussed.'

With the sharp-edged February air nipping her cheeks, Joan rubbed her gloved hands together as she hovered on Steven's mum's doorstep, anxious to knock yet dreading the reception she might receive if he had told his parents about them. He might have felt he had to, after being caught by Gran. What would Mrs Arnold think? She had been ever so fond of Letitia, probably viewing her as her daughter-in-law elect. Mr Arnold had helped Steven dig the hole for the Fosters' Anderson shelter and he sometimes sent Gran leeks or a cabbage from his allotment.

'Joan, how long have you been standing there waiting for me to answer the door?'

Turning, Joan found Mrs Arnold behind her. She stood aside while Mrs Arnold fiddled for her key.

'I'm normally home at this time, but I had to nip round the corner shop for a box of candles. It's amazing how much they've gone up in price. They were all of tenpence a box before the war.' Pausing in the doorway, Mrs Arnold looked at her. 'Are you coming in? You look like you've taken root.'

'I was hoping for a word with Steven, to see how he's getting on now he's back at work. I'll come another time if he's not here.'

'He'll be back in twenty minutes. Come in and wait. You can talk to me while I peel the potatoes.'

Joan couldn't meet her eyes. 'No, I'm sorry, I haven't got that long. I'll see him another time.'

She backed away with what she hoped looked like a polite smile, though her face felt like a mask. She hurried away, stopping as she reached the corner. Should she hang about until Steven came by on his way home? No, she didn't want the neighbours mentioning it to his mother, which meant she'd have to wait outside the police station. Besides, walking there would kill a bit of time.

The front of the police station was covered by a wall of sandbags. When Steven came down the steps, he was with a colleague. Joan was taken aback to see him smiling and chatting as if he hadn't a care in the world. She stepped forwards and Steven stopped mid stride.

He said to his companion, 'This is Letitia's sister.' Not 'This is my girlfriend' or even 'This is my friend', but 'This is Letitia's sister.'

The other policeman's smile switched to a sombre expression. 'I'm sorry for your loss.'

'Thank you.' Grief, swirling up from the dark place where she kept it, threatened to engulf her. She hated having to thank people for their condolences. Losing her beloved sister wasn't something that should involve thanks.

'See you tomorrow, Arnie,' Steven's colleague said as he went on his way.

'Arnie?' Joan asked as she and Steven set off. It was easier, safer, than saying, 'You didn't say I was your girlfriend.' Anyway, she had no business saying that, not when she hadn't finished with Bob. A crackle of nerves left her feeling uneasy. Was she really going to part with Bob and never see him and his family again?

Steven laughed. 'Constable Arnold, at your service.' He paused and his voice turned serious. 'I'm glad to see you. I wanted to come round, but I didn't want to make things worse.'

'I had to leave home.'

'What?'

'Keep walking – and keep your voice down. People will stare. Gran chucked me out.'

'That's appalling. You don't deserve it.'

'It's turned out all right. I've moved in with Mrs Cooper – Lizzie's mother, the girl who was killed in the park-keeper's house. A good friend advised me to tell Mrs Cooper the truth about why Gran didn't want me any more, and she doesn't hold it against me. She was very understanding, actually.'

'That's good. You must give me the address. I've been beside myself with worry.'

'I've just been to your house. I hoped to find you off duty, but I was too scared to knock in case you'd told your parents about us and your mum had taken it badly.'

'I haven't told them,' said Steven.

'I know. I saw your mother. She came back from the corner shop while I was standing there.'

'I haven't told anybody.'

'I've told Mrs Cooper and Mrs Grayson, the lady who lodges with her.'

Steven stopped. He didn't touch her, not in public, but she stopped as readily as if his hand had drawn her to a standstill.

'I haven't kept quiet about us out of cowardice or any lack of feeling for you,' said Steven. 'It's too soon after

Letitia for us to announce anything. But there is one person who needs to know.'

Her chin quivered. 'Bob.'

'Until you tell him, I don't know where I stand,' said Steven. 'We had that brief time together, then you changed your mind and I tried to convince myself it had been a mistake on both sides. But I didn't mean it, not deep down. I longed for you to come back to me – and you did.' He half laughed. 'If I'd known that all I had to do was fling myself under a collapsing ceiling, I'd have done it sooner.' His hand moved as if to touch her, then fell away. 'I know this is harder for you, because you've got Bob, and I understand that you need time to think things through and make the right decision. I can wait. I just want you to be sure.'

Joan stood beside Letitia's grave. What she really wanted was to kneel down and feel closer to her sister, but the ground was cold and damp. She tried crouching, but after a while that made her legs ache, so she stood up again, hating to feel distanced. But then, what greater distance could there be than death?

'I've been thinking about how Gran judged Estelle,' she said quietly, 'and the way she brought us up to judge her. I know now from my own experience that life and love aren't always straightforward. I should be ashamed for thinking I'm perhaps starting to understand the mother who abandoned us, but there you are. Is understanding Estelle as good as admitting we're two of a kind? I don't want to resemble any woman who could walk out of her marriage and leave her children behind. And yet here I am, torn between two men, and maybe . . . maybe that was what it was like for her. If so, and if she had chosen to stay with Daddy, nobody would ever have known of her struggle. But she chose to run off with her fancy man and I can never forgive her for that. I've never told anyone this, not even you, but I've always been afraid that I wasn't worth staying for. It happened before I was old enough to remember, yet it hurts as if it happened only yesterday.'

Drat whether it was cold and damp. She was jolly well going to kneel down and take off her gloves so she could touch the earth that lay between her and her sister.

'Do you think Gran wanted us to feel hurt, so we'd hate Estelle for leaving us and making Daddy die of a broken heart? She wants us to be angry with Estelle the same way she is. I'm hurt and I always have been, and now I'm in the position of hurting other people. Gran never wants to see me again. Steven is being unbelievably patient and kind, but it hurts him that I'm struggling to sort out the right thing to do. And the very thought of letting down Bob and the Hubbles makes my heart turn over. But now that Gran has slung me out, I'll have to tell him. I have to make my decision. When did it all get so complicated?'

She didn't say so to Letitia, but the question was there in her head.

Had Estelle asked herself the same thing?

# Chapter Twenty-Nine

'It's good to feel a trace of spring in the air at last.' Bernice positioned her pickaxe under the sleeper, adjusted her weight and heaved. 'I was getting heartily tired of those sharp winds.'

'You and me both,' Mabel agreed. 'The days are getting longer too.' Stepping forward with her spade, she half shovelled, half scraped the stones back underneath where the sleeper had been, using the back of her spade to pack them down before Bernice lowered the sleeper into place again.

For once they were working beneath a blue sky. When had they last done that? But you couldn't be wholeheart-edly pleased about the coming spring, because each fine day brought the threat of invasion further into the realms of possibility. It also meant Harry was more likely to be flying. He was a bomb aimer, which was dangerous work. His place was right inside the nose of the Lancaster, from where he provided information to the navigator and had to climb into the lower section of the nose to release the bombs.

'It might be the back end of winter,' said Bernice as the four of them stopped at the end of the morning's work, 'but it's still parky enough for me to be glad we're not far from a hut today, so at least we're guaranteed a warm fire and a hot drink.'

Bette agreed. 'And the lingering aroma of male sweat. Look, the coltsfoots are out.' She nodded at a clump of flowers that Mabel would have taken for dandelions except for the time of year. 'I never know whether I should call them coltsfeet. It doesn't sound right to say "coltsfoots".'

'Fancy you knowing wildflower names,' said Louise. 'Where I live, there's not a flower to be seen. I reckon I'd have trouble recognising a daisy.'

They approached the lengthmen's hut, which was built from railway sleepers standing up like planks of wood. This hut boasted the ultimate luxury. It had been here long enough that the men had built an extra piece at the side with a bucket in it, which acted as an outside lavatory.

Inside the hut, it was a squeeze, even more so because four blokes were already in there. Mabel had heard about lengthmen who, in this situation, jokingly offered to let the women sit on their laps, but Bernice wouldn't stand for any nonsense of that kind – 'and if you're in my gang, neither must you,' she had made clear to Mabel on her first day. 'Any girl who wants to flirt can go and find another gang to work with, because she won't be welcome in mine.'

Whether Bernice had the authority to chuck a girl out, Mabel didn't know, but she wouldn't like to be in the foreman's shoes if he didn't want to comply with Bernice's wishes.

The four of them removed their heavy overcoats before squatting down on the makeshift benches, which were far from comfortable but an infinite improvement on sitting on the ground in a nippy breeze.

'Shove up, Lou,' Bette said cheerfully. 'For a skinny one, you don't half take up a lot of room.'

Bette dug her elbow into Louise's arm and Louise squealed.

'Eh up!' Bette exclaimed. 'I didn't do it that hard.'

Louise rubbed her arm and flinched.

'Are you all right, love?' Bernice asked.

'It's nowt. Bette took me by surprise, that's all.'

'Give over rubbing your arm, then,' said Bette. 'You're making me look bad.'

They chatted with the men as they tucked into their barm cakes. There was nothing like physical work in the fresh air to give you an appetite.

The four men finished their meal break and a cool breeze rushed inside as they left. When the women finished eating, they used the facilities. You had to have someone with you to stand guard outside in case a chap who had been caught short came along. Leaving Bette and Bernice to guard the door for one another, Mabel returned to the hut for a final warm beside the brazier.

The instant she walked in, Louise pulled down her sleeves, but not before Mabel had seen the bruises on her arms.

'No wonder it hurt when Bette nudged you,' she said. 'What did you do?'

'Nothing.' Louise dragged on her coat, bending her head as she fastened the buttons. 'I fell against the wall in our backyard, that's all.'

'Nasty,' Mabel said sympathetically.

The other two came in.

'Ready, girls?' asked Bernice. 'Back to work and don't leave owt behind.'

Bette, who had a good singing voice, gave them a few lines of the dwarf' 'Heigh-ho' song, but instead of joining in, Mabel frowned. If Louise had fallen against a brick wall, shouldn't she have scrapes and grazes rather than bruises? And what kind of fall was it that left bruises up and down both arms? A sideways fall would have injured one arm. To bruise both suggested a forwards fall, but if you fell forwards and raised your arms to protect yourself, it would be your forearms that took the force of the accident, and Louise had bruises on her upper arms as well. It didn't make sense.

Yes, it did. Louise had lied. She had also made it crystal clear that she had no intention of discussing it.

After some heart-searching, Mabel had a quiet word with Bernice.

'Not again.' Bernice sighed. 'It happens from time to time.'

'What does?' Mabel glanced along the permanent way to where Bette and Louise were working, making sure they were out of earshot.

Bernice leaned on her spade. 'Our Lou's brother is a nasty piece of work and he's not afraid to knock her around, and the rest of the family an' all.'

'Can't something be done?' Mabel whispered.

'Like what? Tell the police? They'd say what happens behind closed doors is a private matter. Even if they did have a word with him, what d'you imagine would happen afterwards, eh? Think he'd mend his ways, do you?'

'Poor Louise.'

'Take my advice, love. Leave well alone. There's nowt you can do.'

It was Mabel's turn to sigh. She glanced at Louise, who, looking scrawny in spite of her big overcoat, was hefting a pickaxe to force the sleeper up for Bette to repack the ballast.

Leave well alone? There was nothing 'well' about it.

The wireless was on in Cordelia's sitting room. On the Home Service, Arnold Richardson was playing works by Marcel Dupré on the organ. Mabel stifled a sigh. Cordelia, wearing spectacles for close work, was doing a piece of intricate embroidery and Mr Masters was reading his newspaper. Mabel had chosen Agatha Christie's *Dumb Witness* from the mahogany bookcase that had fruits and leaves carved into the columns on either side. This was the bookcase Cordelia and her husband used for their novels. The serious stuff – the leather-bound *Encyclopaedia Britannica*, the complete works of Shakespeare – had pride of place inside a glass-fronted bookcase of solid walnut.

Mabel was enjoying the story, but at the same time couldn't help being aware that at home in Kirkland House she might have swung her legs over the arm of the chair. Here, she kept both feet on the carpet, one ankle hooked demurely behind the other, like one of the illustrations in Mumsy's etiquette book.

What would it be like in this house when Emily Masters was at home? She was away at school and was due to sit her School Certificate this summer. A formal photograph on the mantelpiece showed her to be a pretty girl with dark hair. There was another photo in the dining room, showing her in a summer dress at the beach. She was laughing as she pushed her hair out of her eyes on what was apparently a breezy day. Was this the real Emily? Would her presence in the house soften the formal atmosphere or would she sit with her feet demurely side by side?

Mabel glanced at the clock. It was a brass skeleton clock, all its workings on show beneath the elegant glass dome that covered it. The clock stood on four little bun feet on a wooden base, to which a small silver plaque had been fastened. On her first day here, Mabel had read the words on it.

*Presented by his colleagues*
*to Mr Kenneth Masters*
*on the occasion of his marriage.*
*24th January 1920*

Mabel was dying to know what Cordelia thought of not being mentioned by name on an inscribed wedding gift.

Without looking up from her embroidery, Cordelia said, 'I meant to mention to you, Kenneth. I saw Mrs Morgan yesterday. She says they are considering closing up the house and moving somewhere safer for the duration.'

'That's hardly the sort of spirit we want to foster.'

'They're elderly,' Cordelia said mildly. 'It's not as though they'd be shirking war work.'

'One hears of these people sitting out the war in smart hotels in Torquay,' Mr Masters said disapprovingly. 'It's an abuse of privilege, if ever I heard of one.'

'It's interesting how people usually associate privilege with rank and wealth,' Mabel put in.

'With what else would you associate it?' enquired Mr Masters.

'I realise how privileged I am to have loving parents who have always treated me kindly.' Too right. The thought of Louise's brute of a brother had been lurking in her mind.

'That's the most important thing of all,' said Cordelia.

Yes, it was. The need to be with Mumsy and Pops coursed through Mabel. She hadn't been home in yonks, not since Pops had spirited her home to recuperate following that nasty spell of blood poisoning.

'I wonder if I could wangle some leave.'

'The use of the word "wangle",' said Mr Masters, 'suggests you are not entitled to it.'

Did he equate her with those yellow-bellies of private means in Torquay? 'I expect I'm due some holiday. It's just that having been off sick last year, I feel as if I shouldn't take any more time.'

'Nonsense,' said Cordelia. 'You were very poorly.'

'I'd love to see my parents, just for a day or two. Perhaps I could tack on a day either side of my next day off.'

As she pictured it, her heart gave a great leap of anticipation. In that moment, she could think of nothing she wanted more than a warm, tobaccoey hug from Pops to make her feel like his little girl again. Oh, and the bliss of a girly chat with Mumsy, all about Harry. Mumsy would adore that. Mabel smothered a grin. So would she.

She remembered that thought when she saw Harry that Saturday and had to hide her face against his broad chest so as to conceal her delighted blush.

It was St David's Day and Harry had arrived with daffodils for Cordelia. It was a fine afternoon and Mabel felt floaty with happiness as they strolled out together, arm in arm. She was wearing her brimless green felt hat, which showed off her dark brown wavy hair so flatteringly. Harry loved her to wear her hair loose.

She told him of her plan to go up to Annerby, work roster permitting. When Harry didn't immediately reply, she looked up at him, her tummy doing its usual little flip at the sight of his handsome features. All the girls fancied him. Wherever they went, the other girls could barely keep their eyes off him, and the cherry on the cake was his RAF uniform and the badge on his tunic with the letter B and a wing.

'Don't you think it's a good idea?' she prompted when he still said nothing.

'It's grand. I didn't say anything because – well, I hoped you might be about to invite me along.'

This time it was Mabel's turn to delay her reply.

'It would save me turning up unexpectedly like last time,' Harry said lightly. 'After all, you did say I could well be the man for you.'

Mabel felt a flutter of, not uncertainty, but – but what?

Excitement? Elation? Both of those, yes, but something else too. It couldn't be uncertainty – could it?

'It's not as though you come from Manchester and I can pick you up from your parents' house to take you dancing,' said Harry. 'Don't you think your parents ought to get to know me?'

'Of course I do, but I live such a long way from here and taking you there suggests . . .'

'It suggests something serious. Is that a problem for you?'

'No, but . . .' She felt a wild fluttering inside.

'The fact is, I have to go up to Annerby whether you take me with you or not. I respect your parents and I don't want them ever to think anything untoward went on behind their backs. I've told you how serious this relationship is for me. I don't want to push you into anything before you feel ready, but it would be ungentlemanly of me not to ask your parents' permission to court you, and unless you tell me here and now that you don't want to see me again, that's what I'm going to do.'

'I say – Miss Foster!'

Having taken a passenger's suitcases to Left Luggage, Joan was wheeling her empty trolley to meet the Blackpool train. She paused at the sound of Persephone's voice, then altered direction and headed towards her friend. Persephone wasn't allowed to leave her post at the entrance to the platform.

'Are you free to go to the flicks this evening?' Persephone asked. '*The Women* is on at the Rivoli. I could meet you there – unless you're seeing Bob tonight. I know Harry is collecting Mabel this afternoon and they're spending the evening together, and Alison is out with Paul.'

'Sorry,' said Joan, 'I'm not seeing Bob, but I am on first-aid duty.'

'What, again?'

'I volunteered for extra shifts. There's a girl whose boyfriend has got a forty-eight-hour pass, so I said I'd do her stint for her.'

'That was kind of you, especially on a Saturday, and doubly kind if it means you don't get to see your own chap.'

Joan squirmed inwardly. It wasn't kind at all. It was a means of escaping from her tangled situation. She would have enjoyed going to the pictures, though it was just as well that she couldn't. It wasn't only Bob she was keeping secrets from. By pretending all was normal, she was deceiving her friends too.

Leaving Persephone, she returned to her duties. The station wasn't back to normal yet following the blitz, but it was both surprising and reassuring how close to normal it was. The railways and the people who kept them running were amazing. Joan was proud to be part of something that was essential to the war effort. How else could such numbers of troops, and such quantities of goods and munitions, be moved from place to place? She had even heard of pretend tanks being ferried about on flatbed wagons to fool Jerry planes on recce.

On top of all that, they still had to transport ordinary passengers, though the posters reminded everyone to ask themselves *Is Your Journey Really Necessary?* and *If You Must Travel, Travel Light*, accompanied by a cartoon picture of a soldier with all his kit beside the words *I Can't – You Can*. It was all about doing your bit. Sometimes your bit meant tolerating long delays to your journey, but what felt like a long delay to you meant swift passage to a troop train or priority movement to munitions.

And she, Joan Foster, was a tiny cog in this extraordinary machine. In the turmoil of her personal troubles, Victoria Station felt like the one constant in her life. She might have made a huge mess of things since Letitia's death, but her portering job anchored her to something far bigger than herself. She was taking part in something of such scale and significance that it would shape the history of the world for generations to come.

A tiny cog – and a proud one.

Joan rose from her seat with a murmured 'Excuse me' and the man beside her stood up, stepping into the aisle so she could get past. Careful of her footing as the vehicle swayed, she walked down the bus's central aisle and stepped down onto the platform at the back, the cool air rushing past as she held on to the pole in the centre.

The bus drew into the kerb and she stepped onto the pavement as two people in the queue stood aside to let her through. She headed for home – was it cheeky to call Mrs Cooper's house home? She didn't want to take anything for granted. Would Gran get over her fury and ask her to come back to Torbay Road? Ask her – or order her?

Did Gran miss her?

Did she even want to go back? If Gran wanted it, she would have to. It would be expected of her, not just by Gran, but also by Mrs Cooper and Mrs Grayson. There wouldn't be a choice. Would she like to have a choice?

It wasn't far to Mrs Cooper's. There would be something delicious for tea before she went to St Cuthbert's. Mrs Cooper had come to an arrangement with Mrs Grayson whereby they shared the housework and the cooking. Mrs Grayson was a wizard with the saucepans. A spoonful of Bovril here and a dab of Colman's mustard there added depth to the flavour of stew or gravy. Grated apple was mixed with marmalade to make a whipped pudding and bits of cheese were transformed into cheese straws. Gran was a good cook, but she believed in plain meals. Mrs Grayson's skill had come as a revelation.

Joan turned the final corner – and stopped dead.

There, hands in pockets, watching some lads playing marbles in the gutter, was Bob. As if he felt her shocked gaze upon him, he lifted his head and looked at her.

Joan forced herself to walk towards him. Removing his hands from his pockets, Bob left the boys and walked in her direction. Instead of the usual broad smile that made him appear boyishly handsome, his mouth was a straight line. His gaze was on the flagstones more than on her.

He stopped a few paces from her, his expression strained.

'I went round to your gran's. I thought we could have half an hour together before you set off for first-aid duty.' His jaw tightened and he drew a ragged breath. 'She told me about – about you and Steven.'

'Bob, I'm so sorry. I never meant you to find out like that.'

'Well, I did, so what's next?'

'Could we go somewhere and talk?' she suggested desperately. How could she ever have treated this darling man so abominably?

'No,' said Bob, surprising her. Easy-going Bob was always flexible, but not today. 'I can't bear to drag this out a minute longer than necessary. Mrs Foster said all kinds of things about you, horrible things, but I walked away and left her ranting. I couldn't believe what I was hearing. I *don't* believe it. What I believe, what I hope with all my heart, is that you and Steven, somehow, because of Letitia . . . I could understand that.' His gaze searched her face. 'I know how much you loved her. It would tear me apart to lose one of my sisters. So I would understand if that was what happened.'

Her mouth was dry. 'We never planned it. It just ... happened.'

Bob nodded slowly. Then he heaved a deep breath. 'I believe you. If you say that was how it happened, I believe you; and if you promise not to see Steven again, I'll believe that too and I swear I won't hold it against you. What do you say, Joan? Will you promise never to see Steven again?'

# Chapter Thirty

'Excuse me.' Dot stopped a middle-aged man who was all togged up in pinstripes. 'I'm looking for Miss Emery's office.'

'Down to the end and round the corner. You can't miss it.'

'Thank you. Is her name on the door?'

'As I said, you can't miss it.'

He went on his way. Dot resumed walking along the corridor. She passed a few other people, the men smartly suited, the more mature women in plain dresses or sober blouses and skirts with neat jackets or cardigans, the younger ones in pretty colours. Dot was in her Sunday best, an A-line skirt, box-pleated from the knee, and a long-sleeved blouse, together with her best winter-weight cardigan. If only she had a jacket. She had toyed with the idea of buying one for the occasion but had rejected the notion as a criminal waste of money. Though now that the time had come, she thought maybe she should have.

Rounding the corner, she expected another corridor with lines of doors, and that was what it was like a little further down, but here, at this end, was a wider part with a large alcove off the staircase. Part of the alcove was sectioned off, at the back and along the far side by plastered walls, and on this side by wooden panelling with windows. Where the fourth wall and the door ought to have been, there was nothing. The enclosed area contained a desk that butted up against one wall and, against the wood panelling opposite, a small table just big enough for a typewriter. The upright wooden chair at the desk, if turned around, would be in exactly the right place for the sitter to use the typewriter. A second upright chair stood against the wall beside the typewriter table.

At the rear of the space, looking in a battered old cupboard, was Miss Emery.

'This is never your office.' The words were out of Dot's mouth before she could stop herself.

'Welcome to my domain.' Miss Emery's voice was dry.

'Well, I think you ought to have a proper office,' Dot declared. 'You're in charge of all the women, for heaven's sake.'

'Not exactly, but thank you for the thought. I had a proper office until quite recently, but it was needed for other purposes, so here I am.'

'It's disrespectful to all the women to put you here.'

'Please don't adopt that tone in your interview, Mrs Green. It won't go in your favour. Would you like to hang up your coat? I may not have a front wall or a door, but I do possess a couple of pegs.'

Dot shrugged her way out of her trusty old coat, feeling unexpectedly self-conscious after having seen the nicely dressed women on her way here. Miss Emery looked smart in a tweed suit with a discreet row of graduated pearls.

'Please don't take this amiss,' said Miss Emery, 'but Miss Hutchins in Accounts has a rather nice jacket that I happen to know she's wearing today and I think it might suit you.'

'Nay, you're never going to ask her for a lend.'

'It's important to appear as smart as possible and I don't mean to offend, but a jacket is more likely to give the right impression. Excuse me.'

Miss Emery disappeared before Dot could stop her. Well! Just when she had been trying to feel good about herself an' all. Every man and his dog might be mucking in and doing their bit for the war effort, but when all was said and done, she was still a working-class housewife.

When Miss Emery returned, she had the jacket over her arm. She held it up and Dot noted the silky lining before she allowed herself to be helped into it. It was a tad tight across the shoulders, but that didn't matter. It was well made and she didn't need a mirror to tell her it improved her appearance.

Miss Emery consulted her wristwatch. 'Let me tell you what to expect. You'll be interviewed by two gentlemen: Mr Mortimer, whom you may remember from your first day, and Mr Prescott, who is our liaison with the Ministry of Labour. I have permission to be present and I can help you to answer their questions.'

That came as a surprise. 'I thought your job would be to put forward my side of it.'

'Unfortunately not.'

'Oh good, you're still here.' It was Cordelia. 'I was afraid we might have missed you.'

Looking willowy and elegant in her wine-coloured coat and grey felt hat with its upswept brim, Cordelia was accompanied by a severe-looking gentleman some years her senior. He wore a grey wool overcoat, silk scarf and a dark grey trilby with a petersham band. He was carrying a leather briefcase.

'May I introduce my husband, Mr Masters,' said Cordelia. 'Kenneth, these ladies are Miss Emery and Mrs Green, whom I've told you about.'

'How do you do?' Mr Masters raised his hat. 'You'll excuse me for being blunt, but I'm a busy man and I don't have a lot of time. My wife has prevailed upon me to assist Mrs Green, so I'd be obliged if we could expedite matters.'

Prevailed upon? Expedite? Crikey, his tongue was even fancier than Cordelia's. Honestly, who said 'prevailed upon'? What was wrong with plain old asking?

'I'm sorry.' Miss Emery looked from Mr Masters to Cordelia and back again. 'I don't understand.'

'I'm a solicitor, Miss Emery.' Putting down his briefcase, Mr Masters unbuttoned his overcoat and fiddled with the buttons of his jacket. 'Mrs Green is my client for the next . . .' he produced a silver watch from the small pocket in his waistcoat,'. . . fifty-five minutes at the most, which is why I should be grateful to get matters under way immediately.'

'The matter is already under way,' said Miss Emery. 'Mrs Green hasn't been sent for yet.'

'I, for one, will not wait to be summoned. My presence is required throughout the proceedings.' Mr Masters removed his hat, coat and scarf, thrusting them into Cordelia's arms. 'Would you mind, my dear?' He picked up his briefcase. 'Kindly take us to the relevant office, Miss Emery. Mrs Green, if you're ready?'

Miss Emery took them along a couple of corridors and up a flight of stairs. She knocked on a door and opened it.

'Excuse me—' she began.

'We aren't ready for you yet,' said a man's voice from inside.

Mr Masters reached past Miss Emery to open the door further. 'Please enter, ladies. Good morning, gentlemen. My name is Masters, from Wardle, Grace and Masters, a long-established firm which started life as Grace, Wardle and Grace in the last century. I am here to represent Mrs Green in this matter.'

The men's mouths dropped open. Mr Mortimer, in

pinstripes and a bow tie, sat behind the desk while another gentleman, who must be Mr Prescott, was seated beside the desk, facing into the room. With his back to the new-comers was a third man. He turned round in his chair to look at them. It was Mr Weaver, the porter who had wit-nessed Dot's humiliation at Edie's hands.

'This is highly irregular,' said Mr Mortimer.

'I agree, sir,' said Mr Masters. 'It is deeply irregular that my client has been excluded from these proceedings, even though it is her good name that is under discussion.' He addressed Miss Emery. 'Might I trouble you to organise some more chairs?' Then he looked at the two men sitting in judgement. 'Perhaps you would kindly bring me up to date with what has transpired thus far.'

Mr Mortimer and Mr Prescott gawped at him and then at one another. Dot realised she was gawping an' all and snapped her mouth shut.

'Mrs Green,' said Mr Mortimer, 'you have a solicitor?'

'Indeed she does, sir.' Mr Masters waved a hand in Mr Weaver's direction. 'What are you doing here, my man?'

Mr Prescott cleared his throat. 'Thank you for your assistance, Weaver. You may go.'

As the porter left, Mr Mortimer, possibly trying to gain control of the situation, introduced himself and his col-league. Miss Emery reappeared, followed by a lad carrying a couple of chairs.

'If they could be placed over there, please, for the ladies.' Mr Masters took the seat Mr Weaver had vacated in front of the desk and opened his briefcase to take out a note-book and fountain pen. 'What stage has this enquiry reached, gentlemen?'

The two men exchanged glances before Mr Prescott spoke.

'We have heard from Mr Bonner—'

'Ah yes, the train guard. He dislikes having a woman working on his train, but this is wartime. I personally dislike having my wife dirtying her hands cleaning railway lamps, but, as I say, this is wartime.'

'Whatever Mr Bonner's opinion of having women working on the railways, the issue today concerns Mrs Green's, um, personal conduct. An incident occurred in the presence of colleagues and passengers, who were deeply embarrassed when—'

'I believe we are all au fait with what transpired,' cut in Mr Masters. 'From whom have you heard thus far?'

'Mr Bonner, the train guard who is directly responsible for Mrs Green's performance in the workplace; Mr Chapman, the ticket inspector, a senior figure; and Mr Weaver, one of the station porters.'

'All of whom were, no doubt, suitably shocked at the accusation levelled against my client. Tell me. Has any member of the public made a complaint?'

'No, sir,' said Mr Mortimer.

'I'm pleased to hear it. It injects an element of good taste into the matter.'

'An embarrassing and distressing matter,' said Mr Prescott, 'and one that does not in any respect conform to the way we wish our passengers to view us.'

'Precisely. Do you have a rule against members of staff getting along with one another?'

'Of course not.'

'Why, then, are you pursuing my client when the person at fault is the silly female who caused the scene? What grounds do you have for taking evidence from three men who, I assume, are not in favour of allowing women to work on the railways, and not from the one gentleman in the case who might be supposed to be on my client's side?'

Dot almost jumped to her feet, but had to content

herself with leaning forwards. 'I specially said I wouldn't have Mr Thirkle involved. It wasn't his fault and he doesn't know this is happening today.'

Mr Masters heaved a sigh that rumbled with annoyance. 'God preserve us. Gentlemen, is this Mr Thirkle on duty today? I insist upon his being summoned this instant, so that this matter may be drawn to a conclusion.'

'There's no need,' said Mr Mortimer. 'I have already spoken privately to him.'

'But . . .' Something inside Dot slumped. She desperately hadn't wanted Mr Thirkle to be involved.

'Kindly desist, Mrs Green,' ordered Mr Masters. 'I am acting in your best interests.'

'Mr Thirkle confirmed that his daughter got hold of the wrong end of the stick,' said Mr Mortimer.

'And yet here is my client, embroiled in what I very much hope is *not* a disciplinary interview.'

'We have a duty to investigate all complaints, sir,' sniffed Mr Prescott.

'It is important,' added Mr Mortimer, 'that those men who believe it is ill-advised to have women working on the railways feel their concerns are taken seriously.'

'Quite so,' said Mr Masters. 'It seems to me quite clear that Mrs Green has not, after all, behaved in an inappropriate manner. Are we in agreement on that point?'

'Indeed, sir,' said Mr Mortimer.

'And my client may leave this room without a stain upon her character?'

'She may.'

Mr Masters replaced his notebook and pen inside his briefcase and snapped the brass lock shut. He rose to his feet.

'Thank you for your time, gentlemen. Ladies, shall we depart?'

325

'I'll find someone to take the chairs back,' murmured Miss Emery and hurried away.

Dot stopped in the corridor as Mr Masters shut the door behind them. She opened her mouth to thank him, but he forestalled her.

'Mrs Green, you are a foolish woman and you have got off more lightly than you deserve. Why my wife was determined that I should assist you, I have no idea, but please listen carefully to what I am about to say. In future, you shall not make any attempt to impinge on my wife's charitable nature and you shall never again expect to benefit from my professional services. Do I make myself clear? In future, kindly keep your grubby peccadilloes to yourself.'

# Chapter Thirty-One

Mabel couldn't stop thinking of what Harry had said. 'It would be ungentlemanly of me not to ask your parents' permission to court you, and unless you tell me here and now that you don't want to see me again, that's what I'm going to do.'

'You know I can't say that,' she had replied as vibrant pulses jumped beneath her skin. 'But—'

'No buts.' He had feathered tiny kisses over her face and across her lips, drawing little gasps of eagerness from her. 'I'm crazy about you, you know that, but I'm not so crazy that I've lost sight of what's right and proper. Your parents deserve to know that this isn't a fleeting wartime romance. You want them to think well of me, don't you?'

'Of course,' she breathed, 'but—'

He stopped her with a kiss. 'That rotten word again. I don't want to hear it. Every time you say it, I'll be obliged to kiss you.'

'Really?' Delight radiated urgently through her body. 'In that case: but, but, but . . .'

That had been last weekend. A few days had passed since then and Harry couldn't come to Manchester this coming weekend, which, much as she missed him, was probably a good thing, because it allowed her more time to make up her mind. Should she take him to Annerby with her? She hated herself for hesitating. She adored Harry, but it was such a big step to take.

After some thought, she vowed to share her woes with

her friends. They were meeting in the buffet that evening, as a result of urgent messages written in their notebook about poor Dot's interview that day.

*Even if you can come for only 10 mins, please come,* Cordelia had written and she had listed their names underneath – well, all except Colette's – for them to tick if they could attend. There was now a line of ticks down the page, and at the bottom, Colette, bless her, had added her name with a tick beside it.

That evening, when Mabel, Bette, Louise and Bernice arrived back at Victoria, they made their usual beeline for the Ladies to use the cubicle with the Out of Order sign on the door and check their faces and comb their hair. Bette and Louise often spent the day wearing rollers beneath their turbans.

With a hasty goodbye to her gang, Mabel hurried to the buffet, where Persephone and Alison were pushing two tables together to accommodate everyone. The three of them took turns to guard their tables and fetch cups of tea. Soon the others appeared, Dot arriving last, accompanied by Cordelia, as the rest watched anxiously.

'It's good news,' said Cordelia before she and Dot sat down.

The anxious expressions vanished, replaced by smiles and relief.

'Congrats,' said Persephone.

'From all of us,' Colette added.

'What happened?' asked Alison.

Dot looked emotional and her voice wavered. 'You tell them,' she instructed Cordelia.

'Very well.' Cordelia smiled. 'You may recall that my husband is a solicitor. He kindly escorted Dot into the interview room to ensure that she had someone to speak up for her effectively.'

'Aye,' said Dot. 'He did that all right.'

'And you were let off?' said Alison.

'It wasn't a case of being let off,' said Cordelia. 'Dot had done nothing wrong in the first place.'

'Anyroad,' said Dot, 'it's all over and done with. Please let's talk about summat else – though, before we do, I want to thank you all for being here. You don't know what it means to me, especially seeing you, Colette. I know you'll have had to make a special arrangement with your husband to pick you up later than usual.'

Colette's fair skin took on a rosy flush. 'Whatever today's outcome had been, I wanted to be here to give you my support.'

Dot pretended to slap Colette's wrist. 'Less of that. I told you – we're not talking about that any more. Has anyone got any good news?'

They glanced at one another. Then Joan spoke, and was it Mabel's imagination or did she take a deep breath?

'I've got something to tell you. I've – I've moved. I've left home.'

'You dark horse!' Persephone exclaimed. 'Where have you moved to?'

Joan closed her eyes for a moment. 'I'm sorry. The way I phrased that was rather misleading. Yes, I've moved, but it wasn't my decision. It was Gran's. She wanted me to go.'

'Why?' asked Alison.

'And you still haven't said where,' Colette added.

'I'm living at Mrs Cooper's.'

'Mrs Cooper's?' A flash of envy made Mabel's heart beat harder as she relived that moment when she had realised how lucky Mrs Grayson was to live there.

'Mrs Cooper's?' A smile transformed Colette's face. 'In that case, I might bump into you. I visit her once a week.'

'Do you?' Mabel asked.

'I have done ever since Lizzie . . .'

'You're a good lass,' said Dot. 'I drop in on her now and then, but not nearly as often as I ought.'

Colette smiled at Joan. 'I probably missed you because of your shifts.'

'So what took you to Mrs Cooper's, Joan?' asked Alison.

'It's because . . .' Joan's chin dipped.

'Go on, chick.' Dot's voice was quiet. 'You're among friends.' She looked round the table. 'Listen to what Joan has to say and then think before you say owt.'

Alison looked at Dot. 'You already know about this.'

'Let Joan speak,' said Dot.

'I've got myself into a sticky situation.' Joan kept her gaze fixed on the tabletop. 'You all know I've been seeing Bob since last summer, and – and Letitia had a boyfriend called Steven. Well, a while back, Steven and I grew closer, because of our shared grief, I suppose, and—'

'One thing led to another,' Alison burst out. 'Oh, Joan.'

'I've shocked you.' Joan raised her eyes.

'Well – yes,' said Alison. 'I never had you down as the flighty sort.'

'That's because Joan isn't flighty,' said Dot. 'This happened because of losing her sister.'

'Gran was shocked when she found out,' said Joan. 'She made me pack my bags.'

'And Joan is stopping with Mrs Cooper,' said Dot, 'until such time as she and her gran make up.'

'Don't hold your breath,' Joan murmured.

'Does this mean you've finished with Bob,' asked Persephone, 'and you're seeing Steven instead?'

Joan's eyes were dark with misery. 'I've been seeing Steven on the sly and stringing Bob along. There. Now you know.'

'I can appreciate how both of you being so unhappy could bring you and Steven together,' said Cordelia, 'but it's artificial. You can see that, can't you? You mustn't lose Bob because of it.'

'You've always said such wonderful things about Bob,' said Mabel, 'and about his family.'

'I know, and all those things are still true,' said Joan. 'But then there's Steven.'

'Then you must tell Bob,' said Cordelia.

Joan shook her head. 'No need. Gran already told him.'

'Crikey,' Persephone murmured.

'What does Bob have to say about it?' asked Colette.

'And Steven?' added Alison.

'They want me to choose and they're both prepared to give me time to sort things out. In a way, I wish one of them had lost his rag and marched out of my life for ever. Then the matter would have been settled.'

'We'll have none of that, thank you,' said Cordelia. 'It's better to make your own choice, no matter how difficult.'

'You need time to mull things over, chick,' said Dot. 'It'll all come out in the wash.'

Joan smiled tremulously. 'I hope so.' She looked at Mabel. 'Has Mrs Hubble said anything to you?'

'Not a word,' Mabel hastened to assure her. 'Maybe she doesn't know.'

'It would be like Bob not to tell his family,' said Joan. 'He'll be hoping there's never any reason for them to know.'

'Which is precisely why you should stay with him,' said Persephone. 'He takes such good care of you.'

'That's enough, Persephone,' said Cordelia. 'Joan has to decide for herself.'

Alison looked uncomfortable. 'I shouldn't have been sharp with you,' she told Joan. 'You're right: I was shocked.

It's so completely different to my relationship with Paul. Neither of us would ever . . .'

'Quite,' said Dot. 'Now that Joan's been brave enough to tell us the reason behind her moving house, I suggest we leave her alone and talk about other things. We can talk about Joan's troubles – if she wants us to – another time.'

'Exactly so,' said Cordelia, 'but before we move on, I'd like to add, on behalf of us all, Joan, that if you need a shoulder or a sounding board, the rest of us are here to support you – aren't we, girls?'

Mabel joined in the chorus of assent, pleased to see how Joan's face glowed.

'Thank you,' said Joan. 'Dot told me I should confide in the group and she was right.'

'I always am, love,' Dot quipped, causing smiles all round. 'Make sure you tell my husband and daughters-in-law, if you see them.'

Joan's courage in confiding in them spurred Mabel to share her own situation. In a jokey voice, she asked, 'Do you want to hear about my love life?'

'Goodness me,' Cordelia murmured, 'do you think they've put something in the water?'

'Harry hasn't proposed, has he?' Alison demanded.

'No, but I'm going to visit my family soon and he wants to come too.'

There was a breathless silence around the table as her friends took in the meaning of this.

'What do you all think?' asked Mabel.

'Don't ask me,' said Joan. She managed to laugh as she said it, but the look in her eyes was bleak. 'I'm the last person to give advice about relationships.'

'Count yourself lucky to have a boyfriend who's so keen,' said Alison. 'That's what every girl wants.'

Persephone's beautiful features settled into a serious

expression. She looked straight into Mabel's eyes. 'I don't want to sound morbid, but might your reluctance be linked to having lost your best friend? Her death hurt you deeply. Are you trying to hold back from Harry as a way of preventing yourself from possibly getting hurt again?' She shrugged. 'Sorry. I don't mean to cast a shadow.'

'Don't forget that you haven't known him all that long,' said Dot.

'That doesn't matter if he's the right one,' said Cordelia.

Words swirled in Mabel's head from a conversation a few weeks ago when they were talking about some couples madly taking the plunge while others waited. *'If you don't grab your chance while you can . . .'* That was what she had said. Now that she had the opportunity to take this big romantic step, was she wrong to hesitate? If she didn't take Harry with her to Annerby, and then the worst happened and he didn't come home from his next mission . . .

'In any case,' said Colette, 'you can't truly know someone until you're married and you live with them.'

Mabel laughed. 'That sounds ominous. Anyway, just because I'm thinking of taking Harry home with me doesn't mean there should be any expectations. He won't be asking for my hand in marriage.'

'That's a specious argument,' Cordelia stated flatly. 'Of course it will raise expectations. It would be the modern equivalent of a Victorian understanding.'

'Victorian understandings are just that – Victorian,' said Alison.

'Don't be so sure,' said Dot. 'You can't stop people having expectations and those old understandings were a prelude to marriage.'

'Can we please stop talking about understandings?'

said Mabel. 'You're making me feel as if I'm going to be pushed into something.'

Cordelia leaned forward. 'You mustn't let that happen,' she said seriously. 'This is your future we're talking about and you're right to give it careful consideration. It doesn't matter what any of us says or thinks. You have to decide for yourself and feel sure that it's the right thing.'

Surrounded by murmurs of agreement, Mabel felt her doubts fall away, to be replaced by calm confidence. She knew what to do. She wanted her parents to understand that her relationship with Harry was serious. She had never told them about Gil. Well, that relationship, such as it was, hadn't lasted long and it had been complicated. But that made it all the more important for her to share this new happiness. She wanted to be open and honest. She wanted to include Mumsy and Pops in this important part of her life.

She blew out a breath, feeling shaky as excitement rippled through her.

'Thank you all. You've helped me decide what to do. I'm going to invite Harry to accompany me to Annerby.'

'And if your mother immediately rushes to her favourite milliner?' asked Cordelia.

'If Mumsy buys a new hat, I shall look the other way.' A smiled tugged at Mabel's lips. She tried to resist, but then gave in and let the smile spread across her face. 'For now, at any rate.'

'Now that Dot's interview is over,' said Cordelia, 'there's one more thing we need to discuss. It's time we made a plan to catch the food-dump thief.' She looked at Dot. 'I hope you don't think I'm sticking my nose in.'

'Not at all,' said Dot. 'I'm glad you brought it up. It makes me feel I haven't pushed you into it.'

'There's only one way to catch the thief,' said Alison, 'and that's to keep watch.'

'We can't do that non-stop,' said Dot.

'Presumably the thief comes at night,' said Alison. 'During the day, there are lengthmen and lampmen around, and trains going past. I'm not saying the thefts couldn't happen in daylight, but why take the chance?'

'That makes sense,' said Joan. 'We have to be there at night.'

'What, every night?' asked Mabel. 'I suppose if we all took turns . . .'

'No,' Dot said. 'Nobody does owt alone. Keeping safe is the most important thing.'

'Let's agree on a minimum number of people,' said Cordelia.

'Two?' suggested Alison.

'Four,' said Dot. 'That's safer.'

Persephone looked dubious. 'Four of us, all available on the same night? It's difficult enough meeting here after work.'

'Four,' said Dot in a voice that brooked no argument.

'That automatically cuts down the number of nights we can do,' said Joan.

'We'll have to take that chance,' said Cordelia. 'If we can manage a couple of times a week, or even once a week, in the end we'll be there on the night something happens. I suggest we don't stay all night. It'll be easier to make up a foursome if it's only until midnight or one in the morning.'

'And we'll need excuses for being out that late,' said Alison. 'Dot, Joan and Persephone can pretend to have late shifts. I'll say I'm helping out with paperwork at our first-aid depot, or something of the kind.'

Mabel couldn't resist. She gave Cordelia a cheeky glance. 'I'll fob off my landlady with some story or other.'

Colette shifted uncomfortably. 'I hate to let you down, but I really can't manage this. Tony would never let me go out at night in case of an air raid.'

'That's all right, love,' Dot said. 'We all know he dotes on you, and quite right an' all. This is a nasty business to be involved in and I'm sorry to have brought it on everyone. If any of you want to drop out, that's fine.'

They all looked at one another. No one spoke. Beside Dot, poor Colette bit her lip and dropped her gaze.

'We're all behind you, Dot,' said Cordelia.

'Aye, and thank you all,' said Dot. She reached for Colette's hand and gave it a squeeze. 'Don't feel bad, chick. You're lending – what's that fancy expression, Cordelia?'

'Lending moral support.'

'So don't you go thinking you're less important than the rest of us,' said Dot, and she received a watery smile. 'We'll have to do our lookout duty outside the shed, not inside. We don't want to get caught inside by the thief.'

'It'll be jolly cold outside,' said Alison.

'It'll be jolly cold inside that shed an' all, if that makes you feel any better,' said Dot.

'If we see the thief—' Cordelia began.

'You mean "when",' said Persephone.

'Very well. When we see the thief, two of us should keep watch while the other two cycle to the nearest signal box to raise the alarm.'

'The signalman can ring the police,' said Alison.

Joan shook her head. 'I know a bit about signal boxes from Bob. They do have telephones, but they don't connect with the outside world, only with the line controller.'

'So the signalman will have to ask the line controller to alert the police,' said Mabel.

'How do we stop the thief getting away while we're waiting for the boys in blue?' asked Cordelia. 'Bearing in mind that we don't want to put ourselves at risk.'

Inspiration struck Mabel and she sat up straight. 'There are bits and bobs lying around outside the shed, including old sleepers. If we shift some of them along near to the outside privy, the two who stay behind can "walk" them into the privy and barricade the inner door. I know sleepers are heavy, but if they were dumped outdoors a long time ago and they've been there in all weathers, they'll have got a bit worn down and that'll make them lighter.'

'Good idea,' said Dot. 'While we're at it, we can use some sleepers to build a bench of sorts for us to sit on while we're on watch.'

'She'll have us building a hut next,' teased Persephone.

'With gingham curtains at the windows,' added Alison.

'And roses round the door,' said Joan.

'Cheek!' Dot pretended to take umbrage, but after a moment her face split into a huge smile. After the strain she had been under when her interview was hanging over her, it felt good to smile again. 'You know what, girls? With friends like you to back me up, that thief doesn't stand a chance.'

# Chapter Thirty-Two

Talk about déjà vu. The last time Joan had been in this vicinity was during the Christmas Blitz, when the public shelter in Erskine Street had been damaged by the blast from a bomb and yet, against all the odds, every single person had emerged alive from the overcrowded building. But that was where the déjà vu ended.

This time it was houses nearby that had been hit and the chances were high that there would be casualties. The simple fact that a Withington first-aid party was here was evidence of that certainty. The Hulme first-aid depot, stretched thin tonight, had put in a call for assistance.

The night air was dense with the drone of aeroplane engines and the sharp bursts of ack-ack fire, searchlight beams criss-crossing the black skies. The Luftwaffe was back with a vengeance and had Manchester and Salford once more in its sights. Before Joan's party had set off from St Cuthbert's, a telephone report had already been received detailing the damage to warehouses and other buildings, shipping, railways and rolling stock along the Manchester Ship Canal.

A tin-hatted ARP warden appeared beside Mr Brannock's motor.

'First aid? Rutland Street and Erskine Street have taken direct hits. I'll show you the way.'

Mr Brannock turned to his party. 'Mr Flynn and Miss Bradshaw, help in Erskine Street. Mr Umber and Miss Foster, we'll go to Rutland Street.'

As they hurried into Rutland Street, rescue workers were clambering on the rubble, moving slowly, testing each footstep before transferring their weight to it. In a series of black silhouettes, a human chain shifted clumps of brickwork and lengths of timber down to the debris-strewn pavement. There was something hypnotic about it, but Joan pulled herself away to tend to a couple of walking wounded.

At last she was called forward to assist with the casualties. A fierce alertness pumped through her. She was going to help these people survive this terrible incident. She didn't want any other family to suffer the never-ending sorrow that she and Gran had to live with every single day.

But there was almost nothing she and the other first-aiders could do. There was one, just one, surviving casualty in each house. The gentleman from number 5, who an hour ago had been a married man, was now a widower, and his poor neighbour would wake up in hospital to the news that the other three people inside number 7 had perished. One of them, Joan saw as she tenderly covered his face, was a lad of no more than fourteen.

'There's nothing more we can do here,' said Mr Brannock. 'Let's go to Erskine Street.'

Halfway there, they met up with Mabel and Mr Flynn.

'Report,' said Mr Brannock.

'Four—' Mabel started to say.

'Four rescued alive from the debris,' interrupted Mr Flynn.

'Thanks, Flynn. I'll see if the local first-aid party requires further assistance. If not, we'll head back to the depot.'

'Lucky Erskine Street,' Mabel said to Joan. 'First, all those people survived that business in the blitz – and everyone survived tonight as well.'

'Tonight isn't over yet, Miss Bradshaw,' said Mr Flynn.

He was right. Even though the Luftwaffe disappeared three times and the all-clear sounded on each occasion, it wasn't long before the warning sirens wailed into the night again. When the all-clear sounded at two thirty on Thursday morning, Joan and Mabel shared a glance. Was it really over this time?

'It's a good job tonight wasn't chosen for keeping watch on the railway shed,' said Mabel. 'Imagine being pinned down out there during a raid.'

'Don't even think about it,' Joan whispered, suppressing a shudder.

Since dreaming up their scheme last week, they had between them managed a single night of keeping watch. It should have been two nights, one of which would have been Friday, but there had been daytime raids that day, so they had cancelled their arrangements, only for the night to be air-raid-free.

There were no further sirens tonight. As six o'clock approached, most of the rescue teams were back inside St Cuthbert's. They started putting things away and gathering their belongings.

Mr Wilson called Joan over.

'A private word, if I may, Miss Foster. You live in Chorlton, don't you? Which road?'

'I don't live there any more. I've moved to Whalley Range.'

'Indeed? You haven't furnished me with your new address. That was remiss of you.'

Joan's chest felt tight. 'Has something happened in Chorlton?'

'Yes, but if you no longer live there . . .'

'My gran is still there. Where did the incident happen?'

'Where does your grandmother live?'

340

'Torbay Road.'

'Ah.'

One simple word, hardly a word at all really. A sour taste filled Joan's mouth and throat.

'I'm sorry to inform you, Miss Foster, that there were direct hits to both Dartmouth Road and Torbay Road during the night.'

Joan had never pedalled harder in her life. As she came to the end of Torbay Road, she stumbled from her bicycle, fear coursing through her, tightening her shoulders. The damage was on her side of the road, but – thank heaven above – further down from her house. Relief brought her faltering to a halt. One hand fell away from the handlebar and she pressed it to her chest. It might be wicked to be grateful that it wasn't her house, but that didn't stop gratitude turning her giddy.

Mr Cleeves, their local ARP warden, left the men working on the stricken house and came to meet her. Before the war, Gran, who was no spring chicken herself, used to refer to Mr Cleeves as an old man, but the war seemed to have given him a new lease of life.

'How bad is it, Mr Cleeves?' Joan asked.

'Peter Goodyear has copped it, poor blighter, and Ida and Barbara Teer from Dartmouth Road have been killed an' all. Eh, you always hope it'll never happen on your own patch. Quite a few have been taken to hospital.'

'From here, you mean?' Joan gazed along her road.

'Aye, and from Barlow Moor Road and Wilbraham Road and others. I'm sorry to say Mrs Foster is among them.'

'Gran!' Joan exclaimed. 'But our house . . .' It looked intact.

'She was up the road with old Mrs Rigby, who was on her deathbed. Her granddaughter is expecting a happy event, so when the siren sounded, Mrs Foster and Mrs O'Leary sent young Mrs Carver down the Andy while they stopped with the old lady.'

'Through the air raids?' Daft question. Of course they had stayed. Gran was an old bag in many ways, but it was easy to imagine her staying put in those circumstances. 'Was Mrs Rigby's house hit?'

'Nay, lass. Mrs O'Leary told me she passed away peaceful like and they were going to leave the laying out for the morning. She and your gran headed for home – and that was when the bomb dropped.'

'Gran,' Joan whispered. 'Is she . . .'

'I don't know anything more than that, lass. Mrs O'Leary's fine, but your gran was taken away by ambulance.'

Weighed down by fear, Joan turned her bicycle round and, putting one foot on a pedal, pushed herself onto the seat. Mr Cleeves called after her, but she was already cycling away. All she knew was that her conduct had upset Gran dreadfully and she had to get to Withington Hospital as quickly as she could. Back she went down Barlow Moor Road, past the terminus, the park, Southern Cemetery.

When she reached the hospital, she propped her bike against a wall and dashed inside. There were others queuing, waiting for information. Some hovered beside the noticeboards, waiting for lists of names to be posted. The clerks behind the counter looked tired and drained.

When it was her turn, Joan failed to keep her voice steady as she asked, 'Has Mrs Foster of Torbay Road been brought in?'

The clerk consulted her lists. 'Nobody by that name, I'm afraid.'

'I was told she'd been taken to hospital.'

'Not Withington – unless . . .' the clerk lifted her

eyebrows,'. . . she had no identification. We do have a couple of unidentified casualties.'

'That wouldn't be her. Gran has all the family papers in her handbag and she keeps that with her at all times. I'll try the Infirmary.'

At the Royal Infirmary, Joan's heart increased its pace at the sight of the damage that the building had suffered during the Christmas Blitz, when a delayed-action bomb had done its worst.

Once more, she queued up for information.

'Do you have Mrs Beryl Foster of Torbay Road?'

She tried to read upside down as the clerk's finger ran down the list of casualties.

The clerk looked up. 'I can't see her name. Where is Torbay Road?'

'Chorlton.'

'On-Medlock?'

'Chorlton-cum-Hardy.'

The clerk pushed the list aside. 'She wouldn't have been brought here. She'd have gone to Withington.'

'I've already tried there.'

'I take it Mrs Foster was at home last night?'

'Yes. The ARP warden told me she'd been taken to hospital.'

'Then I can only suggest you try Withington again. She definitely wouldn't have been brought here.' The clerk spoke with finality and looked beyond Joan to the next anxious enquirer.

Joan returned to Withington. Her nerves were in shreds, but she was more determined than ever to find Gran. Gran's name was late being added to the casualty list, that was all. It would be certain to be on there by this time.

But it wasn't.

She was stumped. What next? All she could do was wait. She hovered close to the noticeboards, where others peered at the lists.

'When will the next list be put up?' a man demanded.

'I can't say, sir. When it's ready.'

The man tore off his trilby, practically crushing it between his hands.

The clerk leaned across to murmur to her colleague, who nodded. The first clerk quietly slipped out from behind the counter. Joan took a chance and followed her.

Upstairs, the clerk disappeared through a ward's double doors. Joan caught a glimpse of men in the beds lining both sides and hung back. Soon the clerk reappeared. The next ward she entered was a women's ward. Joan waited for her to come out and go on her way.

Then, her insides fluttering, she pushed open one of the doors and went in. There was an office immediately inside. A nurse looked up from her place at the desk, her eyes turning flinty.

Joan spoke quickly. 'I'm sorry to barge in, but I'm desperate to find my grandmother. She's not on the lists here or at the Infirmary.'

The nurse rose to her feet and walked round the desk, apparently intent upon ejecting her.

'Mrs Beryl Foster,' said Joan.

'We have no one by that name, and no unidentified patients either. Please leave.'

She placed one hand on Joan's sleeve, the other on the door. Joan looked down the twin lines of beds on castors – and saw Gran.

'There she is!'

'Wait,' the nurse ordered, but Joan slipped free and hurried to where Gran lay unconscious, her eyes shut, her arms neatly by her sides.

On top of the bedside table was Gran's handbag. Joan snatched it up and snapped open the catch, ignoring the purse and the keys as she felt for Gran's identity card. There wasn't time to scrabble about for it; the nurse had paused to gather reinforcements and now three nurses headed her way. Joan pulled out Gran's old brown envelopes. Each was labelled in her writing. *Letitia, Joan, Donald.* That was unexpected, though it shouldn't be, really. Donald was Daddy. The last one said: *Self.*

Opening it, Joan removed the certificates. It was the marriage certificate she needed, the proof of Gran's surname. It was the first one she unfolded and what she glimpsed in the instant before the nurse twitched it from her fingers turned her cold, right to the centre of her being.

'I told you,' snapped the nurse. 'Now, are you going to hand me the patient's possessions and leave quietly or should I send for the police?'

Joan felt her face go slack with shock. She had caught one detail, just one, from Gran's marriage certificate, and that word, that name was frozen onto the surface of her mind.

Gran's married name was Henshaw.

# Chapter Thirty-Three

Dot was accustomed to crossing paths with staff and passengers from all over the place. If there was owt to be heard, she heard it. Lives had been lost last night in Manchester and Salford. How many, she didn't know, but she had formed the impression – and please God, let it be correct – that the toll was nothing like it had been on the two nights of the Christmas Blitz. Not that that would be of any consolation to the families left behind, newly stunned by grief and possibly homeless an' all, forced to think about what to do next when what they really needed was to concentrate on their bereavement.

Perhaps she ought to be more concerned about the damage to the docks along the Manchester Ship Canal, which would impede the war effort. Nevertheless, it was the deaths of ordinary citizens that touched her the most, her spirit raging against lives cut short, her heart aching for the folk left behind. The trains kept running, no matter what, and in its own way that was a comfort, a sign of determination and fortitude and ordinary, everyday life. Dot went to Southport and back, helping passengers and unloading and taking on parcels at every stop along the way. Before she had come to work today, she had dashed round to make sure Pammy's and Sheila's houses were still standing, which meant she could concentrate on her job without being torn in two with worry.

When she had loaded her second trolley of the day in Victoria's parcels office, it was Mr Thirkle who opened the

346

gate to admit her onto the platform. Dot experienced a flutter of nerves. She hadn't set eyes on him since before that excruciating interview last week when her morals had been under discussion. She wasn't sure how she felt now about having had help from Mr Masters. He had steamrollered the interview along, for which she had been profoundly grateful at the time, but his parting shot had shocked her, not to mention undermined her self-esteem.

'Afternoon, Mrs Green,' said Mr Thirkle, touching the peak of his cap to her.

She stopped her trolley. 'I'm sorry you got roped into that business with Mr Mortimer and Mr Prescott. I never meant for you to be involved.'

'I was pleased to be of service.' Mr Thirkle's kind eyes were grave.

Mr Bonner marched past. 'When you've quite finished socialising, Mrs Green,' he said with a curl of his lip.

Heat stung Dot's face. 'Coming, Mr Bonner.'

With an effort, she got her trolley moving again, trundling it down to the platform and into position beside the guard's van. She wanted to set the record straight with Mr Bonner, but it would be a good idea to load the parcels first.

'Mr Bonner,' she said, steeling herself when the time came, 'I'd like to remind you that Mr Mortimer and Mr Prescott found nothing wrong with my conduct.'

Mr Bonner's face assumed an expression of superiority. 'They are entitled to their opinion, Mrs Green, and so am I.'

With a heroic effort, Dot refrained from casting her gaze up to the ceiling. What a jolly journey this was going to be.

When it was almost time for the train to depart, Mr Bonner descended onto the platform to check that all the doors were securely closed, then returned to stand beside the guard's van, blowing his whistle to get the driver's attention so he could signal that the train was ready. He stepped up into the van and closed one of the double doors, leaning out of the other one to wave his green flag. The train whistle blew in reply and Mr Bonner drew himself inside, closing the door. Dot heard the loud hiss followed by the rushing sound of lots of steam and the *puh . . . puh . . .* started, slowly at first but gradually building up. As the mighty engine drew the carriages alongside the platform, the couplings between the coaches creaked as they shifted and stretched. The train built up speed and the much-loved chuffing sound began.

Once they were on their way, Dot was too busy to fret about what Mr Bonner thought of her. Not that she had much time for gazing out of the windows, but she was pleasantly aware of clear skies and a bright day.

A sharp explosive sound burst out – and another – and a third. Even though Dot knew what this meant, it didn't stop her jumping out of her skin. She was making her way through the coach attached to the guard's van at the time, so her first job, after standing for a moment to absorb the small lurch as the train was brought to a standstill, was to reassure the passengers. She slid open the compartment doors.

'Nowt to worry about, ladies and gentlemen. It's just a signal to halt the train, that's all. We'll be on our way again as soon as we can.'

She walked through the connecting section from the coach into the guard's van.

'Why have we stopped?' she asked.

Mr Bonner had opened the double doors and was peering out. He drew his head back in to say, 'I'll get out my crystal ball, shall I?'

Dot knew what was coming next. Not because Mr Bonner had ever thought it worth his while to explain it to her, but thanks to Mr Emmet on the Leeds train. Rule 55.

A sound from outside sent fear rattling through Dot's body. It was a familiar noise, yet at the same time oddly different. She was accustomed to hearing it at great volume, filling the night skies and accompanied by anti-aircraft fire interspersed with the crump of bombs landing. This was that same sound, only thinner.

Mr Bonner stuck his head out again, hanging on with one hand and leaning right out to peer upwards.

'It's Jerry. Thank God it's only one plane.'

He stopped staring up at the sky and looked along the length of the train instead. Dot joined him. The windows in the top halves of the doors had been pulled down and passengers were leaning out to see what was going on.

'Get back inside!' roared Mr Bonner. 'Take cover. Keep away from the windows. Lie on the floor.'

He pushed Dot aside as he went into the wire cage and headed for the captain's chair beside the circular handbrake. A sharp burst of gunfire spat into the gravel and hammered along the tops of the coaches. Dot threw herself into the corner, making herself as small as she could.

Lifting her head, she watched as Mr Bonner applied the handbrake, opening the vacuum-brake valve so that the train couldn't move. Then he reached inside the small wall-mounted cupboard and Dot knew he was removing three of the half-crown-sized detonators, which he shoved in his pocket.

The plane's engines roared closer as the pilot came down for another pass. There was another burst of gunfire from one end of the train to the other. When it finished and the plane lifted away, Dot dared to lean out through the open doors.

'Don't do that, you stupid woman!'

But Dot's ears had picked up another sound. 'That's another plane.'

'One of ours?'

'I don't know.' What had made her think that learning aeroplane silhouettes was a hobby for schoolboys? She screwed up her eyes. Yes! The RAF roundels on the undersides of the wings. 'Yes, it's ours.'

'One against one. Let's hope it sees Jerry off.'

His face fixed in grim lines that added years to him, Mr Bonner took hold of the metal handgrip at the side of the door and swung himself down to the ground via the narrow step. Dot plastered herself against the inside wall of the guard's van, trying to give herself the widest possible angle to view the outside as Mr Bonner stumbled, righted himself and set off down the permanent way. Sounds from above made Dot shut her eyes. Two engines, two sets of gunfire – Jerry aiming at the ground, the chasing Spitfire aiming at Jerry. Another round of machine-gun fire hit the train and spat its way along the tracks. The planes howled directly overheard, then the drone of the engines lessened as they climbed away.

Dot took a chance and stuck her head outside. How far had Mr Bonner got? He needed to be five hundred yards away before he could fasten the first detonator to the track.

She grasped the handgrip so tightly that her knuckles cracked. Mr Bonner lay stretched out on the permanent way.

Joan hovered anxiously in the corridor. She wanted to stand right outside the doors to the ward so that she could bolt inside the moment they were opened at visiting time, but what if that nurse was still on duty and refused to let her in? So she hung back, near the head of the staircase, questions building up inside her.

She glanced at her wristwatch for the hundredth time. Nearly two o'clock. Had time ever passed so slowly? After leaving here this morning, she had gone home to Mrs Cooper's. She couldn't have Mrs Cooper and Mrs Grayson worrying about her.

She told them Gran was in hospital.

'That's worrying, of course,' said Mrs Cooper, 'but at least it's your day off, so you can visit without any trouble.'

'Don't worry if you don't see me later.'

'First-aid duty tonight, is it?'

No, it wasn't, but Joan had let her think it was. The truth was she had no idea what was going to happen after she had seen Gran. She just knew she needed to be free of any obligations.

The ward doors swung open and Joan made sure she was in the middle of the group of visitors and didn't look directly at any of the staff. Gran was sitting up in bed. Good. There was a dressing on her temple. Her face was pale and looked more deeply lined than usual, but to Joan's eyes it was the absence of her snood that made her look vulnerable. When had she last seen Gran without her snood? Gran kept her hair neat and under control just as she kept everything neat and under control.

'Hello, Gran.'

'Oh, it's you.' Gran's face hardened and she stared at the ceiling.

'How are you?'

It seemed Gran might not answer, but then she said, 'On the mend. I got knocked out, that's all. One minute I was on my feet and the next I was waking up in here.'

'Good.'

'Good that I was knocked out?'

'Good that you're on the mend. It was good of you to sit with Mrs Rigby.' She waited, but Gran didn't respond to this. 'Do you know when you'll be going home?'

'They want to keep me in another night.'

Joan swallowed. Evidently not even getting caught up in a bomb blast was enough to make Gran soften towards her wayward granddaughter, still less forgive and forget. She grasped the back of a chair and positioned it beside the bed. Sitting down, she leaned forward, keeping her voice low.

'I had trouble tracking you down.'

'I didn't want to be tracked down, thank you.'

'I was looking for Mrs Foster and the staff must have gone through your papers while you were knocked out, because they listed you as ... Mrs Henshaw.' Saying it sent a shiver through her.

Silence.

'I've seen your marriage certificate,' Joan persevered. 'I know you're really Mrs Henshaw. Why call yourself Mrs Foster all these years? It doesn't make sense ... Aren't you going to say anything?'

'I would tell you to mind your own business, but it's obviously too late for that.'

'If you're Mrs Henshaw, that makes Daddy Donald Henshaw, and Letitia and I are Letitia and Joan Henshaw.'

'Keep your voice down. I don't want my private business broadcast to the ward.'

'It's my business too, if I've been known by the wrong surname all my life. Or maybe I haven't. Maybe Henshaw is your second married name and Daddy was from your first marriage, so you're a Henshaw and the rest of us are Fosters. Is that what happened?'

Gran shrugged.

'*Gran*,' Joan hissed in an urgent undertone.

'Leave me be.' Gran's voice might sound weary, but her eyes had narrowed. 'It's nothing to do with you.'

'Of course it's to do with me.' Joan's throat tightened with the effort of keeping her voice down. 'This is my name we're talking about, my identity. It's who I am.'

Gran snapped round to look at her. 'Who you are, miss, is who I brought you up to be. I've always done right by you and Letitia. I've protected you.'

'From what?'

'I might as well not have bothered in your case.' Gran's gaze returned to the ceiling. 'You're your mother all over again. Now get out of my sight. I didn't want you in my house and I don't want you at my bedside.'

'I'll go, but only if you give me the envelope with my birth certificate.'

'You'll go when I tell you or I'll summon a nurse.'

'If you try, I'll go straight to Torbay Road and tell the neighbours your name is really Henshaw and you've been living a lie all these years.'

'Even you wouldn't stoop that low.'

'If you give me my birth certificate, I shan't have to. Be reasonable, Gran. Everybody needs their birth certificate. If you truly don't intend to see me again, you have to hand it over.'

Silence. Gran's jaw hardened.

'Pass me my handbag.'

Joan obeyed. Gran opened it in such a way that Joan couldn't see in. She withdrew one of the brown envelopes and flipped it onto the bed without a second glance.

'There – for all the good it'll do you. Now leave me alone.'

This time Gran turned her face in the opposite direction. Joan picked up the envelope and rose to her feet.

'Goodbye, Gran.'

Her heart pounded as she walked down the ward towards the doors. Outside, in the corridor, she stared at the envelope.

Well, who was she? Joan Foster or Joan Henshaw?

Dot stared in horror at Mr Bonner's prone form out there on the permanent way. Shock closed in on her and she couldn't hear owt but the blood pounding in her ears. Her legs were as weak as last week's blancmange, but somehow they held her up.

The world rushed into focus. Jerry strafing the train and the permanent way – Mr Bonner – the battle in the skies – the train in between stations. Urgency pulsed through her. It was essential to administer Rule 55 or the next train on the line might plough into the back of them.

Mr Bonner had done everything that needed doing inside the guard's van. Now it was up to her to finish the job. There was no time for fear. Dot was filled with an acute sense of purpose. Her passengers were relying on her. The engine driver and the fireman were relying on her, and so, did they but know it, were the passengers and crew on the train behind.

She clambered down from the train, landing with a clumsy thud that jarred her ankles and made her stagger like a drunkard before she set off along the track. Each step brought her closer to Mr Bonner. Was he dead? She saw him make a slight movement – or were her eyes playing tricks, showing her what she wanted to see?

She dropped to her knees beside him. He lay face down, his cap a couple of feet away. Was that a darker patch on the back of his jacket? How bad did a wound have to be for blood to seep through every layer of clothing?

She touched his shoulder. 'Mr Bonner, can you hear me?'

As an answer he breathed out a soft groan. There was no time for relief or gratitude.

Dot dug inside Mr Bonner's jacket pocket and retrieved the three detonators. If the next train came along, the sound of three sharp explosions in quick succession would alert the driver to stop the train immediately.

She was about to set off, then stopped, her gaze swinging back to Mr Bonner. She couldn't leave him here, out in the open, but she didn't have much time and she had to execute Rule 55. That had to take precedence. The lives of two trains full of people against the life of one injured man – no question. But she couldn't leave him, she just couldn't. Dot bent almost in two, grasped Mr Bonner under his armpits and tugged him clear of the tracks and into the bushes, hoping she wasn't causing more blood loss as he bumped along.

Now for the detonators. The first was meant to be attached to the track about five hundred yards behind the train. Dot looked back to gauge how far she had come, only to find that it was one thing to measure distance when you were at home in your familiar surroundings, but quite another when you were out in the open with umpteen lives depending on you.

Better to go too far than not far enough. She ran along the track until there could be no doubt she had covered the required distance, then kept going to make sure. At last she allowed herself to set the detonator, fiddling with the strap and cursing her fingers.

Scrambling to her feet, she almost pitched forwards in her haste. Hoisting up her skirt a few inches, she counted ten strides. A stride was meant to be a yard, wasn't it? She added a few extra in case she wasn't tall enough and bobbed down to fix the second charge in position just as the sound of aircraft engines reached her ears, sending fear streaming through her. A few unladylike words escaped from her lips as the straps on the second detonator resisted her attempts to fasten them.

With the German returning and the Spitfire in pursuit, she fixed the detonator in position and bolted for the next place. It sounded as if Jerry was close enough to reach a hand out of the cockpit and pick her up by her collar. Terror swept through her, then instinct took over and she hurled herself sideways, landing with a crunch and rolling over to get as far away as possible. That same moment, a line of gunfire spat gravel and splinters along the permanent way, precisely where she had been running, before letting loose another line of fire along the roofs of the train's coaches.

The Spitfire swooped down and chased Jerry away, buying time for Dot to set her third and final detonator. Never mind her clumsy fingers and her pounding heart. She would finish this job if it was the last thing she did.

And it might be.

Jerry was returning for another pass. Dot heard the machine-gun fire peppering the tops of the coaches as she fixed the detonator. The instant she finished, she hurled herself sideways into the bushes beside the tracks. If Jerry couldn't see her, maybe he would tire of the game.

But he knew where she was, because this time he aimed not at the permanent way but in a straight line alongside it – Dot's side. God in heaven, was this it? Was her time up? In a bush? Would anyone work out where to look for her? *Oh, Archie, Harry, I love you, I love you . . .*

As she watched through the foliage, unable to tear her eyes away, the Spitfire scored a hit, clipping Jerry's wing. It was enough. Jerry pulled the nose of his plane higher and set off to save his skin, the Spitfire in pursuit.

Dot scrambled back to the tracks practically on her hands and knees and stood up, watching the Spitfire see Jerry on his way. Grabbing her cap off her head, she waved it high in the air and cheered like a mad thing.

The air-raid siren went off at half past eight, but Joan didn't move. She was in her old home in Torbay Road, having let herself in with the spare key that hung on a nail inside the coal bunker. She had been sitting in the parlour since arriving back from the hospital that afternoon. This sofa was no longer simply the place where Steven had shown her the engagement ring he had chosen for Letitia. It was now the place where she had found out the truth about herself.

'For all the good it'll do you,' Gran had said and it seemed she was right.

Her name was Henshaw. Joan Henshaw, not Joan Foster. Why had Gran called them Foster?

A memory crept back into her mind. Letitia going on and on about wanting to look after her own birth certificate.

'I know you like keeping them in your handbag, but I'm not sure that's the right place . . . You do remember what my war work is, don't you? I double-check the maths of the engineers responsible for the shells. So I'm clever enough and grown-up enough to do that, but I'm not grown-up enough to be responsible for my own birth certificate . . . I'm sick of not being trusted.'

And almost immediately after that, Gran had changed her mind over another matter and allowed the girls to shorten their dowdy, calf-length hems. Had Gran given in over the hems so as to distract Letitia from the family papers?

Thanks to her own birth certificate, Joan now knew her mother's maiden name was Hopkins and had the address where the family had been living when she was born. She had always known that Gran had brought her and Letitia here to Manchester from down south after Daddy died. Gran had been heartbroken at losing him and had wanted to give herself and her two little charges a fresh start.

Fine. She had wanted to move away. But why lie about their surname?

Had it been part of the fresh start? Was it – was it to make it impossible for Estelle to find them if she ever realised what a terrible mistake she had made and came looking for her daughters to beg their forgiveness?

Somehow that didn't fit in with the brusque, judgemental Gran Joan had known all her life. Gran wouldn't have been scared of Estelle turning up on the doorstep. A pound to a penny, Gran would have given her a piece of her mind and then chased her up the road, brandishing the poker. No, Gran wouldn't have feared Estelle's return. It would have given her the chance to play the part of the avenging angel and she would have relished every riled-up moment. Yes, and used it as a weapon against the girls, something disgraceful about their rotten mother to be held over their heads to ensure their own impeccable behaviour.

But if the change of name wasn't to hide from Estelle, then what was its purpose?

From outside came the sounds of aeroplane engines and ack-ack fire, together with the whistle and crump of falling explosives. Joan was vaguely aware of the destruction that was going on, but she continued to sit there, hour after hour.

If Gran had lied about the family name, what else might she have lied about?

# Chapter Thirty-Four

Clad in her wrap-around pinny and turban, Dot had washed up the breakfast things and made the bed. Now it was time to do the step. Half filling the bucket in the scullery, she walked through the house to the front door, setting down the bucket and putting the doormat on the pavement to kneel on. As she washed her doorstep, she smiled to herself. Hitler could drop as many bombs as he liked. It wouldn't stop good northern women donkey-stoning their front steps of a morning.

She wanted to get her housework done, then dash round the shops – in so far as you could dash in these days of queuing. It was a shame there was no morning visiting at the hospital or she might drop in to see Mr Bonner, who'd had surgery yesterday. She wasn't sure he would want her to visit, but she felt she ought to, out of courtesy, if nowt else.

With her step clean, she set to with the donkey stone, scrubbing the cream colour all over in a pattern of swirls. It was important to have a nice pattern. Mam had taught her that. Finishing, she stood up and stretched her back.

'Mrs Green – I'm that relieved to have caught you.'

Dot turned round. There was Mrs Cooper in her overcoat, her dressing gown hanging down beneath. It could mean only one thing.

'Eh, love, you've never been bombed out.'

Mrs Cooper's lips quivered. She pressed them together. 'Aye. We've lost everything. Everything.'

'What about Mrs Grayson – and Joan? Are they all right?'

'Mrs Grayson was with me in the public shelter and Joan was out all night at first aid.'

'Come in. Let's put the kettle on.'

By, the poor woman looked like she'd been twice through the mangle. Her face was drawn with exhaustion. More than exhaustion – shock, if Dot wasn't mistaken. She had seen it enough times since the air raids began.

Mrs Cooper sat at the table, her handbag on her lap, clutching the handles as if she would never let go. Dot imagined having to prise her fingers apart for her to have a cup of tea.

'Shouldn't you be at the rest centre?' she asked gently.

'It's not that simple. There's Mrs Grayson to think about. It's not easy for her to go to the public shelter, but I made her agree to do that when she moved in with me.'

'Jolly good job you did an' all.'

'When the all-clear sounded, we waited for everyone else to leave. We always do that. It's easier for Mrs Grayson not to feel part of a crowd. We set off for home and our road – I've seen enough bombed streets, but honest to God—' Mrs Cooper knuckled summat from her eyes. Not tears. Her eyes were dry. 'When it's your own house – your own street – your neighbours' houses . . .'

'Was anyone killed?'

'Nay, thanks be for that.'

'That's the main thing,' said Dot. 'The rest is bricks and mortar.'

Mrs Cooper looked straight at her, her eyes huge and haunted. 'Aye, bricks and mortar – and my Lizzie's stuff. Her clothes and her teddy and the lipstick she wanted for her seventeenth birthday even though she wasn't allowed to wear it until she were eighteen. Pink, it was. I said she wasn't allowed red.'

'Oh, love.' Dot's heart creaked. 'I'm that sorry. Did you lose all her belongings?'

'I've got her birth certificate and her baptism certificate ... and her death certificate.' Mrs Cooper's mouth twisted. 'I keep them in the air-raid box – well, the air-raid shopping bag, in our case. I've left it with Mrs Grayson to look after.'

'Is that all you've got of your Lizzie's?'

'A few bits and pieces. A silver cross she had for her first Holy Communion. Her swimming certificate for doing her first length.' Mrs Cooper laughed, a harsh sound. 'Imagine that. Her clothes have gone, her collection of pottery kittens, her film magazines, even her teddy bear, but what does any of that matter when I've got her flamin' swimming certificate for front crawl?'

'That's hard, love,' said Dot, 'but it's not about things, is it? You'll always have your Lizzie with you in your heart.'

'Oh aye? That'd be enough for you, would it?' All at once, there was fire in Mrs Cooper's eyes. 'If, God forbid, you got the telegram and one of your boys had copped it, would you say, "That's all right. I'll always have him with me in my heart"? Give you everlasting solace, would it?'

Dot was appalled. 'Nay, love, of course not. I'm that sorry. I never thought ... It's just what you say when someone dies, isn't it? It's meant to be comforting. But I'll never say it again, not now you've made me think.'

Mrs Cooper slumped as the fight went out of her. 'I'm the one what's sorry. You never meant no harm. You're good to ask about Lizzie. You're good to remember.'

'Of course I remember. I'll never forget her.' Dot let that part of the conversation fade away. 'Shouldn't you be at the rest centre, sorting out what to do and where to go? Is that where Mrs Grayson is?'

'I took her back to the public shelter. I didn't know where else to put her. It's not as though I could have dropped her off at a neighbour's. There aren't any neighbours' houses left. That's why I'm here. I've come to ask if you'll have her while I go to the rest centre.'

'You've walked all the way here for that?'

'I need someone as knows her and understands her ways.'

'You fetch her here, Mrs Cooper. In fact,' said Dot, sacrificing her shopping time, 'give me five minutes and I'll come with you and fetch her myself, so you can go straight to the rest centre. It'd be a poor show if I couldn't make time for a friend.' As she spoke, an idea unfolded in Dot's head. 'You get down that rest centre and put in your claim for what you've lost, but don't fret too much over where to move to. Give me and the girls a chance to come up with summat for you.'

'I couldn't ask that of you.'

'You're not asking, I'm offering. You took in Mrs Grayson and Joan without a murmur. It's time to let someone do summat for you for a change. You're our Lizzie's mam and that makes you one of us.'

Someone had produced a porter's cap for her, but other than that Joan spent her working day in her own clothes. After her long and wakeful night in Torbay Road, she had cycled home to Mrs Cooper's, dogged by an obscure resentment at having to return to normality when her world, already upside down, had taken a further blow, but that feeling had vanished when she saw the flooded crater in the road and the terrible damage done to Mrs Cooper's home, among others. The back wall of Mrs Cooper's was still standing and, bizarrely, much of the roof appeared to be intact, stretching above a largely empty shell. Most of the house and its contents had been reduced to a heap of rubble and timber, pieces of fabric and shards of glass and crockery.

Joan had climbed off her bicycle, which crashed to the ground as she let go, though the sound had barely penetrated her numbed state. It turned out that Mrs Cooper and Mrs Grayson were both safe, though nobody seemed to know exactly where they were just then. Neighbours who were picking through the ruins of their own homes had promised to tell Mrs Cooper that Joan was all right and sent her off to work.

Now she was approaching the end of her working day. It had been a weird day all round. By rights, she ought to be distraught at losing her new home, together with her clothes and the possessions she had taken with her, but all she could think about was her real name. Joan Henshaw. If she thought of it often enough, would she get used to it? Letitia had been Letitia Henshaw, which actually had quite a nice ring to it. She had been buried in the name of Foster, and the undertaker had used this name, so Foster must be on her death certificate.

Letitia and Joan Foster.

Letitia and Joan Henshaw.

'Joan Henshaw,' Joan whispered. It didn't stir anything inside her memory, didn't awaken an instinctive response, but then how could it? She had been less than a year old when Daddy died and Gran had upped sticks and moved to Manchester ... when Mrs Beryl Henshaw had shut the front door for the final time on their old home, taking her two tiny girls, Letitia and Joan Henshaw, with her. When they had arrived at their new home, it was Mrs Beryl Foster, with little Letitia and Joan Foster, who had taken up residence.

Joan had been Joan Foster on the register at school, then Miss Foster when she worked at Ingleby's. Now she was Miss Foster the station porter.

What was she supposed to do with this new knowledge?

'For all the good it'll do you,' said Gran's voice inside her head.

It was a relief to join her friends in the buffet. She had considered ducking out, but what good would that do? She didn't intend to tell them – yet – what she had discovered. She couldn't bear to hear from their lips all the questions that had been tormenting her. But, as she knew from the dark days after Letitia's death, just being with her friends would help. Their company would provide something for her to cling to. Besides, she must tell them about Mrs Cooper's house.

She arrived in the buffet and joined the queue, a glance across the room telling her that she was the last to arrive. They weren't expecting Dot today and, of course, not Colette either.

To her surprise, Alison and Persephone jumped up and hurried between the tables. A chill went through her. How could they know? Were they rushing to sympathise over the shock she had received? Ridiculous idea – they couldn't possibly know. Then she realised they weren't aiming for her, but had veered towards the door, where they were hugging Dot. What was going on?

She purchased her tea and went to the table. Dot was already there. Alison and Persephone had handed her over to Mabel, who also hugged her. Good heavens, even Cordelia took Dot's hand and leaned forward to peck her cheek.

'Is it your birthday?' Joan asked Dot.

The reply came in the form of looks of astonishment on the others' faces.

'Haven't you heard?' asked Cordelia.

'Heard what?'

'Dot's a heroine,' exclaimed Alison. 'No one has talked about anything else all day. How could you not know?'

'I've – I've been preoccupied.' Joan's mind scrambled to catch up. She turned to Dot. 'You're a heroine? What's happened? I'm so sorry not to have heard anything.'

'That's enough of that,' said Dot. 'First off, I'm no heroine. I didn't do owt that anyone else wouldn't have done. One of you can tell Joan later, if she's interested, but just now I haven't got much time. I've a short break before the evening train goes and I'm here because poor Mrs Cooper has been bombed out.'

Amid exclamations of 'Oh no' around the table, everyone turned to Joan.

'Is she all right?' asked Persephone. 'And Mrs Grayson? And you, of course?'

'The ladies are both fine,' said Dot. 'I don't suppose Joan has seen them, as you were on first-aid duty last night, weren't you, chick?'

'Has Mrs Cooper lost everything?' asked Mabel.

Dot nodded. 'The lot. That pretty harebell tea set she was so proud of, and all Lizzie's things.'

'As if she hasn't been through enough,' said Cordelia. 'Where is she now?'

'She and Mrs Grayson have been taken in for the night by neighbours round the corner,' said Dot, 'while arrangements can be made.' She looked at Joan. 'You can stop in my spare room, love.'

'Or I can stay at Gran's while she's in hospital.' As the others turned startled faces towards her, Joan quickly added, 'She'll be fine. They need to keep an eye on her because she was knocked out.'

'Will Mrs Cooper go to live with her sister and

brother-in-law?' asked Persephone. 'And where will Mrs Grayson go? Not to mention Joan.'

'That's why I'm here,' said Dot. 'This is our Lizzie's mum we're talking about. Does anyone have an idea that could help?'

Joan exchanged glances with her friends. They all wanted to help, but it wasn't as though they could pluck a house out of the air.

'I have a suggestion,' said Cordelia, 'though perhaps I'd better keep it to myself until I've spoken to the couple concerned.'

'You have to tell us now,' said Alison. 'You can't leave us dangling.'

Cordelia looked at Mabel. 'Do you recall my mentioning Mr and Mrs Morgan to my husband?'

'The elderly couple who are moving to the seaside?'

Cordelia addressed the group. 'Their son works in London for the Inland Revenue, which has been moved to Llandudno for the duration. The Morgans have decided to move there to be near him and his family, but they're concerned about who might get billeted on their house in their absence.' She looked at Dot. 'Do you think Mrs Cooper would be interested in a post as housekeeper?'

After spending longer than she ought in the buffet, Dot had to dash to get her parcels trolley to the platform. Eh, a year ago, she would have been out of puff if she'd had to hurry with a fully loaded trolley, but now the physical exertion was an ordinary part of life.

'Mrs Green.' Mr Thirkle had opened the platform gates ready for her. 'I'm glad to see you.'

'Sorry. Can't stop.' Dot manoeuvred the trolley onto the platform, calling thank you over her shoulder.

To her surprise, she found Mr Thirkle walking beside her.

'I heard about what you did yesterday. How very brave of you. There was another train on the line, you know. If you hadn't executed Rule 55 . . .'

Dot halted her trolley beside the doors of the guard's van, applying the brake with her foot before turning to give Mr Thirkle her full attention. She hadn't felt comfortable today, being praised and congratulated by all and sundry, but receiving Mr Thirkle's praise was different. It warmed her.

'I have you to thank,' she said, 'and so does everybody on board that train – both trains. You're the one who told me about Rule 55 and suggested I learn about it.'

'That was just good sense.'

'No, it was you doing the decent thing and accepting the presence of women on the railways. There are still plenty who don't.'

'Mr Bonner among them, I'm sorry to say. Maybe he'll think again after what you did yesterday. It isn't easy for men to accept that their wives and daughters might be as capable as they are. Not that I'm setting myself up as a shining example, mind you. I've told you how I denied my late wife the opportunity to work outside the home, and all because I believed it would reflect badly on me as the provider.' He smiled, a touch of humour in his eyes. 'But I've seen the error of my ways.'

'I'm pleased to hear it,' Dot said lightly. She enjoyed his humour. It was gentle and kind. Not like Reg's. Reg's idea of a good joke was to poke fun at his missus.

'Excuse me. I must return to the barrier.'

'I must get on an' all, but if I've time when I've loaded up, I'll pop along for a word.'

She set about loading the wire cage inside the guard's van, double-checking the address labels to ensure that every parcel would be set off at the correct station. Mr Hill, the guard who had taken over from Mr Bonner, climbed on board with a pleasant greeting. Dot had half hoped for a lady guard, but they were rarer than hens' teeth – for now, anyroad, but surely, as the war progressed, women would be given guards' jobs.

With five minutes to call her own, she hurried back to the barrier, smiling at the passengers coming towards her.

When Mr Thirkle had a moment, she said, 'Thanks for your help with the food-dump business, but you needn't worry about it any more. My friends are helping me. We're going to spend whatever hours of darkness we can there.'

'But never alone, I hope,' said Mr Thirkle, alarmed.

'Of course not. Only when four of us can go. When whoever it is comes along, we'll let him get inside, then two of us will barricade him in with old sleepers and the others will cycle to the nearest signal box for help.'

'I can't say I like the sound of it.'

'Steady on.' Dot tried to make light of it. 'Have you forgotten you're all in favour of women doing what's necessary?'

'I never meant anything like this.' Mr Thirkle pressed his lips together. 'If you hang on a moment . . .' He pulled out a small notebook and scribbled something, tearing out the page and handing it over. 'That's the identification number of the railway shed. You'll need to give that to the signalman.'

'Thank you.'

'I know there's nothing I can say, other than be careful.'

'We shall.'

'And also, there's no need for me to drop out.'

'Yes, there is, after that business with your Edie.'

Mr Thirkle drew back his shoulders. 'My dear Mrs Green, continuing to assist in this matter is the decent thing to do, and when the thief is apprehended, it'll show Edie I had a genuine reason for meeting up with you.'

'Aye,' said Dot, 'I can see that.'

Yes, she could. He was going to carry on, not out of friendship or regard for her, but to make things right with his Edie.

Quite right too.

And she really had no business feeling disappointed.

# Chapter Thirty-Five

'Lead the way,' said Mrs Cooper as she and Joan descended from the bus at the Chorlton terminus. 'You know where we're going.'

Joan would have liked to link arms with her, or would it be too much of a liberty? Gran would curl her lip at it certainly, but did she wish to be guided by Gran's rigid rules any more? She was no longer wearing her snood all the time. She wore it for work and at first aid, but she had stopped wearing it at other times.

She and Mrs Cooper walked along Beech Road, turning the corner before the rec.

'There's Mrs Masters.' Mrs Cooper walked faster. 'I hope we haven't kept her waiting.'

They joined Cordelia at the corner of Wilton Close, a small cul-de-sac with two pairs of semi-detached houses on either side and another pair of semis at the top end. Each house had a front garden with a gate and a path to the porch. It was a pretty little road, though it must have looked a lot prettier pre-war when the gardens had beds filled with flowers instead of wartime vegetables.

'The Morgans live at number one,' said Cordelia, leading them to the first house on the right.

The door was answered by an elderly lady in a finely knitted cardigan that fell in silky lines over a linen blouse with a cameo brooch pinned between the wings of the collar. Her grey hair was neatly coiffed and her face discreetly powdered, the powder blurring her lines.

'Mrs Masters, how good of you to come.' Mrs Morgan made this sound like an ordinary social occasion. 'And you've brought your friends. Do come in.'

She showed them into the front room, with its William Morris wallpaper and dark blue curtains hanging from a brass curtain pole above the bay window. A grey-haired man rose from his chair, transferring his pipe to his left hand as introductions were performed and hands were shaken.

Joan sat and listened while the Morgans interviewed – there was no other word for it – Mrs Cooper.

At last, Mrs Morgan said, with a glance at her husband, 'I'd been feeling guilty about leaving, in case anyone thought we were running away, but if you take care of our property, Mrs Cooper, we'll be performing a service to you and Miss Foster.'

'And Mrs Grayson,' Cordelia added.

'Quite so. There's ample room for the three of you. Allow me to show you round.'

As Mrs Morgan and Mrs Cooper stood up, Cordelia nodded to Joan.

'You too. I'll stay and chat with Mr Morgan.'

From the sitting room, Mrs Morgan ushered them into the dining room, which had windows onto a rear garden complete with Anderson shelter. A smaller room led off to the side, with built-in floor-to-ceiling cupboards painted in palest yellow and windows onto the side passage and fence.

'This is the breakfast room,' said Mrs Morgan, 'and through here we have the kitchen and scullery. Beyond the scullery is a little wash house, but you have to go outside to get to its door.'

'Your very own wash house.' Mrs Cooper's voice was reverent.

'Shall we go upstairs?' offered Mrs Morgan.

Opposite the foot of the stairs was an alcove whose pegs and shelves declared it to be a cloakroom. Halfway up, the stairs turned a corner. Mrs Morgan reached the landing and stood there with the others bunched behind her on the stairs, as if she didn't want them invading the privacy of her first floor.

'We have two double bedrooms, which are above the front room and the dining room and therefore have fireplaces. There is also a large single room and a boxroom which could be a small bedroom if required. We used to have a live-in maid and it's where I put her.'

Mrs Morgan moved, allowing Mrs Cooper and Joan onto the landing. She opened a couple of doors, permitting them a glimpse inside. Joan was treated to a flash of the single room, which she assumed would be hers, with Mrs Cooper and Mrs Grayson occupying the two doubles.

'We have a bathroom.' Mrs Morgan waved her hand vaguely at another closed door before adding, 'And all indoor plumbing amenities,' which was presumably a polite way of referring to an indoor WC.

Downstairs once more, Mrs Cooper said to the Morgans, 'You have a beautiful house. If you decide I'm suitable, I promise you won't regret entrusting it to me.'

'I understand you've lost everything,' said Mr Morgan. 'A sorry business.'

'I'm not the only one,' said Mrs Cooper.

The Morgans looked at one another and Joan was aware of a message passing between them.

'It isn't easy to hand over one's home,' said Mr Morgan, 'but, with Mrs Masters speaking highly of you, I'd like to ask you to be our housekeeper for the duration. We'll pay you a small fee, of course.'

Mrs Cooper's hands fluttered. 'There's no need.'

'Yes, there is. It's essential that everything is done correctly. Mr Masters has offered to draw up a contract, so everything will be above board.' He laughed a shade too heartily. 'We can't have you declining to hand the house back at the end of the war, can we?'

'Raymond!' Mrs Morgan exclaimed. She turned to her visitors. 'Please excuse my husband. The number of times I've had to apologise for him over the years.' Leaning towards Mrs Cooper, she said, 'Now that it's definite, would you like to see around the house again?'

Saturday evening out with her beau. What could be better? Dressed in a flowing silk-jersey evening gown with no waist seam, and her hair tumbling in long curls, Mabel felt like the belle of the ball. Harry had escorted her to the Ritz Ballroom on Whitworth Street, where the pillars and art deco features, together with the balcony above, created a stylish backdrop to the bustling, happy atmosphere. Every girl present had spent ages doing her hair and make-up. Every man had polished his shoes and ensured his parting was straight. But it didn't matter how good-looking any of the other couples were. Filled with love and excitement, Mabel knew she and Harry were special.

They danced every dance together, neither of them having any interest in spreading their favours around other partners. Having Harry's attention focused solely on her made Mabel's heartbeat race and she danced more fluidly than she had ever danced in her life.

When they sat out a dance or two, sipping their drinks, Harry only had eyes for her. She felt ultra-aware of everything – the music, the dancers gliding by, but most of all the two of them. They were the golden couple. Even while she was entranced by Harry's nearness, she couldn't help being aware of how they must appear to other people: the well-built RAF johnny and his slender, beautifully dressed companion. Were her eyes sparkling? Was her complexion radiant? They must be, they simply must.

The band struck up the familiar introduction to 'Lovely Lady', which was the signal that the Ritz's famous revolving stage was going to turn round to reveal the other band, which would be playing the same tune so that the dancing need never stop. Harry and Mabel joined the rest on the crowded floor.

After a couple more dances, Mabel left Harry to buy more drinks and excused herself to visit the Ladies. She hummed under her breath as she entered the long room, with its row of cubicles on one side and the basins and mirrors on the other. The scents of Evening in Paris and Yardley's English Lavender talcum powder mingled in the air, together with a costly dash of Chanel that some lucky girl must have been saving for a special occasion. A line of girls stood before the mirrors, leaning forward to check their make-up and touch up their lipstick. One girl opened her handbag and produced a small piece of greaseproof paper from which she unwrapped – was that a slice of beetroot? Before she could apply it to her lips, Mabel offered her own lipstick.

'Are you sure? Thanks.' The girl applied some, then twisted the stick down and snapped on the lid. 'My chap will get a nice surprise when he kisses me and I don't taste of pickling vinegar.'

The girls at the mirrors all seemed to vanish at the same time, bustling out in a cloud of chatter, leaving Mabel to enter one of the cubicles. She heard the door swing open again, followed by the voices and laughter of a new group of girls.

'We shouldn't laugh,' said one. 'Not really. It's frightfully bad luck on the poor girl.'

'It depends what you call bad luck,' said another.

'I know what you mean,' chimed in a third voice. 'If you're going to have that sort of bad luck, it would be a lot worse without the gorgeous Mr Knatchbull.'

They all laughed. Inside the cubicle, about to pull the chain, Mabel froze, the sound of their laughter rooting her to the spot.

'Where did he find her?'

'Picked her up in hospital, would you believe. I was laid up after having my rotten old appendix out and he came to visit me a few times – though, looking back, I'm not sure that I was really the one he kept coming to see.'

'Who is she, anyway?'

'Name of Bradshaw, so I've heard. Daughter of a factory owner somewhere further north. Daddy is busy pulling his weight for the war effort.'

'Plenty of lovely money, then.'

'And plenty more by the time the war's over.'

'So *she'll* get a handsome husband and *he'll* get a life of luxury.'

'Good old Harry. He's worked hard enough for it.'

'Algy will be pleased. At least he'll get to call his motor his own instead of lending it out so Harry can make a good impression.'

More laughter. Mabel cringed.

'Mind you, she is rather a looker, isn't she? Their children are going to be stunners.'

'You're a bit of a stunner yourself this evening. How did you get your hair to do that?'

With wave upon wave of pain passing through her, Mabel remained trapped while the girls twittered on about hair and make-up. Then the door swished open and closed and there was silence.

Shock made it an effort to move, but she had to get out of there. Pulling the chain and unbolting the door, she scanned the shelf beneath the mirrors to make sure none of the girls had left anything behind that they would all come barging back in to retrieve. As she went through the motions of washing and drying her hands, the door opened, sending fear streaming through her, but the new-comers didn't turn silent at the sight of her, so they must be different girls.

Mabel stared at her reflection so as not to make eye contact through the mirror. If she didn't look at these girls, they wouldn't look at her, but she couldn't avoid looking at herself. Her complexion had drained to the colour of paste. Her eyes were huge and dark. There was no beauty in them, just bleakness.

It was the face she had seen in the mirror after Althea's death.

The railway shed was a huge shape of deeper darkness in the stillness of the night. If Joan hadn't been accustomed to the blackout, she might have found the utter blackness scary. She, Dot, Persephone and Cordelia sat close together on the improvised bench they had made out of railway sleepers. The night was chilly and overcast, the stars hidden behind banks of cloud. That was good – less chance of an air raid. Would it also make it more likely to be a night for the thief to visit the railway shed to steal another batch of foodstuffs?

Warmly wrapped up inside the winter coat she had made a couple of years ago for Letitia, she stamped her feet and found a smile flitting across her face.

'This reminds me of stamping my feet and rubbing my

arms to keep warm when I was a fire-watcher on the roof at Ingleby's. These are from back then as well.'

She removed her hands from her pockets to show small metal hand warmers, which had charcoal inside.

'They survived being bombed out, then,' said Persephone.

'They were never in Mrs Cooper's house. I lost all my own clothes and jewellery when Mrs Cooper's was bombed.' A pang cut through her: the locket from Bob and her treasured silver filigree heart from Letitia. 'There were a few bits and pieces of mine still at Gran's, such as these hand warmers, and this coat and some other things of Letitia's were in the running-away suitcase in the Andy at Gran's. I took them from the house while Gran was in hospital.'

'A good thing too,' Dot said robustly. Dear Dot. 'I'm glad you've got some of Letitia's things.'

'She had good taste.' Persephone clicked on her torch and ran its muted beam over the wool coat with its large collar, padded shoulders and flap pockets. 'That's a beautiful coat.'

'Thank you. I made it.'

'Of course,' said Cordelia. 'You used to be a seamstress.'

'A sewing-machinist. "Seamstress" sounds posh.'

'Don't run yourself down,' said Cordelia. 'A good dressmaker will always have work. You wait. Once the war is over, women will be desperate for new clothes.'

Joan was startled. Was it because her troubles had anchored her so firmly in the here and now that it seemed odd to hear the end of the war being referred to? Besides, when the war ended, Letitia would be left even further behind. How was she supposed to face the rest of her life without her sister?

'What is everyone's excuse for being here tonight?' asked Dot. 'Me, I'm meant to be on the late shift.'

'Likewise,' said Persephone.

'Very late,' Cordelia murmured.

'First aid,' said Joan. She leaned forward to look past Persephone and peer at Cordelia. 'What about you?'

'It's my husband's night for fire-watching.'

'Doesn't he know you're out of the house?' asked Dot.

'No. So we'd better not get blown to smithereens.'

Joan hesitated, then plunged in. 'Do you think you might ask him a question for me?'

'Certainly. What is it?'

'It's to do with surnames.' Joan hadn't uttered a word about her family mystery, but now she felt ready to speak up. 'Gran gave me my birth certificate. I more or less made her. She's always kept the family papers and refused to let Letitia and me have our own – and now I know why. Our name isn't Foster. It's Henshaw.'

Exclamations filled the crisp darkness.

'Why did she change your name?' asked Persephone.

'She won't tell me. What I'd like to know from Mr Masters, please, is whether, now I know what my real name is, I have to use it.'

'I'll ask,' said Cordelia.

'You poor love,' said Dot. 'It's brave of you to tell us.'

'If there's one thing I've learned from being part of our group, it's that the support we can give one another is invaluable.'

'I still think it's brave,' said Dot. 'As if you haven't got enough on your plate.'

'Meaning Bob and Steven? I'm not going to think about all that until I've got to the bottom of this name business – no, that's not right. It isn't that I'm not going to. It's because I can't. I know how feeble that sounds, but it's true. I just can't.'

'There's too much going on, isn't there?' said Dot. 'You

miss Letitia. You're torn between those two boys. And now you've found out about your name.'

'A word of warning, if I may,' said Cordelia. 'Be careful about keeping those two young men hanging on. You don't want them to get tired of waiting.'

# Chapter Thirty-Six

Six months ago, she had stood up here on the wind-blown tops with Harry by her side. Mabel inhaled deeply, seeking strength from the rugged beauty of the landscape. Her family had lived in Annerby for generations and, as dearly as she loved Manchester, especially since the Christmas Blitz, nothing could mean more than the love she had for the place of her birth, the place where she truly belonged.

The place she had run away from after Althea's death. And now the place to which she had returned following this new heartbreak.

But the pain was different this time. Even though she felt more like doubling up in misery, Mabel stood tall. This time, she knew that no pain lasted for ever.

That didn't stop it hurting like billy-o here and now, though. How could she have been such a fool? She had fallen for everything Harry had said, all that tripe about being the only girl for him. Huh! It was Pops and his money Harry had set his sights on.

That evening at the Ritz, she had urgently wanted to rescue her belongings from the cloakroom and escape into the night without a word, but then he would have come looking for her and would have turned up on Cordelia's doorstep. She had still intended to escape, though. If she could jiggle around her leave with someone else's, she could hightail it to Annerby without Harry being any the wiser.

Was it cowardly not to have confronted him on the spot? She didn't care if it was. She had simply announced she had a headache and wanted to leave. When Harry tried to put his arm around her, she had wriggled free, muttering something about needing to be left alone. Harry, ever the gentleman, had backed off.

Now here she was at home again. Mumsy and Pops had been so thrilled to see her that her love for them had filled her eyes with tears.

'I promise not to leave it so long next time,' she'd whispered.

'We did wonder if you might bring that charming young man with you,' said Mumsy.

'*We* didn't think any such thing,' said Pops. 'Don't drag me into your schemes, Esme. Mind you,' he added, giving Mabel another hug, 'I wouldn't complain if you did.'

Should she tell them the truth? She pictured crying on Mumsy's shoulder as she shared confidences. But she still felt too raw. Besides, she didn't want to spoil this visit, which felt unspeakably precious.

She would come clean next time. Maybe by then she would be able to do so without howling in anguish.

Her chest was heavy with misery, but she was angry too. Harry Knatchbull had taken advantage of her in more ways than one. It wasn't just that he had set out to catch an heiress. Though he didn't know it, he had abused her feelings in another way too. She had endured months weighed down by guilt after Althea died, but with her friends' help she had come to accept that she could live her life without the simple act of doing so being a gross insult to Althea's memory – which in turn had enabled her to form a relationship with Harry. And the lying, scheming rat had trampled all over her hard-won acceptance of life without Althea.

Standing on the tops, with the tang of the moors swirling around her, Mabel imagined the ancient landscape feeding strength into her bones. As hard as it was to bear Harry's betrayal, she wouldn't let it crush her. He didn't deserve that. He wasn't worth it.

He wasn't a cheeky blighter, but a lying, cheating blighter. And not a blighter, either, but an out-and-out bounder. She was determined to get over him and she knew exactly how she was going to start.

Standing outside the hospital ward with the other visitors, Dot looked round at the women, wondering if one of them was Mrs Bonner. When the doors opened and the rest went in, she hung back until last. It felt odd going into a ward to visit a man who wasn't her husband. She didn't want to see Mr Bonner in his pyjamas.

There he was, down the far end. A woman in a patterned headscarf had just arrived by his bedside.

Dot hurried over. 'Pardon me. I don't want to interrupt you before you've even got started, but I wanted to say how do, Mr Bonner, and ask after your health.'

She looked at Mrs Bonner, feeling unexpectedly awkward. Normally, no one could accuse her of being shy. As Reg so elegantly put it, she had been at the front of the queue when mouths were handed out, but right now she was stumped for how to introduce herself. You could hardly say, 'How do, love. I'm the woman what saved your old man's life,' could you? Not without sounding horribly big-headed, you couldn't.

Mrs Bonner, having looked her up and down, looked at Mr Bonner. Dot looked at him an' all.

'This is Mrs Green,' he said.

'Mrs Green?' Mrs Bonner leaped to her feet. Crikey, had Mr Bonner told her about the man-mad female who had been hauled up before the powers that be to have her wings clipped? 'Mrs Green? Oh!' And she burst into tears.

Dot patted her shoulder. 'There, love. It's all right.'

Mrs Bonner gave her a watery smile. 'I can't thank you enough.'

Dot turned to Mr Bonner. 'I hope I find you well.'

'Doing nicely, thank you.' He frowned. 'And, er, thank you for what you did.'

'All in a day's work,' said Dot. 'I'd best be off. I just came to pay my respects.' She nodded to Mrs Bonner. 'Nice to meet you.' To Mr Bonner, she said, 'Take care, love. I hope you're back at work soon.'

Mr Bonner's shoulders stiffened inside his striped pyjamas. 'I told you when you first worked for me not to call people "love", Mrs Green.'

'And I told you,' said Dot, 'everyone is "love" when they need a spot of coddling.'

Heading for home, she was chuffed to bits when she thought of Mrs Bonner's tears. Never mind what a grumpy old stick-in-the-mud Mr Bonner was, that spurt of tears from his wife's eyes made up for everything. It was better than receiving a medal.

Eh, but she wasn't keen on all the fuss folk had made of her. She had only done what anybody else would have in the same situation. Actually, it was rather embarrassing being asked to describe what had happened – but, oh, it was worth it when she realised she had shot sky-high in Jimmy's estimation. And Jenny wanted her to give a talk to the Guides, would you believe.

Honest to God, what could be better – what in the whole wide world could be better than having her two precious grandchildren gazing at her with stars in their eyes?

*

With her handbag and gas-mask box slung over her arm, Mabel carried her carpet bag downstairs. Mr Masters had already taken her suitcase down and placed it on the polished floorboards in the hall. Cordelia emerged from the sitting room.

Mabel put down the carpet bag. 'Thank you for your hospitality. It's been enormously kind of you to put me up.'

Cordelia smiled. 'We wish you all the best in your new home – don't we, Kenneth?'

'Of course,' said Mr Masters.

The doorbell rang.

'Your helpers have arrived,' said Mr Masters.

Cordelia stood aside to admit Joan and Persephone, whom she introduced to her husband.

'How shall you manage everything?' Cordelia looked dubiously at the case and the carpet bag. 'Those are rather large.'

'Joan and I came up with a grand wheeze on our way here,' said Persephone. 'We'll lay the suitcase across your bicycle saddle, Mabel, with the carpet bag on top, then you can steer the bike while Joan and I walk behind to balance the luggage.'

Loading the bicycle, they set off, Mabel pushing the bike, the other two holding on to the suitcase. It wasn't the easiest way of getting about and there was much giggling and grabbing each time they went over a bump and the luggage slipped sideways.

'Did Cordelia mind you leaving?' asked Joan.

'She'd have let me stay as long as I needed, but I think she realises I'll have more fun living with you.'

'It isn't living with Joan that's meant to be fun,' said Persephone, 'it's going out with Harry.'

The words stabbed Mabel and her heart folded in two

to absorb the pain. She didn't want to admit the humiliating truth, but if she failed to speak up now, her friends would think all was well and she would be letting herself in for all kinds of uncomfortable lies – and she would still have to admit the truth in the end.

'Actually, I shan't be seeing him again.'

There was a lurch and a quick flurry as the other two stopped walking and then had to cling on to the luggage in a hurry when Mabel resolutely kept going.

'Mabel!' Persephone exclaimed. 'I thought you were mad keen on one another.'

'Oh aye,' Mabel said bitterly, 'I was mad keen all right. Wildly beating heart, hardly a wink of sleep, desperate to see him, desperate to be kissed. I was embarrassingly mad keen. But Harry – well, he was less keen on me than he was on my father's money.'

'I'm so sorry,' said Joan.

'I thought you two were a sure thing,' said Persephone. 'We all did.'

'As sure as Alison and Paul,' Joan added.

Mabel forced a laugh. 'If you intend to make me feel better, you'd better brush up your technique.'

'How did you find out?' asked Persephone.

'I overheard some girls talking about us.'

'And what did Harry have to say for himself?'

Mabel shrugged, eyes fixed on the way ahead. 'I didn't ask. I went off to Annerby early without telling him. There was a letter from him waiting for me when I got back to Cordelia's, but I haven't opened it.'

'He'll be worried not to have heard from you,' said Joan. 'You write to one another all the time.'

Persephone said cautiously, 'Don't you think you should have had it out with him? You know, given him the chance to defend himself.'

Mabel grasped the handlebars tightly. 'Can't face it. Too humiliating.'

A profound longing to be at home with Mumsy and Pops overwhelmed her. They had made her feel cherished and special. Best of all, they hadn't known anything about what had happened with Harry and that had enabled her to be strong.

'Don't be kind to me,' she said, 'or I'll sit down in the middle of the road and bawl my eyes out.'

'We can't have that.' Persephone put on a cheery voice. 'Shake a leg, you two. Let's get Mabel to her new home. What's your room like?'

This time, Mabel's laugh was real. 'Do the words "not enough room to swing a cat" mean anything to you?'

'Mabel's in the boxroom,' said Joan. 'It's not a bad size for a boxroom.'

'It'll be plenty big enough for me,' said Mabel. 'I wanted somewhere new. Where better than with Mrs Cooper?'

'She's been kindness itself to me,' said Joan, 'and Mrs Grayson's a good sort as well.'

'There was a time not so long ago when I would never have expected to say this,' said Mabel, 'but I like Mrs Grayson. I used to think she was bonkers, but once I understood what she's been through, I started to get fond of her.'

'Joan, have you noticed how she's looking forward to living with Mrs Cooper and Mrs Grayson, but she hasn't mentioned you?' Persephone said mischievously. 'Are you feeling unappreciated?'

'Horribly,' said Joan.

'Joan's the price I have to pay,' Mabel retorted with a dramatic sigh.

But when they arrived at Wilton Close, it seemed that it was Mrs Cooper who would be paying the price.

'I've decided not to put you in the boxroom, dear. It makes much more sense for you and Joan to share the master bedroom and I'll have the single room that Joan has been in.'

'I can't let you do that—' Mabel began.

'I've already moved my things. I hope you won't mind sharing, Joan.'

'I always shared with Letitia,' said Joan, and she must have sensed Mabel's awkwardness because she added, 'Of course, it all depends on you not hogging the bed in your sleep.'

'No need to worry about that,' said Mrs Cooper, throwing open the bedroom door. 'Mr and Mrs Morgan had separate beds. Which would you like, Joan? You get first choice because you've been here longest.'

The Morgans must have had the matching bedroom furniture all their married lives, and it wouldn't have been new when they started out. A small cupboard stood beside each bed. There was a chest of drawers, a dressing table with a triple mirror and a wardrobe with a long mirror inset in one of the doors. And there was the fireplace.

Mabel turned to her new landlady. 'You can't give up a room with a fireplace.'

'I already have.'

'You're too kind.'

'It makes sense, that's all.' Mrs Cooper sounded brisk, but was that a flush of pleasure? 'And while we're on the subject of making sense, the house rule is that girls here are called by their first names. I know Mrs Grayson always addressed you as Miss Bradshaw, but I want a homely atmosphere, so from now on, you're Mabel. I hope you don't object.'

Persephone slipped a slender arm around Mrs Cooper's bony shoulders. 'Is this you laying down the law, Mrs C?'

Mrs Cooper attempted to look stern. 'Yes, it is, miss.'

Mabel smiled. She might be Mabel and Joan might be Joan, but Mrs Cooper was never going to call the Honourable Miss Trehearn-Hobbs anything but 'miss'.

The door opened and Mrs Grayson looked in. 'Welcome to your new home,' she told Mabel.

Persephone lifted her chin and sniffed. 'Something smells rather delish.'

Mabel's smile grew into an outright grin. 'And now you know the real reason I wanted to come here: Mrs Grayson and her magic mixing bowl. What are you making?'

'Marmalade pudding, to celebrate your arrival.'

'You're a darling. Thank you.'

'I'll enjoy having another person to cook for. Don't forget to hand over your ration book.'

Mrs Cooper and Mrs Grayson disappeared downstairs. Before they brought her bags up, Mabel insisted they should move Joan's belongings so she could have the first choice of drawer and wardrobe space. Mabel had never pictured herself sharing digs with another girl, but if she had, it would have been with Althea. The old guilt twisted inside her, not tearing her apart as it had once done, just reminding her it was here to stay.

Once it would have robbed her of her ability to breathe, but now she could, not set it aside, but ease her way around it. She badly needed this move to be a success and that would only happen if she concentrated on the future.

The future. Not just without Althea, but now without Harry. Another pang of distress assaulted her – deeper, sharper. Fresher. She had to treat it the same way as her guilt. Ease around it. See what's on the other side. Focus on that.

'There, that's all my things,' said Joan, shutting a drawer. 'I say mine, but mostly they're Letitia's.'

And part of getting through her own difficulties would be remembering that others had troubles too.

'That must be hard.' Standing at the open wardrobe, Mabel touched a lilac dress that had elbow-length sleeves, a round, collarless neck and matching belt. 'I remember her wearing this.'

'I made it for her. I ought to alter it to fit me properly, but I can't bring myself to change it at the moment.'

'There's no hurry,' said Mabel.

'I know,' said Joan. 'Don't let's be miserable today. Let's bring your bags up, Mabel. If you two fetch the luggage, I'll take the bike to the garden shed.'

They clattered downstairs. While Mabel and Persephone tussled politely over who should lug the case upstairs and who should bring the lighter carpet bag, Joan opened the front door and disappeared. A moment later, she was back.

'Mabel – Harry's here.'

Mabel barely had time to feel more than a wild fluttering in her stomach before the door to the front room opened and Mrs Grayson appeared and practically dragged Harry over the threshold, greeting him like an old friend – which, to her, he was. To her, he was the handsome young man who had charmed her in her knitting-bedecked parlour and then helped her move to Mrs Cooper's old house. With Mrs Grayson gushing on one side of her, and Joan and Persephone looking daggers at Harry on the other, Mabel felt trapped in the middle. When Mrs Cooper appeared, cooing welcomingly, all Mabel could think was that she had to eject Harry toot sweet.

'You've arrived at precisely the wrong moment.' Her voice was artificially bright. This wasn't a matter of just getting rid of Harry. She had to do it in such a way that Mrs Cooper and Mrs Grayson wouldn't ask awkward questions afterwards. 'I haven't even unpacked yet. Would you mind coming back later?'

To her relief, Persephone was ushering Mrs Grayson into the front room and Joan had distracted Mrs Cooper.

'Shall we . . . ?' Mabel indicated to Harry to step outside. She pulled the door to behind them. 'I'm busy at the moment, but I do want to see you. Can you come back this evening?'

A frown clouded his handsome face. 'Can't I see you now?'

'No. I'm sorry.'

Self-consciousness trickled like icy water down her spine and she could hardly meet his gaze as they made arrangements for later on. When Harry, with obvious reluctance, disappeared, Mabel took a deep breath to prepare herself to feign bravery in the face of her friends' concern.

# Chapter Thirty-Seven

Joan felt unsettled – well, that was pretty normal for her these days, but instead of her own situation causing it, it was down to Harry's unexpected appearance, which had taken the gloss off Mabel's moving in.

'Thank goodness you told us about him beforehand,' said Persephone after Mabel had seen Harry on his way, 'or we'd have welcomed him with open arms. Are you sure you want to see him tonight?'

'I'm not sure that "want" is the right word,' said Mabel, 'but I think I ought to.'

Shortly afterwards, Persephone departed and Mabel went upstairs to unpack. Joan followed her and opened the wardrobe.

'Don't worry. I'm not going to stand over you to make sure you don't encroach on my space. I've just come to fetch this. It's my new porter's uniform, only it's huge so I have to alter it.'

She took it downstairs. She had already asked Mrs Cooper's permission to use the dining table. She didn't actually require the table for unpicking the seams, but she didn't fancy making small talk in the front room with Mrs Cooper and Mrs Grayson. She wanted to be on her own so she could think, although what was the point when her mind kept going round in circles? 'For all the good it'll do you,' Gran had said.

The doorbell rang and she heard Mrs Cooper answer it. Might it be Colette, on her weekly visit? She would enjoy getting to know Colette better. There were voices in the hall. Was that Cordelia? Presently, the dining-room door opened and Cordelia and Mrs Cooper looked in.

'Sorry to disturb you,' said Cordelia and they withdrew.

Joan picked up the tape measure she had borrowed from Mrs Morgan's sewing basket, holding it taut against the side seams of the jacket and its lining. If she could get the jacket and skirt tacked today, she could get to work with Mrs Morgan's treadle sewing machine tomorrow afternoon. Sewing everything together would be the easy bit.

The door opened again. This time it was Cordelia on her own, looking as discreetly expensive as always in a dove-grey costume and pearls.

'I hope I'm not interrupting, but I'd like a private word, if I may.'

Joan put down her sewing.

Cordelia sat at the table with her. 'I'm glad that's over.'

'What's over?'

'Checking the house. Since I recommended Mrs Cooper, Mr Morgan took it into his head that he'd hold me partly responsible for the condition of the house during her tenancy. I have to inspect it every month. Anyway, that isn't what I want to talk to you about. I'm here to tell you what my husband said about your surname.'

A chill rippled through Joan from somewhere inside her chest all the way down to her belly.

'It's simple,' said Cordelia. 'You've been known as Foster practically all your life, so it is quite in order to continue using the name, though should you marry, you would need a formal letter of identification from a solicitor or a magistrate.'

'So I'm allowed to carry on being Joan Foster.'

'You're equally entitled to change your name to Henshaw, in which case you'd need to place a notice in the newspaper to that effect as well as inform everyone who needs to know. You wouldn't have to change your name by deed poll, because the name is already yours, even though it hasn't been used since you were a baby. Does that help?'

Did it? Not really. Yes, it clarified the legal situation, but it didn't answer her deep need for information about *why*. That was what she wanted to know. Why had Gran changed the family name from Henshaw to Foster?

Endlessly fretting over it hadn't helped. Securing supposedly useful guidance from Mr Masters didn't help. She had known since the middle of last week, and now it was the Saturday of this week, and she was no further forward.

There was nothing else for it. She had to tackle Gran.

Mabel and Harry, her erstwhile boyfriend, the rotter who had duped her into falling in love, sat on a bench on Chorlton Green in the pitch-darkness. Not long ago, she would have grabbed the opportunity to snuggle up close, but not now. Never again.

'It didn't take you long to find me,' she said. Of course it hadn't. He wouldn't let go of his meal ticket so easily.

'It isn't the first time I've tracked you down.' Harry's voice was light, but there was confusion beneath the lightness. 'D'you remember my arrival at Kirkland House while you were recuperating?'

Her heart lurched. 'I'm not likely to forget.'

If he hadn't done that, he would have been nothing more than the cheeky blighter who had gingered up her stay in hospital. By turning up at her family home, he had made it impossible for her to sidestep the attraction she felt to him. Heat coursed through her veins as anger flared. He had invaded her home. Mumsy had sat on her bed, saying archly, 'You can't blame me for wondering.' It wasn't just Mabel who had been duped.

'Mrs Masters gave me your new address,' Harry continued. 'She was surprised I didn't know it. I felt rather a chump, I must admit.'

A chump? Bully for him. That was nothing compared to the hollowed-out husk of her former self that she had been reduced to. Should she say all this? Yell it at him, as he deserved? But fury, humiliation and despair clogged her throat.

'And you haven't written all week,' Harry added. 'I've been worried sick. What's going on? Talk to me.'

All she wanted was to lick her wounds in private, but Joan and Persephone were right. She had to have it out with him. He wasn't going to let her go so easily. She had been stupid to imagine he might. Not stupid – desperate.

'If I didn't write to you, and I didn't pass on my new address, doesn't that tell you something? If I say I also went up to Annerby without you, does that help you understand?'

'You've been to Annerby?' Harry's voice rose in surprise. 'But I was meant to go with you.'

'Change of plan.'

'You changed your mind about wanting me to see your parents?'

'I changed my mind about a lot of things.'

Harry reached out to her and she shot to her feet.

'Don't touch me.' She sat down before he could rise. She didn't want him towering over her. 'How did you get here today? Did you drive over in your Austin Ten?'

'You know I didn't. It's up on blocks for the duration.'

'Is it? Are you sure?' Her heartbeat was a thin, cold

chime. 'Only, I thought maybe Algy must be using it. It is his, isn't it? Your friend Algy's?'

There was a moment of – what? Shock? Embarrassment? But when Harry said, 'Now see here, Mabel,' his voice, damn him, was utterly reasonable.

'No, you see here, Harry. You let me think that motor was yours and it isn't, is it? It's Algy's, whoever he is.'

'He's a friend, a good friend. And I never actually said the Austin belonged to me.'

'You let me think it. You let my parents think it. You know you did.'

'Can you blame me for wanting to impress them? To impress you? For wanting you to think well of me?'

'I'd think more highly of you if you'd told the truth.'

'Is that what this is about?' Harry asked. 'The ownership of an Austin Ten? I apologise if I misled you—'

'If?' she demanded. 'And that isn't what it's about, or at least that's only part of it. I . . . I overheard some girls talking about you – about us. They said you were after my family's money.'

'And you believed them?' Harry rubbed his face with his hands. 'After everything we've meant to one another, you chose to believe *them*?'

'Was I wrong? I've remembered a couple of things. I remember how you winked at me that time on the hospital ward.'

'Of course I did. A pretty girl like you – I couldn't help myself.'

'The next time you saw me, you apologised. I thought that was because I was on the respectable side of the ward by then with the other middle-class patients – but you wouldn't have known how the ward was organised, would you? So that wasn't the reason you apologised. But I've remembered that the day you winked, you were on your way along the ward to ask a question at the office. I bet you anything that when you were there, you heard Persephone asking the nurse to get in touch with my parents. All she knew was that my father owned a factory in Annerby. You overheard that, didn't you? And you used the information to find out that I had precisely the quality you were looking for in a wife, namely a wealthy father.'

'You can't seriously believe that?'

'Why not? Those girls did. They laughed about it. It was common knowledge as far as they were concerned.'

Harry's silence merged with the blackout. Shivers built up inside Mabel as it hit her that somewhere inside her, hope had lurked, wanting him to make everything right.

'You aren't falling over yourself to deny it,' she said.

'I can't deny it.'

With a cry, she almost doubled over, then sat up straight, moving aside as Harry made to reach out to her.

'Hear me out,' he begged.

Her voice roughened. 'Believe me, there's nothing you can say.'

'Yes, there is. I swear that every word I said to you about my feelings was true. Please listen – not for my sake, but for yours.'

'How can it possibly be for my sake?'

'It can, if everything you said about your feelings for me was true.'

The trap snapped shut. She was forced to listen. If he had played fast and loose with her, she hadn't exactly been a hundred per cent honest with him, had she? She recalled how she had dodged the question about whether Harry was her first boyfriend, her first serious love. That might not be on the same scale as the trick he had played on her, but it showed she wasn't exactly a shining example of honesty and integrity.

'You want the truth, so here it is. Those girls you over-heard – I don't know who they were, but I can make a pretty good guess. I used to be in with a crowd, none of whom had much money, and we used to joke about making advantageous marriages.'

'I don't want to hear this.'

She started to get up, but Harry pulled her back.

'You can't leave now, when I've made myself sound like the worst sort of rat. Give me the chance to redeem myself. You're right about what happened in the hospital. I did overhear Persephone, but remember, that was after I'd winked at you and I wouldn't have done that if you hadn't caught my eye.'

'Me and a hundred others, no doubt.'

'Your family circumstances mattered to me in the beginning, but the more I got to know you, the more deeply involved I became, the more I developed true feel-ings for you. Everything I've ever said to you about how much you mean to me is true. I had no idea I could feel this way. I thought all I wanted was a comfortable life, but I swear that if your father lost every penny, I'd still want to spend my life with you. You're clever and caring, and God, when I think how brave you were during the Christ-mas Blitz, my heart almost explodes. You make me feel like the luckiest man in the world. If anything were to happen to you, I don't know how I'd manage. Yes, I didn't exactly have honourable intentions when I started out, but think how long ago that was. I love you, Mabel Bradshaw. I honestly love you and I'd do anything to win you back. Please don't let this come between us. I was an absolute ass and if you walk away, it'll be what I deserve, but if you take me back, I'll spend the rest of our lives together mak-ing it up to you. I promise I'll never let you down again.'

# Chapter Thirty-Eight

Mabel and Joan cycled home side by side after a night on duty at St Cuthbert's. There had been no air raids since this time last week. The girls had been on duty three nights running and Mabel was sure she had been wide awake the entire time. Would there be another letter from Harry today? Or more flowers? A splendid bouquet had awaited her when she arrived home from work on Monday. She hadn't wanted to be impressed, but she was. It must have set him back a bit. Before everything went wrong, she wouldn't have thought twice about flowers because she had assumed Harry was well heeled, but now, just when she should have scorned this blatant attempt to win her round, she worried whether he could afford it.

Tuesday had brought a letter.

> *My darling Mabel,*
> *No matter what happens, no matter what decision you make, you are my darling, my dearest, my one and only true love . . .*

Warmth had flooded her face. He knew how to write a jolly good letter, she had to give him that. But could she trust his apologies and explanations, his protestations of love? Had he truly written from his heart? Yet if the letter wasn't genuine, why would he bother? If he had never loved her, if the whole thing had been a sham from start to finish, wouldn't he simply shrug his shoulders and walk away?

Then yesterday, Wednesday, another letter had arrived, again filled with love and remorse. He wrote so fluently. The fluency of a confidence trickster or of a desperate lover?

If he kept bombarding her with attention, would she be able to resist? Did she want to resist? Never mind what she wanted. What was the sensible thing to do?

But, as she knew all too well, being in love and being sensible didn't necessarily go hand in hand. And Althea had paid a terrible price.

Arriving in Wilton Close, she and Joan wheeled their bicycles up the passage and through the gate into the back garden. The kitchen door opened and Mrs Cooper looked out.

'You shouldn't be hauling yourself out of bed this early,' Mabel scolded her.

'Yes, I should. Put your bikes away. Breakfast is almost ready.'

When they were seated at the breakfast table, Mabel, determined to avoid any speculation on Mrs Cooper's part as to whether she would hear from Harry today, started a conversation.

'How are you settling into your new neighbourhood, Mrs Cooper?'

'It's not the easiest thing. I moved into my old house the day I got wed and I'd grown up around the corner.'

'Coming here can't have been easy.'

'Coming here was a blessing. I've got a smart house and you two lasses to look after and Mrs Grayson to keep me company. You have to look on the bright side. I'm getting to know the folk around and about, not least through queuing up at the shops. I met a very nice lady the day before yesterday, a Mrs Shires, who lives in Claude Road. She was saying it's her son's birthday on Thursday – well, today, in fact. His name's Peter and he's fourteen today. Her biggest hope is that the war will be over before he's old enough to be called up.'

What a sobering thought. Would the war be over before Peter was called upon to fight? Look how long the last war had gone on.

'Anyroad,' said Mrs Cooper, 'that's enough of me gassing. Joan, you can have first crack at the bathroom, because you have to get to work. Mabel, you've got the morning off, so why not go to bed for a couple of hours?'

Mabel laughed. 'I was thinking that all the way home, but now I'm here, I'd rather press on. It's April next week and I have to plant the early potatoes and protect them from frost.'

'I didn't know you knew about gardening,' said Joan.

'I don't, but I told Mumsy about having a proper garden here and she got our gardener to list all the jobs I should be doing.'

'Steven's dad is a keen gardener,' said Joan. 'He used to get Steven to tell Letitia and me what to do.' She ducked her head, but not before Mabel had glimpsed tears.

'It's not easy, is it, chuck?' said Mrs Cooper. 'We all try hard to be all right, and you've had more to cope with than most.'

'For what it's worth, you seem to be coping pretty well,' said Mabel.

'There's no choice, is there?' said Joan. 'Bad things happen and you have to deal with them. You can't crumble, especially not in wartime.'

'Shall I tell you how I sometimes feel since losing my Lizzie?' said Mrs Cooper. 'I feel as if I haven't got room inside my head for even one more thought. There's so much crammed in there that I hardly dare think in case it jumbles everything up.'

'That's it exactly,' Joan whispered, gazing at their land-lady as if she had uttered a magic spell.

The doorbell rang.

'That'll be the milklady,' said Mrs Cooper, getting up. 'I must go and pay her.'

'Is that why you still haven't chosen between Steven and Bob?' Mabel asked Joan.

'I was agonising over them all the time, and then I found out about my name and now that's all I can think about. Cordelia says I shouldn't keep them hanging on in case they get fed up, but finding out about my name has thrown up so many questions.' Joan sat up straight. 'Hark at me, carrying on as if I'm the only one with problems when you've had your big upset with Harry.'

'Don't change the subject.'

'I want to change it.'

'You mean you'd rather poke around in my sore spot than have me poke around in yours?' Mabel spoke in a jokey way, wanting to ease her friend's burden. 'What is there to say? I trusted him and gave him my heart and then it all turned out to be a big fat lie . . . except that maybe it wasn't a lie after all. Whatever his motives were in the first place, he swore to me last Saturday, and in his letters since, that he loves me and I'm the only girl for him.'

'Do you believe him?'

'He's very convincing.'

'Do you want to be convinced?'

'I feel . . . frozen. I loved him so much. If I let my feel-ings thaw, will we live happily ever after? After what he did – can we?'

*

Friday was Joan's day off. When she dressed and did her hair, she put on her snood. Was that cowardly? But there was no point in annoying Gran when it could easily be avoided.

It didn't take long to walk to Torbay Road, just a matter of minutes. It was strange to think of her and Gran living so close. For a moment, she wished they were miles apart. That would feel more natural after all the upset there had been between them.

Maybe her peace offering would help. After she had altered her new uniform last weekend, she had dug out the piece of material she had rescued the day she had helped herself to Letitia's clothes. It was an oddment left over from a dress she had made for her sister, big enough for a bolero jacket or something else that didn't require much fabric. After some thought, she had used part of it to make a cover for Gran's prayer book. Surely Gran wouldn't refuse a gift with such a strong connection to Letitia.

Joan walked along the road, enjoying the morning sunshine on this mild spring day. It would be April next Tuesday. Longer days, warmer weather, a late Easter: people must be looking forward to that, but not Joan. When March ended, that would mean she had lived through another full month without Letitia.

She opened the wooden gate and walked through. Her heart thumped as she rang the bell. She took a step backwards in case the sight of her unleashed Gran's tongue.

The door opened. Gran was dressed in a calf-length skirt with a blouse and a brown cardigan, her iron-grey hair tied back in a bun. Joan caught the faintest metallic whiff of silver polish. Friday was Gran's morning for cleaning the brights. She had removed her pinny before coming to the door.

'What do you want?' Gran asked.

Joan hung on to her pleasant expression for dear life. 'Hello, Gran. How are you?'

'Fine, thank you. What do you want?'

All the muscles in Joan's body seemed to have set like rock. She swallowed. 'May I come in?'

Gran's gaze shifted. Joan glanced over her shoulder. A couple of neighbours passed by, shopping baskets on their arms.

'Get inside,' Gran hissed, pulling her over the threshold.

Joan went straight into the parlour, not waiting to be invited in case she wasn't. She had forgotten how dingy it was, with its old furniture and those thick net curtains.

Gran followed her in and took her customary seat by the fireplace. Joan sat opposite.

'I need to give you my new address.'

'Has Mrs Cooper thrown you out, then? I can't say I'm surprised.'

Joan held on to her temper. 'We were bombed out. Mrs Cooper lost everything. She's acting as housekeeper in a place in Wilton Close now. The owners are away for the duration.'

'Cowards,' said Gran. 'Wilton Close? That's a step up for the likes of Mrs Cooper.'

'That's where I'm living. Number one, Wilton Close.'

Gran looked away.

Finally, Joan added, 'So I'm nearby if you need me.'

Gran huffed out a breath. 'I told the neighbours you'd moved out to be closer to your job and now you've ended up practically on my doorstep.'

What was she supposed to say to that? She produced her gift. She had put it inside a brown paper bag, but hadn't tied it, hadn't tried to make it look like a gift. Something so closely associated with Letitia's death had no business looking festive.

'This is for you.'

'I don't want it, not after the way you let me down.'

'It's a keepsake. I made it in memory of Letitia. Look.'
Joan unwrapped it. 'It's a cover for your prayer book. Do
you recognise the material?'

'Her favourite dress.'

'Won't you please accept it? For her sake.'

'I don't need folderols to remind me.'

'Neither do I, but it's good to have them all the same.'

Gran's eyes clouded. Then she reached out and took it.
'Thank you.' She bent her head over it. 'I'll give you this:
your work is as neat as ever.'

'Thank you.'

'But if you've brought me this to butter me up, it won't
work.'

Self-consciousness tightened Joan's skin. 'Of course I
didn't.'

Gran's lip curled in open disbelief. 'I told you it'd do
you no good to have your birth certificate.'

'Won't you please tell me why you changed our name
to Foster? I need to know.'

'No, you don't.' Gran spoke so sharply that Joan froze.

'But, Gran—'

'No.' Gran might have been reprimanding a disobedi-
ent dog. 'You don't.'

'This is altogether too comfy,' said Bette, leaning against
the back of the long wooden bench and stretching her legs
in front of her in a way that would have made Mumsy
have kittens should Mabel have done the same thing in
public.

'It's come to something when a station waiting room
feels like luxury,' said Louise.

Mabel and her gang had been allocated a length of

permanent way near enough to a small station for them to take their midday break 'in a real room with real furniture', as Bernice put it, and who cared if the furniture was wooden benches?

'Time to get back to work before you all start snoozing,' said Bernice, putting her flask in her knapsack.

'Not until we've visited the Ladies,' said Bette.

'We've got to enjoy the glamour while we can,' said Mabel.

When they set off for their allotted section of track, Bernice said, 'We'll swap partners for the afternoon. Mabel, you'll be with me.'

The two of them soon settled into the routine, Mabel lifting the sleepers and Bernice packing the ballast underneath.

'I don't want to put you in a bad position,' said Bernice when they were between sleepers, 'but I need to ask you a question.'

'That sounds ominous.'

'It's about Joan. I know it's not fair to ask you, but I'm worried about her and Bob. I don't think they've been seeing one another recently. Bob says it's because of their shifts and first-aid duties, but I wonder if there's more to it.'

'You're right,' said Mabel. 'It's not fair to ask me.'

'Then there is summat going on?'

'I didn't say that.' Mabel bit her lip. 'But if there is anything, it's their business.'

'Oh aye?' Bernice's normally kind eyes hardened. 'Wait until you have children.'

That stung. Mabel bent over the next sleeper and resumed work, feeling the pull inside her muscles as she lifted it.

If Bernice was miffed with her, it didn't last. Mabel had learned early on that Bernice knocked any sign of grumpiness on its head, and evidently she didn't allow herself to be grumpy either. Nevertheless, Mabel felt uncomfortable at having been so blunt with someone who wasn't just her senior in years but also her boss.

'I'm sorry for speaking out,' she said as they tackled their final sleeper before stopping for their afternoon tea break. 'I hope you didn't think I was rude.'

'I did at the time, but I was the one who said I didn't want to put you in a bad position.' Bernice smiled ruefully. 'I couldn't resist asking. It's not every mother who works alongside her son's girlfriend's friend.'

Mabel was glad things had been smoothed over, but it had given her something to think about. Joan was locked in a state of indecision over her two blokes, and that wasn't helping anyone. Not Bob or Steven, and not Joan either. Now it had affected Bernice too – and she had taken it out on Mabel.

That settled it. Mabel wasn't going to let her own situation with Harry trundle on while she agonised over what to do. She was going to make her choice and abide by it.

She would write to Harry this evening.

# Chapter Thirty-Nine

After Mabel had posted her letter to Harry last Friday, he had raced to her side on Sunday, not exactly on a dashing white charger, but he might as well have been. She had seen him from the window, striding purposefully up the path as if meeting her was the only thing in the world that mattered. It was impossible not to be flattered. There had been a spurt of anger too, because he had spoiled what they'd had, but that had been swamped by a surge of desire deep in her belly. Was she weak still to have feelings for him?

She hadn't let him take her out on Sunday. Instead, she had made him stay in and play whist with Mrs Cooper and Mrs Grayson and he had delighted the two of them with his easy banter. She had sent him on his way early, too.

'I was hoping we could talk,' Harry had said as he lingered on the doorstep.

'Nothing to say. You said it all last weekend and in your letters.'

'Now I'm confused. Are we on again?'

'I can't leap back in as if nothing has happened. I want to go out with you, but you hurt me badly and I need time to recover from that.'

'We'll take it as slowly as you like. I'll agree to anything as long as I can be with you.'

'Are you free on Tuesday evening? The Midland Hotel is hosting a dinner and dance to help raise money for a Spitfire. Would you like to take me?'

Did Harry realise what the date would be on Tuesday? Should she be worried about being an April Fool?

Getting ready now, she couldn't have been more nervous if this had been her first night out with a man. With her hair in rollers, she poured the dregs of her bath crystals into the basin and gave herself an all-over wash, then dried herself and removed the circular lid from the box of Bronnley dusting powder Mumsy had popped into her stocking a couple of Christmases ago, using the puff to brush the fine, scented powder over her skin.

She had brought three day dresses and a couple of formal evening dresses back from Annerby and now she chose her pearl-grey silk-crêpe evening gown, its sweetheart neckline and simple lines appealing to her with their lack of fussiness. After applying a little make-up, she removed her rollers, brushing the resulting mass of curls into loose waves that she fastened back from her face with mother-of-pearl clips. It wasn't the most fashionable way to wear her hair, but Mabel knew what suited her. At heart, she was an outdoor girl who, in spite of her made-to-measure wardrobe, looked her best, as well as felt at her most comfortable, when her appearance had a casual air.

'You'll knock his socks off,' said Joan.

And she did. The dazzled look in Harry's dark eyes told her so.

His conduct all evening was impeccable. He was attentive, considerate and charming. They must appear the perfect couple, but Mabel could see Harry wasn't taking anything for granted, which was as it should be.

The evening was hosted by a master of ceremonies. Mabel waltzed and quick-stepped in Harry's arms and, during a gentlemen's excuse-me, found herself changing partners time after time as each partner was excused by the next. Was it petty to hope Harry had seen how many men wanted to dance with her? Shortly afterwards, there was a ladies' excuse-me, which she made the most of, moving swiftly to find a new partner each time a girl tapped her on the shoulder and said 'Excuse me.'

As well as the ballroom dances, there were old-time dances. Mabel didn't know all of them, but she could do the military two-step and during the veleta she murmured, 'One-two-three, one-two-three, one and two' under her breath, just as Grandad had done when he'd taught her this one when she was a little girl.

'Having fun?' Harry asked as they returned to their table to sit out the next one and have a drink.

'It's a wizard evening. Thank you for bringing me.'

'Thank you for giving me another chance.'

How handsome he was, with his dark hair, his broad forehead and strong jawline. And those eyes. Oh, those eyes, so dark and intense, but just now with a question in them, a question he hadn't put into words all evening.

Mabel wasn't the sort to play games and keep him dangling. It was time to answer his question.

She caught his hand. 'This is what I want. You were a dunderhead to chase me for my money, but the feeling that grew between us is real and I believe you when you say I'm the girl for you.'

'You are, I swear it.'

'There.' Elation threaded through her, sending the little pulses jumping in her wrists and at her throat. 'I've said my piece.'

'If that's all you're going to say,' Harry murmured, leaning towards her, 'I can think of something else that pretty mouth of yours can do to keep busy.'

He kissed her in full view of anyone who wanted to watch.

And Mabel, not caring if the dance spotlight caught them, kissed him back.

Joan had wanted to spend some of the hours of darkness at the railway shed, but she wasn't needed. Dot, Alison, Persephone and Mr Thirkle had already made arrangements to go and four was what their plan required. Instead, Joan went to St Clement's School, where a knitting evening was being held in one of the classrooms. In the confines of the Morgans' house, Mrs Grayson was churning out knitted garments for bombed-out families and she had asked Joan to deliver them to a collection place. Joan hadn't liked to take them to the WVS station at MacFadyen's Church, because that was a stone's throw from Gran's house and she felt awkward at the thought of bumping into some of her old neighbours, so she had gone to St Clement's instead, where the skilful stitching in Mrs Grayson's garments had been exclaimed over and a pair of needles was thrust into Joan's hands before she had a chance to explain that she wasn't responsible for making what she had brought. Not that it mattered. She was a competent knitter and she was happy to spend the evening chatting and stitching.

Or so she thought. She soon realised that there were several mother-and-daughter pairs here, working side by side, and it brought home to her the loss with which she had grown up. Could you miss what you had never had? Yes, you could, absolutely. She had never had her mother's love. She gave herself a moment to hate Estelle, but no hatred bubbled up. All she felt was a profound sadness. She had never hated Estelle. Gran had done her utmost to teach her to, and Joan, obedient to the last, had pretended she did. But what she felt for Estelle had always been a weary, never-ending longing.

Her heart still felt heavy, and her mind preoccupied, as she left to go home. She walked to Chorlton Green, then onto Beech Road. Head down, she stepped off the white-edged kerb to cross over, aware, too late, of the motor coming at her. Her mind froze, but her body didn't. She leaped backwards, but she stumbled against the kerb and toppled hard to the ground, banging her hip and her elbow. Pain darted through her at the same time as her head bashed against the street lamp, sending shock vibrating throughout her body, depriving her of breath and the ability to think.

A figure loomed over her. 'Great Scott! Are you all right?' A man's voice. 'Where's your road sense, you little idiot?'

Another voice. A woman this time. 'Leave her be, Richard.' A whiff of perfume as the woman crouched beside her. 'Don't try to move. Richard, the police station's just over there. Fetch help.'

'There's no need,' said Joan.

She tried to get up, but her legs wouldn't hold her. Her head felt swimmy. Then there were more people, more voices. She was lifted into someone's arms – Steven's. She curled against him so as not to be jolted as he carried her into the police station.

'Fortunately for you, there's a doctor here tonight,' said Steven.

He set her down gently on a chair. She still felt woozy, but she was also starting to feel like a prize twit. All those air raids she had attended without being injured, and now she had all but hurled herself into the teeth of an approaching motor car.

'Leave us, please, while I examine the young lady.'

The doctor was a middle-aged man with a clipped moustache. He tested her limbs, examined her skull and prodded her side, making her flinch, but when he felt more carefully, he declared she hadn't broken anything.

'You'll be black and blue in the morning. If you feel sick or dizzy, see your doctor.'

He opened the door to leave. At once Steven came in.

'How is she?' he asked.

'She'll do,' said the doctor as he left.

'I've brought someone you'll want to see,' said Steven.

Bob! Suddenly Joan's mind was crystal clear and so was her heart. Bob was the one she wanted, the one she needed, now and always. She half rose, arms already reaching out.

In walked Mrs Cooper.

Together with Alison, Persephone and Mr Thirkle, Dot was here for a few hours of waiting near the railway shed, in case the thief returned. They were stopping until midnight, so they had about another hour to go. Sitting on the makeshift bench constructed from railway sleepers, Dot shifted a fraction so that her arm brushed Alison's. To her dismay, Alison murmured 'Sorry' and moved away, as if it was her fault for sitting too close.

'Nay, love, that were me,' said Dot. 'I needed to feel I've someone close by, that's all.'

'In that case . . .' Laughing, Persephone budged up closer on her other side and tucked her arm through Dot's.

Alison followed suit. Did Mr Thirkle, on Persephone's other side, feel left out?

'I heard a good April Fool's trick that was played on a new lad in the work sheds today,' said Mr Thirkle. 'One of the lady steam-hammer operators told him she needed a replacement part and she sent him to the stores to ask for a long weight.'

Persephone laughed, though it took Dot a moment to

catch up. Of course. The boy would have been kept hanging about for ages. A very long wait.

'That's clever,' said Alison.

'I hope he saw the joke,' said Dot.

'It's part of being new,' said Mr Thirkle. 'I wonder what jokes your grandson got up to.'

'I just hope he played them on the other kids and not on his teacher,' said Dot.

The low hum of an engine purred through the darkness and a chill trickled through Dot.

'Hide behind the bench,' said Mr Thirkle.

They crouched behind it, peering over the top as the sound grew louder. Over to their left, a muted beam of light scraped the ground and then stopped. The engine fell silent. The motor car was at the front end of the building, where the big double doors were securely padlocked. There was the sound of a door opening and slamming shut, then a torch beam, a proper beam, not one muffled by tissue, swam around, crossing the side of the vehicle.

Dot had seen that motor before – on the day she had helped set up the food dump.

'It's Mr Samuels,' she whispered. 'He's the LMS bigwig who came here the day we delivered the food.'

'I'm glad it's him,' said Alison, 'and not one of Mabel's gang.'

But Dot didn't feel the same. She couldn't be glad that anyone who worked for the railways was a thief.

Joan sat up in bed, propped up in a nest of pillows. A hot-water bottle took the edge off the ache in her side and there was a glass of fruit cordial on her bedside table, together with a small tin of Howards' aspirin. Mrs Grayson had produced a bottle of arnica ointment and insisted

Joan rub it into her sore places. The two ladies now sat one on each side of the mattress.

'You're both very kind,' said Joan, 'but I don't need all this looking after.'

'Don't be silly,' said Mrs Cooper. 'Of course you do.'

'Be grateful this is all there is to it,' Mrs Grayson added. She was wrapped up in her dressing gown, with her curlers under her hairnet. 'You might easily have ended up in hospital.'

'It doesn't bear thinking about,' said Mrs Cooper. 'Mrs Grayson, would you mind making Joan some cocoa?'

'I'll make us all some.' Mrs Grayson left the room, pulling the door to.

'Thank you for coming to my rescue at the police station,' said Joan.

'My dear girl, if only you knew what a shock it was when I opened the door and saw a policeman.'

Was she recalling the knock at an unexpected time that had heralded the news of Lizzie's death? Or hearing that Mr Cooper had been knocked down in the blackout? Joan's fingers twitched across the counterpane to entwine with Mrs Cooper's.

'I'm glad you sent for me, Joan.'

'I didn't,' Joan confessed. 'Steven came for you off his own bat.'

'When I walked in, there was such a look of hope and – and brightness on your face, but then the expression vanished.'

'It's not that I wasn't pleased to see you,' Joan assured her.

'I know, love. But who were you hoping to see?'

The door swung open and Mrs Grayson appeared with a tray. She placed it on Mabel's bed and handed mugs to Joan and Mrs Cooper before taking the third one for herself and returning to her place on the bed.

'There's no need to stop talking on my account,' she said.

'You don't have to say anything if you don't want to,' Mrs Cooper told Joan. 'Maybe you need to think about it.'

'Mrs Cooper,' said Mrs Grayson, 'you might have been blessed with the clairvoyant powers to know what's in Joan's mind, but I haven't. What's happened?' she asked Joan.

Joan felt wobbly and it was nothing to do with her bumps and bruises.

Mrs Grayson touched her hand. 'I don't want you to think I'm being a nosy old bat.'

'Huh,' Mrs Cooper muttered.

'But not so long ago,' said Mrs Grayson, 'half of Manchester witnessed me being forced out of my home with my husband and Floozy queuing up outside to push their way in, so if anybody knows what it feels like to have their dirty linen washed in public, I'm that person, and I'm telling you that as horrible and upsetting as it was, the thing that got me through it in one piece was having good folk around me taking my side and doing all they could to help me. And if I'm a nosy old bat, then I'm a nosy old bat with your best interests at heart.' She gave Mrs Cooper a *so there* look.

Emotion swelled inside Joan. She pushed her mug into Mrs Cooper's hand and fumbled about, trying to fish out her hanky from under her pillow, only for a twang of pain to shoot up her side as she tried to twist. Mrs Grayson thrust her own handkerchief into Joan's hands for her to pat her overflowing eyes.

'I think our Joan has realised what she needs to do regarding her personal life,' said Mrs Cooper.

'About time too,' said Mrs Grayson. 'Now, is one of you going to tell me what?'

*

415

Dot watched as the beam of torchlight progressed along the ground for the length of the railway shed, dipping out of sight now and then as Mr Samuels made his way behind the bushes.

'It's horrible to think of an important railway official being a thief,' said Dot. 'This will give the entire company a bad name.'

The figure arrived at the privy. Torchlight flashed up and down the wonky door. There was a grunting sound as Mr Samuels applied himself to the task and wrenched it open, sending a grinding noise into the darkness. The beam of light zigzagged as he jumped back when the door tilted towards him, the light catching his profile.

'He looks young to be in an important position,' said Alison.

'I think you've got your wish, Mrs Green,' said Mr Thirkle. 'That's not Mr Samuels.'

Dot was concentrating too hard to feel relieved. The torchlight had afforded her the merest glimpse, but she was sure she recognised the man.

'It's the chauffeur,' she hissed. 'Mr Samuels's driver.'

The chauffeur disappeared inside the shed. Through the still night air, the watchers heard the inner door opening. Dot went very still and sensed the others doing the same as they all prepared themselves for what was coming next.

'I should take the rotor arm out of the engine,' Persephone whispered, 'so the motor won't start.'

'You shouldn't need to,' said Mr Thirkle, 'if we trap him in the shed.'

'But—' Persephone began.

'It isn't part of the plan,' said Dot. 'Don't start changing things now.'

'You two girls,' Mr Thirkle said softly, 'you know what

416

to do. Creep back to your bicycles, take them to the path and cycle like fury to the signal box. Go up the steps and bang on the door until the signalman lets you in. Have you got the paper with the shed number and location?'

'In my pocket,' said Persephone.

'Explain what's happening and tell him to get on the blower to the line controller. Then the line controller can send for the police. Meanwhile, Mrs Green and I will fasten the thief inside.'

The girls clicked on their muted torches and slid away, their progress marked the occasional rustling.

'Come along, Mrs Green.'

Torches on, they made their way to the pile of sleepers the railway girls had moved close to the privy door.

'You hold that end steady,' said Mr Thirkle, 'and I'll swing this end round and down to the ground, then lean it up against the wall.'

'Let's get them all standing up before we start walking them.'

With Mr Thirkle taking most of the strain, they got eight sleepers standing up against the wall. Dot had walked any number of long parcels and boxes as part of her job, but that had always been on flat station platforms. The ground here was bumpy and walking the sleepers was tricky, not least because even though, being old and weathered, they were meant to be light, they were still jolly heavy. But Dot didn't care how difficult it was. She had fretted herself silly over these thefts and she wasn't going to fail now.

They walked the first sleepers to the privy. Thank heaven the chauffeur had wrenched open the outer door. Little did he know that he had helped trap himself. Dot leaned her sleeper against the outer wall and had a breather while Mr Thirkle manhandled his sleeper inside. Dot squeezed in after him and they fumbled the sleeper down to the floor across the inner doorway before doing the same with Dot's.

'Back we go,' said Mr Thirkle and they returned to where the rest of the sleepers were standing.

They repeated the process, and then did it again. It wasn't true what folk said about things getting easier with practice. Shifting the fifth and sixth sleepers felt every bit as tricky and bumbling as moving the first two.

When they returned for the fourth pair, Dot caught a faint whiff of something in the air. Tobacco! She was about to whisper to Mr Thirkle when a strong hand grabbed her arm and half dragged, half flung her backwards. With a yell that sounded like she was whooping a battle cry, she staggered back, desperately trying to evade the inevitable fall. She had barely landed on her back, the air rushing from her body, when she was kicked in the ribs so hard that the bones bent inwards. Shock and pain rendered movement impossible, but then instinct took over, curling her into a protective ball.

She tried to roll away before a second kick could find its mark. Then there was a fresh commotion. Mr Thirkle had hurled himself at the attacker, barging him aside and giving her the time she needed to scramble to her feet, clutching her side.

The attacker quickly righted himself and charged at Mr Thirkle, young man versus old. The two of them hit the ground, with Mr Thirkle underneath. The attacker drew back his fist and slammed it down on Mr Thirkle, then raised it again for a second blow. Dot bent down, her hands scrabbling around. When one hand banged against something hard, she brought her other one across to explore the shape. A cube, more or less, with some knobbly bits and a handle – a railway lamp!

She grabbed it with both hands. Who cared if its glass

was broken, if her gloves got ripped, if her hands got shredded to pieces? She plunged towards the two men, dodging backwards as their combined shape lurched in her direction. Good for Mr Thirkle – he was fighting back.

She raised the lamp high above her head and brought it crashing down on the attacker, bashing his shoulder. With a furious yell, he swung towards her. She drew back her weapon and smashed it into his face. He yelled again, doubling over before lurching upright again. It took all Dot's courage not to retreat, but more heroics were unnecessary for the man staggered away, picking up speed.

Casting the lamp aside, Dot dropped to her knees beside her friend.

'Are you all right?'

Mr Thirkle blew out a sharp breath and pushed himself up on his elbow. 'Never mind me. Are you all right?'

Dot touched her ribs. 'It's nowt. You're the one that went ten rounds with Jack Dempsey.'

They rose to their feet, helping each other.

'What a pair,' chuckled Dot, but then she stopped chuckling, practically stopped breathing.

They were standing very close. Not on purpose, but just through having assisted each other to their feet. Dot's fingers tingled with the need to touch Mr Thirkle's face. They looked at one another. Dot's pulse raced.

Then the sound of the motor's engine starting broke into the moment, making them look round. The motor reversed, executed a turn and drove away.

'Perhaps we should have let Miss Trehearn-Hobbs remove the rotor arm after all,' said Mr Thirkle.

'Certainly not,' said Dot. 'She'd have walked straight into that man's arms. Did he hurt you badly? You were so brave to come to my rescue.'

'What a brute, attacking a lady.' Mr Thirkle made a

move. Was he about to reach towards her? But no, he cleared his throat and turned away. 'We'd best finish blocking that door.'

'Do you think the chauffeur will have heard the kerfuffle?'

'No, those walls are pretty thick.'

When they got the fourth pair of sleepers up onto their makeshift barrier, Dot's shoulders protested, and as for her ribcage, well, she wouldn't worry about that now. The beating Mr Thirkle had taken was far worse.

As they stepped back outside, she said, 'Mr Thirkle, I owe you an apology.' Was she trying to create another moment of intimacy? She refused to examine that possibility too closely. Besides, she genuinely wanted to say this.

'I'm sure you don't.'

'I do. The first time I saw you, I thought you had a receding chin.'

He smiled. 'You could say that. My Edie says I look like a tortoise.'

Ruddy Edie. Dot wasn't having her spoiling the moment.

'And I thought – well, I thought a chin like that makes a man look like he isn't strong, but that's not true. You may not have much chin, but, by golly, you've got plenty of backbone. I'll never forget the way you took on that man to save me.'

'Any man would have done the same. Now, before our shoulders seize up, I suggest we put these against this outer door and shut it as best we can.'

'Do you think the thief will manage to get out?'

'I doubt it,' said Mr Thirkle, 'but if he does, the moment he shows himself, I think one bash on the head from you with your trusty lamp will send him scuttling back inside.'

# Chapter Forty

Dot, Mr Thirkle and the girls spent much of the night in the police station, explaining again and again what had happened. They were separated from one another, which made Dot feel twitchy, as if they were the criminals.

'So you're the one who started it all?' asked Inspector Stanhope.

'No, the thief started it.'

'And you instigated your own investigation. Why didn't you come straight to the police?'

'I've already explained why not.'

'Indulge me.'

'I was worried you might not believe that I didn't see the cross on the label until after we'd eaten the corned beef. I didn't want to be accused of feeding stolen food to my family and I didn't want to get into trouble for buying the corned beef in the first place. I've heard of a magistrate who punishes folk who buy off the black market.'

'You say you bought the corned beef?'

'Aye.'

'But Mr Thirkle is under the impression it was your daughter-in-law who purchased it.'

Drat. 'I was trying to keep her out of it.'

'Taking the blame for her misdemeanour, you mean?'

'She hasn't committed a misdemeanour. She bought those tins in good faith.'

'Let's go back to the beginning, shall we?'

And so on. At last, Dot was escorted to the front desk, where the other three jumped up from a long bench.

'You've been ages,' said Alison.

Inspector Stanhope addressed them all. 'Because of you, we've apprehended a thief who made use of his employer's motor. He hasn't given us the name of his accomplice yet. Thank you all for your assistance, but next time kindly put the matter in the hands of the police immediately.'

'I hope there won't be a next time,' Dot murmured.

'We shall, sir,' said Mr Thirkle.

'One last thing,' said the inspector. 'Keep this to yourselves.'

'Must we?' asked Persephone. 'I'm a reporter and I'd like to write about it. Mrs Green is a heroine, and not for the first time, I might add.'

Dot nudged her. 'Give over.'

'No talking and no reporting,' said Inspector Stanhope. 'There's a question of morale here. We don't want the general public getting upset over wartime thefts. Neither do we want them knowing about food dumps.'

'Why not?' asked Alison.

'Had you heard of them before this?'

'No.'

'Quite. There are some things we don't want getting about.'

'The food dumps are in case of invasion,' Persephone whispered and Alison nodded.

'So keep mum,' ordered Inspector Stanhope.

They spilled out onto the pavement. Alison and Persephone headed down a side passage towards the bicycle shed.

Mr Thirkle sighed. 'That's made me feel I should apologise all over again for what my Edie said to you.'

Dot looked at him in surprise. 'What's your Edie got to do with the price of fish?'

'I'd intended, when the thief was caught, to tell her why we were seen at the Worker Bee together, so she'd understand how wrong she was to make those accusations.'

'Never mind,' Dot said flippantly. 'You can tell her when the war's over.'

She turned away. Best not look at him. In fact, best to keep her distance in future.

Because if there was one thing Mr Thirkle's bravery in trying to save her from the thief's accomplice had taught her, it was that his Edie had been spot on.

Joan had never been more glad of shift work and a morning off. She had stayed up half the night talking with Mabel, sharing her friend's happiness and her own revelation. They had eventually settled down, but Joan had barely slept and she imagined Mabel hadn't either. Even so, Joan felt energised this morning, even though the first thing she must do was going to be far from easy.

'Chin up,' said Mabel. 'Here, allow me.' She eased Joan's coat sleeves up her arms and settled the coat on her shoulders. 'Be brave,' she whispered.

Joan set off for the police station. She was stiff and achy, but that wasn't going to stop her. Steven's night shift would finish at seven o'clock and she must meet him as he came out. As hard as this was going to be, it would be ten times worse if she missed him and had to follow him home.

As she walked along Beech Road, past the recreation ground, she saw him coming towards her. She almost stopped dead, but managed not to. If she stopped, if she looked reluctant, he might guess what she was going to say and that wouldn't be fair. He deserved to be told face to face as kindly as possible.

'I was on my way to see you,' Steven said as they met up. 'How are you?'

'Fine, thanks. A bit sore. I was on my way to see you too.'

Steven smiled. 'That's good.'

No, it wasn't and she mustn't let him think it. Oh, but the thought of hurting him made a knot form inside her chest.

'Steven, I'm sorry. I've kept you hanging on all this time while I tried to decide what to do.'

'What to do? Which of us to choose, you mean.'

'I felt I was being torn in half, but last night, just before Mrs Cooper walked into the room in the police station, when you said you'd brought someone I'd want to see – all I wanted in that moment was Bob. It wasn't a question of thinking about it or making up my mind. It was there, in my head and in my heart, and I knew.'

'In the emotion of the moment, maybe—' Steven started to say.

'Not just in the moment,' she put in. 'It's for always and I know it's right for me. Bob is right for me.'

'But last night, when I picked you and carried you inside, you – you cuddled up to me. I felt ten feet tall. It seemed like a public declaration of your feelings.'

'I'd just thrown myself out of the way of a motor and bashed my head on a lamp post. I'd have pressed close to anyone who picked me up, because I was trying to stop my head spinning.'

'Well, that puts me in my place.'

'I didn't know then about Bob. I didn't realise that until Mrs Cooper appeared.'

'I see.' Steven stared at the pavement.

'Steven, I care about you dearly and I always will, but Bob is the one I want to spend my life with. He always was the right person. I just lost sight of it for a while.'

Glancing up at her, Steven faked a laugh. 'There's no need to rub it in.'

'I'm not trying to. I want you to understand. You and I – that was all part of grieving for Letitia.'

'For you, maybe, but not for me. For me, it's real, but I suppose if your mind is made up . . .'

'I told you,' said Joan. 'I didn't make up my mind. It was my heart that decided.'

Mabel felt fired up, as if her blood was pouring through her veins at twice the normal rate. She wouldn't require a partner on the permanent way at this rate. She could jack up a sleeper with one hand and pack ballast with the other.

But she came down to earth with a bump when she met up with her gang. Bette and Bernice smiled as she approached them on the concourse, but the smiles dropped off their faces, giving her a moment of confusion before she twigged that they weren't looking at her any more. They were looking beyond her. She glanced over her shoulder – and shock thudded through her. Louise.

Mabel ran to her. 'What happened?'

'Nothing.' Louise kept on walking. 'Don't fuss.'

Mabel hurried to keep up. 'That is definitely not nothing.'

Louise was sporting a massive black eye. The skin around her eye socket was puffed up and stretched tight beneath the purple discoloration. It must hurt like the devil. One side of her jaw was heavily bruised and the way she was moving suggested it was more than her face that had suffered injury.

'Bloody hell, Lou,' said Bernice.

'It's nowt,' said Louise. 'I fell downstairs.'

'Don't give me that,' said Bernice. 'It was that brother of yours, wasn't it?'

'The brute,' said Mabel.

'I can think of better words for him than that,' said Bette, 'and when I say "better", what I mean is words that are a lot worse.'

'I told you. I fell downstairs,' Louise insisted. 'It's my own fault for being clumsy.'

'For clumsily stumbling where your brother's fist happened to be,' said Bernice. 'I'm sorry, Lou. I've seen you sporting bruises from time to time and I've bitten my tongue because you made it clear you didn't want to talk about it, but I'm not standing by and saying nowt this time. Look what he's done to you. Come on. We can't discuss this out here.'

'Where can we go?' Mabel asked. There wasn't anywhere. The mess was the only place reserved for staff and it was always occupied, mostly by men.

'The ladies' waiting room,' Bette suggested.

She led the way and opened the door. There were two women inside, each with a cardboard suitcase by her feet.

'Pardon us, ladies,' said Bette. 'We're the cleaners and we've got to give this room a good bottoming, so if you wouldn't mind leaving . . . Let me help you with that suitcase, madam.'

Soon the door was shut and the four of them were alone. Louise looked mutinous and refused to sit down, but finally she gave in and sank onto a bench. Bernice sat beside her. Louise stared at the floor.

'It isn't just your face, is it?' Bernice asked. 'It's your ribs an' all. I notice you don't deny it,' she added when Louise didn't answer.

'You have to go to the police,' said Bette. 'We'll all come with you after work.'

Louise laughed bitterly. 'If he was a stranger, the police

might do summat, but Rob's my brother. The police won't want to know. They say what goes on inside the home is private. Believe me, my mum used to have that conversation about my dad.' She shook her head. 'I thought life would get better when Dad slung his hook, but our Rob has taken over where he left off.'

'What made him do it?' asked Mabel.

'How should I know? I was in bed asleep and I woke up to find myself being dragged across the floor. He was yelling and thumping me and Mum was trying to pull him off, and then he walloped her as well, and the kids were screaming.' Louise breathed heavily. 'Another peaceful night in the Wadden household.'

'Was he plastered?' asked Bette.

'I don't know. You can normally smell the booze on him when he's had a few, but I were too busy trying to protect myself to notice. Every time he belted me, he yelled, "That's for blabbing. That's for not keeping your mouth shut." I don't know what he were on about.'

'You must have some idea,' said Bette.

'Well, I don't. Leastways, he did say summat, but it didn't make any sense. He were banging on about a railway shed.'

'But he doesn't work on the railways,' said Bernice.

'I told you it made no sense. But he kept going on about it. When I tried saying I didn't know what he was on about, he punched me.'

Mabel's skin prickled. 'A railway shed?'

'Aye. He made it sound like I talk about sheds all the time, but the only time I can remember talking about one must have been a year ago. It was the day we found that outside lav – d'you remember?'

'I remember it stank to high heaven,' said Bette.

'You should come to our place,' said Louise. 'We share

with five other families. Mum reckons if Hitler bombs our road, he'll be doing the world a favour.'

'And you mentioned the shed at home?' Mabel's pulse was building up speed.

'My kid brothers are keen on owt with an engine inside it, so I told them about the Scammell we saw that day, hauling the trailer with the tarpaulin over it.'

'Whoa there,' said Bernice. 'How did we get from your no-good brother to talking about a flamin' Scammell? Is this you trying to dodge the subject, Lou?'

Mabel chipped in quickly. 'Was your brother there when you had this conversation?'

'I dunno. Maybe. Probably. Put it this way. It were before opening time, so he couldn't have been down the pub – unless he were in the pub yard, doing a deal.'

'And he accused you of talking freely about this shed?' asked Mabel.

'I told you. I don't know what he were on about. Like I say, the only time I can ever remember talking about a railway shed at home was when I told the boys, and it wasn't really the shed I was telling them about. It was the Scammell.'

'What's this got to do with anything?' Bette demanded. 'You need to see a doctor, lady.'

'What I need,' said Louise, getting up and trying not to wince, 'is to get to work. If we don't look sharp, we'll miss the train and then we'll all be in the soup.'

The others looked after her in dismay as she headed for the door.

'What should we do?' asked Mabel.

'There's not much we can do if she won't let us,' said Bernice. 'We'd best catch that train.' She placed her hand on top of Louise's to stop her opening the door. 'Before we go, what did your brother have to say for himself this morning?'

'Nowt. There was no sign of him. He'd gone.'

'Gone out early?'

'Packed his clothes, emptied the housekeeping jar and hopped it.'

'That's barmy,' said Bette, 'unless he thought he'd killed you.'

'If he's gone,' said Bernice, 'that's a relief.'

'Aye,' said Louise, 'but he can always come back, can't he?'

Dressed in her porter's uniform, with her gas-mask box slung across her back and her handbag in the wicker basket on the front of her bicycle, Joan pedalled along the old road she and the others travelled when they were going to the railway shed. This was the first time she had come this way in daylight. She cycled past her usual turn-off and kept going.

She knew which was Bob's signal box. He had taken her there once, eager to show her his place of work. She was proud to think of him pulling the long levers, logging each train that passed and using bell codes to communicate with other signal boxes.

When the box came in sight, she looked for the turn-off that led to it and pedalled down a scrubby path that ended at the foot of the staircase. Dismounting, she propped her bike against the brick wall and perched on one of the lowest steps. She knew Bob's shift pattern because he had written it into her pocket diary ages ago, when the 1941 diary was brand new – before Christmas, before the blitz, when Letitia was still here; before everything went so dreadfully wrong.

Presently, a middle-aged man with a beer belly cycled up to the box, swinging his leg over the crossbar as he dismounted. He had a knapsack as well as his gas mask.

'Blimey, you gave me a start,' he exclaimed as his gaze landed on her. 'Don't tell me they've sent me a slip of a lass to train. No one said owt about it to me.'

Joan scrambled to her feet and moved out of the way. 'I'm waiting for Bob Hubble.'

The man's face creased into a smile. 'Are you Joan? Reet fond of you, is young Bob. Can't stop talking about you.'

Hope leaped inside her.

'Though he hasn't mentioned you recently, come to think of it.'

The hope vanished beneath a heap of remorse. Had she spoiled things between them for ever?

The man climbed the steps, holding the handrails on either side, and disappeared through the door at the top. Would he tell Bob she was waiting? Would Bob fling open the door and . . . ?

Of course not. There was a procedure involved in handing over signal-box duty and Bob would follow it to the letter. For all that he was easy-going by nature, he wasn't one to cut corners in his job.

Joan hovered a few yards from the foot of the steps. At last Bob emerged. She took a step forward as he saw her. He came down the steps and walked towards her. She wanted to run into his arms, but forced herself to hold back. He stopped a short distance away.

'This is unexpected.' Bob frowned. Uncertainty? Or unwillingness to be with her because he had already made up his mind he was better off without the heartache she had caused? 'I would ask what brings you here, but I'm not sure I want to know.'

'Bob, I'm so sorry . . .' she began, emotion clogging her heart.

He shook his head. 'Good grief. I don't know what to say. I've been dreading this. I wish you well, Joan.'

Shock washed through her. Had he got over her to the point where all that was left was the sorrow of telling her it was over? Just when she had come to make up with him?

'I suppose I can understand if you've taken against me,' Joan faltered, 'but – but can't we at least talk about it? Please?'

'Taken against you? I could never do that, no matter what you did. If being with Steven is what makes you happy—'

'But I don't want him. I want you.'

'But you said you were sorry.'

'Sorry for hurting you, not for – for deciding against you. When you said you'd been dreading this, I thought you didn't want me any more and hated having to tell me.'

'Not want you? You're the only girl for me. I've been driving myself mad since I found out about Steven. I wondered if it was my fault for not providing enough support after Letitia died. I wondered if I drove you into his arms.'

'Oh, Bob.' Joan took a step forward, but Bob made no move towards her, so she stopped. 'It's not your fault. It's no one's fault, if you can believe that. It happened out of grief for Letitia. You once told me you would understand that. Do you? Can you?'

'Are you saying you're over Steven?' Bob's brown eyes, which she was used to being warm when he looked at her, were wary.

'It was a kind of madness.' The words emerged barely above a whisper. She gazed at him, willing him to believe her. 'It felt real and right at the time – but I never stopped loving you. It never pushed you out of my heart. It couldn't, could it? Because it wasn't real. What I feel for you is real and true and will last me for the rest of my days.' She realised she had moved closer to him. 'What about you?'

'I've spent all this time trying to prepare myself for you to choose Steven, but I've discovered I could never be prepared for that, because it would break my heart in two.' Bob's eyes softened as he opened his arms to her. 'Come here, Joan Foster. Come back where you belong.'

Thank heavens the girls were due to meet up that evening. After spending last night wide awake, her mind filled to bursting with thoughts of Harry, Mabel had spent all day thinking about Louise. Could her lousy brother be involved in the thefts from the food dump? It sounded like it. She couldn't wait to tell the others.

It was a tough day for Louise out on the permanent way, but the others spared her as much as they could. Even so, she went dead white at one point and Bernice made her sit down until she felt stronger.

'Don't come to work tomorrow if you still feel ropy,' Bernice ordered, but they all knew she would.

At last it was time to catch the train back to Victoria Station. When they arrived, Louise walked off with barely a goodbye, leaving the others to exchange looks.

Bernice shook her head. 'There's nowt to say, is there?'

Actually, there was plenty to say, but not to Bernice and Bette. Mabel felt a twinge of guilt at excluding them, but she had to keep the secret.

She went to the buffet. As she queued up, she could see an animated discussion was under way at her friends' table. Was she the last to arrive? No, Cordelia wasn't there yet, but the others were – Persephone, Alison, Joan and Dot. She would wait for Cordelia to come before she voiced her suspicions.

She had just taken her place when Cordelia arrived at the table.

'Look who I found on the concourse.'

'Colette!'

The delighted exclamation echoed around the table. Colette blushed, but it was obvious she was pleased. She looked trim and smart in a fitted coat with the belt buckled, her felt hat trimmed at the side with a bow. Her fair hair sat in a tidy roll on her shoulders. Seeing her made Mabel realise she had yet to be at home at the same time Colette paid one of her weekly visits to Mrs Cooper. She would like to get to know Colette better. Perhaps they could go out as a foursome, her and Harry, Colette and – what was his name? – Tony.

'You didn't write in the book that you'd be here,' said Alison.

'I didn't like to,' said Colette, sitting down, 'in case I couldn't come at the last minute. It would have been awful to let you down.'

'Well, you're here now,' said Dot, 'and that's what counts.'

'Have you heard?' Alison's excited gaze swept over Mabel, Colette and Cordelia. 'The thief's been caught – well, one of them has. The other got away.'

'But not before our darling Dot bashed him over the head,' added Persephone.

'Tell us from the beginning, Dot,' said Cordelia.

Mabel listened in astonishment and growing pride as Dot related her story.

'It makes what Persephone and I did sound rather piffling,' said Alison.

'Don't be soft,' said Dot. 'Without you, the police wouldn't have come, and without them, me and Mr Thirkle would still be there now, guarding that door.'

'Fancy clobbering the accomplice,' said Mabel. 'You're a heroine, Dot.'

'Get away with you,' said Dot. 'I just wish the other fella hadn't got away.'

Mabel drew a breath. 'I may know who he is.'

Now it was her turn to have all eyes upon her as she explained about Louise's injuries and the way Rob had yelled at her for blabbing about the railway shed.

They all looked at one another.

'It must be him,' said Joan.

'It sounds like it,' agreed Colette.

'We have to get Louise to tell the police,' said Alison.

'She's already refused to tell them,' said Mabel.

'That was about being beaten up,' said Alison. 'This is about the theft.'

'She still might refuse,' said Joan, 'especially if she thinks her brother might come back at some point.'

'There's another thing,' said Persephone. 'We might get into trouble if we tell her about the food dump and the theft. It's a war secret. Inspector Stanhope was adamant that we had to keep it to ourselves.'

'Aye,' said Dot. 'He'd have kittens if he knew that all of you lot are in on it an' all.'

'Maybe we don't have to tell Louise.' Cordelia looked thoughtful. 'If we tell the inspector that we've heard that this Rob Wadden is friendly with Mr Samuels's chauffeur, they can look into it. It might be that the police have already heard of Rob Wadden.'

'They'll turn up at Louise's house,' said Mabel, 'but he's already disappeared. Nothing will be achieved beyond upsetting Louise's family.'

'But at least the police will know,' said Cordelia.

'I'll go to the police station,' said Dot.

'I'll come with you,' Persephone offered.

'Nay, love. You told the inspector you're a reporter, so he'll think you've been digging about for a story. I'm the one what started this off in the first place, so it's up to me to do it. In fact, I'll get off and do it now before I go home.'

Dot got up to leave. Cordelia watched her all the way to the door, then leaned forward, gathering everyone's attention.

'I'm glad Dot's gone. I've had an idea.'

'An idea that doesn't include Dot?' Mabel wasn't keen on the sound of that.

'Don't look so disapproving.' Cordelia smiled. 'Dot's included. Very much so.'

# Chapter Forty-One

Dot looked at herself in the mirror. 'Wear something special,' Persephone had said. Dot didn't have much in the way of special. Women didn't, not in her rank of life. Money went on the home and the family. It went on keeping the man of the house decently fed so he kept his strength up and fulfilled his duty as provider.

Dot's best clothes had been her best since 1937. A bluey-grey A-line skirt with box pleats, teamed with, in cold weather, a long-sleeved blouse or, in warm weather, an elbow-length-sleeved blouse in soft pink with pink buttons and gentle gathers at the shoulder seams.

'Short sleeves, Mother?' Pammy had asked when Dot had proudly shown off her acquisition, nearly new, off the market. 'Do you think that's wise at your age?'

At her age! She had been all of forty-three. She might have taken the blouse back except for knowing that the stallholder would never buy it back for the same price and she couldn't afford to waste money.

Looking at herself now, she recalled Pammy's remark. Could arms look old? All right, maybe her elbows were more wrinkly than they used to be, but who looked at them? Years of energetically possing, wringing and mangling the bed linen and clothes every Monday had prevented her arms from getting flabby. They weren't bad at all, actually.

To complete her ensemble, depending on the time of year, she had two long-sleeved cardigans in different weights of wool, both made from patterns in *Woman's Weekly*. The lightweight cardy, which she was wearing today, was in a cream Sirdar wool and had a Peter Pan collar and dainty puffs at the shoulders. Early April wasn't perhaps warm enough for elbow-length sleeves and two-ply wool, but it seemed dressier than the alternative garment and she wanted to look her best when she was going to be seen in public with the perfectly groomed Persephone. It was a shame her only footwear was a pair of sturdy lace-ups. Pretty courts would finish her off nicely. Mind you, if she wore owt with heels, she'd probably fall off them and sprawl flat on her face.

Persephone had invited her out for tea.

'My treat,' she'd insisted. 'I might not be allowed to write about the food dump just yet, but I will one day, so I need to gather the information while it's fresh in your mind. Please say yes. You'll be doing me the most enormous favour.'

'Ruddy heck, Dot,' Reg called up the stairs. 'Have you seen what's pulled up outside?'

Dot went to the bedroom window. Miss Brown's Bentley was outside their house. The neighbours' eyeballs must be out on stalks. She belted downstairs, threw on her hat and coat and ran outside so that wagging tongues couldn't accuse her of spinning out the moment.

'This is very kind of you,' she said as she climbed in.

'Not at all. Before we have tea, we've been invited to Mrs Cooper's for you to see the house.'

Dot settled back to enjoy the ride. Reg would call her a nosy old bat, but she would enjoy a tour of the house.

When they arrived in Wilton Close, she was impressed by how smart the houses looked. She and Mrs Cooper were two of a kind, both working-class lasses, and this was proper posh. Well, if anybody deserved to land on her feet, Mrs Cooper did.

Persephone held the garden gate for Dot and shut it behind them. The front door opened before they reached the porch and Mrs Cooper appeared, smiling in welcome.

'Come in. Let me hang up your coat and hat.'

'I'll do that,' said Persephone. 'You two go in.'

Mrs Cooper ushered Dot into the front room. Before she realised what was happening, there was a burst of clapping. She looked around in astonishment. All her railway friends were here, their eyes bright, laughter not far away – Cordelia, Alison, Joan, Mabel, even Colette, her face lit up for once, showing how pretty she was when she wasn't feeling shy.

'We're here for a special afternoon together,' said Cordelia, 'to celebrate what a brave lady you are, Dot.'

'You saved Mr Bonner's life,' said Alison, 'and you saved everyone on the train when you set the detonators.'

'And then you bashed a thief,' said Joan, beaming at her.

'A thief?' said Mrs Grayson. 'I didn't hear about that.'

'And you won't either.' Mabel, sitting on the arm of Mrs Grayson's chair, dropped a kiss on the top of her head. 'It's hush-hush and we shan't mention it again.'

Everybody looked at Dot. She stared at all the faces.

'I don't know what to say.'

'That's never happened before,' said Alison, which provoked laughter.

Dot turned to Persephone. 'You naughty girl. You told me we were popping in here before tea.'

'And we are,' said Persephone. 'It's just that tea happens to be here as well.'

Recovering from her surprise, Dot looked around properly. As well as the residents of the house plus the railway girls, Mrs Mitchell, the housekeeper from Darley Court, was here and also a robust-looking elderly lady, whom

Cordelia introduced as Miss Brown, the owner of Darley Court.

'We've made use of the Bentley on various occasions,' said Persephone, 'so we thought we really should invite her.'

'And we couldn't leave out Cousin Harriet.' Mabel smiled at the housekeeper.

'Sit yourself down, Mrs Green,' said Mrs Cooper, 'and I'll put the kettle on.'

'Aye, I could do with a cuppa for the shock,' said Dot. 'I'll give you a hand.'

'No, you won't.' Mabel stood up. 'Joan and I will help in the kitchen.'

'We saved this seat for you.' Colette indicated one of the armchairs.

'Nay, there's no call for me to have that.'

'Yes, there is,' said Persephone. 'You're the star attraction.'

Dot sat down. It was a large room, big enough for a three-piece suite with a three-seater sofa, on which Cordelia was sitting with Miss Brown and Mrs Mitchell. Mrs Grayson was in the other armchair. Alison and Colette perched on chairs from the dining room and Joan had been sitting on the hearthrug. There was an empty dining chair, which was presumably awaiting Mrs Cooper's return.

'It's a bit of a squash with so many of us,' said Mrs Grayson.

'It reminds me of growing up.' Nostalgia warmed Dot's heart. 'My parents fetched up eleven of us and our cottage was a darned sight smaller than this. I like rooms to be full of folk. It feels right.'

'Speaking as one who spent years on her own,' said Mrs Grayson, 'I feel better for having company.'

'You've gone through a lot of change in a short space of time,' said Mrs Mitchell.

'I have, and I'm sorry if I've been a drag on anybody.'

'The main thing,' said Cordelia, 'is how are you coping now?'

'Fair to middling. Being stuck indoors by your own fears isn't summat you get over just like that.' Mrs Grayson snapped her fingers. 'I used to look out of the window and feel small and trapped and useless. Now, living here, I look out and sometimes I feel . . . tempted.'

'You've got plenty of new friends,' said Cordelia, 'who'll be happy to help you when you're ready to step outside.'

'Are you still doing your knitting?' Dot couldn't help glancing around. The room wasn't festooned with woollen articles like Mrs Grayson's old house had been.

'I'm concentrating on clothes for folk who have been bombed out.'

'I hope you include yourself and Mrs Cooper in that,' said Miss Brown.

Mrs Cooper came back in, holding the door for Mabel and Joan, who carried trays. Tea was poured and the cups and saucers were handed round. Dot spared a thought for the harebell tea set that had been Mrs Cooper's pride and joy, smashed to dust beneath a bomb. Eh, was that what war came down to? Smashing pretty tea sets.

After they'd had a cup of tea and a chat, Mrs Grayson excused herself to attend to the Victoria sponge and the apple upside-down cake she was baking.

'I'll lend a hand.' Mrs Mitchell pushed herself up from the sofa. 'We can have a bit of a chinwag.'

Of course. Dot recalled the friendship between Mrs Mitchell and Mrs Grayson that had led to Mabel's becoming Mrs Grayson's tenant last year. She smiled to herself.

They were probably going to give Mr Grayson and Floozy a good roasting.

'Mrs Cooper, I'd enjoy seeing the garden, if you'd like to show me round,' said Miss Brown.

'Charmed, I'm sure, madam.' Mrs Cooper scrambled to her feet.

Left to themselves, Dot and her friends looked at one another.

'We won't have long on our own,' said Alison, 'so let's make the most of it. Dot, we haven't seen you since you went to the police about Louise's brother. What happened?'

Dot shrugged. 'Not much, to be honest. I was allowed in to see Inspector Stanhope, which was good in a way, because he knows about the food dump.'

'But not good in another way?' suggested Persephone.

'He's a shrewd man. There's me saying I'd heard on the grapevine that the chauffeur was friends with this Rob Wadden, but I'm sure the inspector thought there was more to it than that – or maybe that was just my guilty conscience.'

'So we've done all we can,' said Joan.

Colette started to speak, then stopped.

'What is it, love?' asked Dot.

'I was about to ask something, but it's probably something the rest of you know inside out.'

Dot was quick to understand. 'It's because you don't come to the buffet as much as the rest of us, isn't it, chick? The rest of us know the lot and you feel left behind. Is that it?'

'What do you want to know?' asked Alison.

'Will you put the pieces together for me about the chauffeur and Rob Wadden?'

'Actually, I'd like to get it straight too,' said Joan. 'Let's go back to the beginning. The chauffeur didn't necessarily know about the food dump. He'd have known the railway shed had a special purpose, but unless he overheard Mr Samuels and the other VIP talking about it, he wouldn't have known what that purpose was.'

'Then Louise talked at home about the shed and the delivery Scammell,' said Mabel. 'She was telling her little brothers, but it's safe to assume Rob heard too.'

'Rob and the chauffeur were friends and, at some point, they must have compared notes,' said Persephone.

'And Rob knew about the outside privy,' said Mabel, 'because Louise told her mum. So he and the chauffeur must have gone to the shed to see if they could get inside through the privy.'

'That was when they found the food dump,' said Dot. 'They must have thought they'd stumbled across a gold mine.'

'Then, the other night,' said Cordelia, 'Dot and Mr Thirkle trapped the chauffeur inside the shed, not knowing there was an accomplice still in the motor. Rob Wadden attacked them, then drove away. He went home and played merry heck with Louise, thinking that, after the way she'd talked freely at home about the shed, she must have talked freely elsewhere too.'

'And having beaten her black and blue,' said Mabel, 'he did a disappearing act.'

'Inspector Stanhope told me the police found Mr Samuels's motor,' said Dot, 'so, however Wadden got away, it wasn't in that.'

'A bloke of his sort wouldn't look right in a fancy motor like that,' said Alison. 'I'm not surprised he dumped it.'

'He's long gone by now,' said Mabel.

'Aye, and let's hope he stays gone,' said Dot. 'I can't

abide men who hit women. It's a relief to me that it's over, I don't mind telling you. I never intended to do owt wrong, but I was that worried about getting blamed for feeding the evidence to my family or getting our Pammy into hot water for buying the tins in the first place.'

'No one who knows you would ever imagine you'd do something wrong on purpose,' said Persephone.

'Oh, that's me all right,' Dot said flippantly. 'A shining example.' They were going to start praising her again in a minute and she didn't want that. 'What about the rest of you? Are you nicely settled with your Harry, Mabel?'

To her surprise, Mabel blushed, half laughing. Dot leaned forward, excitement bubbling up inside her. News from a girl in love could mean only one thing. She clamped her lips together so as not to steal Mabel's thunder.

'We're very nicely settled, thank you,' said Mabel. 'There was a bit of a bump in the road, but that's been smoothed over and . . .' She shrugged, but it was no good her trying to look casual, not with her eyes shining like that.

'. . . and everything's tickety-boo,' Persephone finished for her.

Dot pressed her hand to her chest. To think she had almost blurted out summat about getting engaged. To cover her almost blunder, she turned to Joan. 'Have you decided between those two young men yet, lovey?'

'I didn't have to – not the way you mean. The decision was made for me in an instant without any conscious thought on my part. I was very silly. I stepped out in front of a motor, but pulled back in time, though I landed with a wallop. This was near the police station and Steven carried me inside.'

'So he's the one?' asked Alison.

'No. He disappeared and when he returned, he said

he'd brought someone I'd want to see – and I wanted Bob. Simple as that. Everything slotted back into place. Steven and I . . .'

'That was all mixed up with losing Letitia,' said Dot.

'You lost your way for a while,' said Cordelia.

'I don't want to sound unfeeling,' said Persephone, 'but Steven's a fine chap. He'll meet someone else eventually.'

'He needs to recover from losing Letitia first,' said Cordelia, 'and he was never going to do that by getting together with her little sister.'

Joan's blue eyes were wet. 'You're all so kind. I feel I've caused so much trouble and here you all are, being lovely to me, and I'm sure I don't deserve it.'

'Yes, you do, chick,' said Dot. 'As for causing trouble, it was the war what did that, not you.'

'Now that you're happy with Bob,' said Alison, 'are you going to see what you can find out about your family name?'

'Give her a chance!' said Dot. 'She's only just got her romantic life sorted out. Let her enjoy that for a while before she thinks about owt else.'

'Hush now,' said Cordelia as the door opened.

The group broke apart as Mrs Cooper and Miss Brown returned from the garden, bringing a dash of fresh air with them to mingle with the delicious smell of baking that wafted in from the kitchen.

'Would you care to see around the house, Mrs Green?' Mrs Cooper offered.

'Nay, love, there's no need for that,' said Dot. 'I know that were only a ruse to get me here. I don't want to be nosy.'

'Don't you?' said Miss Brown. 'I do. Lead the way, Mrs Cooper.'

Laughing, Dot got to her feet and went with the other

two. She enjoyed her tour and heaped compliments on Mrs Cooper for having such a smart house to take care of.

When they came downstairs again, the front room had been rearranged. Two more dining chairs had appeared and some small tables, on which stood an array of plates with sandwiches as well as a three-tier cake stand bearing pieces of upside-down cake, each with a slice of apple on top, and Victoria sponge.

'Though I'm not sure it qualifies as a Victoria sponge without the cream,' said Mrs Grayson.

'Don't worry about that,' said Mabel. 'It won't last long enough for it to matter.'

Alison was at the window, looking out. 'She's back.'

'Who's back?' asked Dot.

'Persephone,' said Joan. 'She took the Bentley on an errand while you were looking around the house.'

Cordelia joined Alison at the window. 'She's brought someone to make the occasion complete for you, Dot.'

Mr Thirkle! Dot's heart bumped. He'd been part of the food-dump palaver, so why not invite him? And if she was extra pleased to see him, that was for her to know and no one else to find out. To hide the colour stinging her cheeks, she went to the window to look out. There was Miss Brown's Bentley at the kerb and getting out of the front passenger door was – Reg. Reg! Her heart bumped again, but for a completely different reason.

He opened the back door and out spilled Jimmy and Jenny, followed by Sheila and, as graceful as you please, Pammy, all of them in their best clobber. The girls must have sat on Jimmy during the ride in the motor. How else had he arrived without his tie askew and his socks round his ankles? Jenny looked like a little angel in a primrose-yellow dress, with ribbons in her hair.

Reg opened the garden gate and they all walked up the path.

'We couldn't leave your family out of this special occasion, Mrs Green,' said Mrs Cooper, and went to let them in.

And there she'd been thinking it might be Mr Thirkle. It just showed what a daft bat she was.

There were voices in the hall, then the door opened and Dot wound her way between the assortment of chairs and tables to greet her family. Jimmy hugged her. He hadn't hugged her since he had come home from being evacuated.

'You're a corker, Nan.' He tilted back his head to gaze up at her. 'No one else has a brave nan who saved a train full of people.'

Dot exchanged smiles with Sheila. 'If I'd known that was all I had to do to get a hug, I'd have done it a lot sooner. Now where's that granddaughter of mine?' She reached out for another hug.

Pammy winced slightly. 'Don't muss up her hair, Mother.' She presented her delicately powdered cheek for a kiss. Not that Dot was allowed actually to plant the kiss on her skin. Pammy wasn't quite close enough for that. She never was.

And there was Reg. He didn't get close enough for a public kiss and she didn't expect it. A nod from across the room was what she got, together with a sort of upside-down smile. It made him look as if he approved of her, for once in his life.

There were introductions all round.

'You must be very proud of your wife, Mr Green,' said Cordelia.

'Aye,' said Reg. 'Aye, I am that.' And there was that upside-down smile again.

'When I grow up,' announced Jimmy, 'I'm going to marry a girl who saved a train.'

'There's no higher praise than that, Mrs Green,' said Mrs Grayson.

'Or I won't get married at all,' Jimmy added.

Pammy murmured something to Sheila.

'Pipe down, our Jimmy,' said Sheila.

'Let's find you all somewhere to sit,' said Mrs Cooper.

'Before that,' said Dot, 'I want another hug from my grandchildren.'

She held out her arms and gathered them to her. Truth to tell, she didn't need one from Jenny, who was always happy to be hugged in spite of Pammy's finicky ways, but she had to make the most of Jimmy's willingness. She met Mrs Cooper's eyes across the top of her beloved grand-children's heads.

'You're a lucky woman, Mrs Green,' Mrs Cooper said softly. Her gaze was clouded with sadness.

'Aye,' said Dot. 'I am that. I never forget it neither.'

She was lucky an' all. Her two boys were alive and well, and, God willing, would stay that way. She had her boys' children with her now, cuddled up close. Her dear friends were all around her. Not only that, but they had seen fit to hold this tea party in her honour. Whoever would have thought she would be deemed worthy of summat like that? Her, Dot Green, Dot Simpson-as-was, loving mother, besotted grandmother, housewife and parcels porter. How her life had opened up this past twelve months. Dot Green – railway girl.

Welcome to

# Penny Street

where your favourite authors and stories live.

Meet casts of characters you'll never forget,
create memories you'll treasure forever,
and discover places that will stay with
you long after the last page.

Turn the page to step into the home of

# MAISIE THOMAS

and discover more about

Secrets
*of the*
Railway Girls

Dear Readers,

As I write this, the UK is in lockdown to keep everyone as safe as possible during the Covid-19 pandemic. It was the 75th anniversary of VE Day on the 8th May. Did you see the wonderful, heart-warming rendition of *We'll Meet Again* that was broadcast by the BBC that evening after the Queen's speech? I don't mind telling you that I shed a few tears and I'm sure I wasn't the only one.

In the media there have been many comparisons between the current situation and what the country went through during the Second World War, and the way in which similar qualities have been needed – determination, cooperation and endurance.

Endurance plays a significant part in *Secrets of the Railway Girls*. I've been told I must be careful not to give anything away in this letter because some readers turn to the back of the book first to read the letter before starting on the story. All I'll say here is that the book includes the Christmas Blitz, which took place on the nights of December 22nd and 23rd 1940, when high-explosives rained down on Manchester and Salford. Afterwards thirty-one acres of buildings lay in ruins around Albert Square in the city centre. What made the Christmas Blitz worse was that on December 21st, there was a blitz over Liverpool and fire-fighting resources from all over the north-west had been sent there ... which meant that when Manchester was bombed the following night, there were inadequate resources.

If you'd like to know a little about how I used real events from the Christmas Blitz in this story, turn a couple of pages to read a piece I've written called *Weaving the Facts into the Fiction*.

Another theme that runs all through *The Railway Girls* series is that of staunch friendships between women. If you read the dedication at the front of this book, you'll see the names of two dear friends of mine, Annette and Jacquie. Their friendship has been a constant in my life for many years and, together, we have gone through all kinds of ups and downs. Jacquie and I have been friends for over forty years, ever since our mums occupied next-door beds in the maternity ward – well, that's our story and we're sticking to it! How else could we possibly have been friends for such a long time? I haven't known Annette quite as long, but she is every bit as important to me.

My hope for the characters in this series is that they will forge friendships that will last a lifetime, because I know from personal experience that strong friendships between women can provide support and comfort, not to mention loads of fun. I hope that you, my readers, have just such special friendships in your lives too.

Until we meet again.

Much love
*Maisie xx*

# Dot Green – mum, nan and railway girl

I'm writing this for you a couple of weeks after publication of *The Railway Girls*. The reviews are coming in and it is clear that readers have taken Dot to their hearts. I'm very happy about this because as I explained in my first letter to you, unlike Joan and Mabel, who had lived in my imagination for some time before I started writing, Dot was a brand new character, so it feels extra special to know she is so popular.

What is it about Dot that makes readers warm to her? They love her common sense, her good humour and her generous heart, as well as sympathising with her frustration at being married to Ratty Reg. Dot is the kind of person we'd all like to have as our next-door neighbour.

The other railway girls value her because they can see how hard she works, not just as a parcels porter, but also at home, looking after her house and family. Always on the go, that's Dot. She's always hurrying to keep one step ahead, chopping that evening's vegetables before she sets off for work in the morning, starting her spring-cleaning early to ensure it gets finished at the right time, as well as squeezing in time for queuing at the shops. The country was full of women like Dot during the war.

She is a good friend too, a real looker-after, who keeps an eye on everyone around her and is happy to help. Dot is good at tea and sympathy, but she isn't just someone you go to for a shoulder to cry on. She is very practical in a crisis.

But first and foremost, Dot is a mum and a nan. Her two boys – Archie and Harry – mean the world to her, and have done ever since she fell head over heels in love with each of them as newborns. Dot would have loved to have more children but, sadly for her, it wasn't to be. She could never imagine loving anyone as much as she loves her sons – until her grandchildren came along and she fell in love all over again. Archie and Harry, Jimmy and Jenny, are the reasons Dot keeps going.

She longs for her sons to come home safely when the war is over. Meanwhile she does everything in her power to support Pammy and Sheila while keeping her reservations about her daughters-in-law hidden deep inside. She worries about Jimmy and Jenny. After the anguish of separation when they were evacuated during the Phoney War, Dot adores having them home again – but is it the right decision? Would they be better off being evacuated again?

Her job as a parcels porter has given Dot a fresh sense of her own identity. Yes, she loves every moment of her home life – well, not every moment of Ratty Reg's company, but you know what I mean. She is a proud housewife with a spotless front step, but having a job outside the home has instilled in her a new sense of self-worth, a realisation that, as deeply as family life matters, it is important to her to have something more. Yes, it's her way of contributing to the war effort, but it has also given her a sense of quiet pride in herself as an individual.

# Weaving the Facts into the Fiction

As with *The Railway Girls*, all the air raids that occur in *Secrets of the Railway Girls* took place. I am indebted to Peter J C Smith's book, *Luftwaffe Over Manchester: The Blitz Years 1940–1944* (Neil Richardson, 2003), for meticulous details of the dates and times of the air raids, as well as the human cost. It was sobering to read the long lists of the dead and injured and I had some emotional moments recognising the addresses close to where I grew up – roads that I had walked along many a time.

The Christmas Blitz plays a major part in this story and *Blitz Britain: Manchester and Salford* by Graham Phythian (The History Press, 2015) was an invaluable source of information, as was *Our Blitz: Red Skies Over Manchester: A Wartime Facsimile*, which was prepared and organised by Cliff Hayes in association with the *Manchester Evening News. Manchester at War 1939–45* by Glynis Cooper (Pen & Sword Military, 2018) also provided useful information.

For the purposes of the story, I have taken the liberty of moving two events of the Christmas Blitz, so that Mabel could take part in the rescues. The real woman who was trapped in her kitchen beside the blazing fire lived in Gorton; and the bus that was driven beneath a bridge, only for the bridge to be bombed, was in Salford.

When Mabel describes to Mrs Grayson the motor car that was lifted up by the blast from a bomb and dumped into a bedroom, she is referring to an incident that did take place in Manchester, but not during the Christmas Blitz. It happened a few weeks earlier. I have to say that a photograph of this is one of the most extraordinary pictures I've ever seen. And you may like to know that there really was a young lad who was trapped beneath a house in the same way that Jimmy was in the book.

If you would like to gain an overview of Manchester's Christmas Blitz, the *Manchester Evening News* website includes a page about it, written in the style of a blog that shows what happened and when. It also includes many photographs. Do an online search for 'manchester evening news christmas blitz blog'.

You may have noticed that I like to describe what my characters are wearing. The history of costume has been an interest of mine for years and I have a large collection of books on the subject. Titles that were of particular use were John Peacock's *20th Century Fashion: the Complete Sourcebook* (Thames & Hudson, 1993) and his *The Complete Fashion Sourcebook* (Thames & Hudson, 2005); and also *Women's Hats, Headdress and Hairstyles* by Georgine de Courtais (Dover, 2006).

I'd also like to mention *Christmas on the Home Front* by Mike Brown (Sutton, 2004), which helped Dot get ready for Christmas; and *The Home Front: The Best of Good Housekeeping 1939–1945* (Ebury Press, 1987), which helped Mrs Grayson with the cooking.

Any historical inaccuracies are, of course, my own. Apologies.

Turn the page for an exclusive
extract from my new novel

# The Railway Girls
# in Love

Coming 2021
Available to pre-order now

# Chapter One

## February 1939

With her gloved hands thrust into the big patch pockets of her rust-coloured wool coat, and her scarf wound snugly around her neck and tucked in beneath the wide lapels, Mabel Bradshaw tramped along, lifting her feet clear of the thick snow so as not to let it spill over the tops of her calf-high galoshes. The benefit of wearing two pairs of thick socks over her stockings wouldn't last long if they got wet.

Beside her, Althea, her best friend, matched her pace.

'Your cheeks are glowing,' said Mabel.

'Which is a polite way of saying they're bright red,' said Althea, 'and so's my nose.'

'Mine too.'

'What would your mother say?' teased Althea.

Mabel laughed. Mumsy was mad keen on etiquette. 'But just think how pale and interesting I'll look when I've thawed out.' She snuggled her hands deeper inside her pockets: only up here on the tops could she get away with such slovenly behaviour.

The two of them crunched through the snow to the edge of the steep hill above Mabel's home and looked down into the long valley below. Behind them stretched the Lancashire moors. Usually its breeze was so full of brisk smells that Mabel could practically taste them as a rich, earthy, green concoction, but not today. Today, as for the past month, the moors had been coated in snow and the air was as fresh as peppermint.

Below lay the town of Annerby. It was still called a market-town, but it had its share of factories too, as well as a railway station. Mabel's gaze was drawn to the building which housed Bradshaw's Ball Bearings and Other Small Components, the factory that represented Pops's life's work. The son of a railway worker, he had made good – and more than good. He had prospered to the extent of purchasing – purchasing, note, not renting – Kirkland House, one of the posh properties high up on the side of the hill. Here, Mabel had grown up.

Now she looked down at Bradshaw's Ball Bearings. Would their factory still be producing small components this time next year? Pops said that when the war came – when, not if, and Mabel had trembled inwardly – factories up and down the country would be called upon to turn over production to whatever they were told to make to help win the war. Mabel had longed to ask a dozen questions, but couldn't, because Pops hadn't been talking to her. It was something she had overheard.

'Here comes a train,' said Althea.

Mabel felt a little burst of pleasure. She liked trains. They made her think of Grandad. He might be gone, but he definitely wasn't forgotten, especially not by her. His son might have risen in the world, but Grandad had stayed put in his cottage near the railway and had never for a single moment considered leaving his job as a wheel-tapper, using his long-handled hammer to tap train wheels, the quality of the ring that was produced telling his experienced ear whether or not the wheel was in good order.

Down on the valley floor, white clouds puffed out of the funnel on top of the front end of the locomotive, which pulled a line, not of coaches, but of goods wagons. Some had names painted on the sides because they belonged to companies that used the railways all the time. At the rear of the line came several unbranded wagons, their contents covered by tarpaulins.

'D'you suppose the train is bringing us our air raid shelters?' asked Mabel. 'Distribution is starting this month.'

'We won't get ours for ages yet,' said Althea. 'It'll be the cities that get them first, and ports and places like that.'

She made it sound almost as if Annerby would have no need of them. Mabel thought of Bradshaw's Ball Bearings and Other Small Components being turned over to war work, but kept it to herself. Would Jerry know where the factories were? If rural Annerby wasn't near the top of the list for Anderson shelters, and war suddenly started, was her beloved hometown in danger of taking a clobbering, with no protection for its citizens? A shudder ran through her.

'Cold?' asked Althea. 'Daft question. It's freezing up here. We should start walking again before our feet turn into blocks of ice.'

She dug her hand into the crook of Mabel's elbow and moved in close, their arms pressed up against one another. Mabel squeezed her elbow against her side, creating a warm nest for Althea's hand as they set off.

They were more than friends. They were as good as sisters, something they had never tired of telling people as they were growing up. As a child, Mabel had wished she too had smooth buttermilk-blonde hair so that they could look like sisters too, but her own hair was dark brown and she reckoned she kept the hair-pin industry in business, since, left to its own devices, her long waves liked nothing better than to fluff up all over the show.

'I wish your family was coming to London for the Season,' said Mabel.

Her brief hope that Their Majesties' state visit to Canada and America in May would mean there would be no London Season this year had been well and truly dashed by the news that the Season was going to commence early.

'Why don't I ask Mumsy if you can come with us?' she suggested.

'No, you mustn't. My parents don't have the same aspirations as yours.'

That was true. Althea's folks were minor gentry and content to remain so. There had never been any question of Althea's being spirited off for a London Season. It was the girls' lifelong friendship that had created the connection between the two families; and if Althea's parents entertained any reservations about the nouveau riche Bradshaws, all Mabel could say was that the girls had never been made aware of it.

Sometimes the thought of the forthcoming Season made her feel as if she had a weight lodged inside her chest, but Pops was determined, so there was no getting out of it. Heaven alone knew how he had brought it about, but he was now in touch with a Dowager Viscountess who made a considerable income each year by presenting debutantes at court if they didn't have a mother or aunt who was allowed to present them. A quick flick through Mumsy's etiquette book had shown that there were more reasons than you could shake a stick at for why a lady wouldn't be deemed eligible to do the presenting. Well, that was a comfort of sorts. If this Dowager made a living in this manner, it meant that Mabel wouldn't be alone in not being presented by her mother.

'I just wish you were having your dresses made up here,' said Althea, 'so I could come with you to the fittings.'

But no, Mabel's wardrobe was to be the product of the most high-class London dress salons. Was it ungrateful not to look forward to that? Possibly. But, honestly, what place was there in the London Season for the granddaughter of a wheel-tapper, even if she had been privately educated and her father had money to burn? Knowing that the Bradshaws wouldn't be the only new money on the circuit was no help. Mabel just wanted to stay at home. Simple as that.

With no Althea to back her up, Mabel had coped alone with dress fittings and curtseying lessons.

*Yes, curtseying lessons!* she wrote to Althea. *Who would have imagined such a thing existed? I am able to sink to the floor with perfect steadiness, but how I'm supposed to rise again without wobbling beats me. I've taken a tumble more than once, I don't mind telling you. The thought of making my curtsey in the presence of royalty is terrifying.*

She shared her coming out ball with a girl whose family was of limited means but impeccable social standing, which meant they could invite all the right people, who were then obliged to acknowledge the Bradshaws. Mabel cringed at the idea of this until she realised it would have been a whole lot worse to have had her own dance and run the risk of not being able to fill the ballroom.

What made it worse was that Althea was having a whale of a time without her.

*The Pentry-Joneses had a dance at their house. There were lots of young men, as Andrew has three chums visiting. It so happens I'd already met them when I was out riding. Andrew introduced them as Will, Ollie and Gil, so I assumed they were William, Oliver and Gilbert, but at the dance it turned out they are Wilson, Ollerton and Gilchrist, but I still think of them as Will, Ollie and Gil and everyone calls them that.*

She seemed to be doing a lot of thinking about Gil in particular. His first name was Iain, with an 'I' in it twice because of his Scottish ancestry. Althea didn't call him Iain because of sounding forward, though it was perfectly acceptable to call him Gil, with that being his nickname. Gil and the others – and it didn't escape Mabel's notice that the others were soon lumped together without individual names – had been chums at Oxford. Gil had ride taken into his family's law firm, but if war broke out he intended to join up.

Gil had hazel eyes and a lean face that was serious in repose, though when he smiled . . . Mabel grinned as she read the rest. *If you're ever in need of extra money, you could always write romance novels,* she wrote back. Gil could ride and shoot and he was very good with children (underlined twice) and had played at lions and tigers with Caroline Walsh's young twins for simply ages. And last night he had played the piano all evening so everyone else could dance, which was utterly spiffing of him, of course, but, oh, how Althea had longed for someone to offer to take over from him so she could drag him onto the floor.

*Are you practising your new signature?* Mabel replied.

She imagined Althea canoodling in the orchard. She wouldn't mind a spot of canoodling herself if the right man came along. Pops was hoping for what Mumsy called a socially advantageous marriage, which was a delicate way of saying that they hoped Mabel would bag herself a young gentleman with an impeccable pedigree and preferably a title. Would said gentleman be permitted by his family to show an interest in the granddaughter of a railwayman? He might well be, if the family was all pedigree and no cash. From wheel-tapper to honourable in three generations, with the highly successful Bradshaw's Ball Bearings and Other Small Components in between. Was that what lay in store for Mabel?

Did all the old families look down on the Bradshaws

because they were new money or were some of the old families eyeing them up for the very same reason? It was impossible to tell, because everyone was faultlessly civil. That was a sign of good breeding, wasn't it? Courtesy to all, regardless of circumstances. But you didn't know what they murmured in private, did you?

With her pulse fluttering in unhappy self-consciousness much of the time, Mabel lapped up Althea's letters, which featured Gil more and more. With the threat of war in the offing, the young Pentry-Joneses seemed to be racketing around having a high old time and the more friends they could persuade to join in, the better. By day, there were rambles across the moors and drives to beauty spots, while the evenings were filled with music and fun.

Meanwhile, Mabel lived more or less in terror of the dances in London. Was she the only girl here whose throat ached in dread at the mere sight of a dance card? First, there was the desperation to have her card filled with the names of partners; but when this had been done, instead of making her feel better, it then engendered a fresh anxiety. Was it a 'pity' dance? Worse, might it be a 'fishing' dance, where a chap requested the pleasure because he had heard about the Bradshaw fortune?

While Mabel endured all this, the young set in and around Annerby was up to all sorts of high jinks.

*We played hide and seek last night,* Althea scrawled. *Can you believe it?*

A faint shiver travelled across the skin on Mabel's arms. It happened sometimes. Mostly she was wryly amused by Mumsy's obsession with the rules of etiquette ('Smile prettily as you enter the room, Mabel ... Don't *shake* hands, Mabel. Apply gentle pressure ... Oh, heavens, I can never remember whether these tongs are for sandwiches or asparagus.'), but occasionally she experienced a frisson of what she thought of as nouveau riche nerves – the feeling that, while proper gentry could stretch the rules to snapping point and get away with it, folk from new money had better watch their p's and q's.

In the game of hide and seek, which had taken place on the ground floor of the Pentry-Joneses' house, there had evidently been a great deal of scuffling and muffled laughter as chaps opened a cupboard or slid behind a potted palm in search of a hiding place, only to discover the place was already taken, obliging them to scuttle off and try somewhere else before time ran out.

*. . . There I was, in an alcove in the rear of the entrance hall, and who should choose the same place but Gil! What wonderful luck! The moment he saw me, he started to withdraw, but just then, Ollie shouted, 'Coming, ready or not!' so I pulled him back and there we were together in that tiny space. My heart was hammering fit to burst. I wanted to snuggle up to him – purely for the purpose of the two of us squeezing into a single hiding place, of course!! – but Sarah Walsh burst in, seeking a hidey-hole, and instead of Gil and myself enjoying a secret moment, we had to put up with Sarah playing gooseberry. I wonder if she realised. Honestly, I could have crowned her.*

Mabel eagerly awaited the next letter, certain that, having been thwarted in the alcove, Gil would get Althea on her own by some other means – but apparently not. Mabel's pen flew across the page in response as she tried to make Althea look on the bright side.

*Don't be down-hearted. It shows he's a gentleman. You don't want a chap who's NST.*

Althea's next letter ended with *PS NST?*

*Not Safe in Taxis*, wrote Mabel. *This London Season might be hell on earth, but at least I've brushed up on my slang.*

Althea's next letter was a heartbroken scrawl. Gil had gone home – he'd had to, because of returning to the office.

She couldn't wait for them to be together again . . . *but of course we can write. I admit to being the most frightful hussy – I wrote first! Imagine what the etiquette book would have to say about that!*

Lucky Althea, having a man to love, even if they were obliged to be apart for the time being. Althea might be down in the dumps, but, to Mabel, she was the luckiest girl in the world.